SWEET VENGEANCE

Chatham's voice was low and hoarse with passion. "No matter what game you play, tonight you will be mine. You will earn that ransom which seemed so important to you, and you will earn it well. I have thought of nothing other than that delectable little body of yours all night and all morning. The tables are neatly turned, my girl, and you are in my power now. Remember that. It is what I want that matters."

He tugged the woolen cap from Alison's head, allowing the honey-gold tresses to tumble down her back. His hands grasped her shoulders and pulled her against him so that her breasts met the iron hardness of his chest. His head bent and his mouth captured hers, his kiss hot and demanding.

Alison shivered, not wholly with fear, finding his kiss teasing and tempting and very pleasurable. Until this moment, she had always disdained sins of the flesh, certain she could easily avoid them. But as sweet torment swept through her body, she learned how wrong she was, and how easy it would be to fall into temptation . . .

ZEBRA BOOKS

KENSINGTON PUBLISHING CORP.

ZEBRA BOOKS

are published by

Kensington Publishing Corp.
475 Park Avenue South
New York, NY 10016

First printing: August 1987

Printed in the United States of America

Chapter One

The night was crisp and clear with cold. Thick fog hovered above the earth, depositing a chilling frost wherever it lingered and touched. Shadows rose and dipped, eerie in the dim light of the forest. The silent stillness seemed unnatural, ominous.

A sudden fluttering of wings overhead rent the air. The cackling of the rook as it ascended the forest startled the slight figure beneath the bare walnut tree. Eyes raised from their original task and followed the bird as it disappeared from sight. The figure wavered momentarily, then reverted all attention to the matter at hand.

Snow blanketed the earth and the forest, spreading beyond, across the road, and through the arches which framed the beginnings of the Jordan estate. Glimpses of a large, Tudor house could be seen through the darkness. A multitude of candles burned in the front windows, bringing the forefront of the house into dim focus.

From her vantage in the forest, the figure had been

waiting, watching and shivering for what seemed like hours.

Cupping freezing hands to her mouth, she breathed warm air there, futilely trying to thaw an icy nose. A patched peajacket and threadbare breeches seemed to have little effect against this latest onslaught of winter. A dark woolen cap covered the head and most of the face of its wearer, making the features indistinguishable. The figure was intent on watching the house and the road across from the forest. Slender gloved hands lifted to opposite shoulders and began to clap a rhythmic tattoo, anything to ward off so much cold. A thick fog wreathed the small figure at every breath, melding into the low-hanging haze created by the early winter frost.

The watcher grew more impatient as the night lengthened. One more effort was made to fight the cold and boredom as she stamped heavy leather boots against the hard ground and again brought fine hands together to make warmth in a cup of breath.

Suddenly all movements ceased. The watcher stiffened as a new sound pierced the night. Her eyes shifted and darkened, seeking to penetrate the depths of the forest. The plodding of heavy footsteps neared as dead leaves, twigs and all were carelessly trampled. If the newcomer intended to be furtive, he failed miserably.

"Jon!" breathed the slight figure as a familiar face descended through the mist. "Can't you be more quiet? We don't want to announce our presence!"

Through a shroud of cold haze, the face appeared. Grey eyes peered at the curious disguise his sister insisted on wearing, the brows raised in a mocking gesture, before turning toward the Jordan estate. The long, lanky body of the young man curled confidingly toward his sister, as though to make amends for the carelessness in his arrival.

"There's no one to overhear," he whispered in grim tones. "Besides, in another hour, I'd be frozen to the seat of that . . . thing. I can't believe anyone ever used that carriage to travel in—not and survived the journey." As the lad spoke, Jon tugged his thick woolen coat more snugly about him, concealing the heavy gold braid of his waistcoat. Black breeches and flaring jackboots were topped off with a nattily angled tricorne from which one flowing feather dangled. Blond hair was tied at the nape of his neck with a black riband. A quantity of Mechlin lace hung at his neck and wrists, just below the thick cuffs of his coat, giving him every appearance of a young man of fashion and breeding.

"Perhaps that's the reason it hasn't been used in so many years," came the halting response.

"Well, the rats love it. It's chock full of 'em."

"Rats?" Alison squeaked, forgetting the cold, her discomfort, even the reason they were here tonight. Her eyes widened and her tongue snaked out to emphasize her distaste. "You won't get me in that thing, not with rats!"

"Don't fret. Every time a wheel turns, a half dozen or so of 'em bale out. Even rats refuse to ride in such a poorly sprung carriage!" Jon spoke scornfully, perhaps with reason. He was the one who'd sat on that miserable driver's seat all this way. "Besides, who asked you to ride in the coach? I didn't even want you along on this escapade. Or did you conveniently forget that little fact? This is no place for a woman."

7

"You need me, Jon. If you weren't so proud you'd admit it," she answered fervently, her head bobbing as she spoke, the movement threatening to dislodge her woolen cap. "Geoffrey is my brother, too, and as much my responsibility to protect."

"I knew I would regret confiding in you."

"Ah, your pat answer. I remind you, if you had not, you would not now have a plan to follow. 'Twas my idea and I mean to see it through," Alison warned.

Jon winced as bright curls tumbled about her nape and temples, leaving no doubt, in spite of her disguise, that she was a female. Stepping in front of her, he withdrew a glove. His fingers worked quickly, tucking the errant strands back into the cap. A rueful smile slowly dawned on his face as he studied his sister's features and comical disguise. She was right. She had always come up with little plots and plans, gleefully. And always it was him they landed in trouble. He might have been wise to keep Geoffrey's trouble from her ears, but Jon was not wise. And when he needed advice, it was his one-year-older sister to whom he turned, just as he'd done all his life. Coming up with this solution to Geoffrey's latest problem had taken her mere moments, a fact which still awed Jon.

"My toes are one frozen mass of icicles," Alison stuttered violently, green eyes bearing accusingly toward the Jordan residence. "We've been here practically the whole night. What can he be doing to take so long?"

Silence answered this question. Jon blinked, wondering what on earth she thought their quarry was doing with Mistress Jordan in the middle of the night. A nostril flared impatiently and Jon replied testily, "If

8

you don't know, I'm not about to tell you."

The bobbing ceased abruptly. Alison turned to face Jon, her eyes twinkling and dimples appearing on either side of her pink mouth. "I wasn't talking about *that!*"

"Good. It's not proper conversation, not even with my sister. Besides, he can't be much longer, not if he wants to be gone before daylight. Even our devilish Marquis wouldn't want to be caught spending the full night with a married lady."

"Especially a lady married to someone else."

Jon's lips thinned as he glared impatiently at Alison. "Of course she's married to someone else. How do you suppose he got his reputation if he spent the night with his own wife? Not that he's got one. A wife I mean. Ally, I swear, sometimes you don't make any sense at all."

Jon sounded thoroughly irate but Alison was not concerned with his anger. She was more concerned that they not be overheard and caught. She tried to shush him but he ignored her, continuing with his small tirade. Finally, Alison quieted and let Jon have his way. He'd been leveling criticism at her head for days now. She knew he was wary of this scheme but could not come up with anything better. She was wary of it, too. She had only met the Marquis as a child and that meeting was disastrous. So long as they were careful, pray God, this next meeting would not end so tragically.

She rested her hand on his arm. "We're both cold and tired, Jon. He will be out shortly and then we can be on our way. A bit of patience will give us the end we need."

9

Jon retorted gruffly, "Well, I wish we had taken Morgan into our confidence. As the moment approaches, I wonder if I really am capable of handling our Marquis by myself."

"You're not," came the unequivocal response. "You need me desperately. We both know his reputation." With her fingers, she counted off what little they'd heard of him. "He's deadly with a pistol, light with a sword and heavy with his fists. You will need my help. And together we need all the help we can get. I pray trickery and deception win this day."

"I wager he's good at those, too."

"Most probably," she agreed ruefully. "He must have been, even as a child. Oh, why did he have to come back into our lives?" Alison grumbled tightly. "He caused trouble enough once. Why couldn't he have left Eileen alone?"

Jon's lips tightened. "It was most probably Eileen who wouldn't leave him alone."

A load of snow tumbled from an overhead branch and landed heavily at their feet. White powder flew in all directions and crept through the girl's stockings and down boots too large for her feet. The cold was growing more unbearable by the moment.

Again she stamped her frozen feet, her eyes wavering from the Jordan house and peeping upwards, toward the dark, heavy sky. Her lips tasted the first of the new snow and she turned to Jon to pass on this latest bit of grim news. The light in the house beyond wavered and beckoned, capturing her attention.

"Jon, look at the window on the upper floor," she squeaked excitedly. "Someone is there. It's a woman . . . Can you see . . . my goodness! What is she wearing?

10

Why, it looks like practically nothing! Jon, can you see through that negligee?" Alison's eyes strained to see better. "Do you suppose that's Mistress Jordan? Where are her servants? And the Marquis? . . . Do you see him? . . ."

Jon took her by the shoulders and turned her, pressing her forcefully toward her horse, unwilling to listen to any more of these artless statements. "But Jon, he's not at the front door yet. We've got time. I did so want to see him kiss her."

"Shut up, Ally, and just do as we planned." He threw her into the saddle and she had to scramble to keep her balance.

The reins were tossed to her and she caught them, responding cheerfully, "As you say, Jon. Just take care of yourself." Booted feet slid into the stirrups and her glance wavered across the road once more. "I hope this goes as planned."

"You haven't seen the size of him lately," came the swift retort. "Do exactly as you were told and I'll be there to protect you. I want no trouble."

"I promise, Jon."

One thought echoed through her mind as she kicked Honey's flanks and together they covered the distance to her destination. This plan must work. For all their sakes.

Turning in the saddle she glanced behind her, but saw no one. The Marquis' leavetaking was time consuming, giving her more time to implement her own plans. Her movements would have to pass careful scrutiny now. Jon was right, this was too dangerous to be taken lightly. Giving a swift kick to Honey's flanks, she rode on.

At the converging of roads leading to London where she and Jon agreed to begin their plan, Alison dismounted and stretched fully on her back, effectively blocking the middle of the road. Sweeping snow aside, she tried to find a more comfortable and natural way to lie. On her side she brought her knees up, but that felt as awkward as lying on her back. She turned to another side, languishing fully. Snow crept through the seams of her coat, melting at the first contact with her warmer skin. Frost numbed her toes.

Still, no sound of an impending rider.

Her side grew stiff with the cold and hurt from her weight on the barren ground. She was rolling onto her back again when the first sounds of another horse came through the night. Now was too late to pose more naturally, too late for second thoughts. She wondered briefly why she had not heard Jon's approach in the carriage, the thought leaving abruptly as hooves neared. The anticipation was overwhelming. Catching her breath she lay still and squinted shut her eyes. After much concentration she forced herself to relax, to breathe normally and loosen the curl of her palms.

The mare was small, gentle and curious. Plodding closer to where her mistress lay, Honey lowered her muzzle to Alison's cheek and, with her soft mouth, began to tickle her.

"No, Honey." Alison whispered frantically, trying not to move. "Go away! Go away, you're bothering me." The words were spoken softly for the other horse and rider were rapidly advancing. All of Alison's resolution was necessary to keep still. Honey reared her head to witness the approach of the newcomers and the reins fell from Honey's neck to land smartly on

Alison's face.

Though her eyes were tightly closed, Alison knew instinctively when the man and his horse neared. The ground reverberated with the rhythm of hooves, and she heard a softly spoken, "Whoa." The hooves came closer still. She was hard pressed not to open at least one eye. Leather creaked as the man dismounted.

"What have we here?" The deep voice was filled with good humor. Too good. He sounded just like Jon when he spent an evening carousing with friends. Great Aunt Seraphina was right, she thought. Liquor was the root of all sin.

Honey was making the little rasping sounds she always made when her muzzle was being stroked. "A fine little filly," that infuriatingly content voice continued, "left completely unattended? Doesn't your master know how tempting this is?"

Alison stiffened, wondering if this Marquis was a horse thief as well as a sinful seducer.

"Such a fine little beast," continued the low, aggravatingly soft voice, "too bad you're not more my size." Honey was lapping up the lavish praise. "And what have we here? A lad? Castaway? What a foolish thing to do. Is this your owner, little filly? This silly boy, to fall from your back here, where he's naught but in my way."

Alison forced herself to remain still while he stood over her. She could feel his gaze sweep her body.

"Foxed," the Marquis affirmed good-humoredly. "I swear the lads are drinking younger and younger each year. Or is it that I'm getting older each year?" He gave a sigh and she knew instinctively that he shook his head. In spite of his drinking, she prayed he wouldn't sink to philosophizing while she slowly froze to death. She soon realized how little philosophy had to do with what was in his mind when he said, "Well, lad, if you must indulge to excess, you must pay the piper. By morning you'll have learned the nasty side of excess drinking, harsh lesson though it may be."

The leather of his saddle creaked again and Alison realized he was remounting. A feeling of horror spread through her. Hooves neared her head and she heard the horse being turned. He was leaving her here alone in the middle of the night! Had he no sense of decency?

Outraged, she realized there was but one option left to her, desperate though it might be. In the deepest voice she could muster, she cried lamely, "H—elp! Oh, please, help me."

Feigning a struggle to sit up, she very effectively collapsed in a heap on the cold ground. Her eyes closed and she moaned as though in severe pain. No one, positively no one, could ignore such a plea.

Alison was rewarded by the hooves returning to her side.

The Marquis could be heard to sigh deeply as he dismounted and stood over her. A furtive peep through eyelashes told her his hands were on his hips and his lips were formed into a thin, impatient line. For good measure, Alison gave another moan of excruciating pain.

"Lad, if your father doesn't give you the hiding you deserve, I will," he bellowed in frustrated tones. "I suppose I can't leave you here, not like this. Tell me, little filly, do you know where home is?"

The Marquis' firm hands slipped beneath her back and shoulders. He slowly began to straighten and rise but the hands groped around the softness of her waist and rear. "What kind of a lad is as soft as you . . ."

The question ended abruptly as a sickening sound of a blow to the back of his head came and he crumpled to the ground, Alison tangled ungainly beneath him.

The heavy weight of the body was shifted from her and she sat up, her eyes focusing clearly now and widening in shock. "Morgan!"

The big man with curling, grey hair glared at Alison as he dropped the Marquis' heavy body to the cold earth. His voice was brusque as the rough, northern brogue rolled off his tongue. "I knew ye and yer brother were up to no good. I just didn't think it could be this no-good."

"You don't understand . . ."

"Ach, I knew yer story about visitin' yer great Aunt Seraphina was malarkey the moment I heard it. Too convenient for ye and Jon to be visitin' her just as I was leavin' to see me sister. Aunt Seraphina, that fusby-faced old dragon!"

With a firm tug on her upper arms, Morgan hauled her to her feet and began dusting the peacoat free of snow. "I've a good mind to let Geoffrey know wot ye've been up to! I'm gettin' too old to chase after ye and yer brother, tryin' to keep ye out of trouble when ye naturally travel toward it. Did ye really think me so easy to gull, me girl?"

Alison blinked rapidly, her mind churning. She and Jon had never intended to involve Morgan in this, more for his sake than for theirs. But now that he was here, she was greatly relieved to see him. With a half sob, she threw herself into his arms and hugged his neck tight. "Oh, Morgan, I'm so glad you're here! We

15

wanted to confide in you, only . . . only we were afraid you wouldn't agree to help us . . . and we have to do something to help Geoffrey! But you can't tell him about this! He'll be too shocked and disappointed in us. Morgan, we couldn't let the Marquis kill him! We just could not!"

"Wot de ye mean, the Marquis would kill 'im?" Morgan demanded.

"In a duel. Geoffrey challenged the Marquis to a duel!"

"Wot? Are ye blarney, girl? They ain't set eyes on each other fer years. Not since the accident!"

"They have. While Jon was in London, Geoffrey returned from the colonies . . ."

"I know that much," Morgan snorted impatiently.

"What you don't know is that the first night he was home, he found Eileen and the Marquis embracing! According to Jon, Geoffrey was in a black rage and slapped the Marquis across the face with his glove and demanded satisfaction!"

Morgan's eyes widened. "Wot? Wot? Are ye sure?"

"Of course I'm sure! Jon saw everything!"

The old man's mouth twisted sardonically. "Are ye sure 'e wasn't foxed at the time?"

"Morgan, it's true. Jon said it's a matter of honor, what with the Marquis cuckolding Geoffrey and all that."

Morgan digested this information slowly. His brows lowered and his brow puckered and the grey eyes glared down on his charge. "So wot's yer doin' in all this? Wot did ye expect to accomplish by . . ." his hand gestured wildly, "this?"

Alison moved closer to the old man to speak more

confidingly. "Well, we thought we'd kidnap him, keep him for a few days until the day of the duel passes. Jon says he'll be scorned when he doesn't show at the duel. He'll have to leave the country to save face."

"Jon says, Jon says! Wot are ye, a parrot?"

"Think about it, Morgan. Geoffrey has been in the colonies seven years. He married Eileen and left for the colonies almost immediately afterward. We know nothing of him for the past seven years other than the paltry missives he writes every month. We don't know if he stands a chance in a duel, let alone one facing the Marquis. And I'm not willing to risk his life, Morgan. No matter what I have to do to protect him."

"No, ye'd rather risk yer own neck than yer older brother's. Did it ever occur to ye as how 'e's more capable of 'andling 'is own moments of madness than ye are?"

"But Morgan, this is the Marquis of Chatham he is to face. *Him.* The same man who murdered Mama and Papa. I don't want him doing any more damage to my family, Morgan."

This last comment had Morgan's eyes widening and the old man stepping back. "Lass, I don't know who ye've been talking to . . ."

"I was there, Morgan. I remember."

"Ye don't remember too well, then. 'Twas an accident, not murder. I've never been convinced 'twas him who ought to have shouldered the blame."

"The magistrate said . . ."

"Bosh! I've 'eard all I want to 'ear of the fool man! Instead of wasting me time arguing over the past, just tell me what you would 'ave done 'ad I not come along when I did. Where's that sorry brother of yer'n? Or

17

were ye supposed to talk the Marquis into agreeing to be yer prisoner?"

"Of course not. I was supposed to do just as I did. Only Jon was to have pulled a pistol on him and forced him into the carriage. He really should have been here by now . . ."

"Wot?" Morgan's voice began in a low roar and swiftly escalated into a loud growl. "The two of ye planned this silly escapade, ye risked yer neck and that dimwit of a brother of yer'n ain't got sense to be where 'e's supposed to be, at the time he's supposed to be there? Wot sort of brainless idiots are ye?"

"Now, Morgan . . ."

"Ye ain't fit to be let out of yer 'ome to take a walk across the park, let alone tanglin' with this mon!" Morgan's hand raised and lowered in a gesture designed to emphasize the prone body between them.

Alison's gaze followed this and guilt spread across her features as she saw the Marquis' body doubled over in the snow, his tricorne crumpled from the effects of the blow Morgan dealt him. Somehow a scene such as this had never entered her mind. "We hadn't planned on hurting him, Morgan."

"Humph. Nuthin' but clodpoles, the two of ye!"

Alison's face burned beneath his mockery. "We thought to keep a pistol on him and he'd do just as he was told. We meant him no harm." She knelt beside the still form and lifted his head to her lap, gently brushing the straight, black strands of hair from his face. "I hope he's not too badly hurt."

Morgan snorted at her words. "Not 'im. Not that great, 'ulking brute. 'e's grown in all directions since I last set eyes on 'im. I doubt anyone could 'urt that 'ard

18

'ead. 'e looks strong as an ox, and as mean, too. I gave 'im a surer blow than intended, but what did ye expect, with ye between us?"

"Ah!" The grated word held a wealth of mockery in it. "And if I ain't mistaken that's yer drizzard brother now!" The noise of the oncoming carriage grew louder by the moment. "But," his face lowered to hers, "if I 'adn't come along, girl, ye two'd be 'is prisoners, not 'im yers!"

Alison stood silently, listening to Morgan. Every word he spoke was correct. They had been foolish and careless. And the Marquis *was* a great hulking brute of a man. Until now, she hadn't realized how large he was. In spite of Morgan's anger, Alison was very relieved to have him beside her.

"Just in case that ain't yer clumperton of a brother, we might be wise to get this'un out of the middle of the road." The unconscious Marquis was a dead weight as Morgan hefted him over his shoulder and struggled to the side of the road. Morgan was breathless as the lumbering vehicle turned the curve of the road and came into sight.

Jon drove recklessly, the musty, squeaky vehicle lumbering precariously from side to side. Alison recognized the carriage instantly as the same one stored in the stable behind Wiltonshire for so many years and came out from her hiding place among the trees. Jon reined to an abrupt stop as he saw Alison, his face clearly drawing a deep breath of relief. Then the old man stepped from the shadows and Jon blinked twice before believing his eyes. A tremor was in his voice as he sought to defend himself from the undefendable. "The coach wheels caught on a tree root. It took me all this time to free them."

"Meanwhile ye leave yer sister to handle the Marquis, alone?"

"I tried to get here as quickly as I could, Morgan, truly. And in spite of everything, the coach was quicker than chasing after her on foot." Jon's mouth dropped open at the sight of their downed quarry and a gleam entered his eyes. "Besides, looking at that, she did just fine without me."

"'Twas me did jest fine, ye mean. Me 'and did the trick. The good Lord alone knows where Alison'd be if I 'adn't followed the two of you."

Tossing the reins aside, Jon jumped from the coachman's seat to get a better look at the inert body. Excitement was thick in his voice as he proudly boasted, "We did it!"

He grinned broadly, his elation waning at the censorious glare of the older man. "I mean you did it, Morgan." He corrected, the gleam still in those eager eyes. A moment later blond brows arched confusedly and once smiling lips turned under as a new worry entered his mind. "He's not dead, is he? He's not moved in minutes."

"Course not. No thanks to you."

"And you, Ally? Are you well?"

"I'm fine. It couldn't have been simpler. Morgan frets so."

"Of course I do, girl," Morgan roared. "I've been worrying about ye since afore ye was birthed, and don't ye ever forget that. Why, if I . . ." Abruptly the flow of words stopped. What he wanted to say, to let these two know how much he did worry about them, sounded too foolish, even in his thoughts. He'd fretted over them

20

like they were his own children and they couldn't have been dearer to him had they been. Their faces now were flushed with guilt and shame. He could rant and rave until this time tomorrow and they couldn't be any sorrier. But Morgan wasn't fooled. They would do the same all over again.

Maybe he should have taken a stick to their hides when they were children, just once.

"Open the door," Morgan ordered gruffly, pulling one of the Marquis' arms taut about his thick neck. He dragged the body to the coach. "'elp me lift 'im in, Jon. 'e's no light weight. Alison, fetch the rope."

Their eyes lit at Morgan's silent agreement to help them with their self-appointed task. Hurrying to him, they were eager to do his bidding.

Somehow Jonathan and Morgan managed to get the heavy body into the coach, but when Morgan situated the Marquis for binding, Alison objected. "He's already terribly uncomfortable. Can't we just bind his feet and arms together so he can at least sleep peacefully?"

Jonathan laughed grimly. "Take a good look at him, Ally. By morning he'll be sore and mad. Would you want to go up against the size of him? Not me. Not even me and Morgan. We bind him as planned."

"It will only make him angrier," she warned.

"I doubt he can be any angrier. I'd be fit to commit murder if I were him."

Morgan tossed Jon three stout lengths of rope and climbed into the carriage, levering himself over the Marquis' body. He had to struggle to pull their prisoner onto the seat, but finally succeeded. He secured the Marquis' wrists to either side of the coach and tethered his feet together, binding them to the floor. Only fingers and hands dangled free.

"You can ride inside the coach for the first few 'ours, Ally, but if 'e shows any sign of rousing, let me know. I don't want ye alone in there with 'im," Morgan warned gravely. As she climbed into the coach, his voice came again, "The moment 'e wakens, ye let me know."

Alison nodded, her eyes wide.

Morgan was not fooled by this easy acquiescence. Deep inside he was still angry over the risks they had taken, in spite of their reasons. Growling, he demanded, "Yer sudden affection for yer Aunt Seraphina 'ad me curious, so I followed ye both from the moment ye quit Wiltonshire house. What pretext did ye use to be rid of those footmen, heh? I want an answer!"

Alison had the grace to flush guiltily. "Jon hired a post chaise and men at the Boondoggle Inn. He claimed our aunt sent them for us and it was perfectly fine for the footmen to return to the manor house. No one questioned our veracity."

"Only because those fools don't know ye as well as I do. In spite of yer one small success, the two of ye make the sorriest criminals I've ever seen. 'Twas me who done the trick, ye both need to remember that. Without my arm you'd be alone with that man, and God knows with what results.

"I can't say as Geoffrey would have bested 'im in a fair duel for I don't know that, but I'd give 'im better odds than the two of ye anytime. I wondered what ye were up to, but kidnapping a fancy lord never came to my mind. I guess I just ain't as devious as ye high born lords and ladies." The familiar, lined face lifted and glared at Alison as she listened from within the carriage. Jon stood on the ground beside her. "But wot's done is done. And as we 'ave 'im, we may as well make use of 'im. So we'll keep 'im and I'll 'elp with yer fribbly plot. But . . . only if ye agree to do exactly as I say. No more no less. Well? Wot say ye? Ay or nay?"

"Oh, of course, Morgan! We'll do whatever—"

"I don't know. We were doing just fine—" Jon's words were cut off abruptly when Alison smacked him on the shoulder and reminded him that if it weren't for Morgan, they would be Chatham's prisoners now, instead of the reverse.

Morgan tugged his tricorne further down his head and stalked off to gather their horses. Honey was tethered behind the coach. The Marquis' animal was skittish at a stranger's handling of him, but Morgan had not spent years working in stables for nothing. The animal was soon calmed and tied beside the more gentle Honey.

Morgan climbed beside Jonathan and, moments later, the coach began its slow, lumbering movements.

Inside, the coach was dark. Alison pulled aside the curtain, seeking light from the moon, but to no avail. Any moonlight was obscured by overhanging clouds.

Alison remembered Jon's rats and grew fretful at each little sound. She did not relax until her body grew so weary that her head dropped against the squabs and her hands to either side of her. Her fingers felt the cracked and torn leather, touching the stuffing which escaped from the musty smelling cushions. The feel of grit was enough to convince her to pull her hands back into her lap and wait until morning when she could better see what she touched.

Her head itched terribly from the woolen cap. She

tugged it off her head and allowed long, thick tresses of honey-gold hair to tumble freely about her shoulders and neck. As she drew slender fingers through it, a contented peacefulness swept over her. Her head dropped against the cushions. A nagging hunger plagued her belly, but her weariness overtook all other sensations. Soon she was asleep.

She wakened to a pale dawn. The wheels of the carriage rolled monotonously along the road. In morning light the worn blue of the leather cushions appeared more shabby than she remembered. The once fine paneling was now scratched and dented, the doors barely hanging onto their latches. All in all, the coach was perfect for their purposes. Just the sort of carriage a criminal might afford. No one would ever connect it with her or Jon or, more importantly, with the Earl of Wiltonshire. Who just happened to be their half brother, Geoffrey.

Miriam Belden, late Countess of Wiltonshire and their mother, had been widowed shortly after Geoffrey's birth. Geoffrey's father died of the same ailment which took his father before him. It was believed to be some sort of inherited stomach malady, and Lady Miriam went to great pains to see that her own son did not fall ill to it.

Ten years after her first husband's death, the Countess married her vicar, Bradwell Asher. Still later, Alison and Jon were born. The country folk around Wiltonshire might have thought it strange for their Countess to be marrying her vicar, but it was soon made clear that the marriage was exactly what she wanted. After raising her son alone for so many years, she loved the role of cherished wife and mother. She loved her husband, and she wanted nothing more than to grow old with him.

Grow old she did not. They died together in a tragic accident one Christmas Eve. Geoffrey was a youth, a student at Eton, and he'd brought his friend Justin Sarrett, the young Marquis of Chatham, home with him to share the holidays. For a lark they decided to build a sleigh and, of course, had to draft Morgan to help them. The sleigh was to be a surprise for the vicar and Lady Miriam. They worked on it the entire vacation, even tried to keep it secret from Alison and Jon and the other children. That Christmas, Geoffrey's great uncle, Naylor Belden, and his two children, David and Eileen, were also there.

They failed to keep the secret. Alison grimaced now to think of the lengths she went to to get one glimpse of the sleigh. She admitted to being a horrible brat at the time, but they might have been a bit more tolerant of the curiosity of a little child.

The sleigh was happily accepted and given its first run by its proud owners. All Alison remembered of the next few moments was the anguish on Geoffrey's face, the tormented cries of pain. The racked sobs gave her nightmares for years after. She knew now how the yoke broke and the sleigh careened toward the soft center of the frozen lake. She later learned how the wood had been sawn too closely for strength. The magistrate held that the young Marquis had been careless, he was the one who shaped the yoke. But the deaths were judged accidental. At the time she only knew something horrible was happening by Geoffrey's agonized expression.

She barely remembered the service for her parents.

The church had filled with her father's parishioners and her mother's friends and relatives, the drawn faces filled with compassion as they looked on her and Jonathan.

Of better recollection was how Naylor Belden and his children moved in with them. That was when she first learned to dislike Eileen and her brother. Two years after her parents died, Alison was seven and Geoffrey was barely done with his studies at Oxford, he announced his betrothal to Eileen. She couldn't understand that either. Geoffrey disliked Eileen almost as much as Alison did!

That was when she and Jon became closer to Morgan, the steady light in their lives. The stables were the only escape from the unpleasantness their home had become.

Shortly after the marriage, Geoffrey purchased a commission in the Royal Navy and was practically gone from their lives. At best they were strangers. Since that time, Alison could count on one hand the number of times she'd seen Geoffrey. Nor had she seen Eileen and her family for that matter. They moved to London and stayed there all these years.

Alison took a deep breath, her gaze seeking and finding their prisoner. She had much reason to hate this man. Because of him her parents were dead. Because of him Geoffrey left his home and remained abroad for seven years.

Until last night, she'd never seen him again.

Still uncomfortably tethered and bound, the Marquis' head hung, insensible against his chest, and his body pitched with every jerking movement of the coach. Black, straight hair slashed across his forehead

26

in disarray. The angle at which she viewed him did not give a clear glimpse of his face. She barely discerned a full lower lip, the curve of which thinned at the corners and made his expression harsher than she remembered. He was every bit as large as she thought last night. There seemed little left of the youth she'd once known.

His hair was almost as black then as now, not so thick perhaps. He had seemed a giant, she remembered, and, compared to her small size, he must have been. Well, he'd grown to fulfill that promise of height and breadth he carried as a lad.

At the beginning of that holiday, he'd teased her unmercifully, his mouth always tilted into a wicked, goading grin—until she fought back.

What was it she had done that time to earn his anger? Hidden his boots and coat? He'd spent hours searching for those. Stuffed the week-old kitten into his valise? He had been angrier over the discomfort caused the kitten than over the mess made of his clothing. Suddenly she remembered. No, he had been angry at her threat to tell her parents of the sleigh and ruin the surprise unless she had the first ride.

Flushing faintly, she admitted it was a perfectly horrid thing for her to do. Perhaps she was as spoiled as he said, over and over again, ranting the words at her. Perhaps she deserved being turned over his knee and whipped, hard. It was the only whipping she'd ever had in her life and she was doubly humiliated that that boor had been the one to give it to her. But Morgan took care of him. Morgan chased him from the barn and told him never to return. He wasn't to lay his arrogant hands on the little one.

Thank heaven for Morgan, her protector, her friend,

27

her confidant. He wouldn't let anyone abuse her. Especially not this man. Not then and not now.

A haunting voice in the back of her mind reminded her that the Marquis had been sympathetic to a kitten and last night to a lad who was perhaps hurt. Not too sympathetic, true, but apparently not willing to let her freeze to death, either. His words came back to her and again she heard the humorous lilt to his voice, its deep and resonant tones.

No, she refused to allow any sympathy for her prisoner to spread. This one needed a lesson. He needed to be away from London, away from Geoffrey, and away from any thought of a duel. He needed to learn respect for the institution of marriage and respect for other people's lives.

Resolutely, she tugged the scratchy woolen cap over her curls and turned from him. Again, she slept.

The carriage lurched to a halt, the sudden jolt tossing Alison from her seat. Rising, she wiped sleep from her eyes and lifted the curtain to peer outside. The sun was high and already warming the day. Before them was a newly whitewashed inn over which hung a sign proclaiming it as the "Foxes' Lair and Pub." In the yard were other traveling carriages and smaller equipages. She noted how Jon stood their carriage a great distance from any others.

Across the yard stood a curricle and beside it a young man Alison assumed to be the owner. He was smartly dressed in grey breeches and topcoat, high black boots and a tricorne with lace dangling around and from the crown. A crop was in his hands which he swished impatiently against his boots. Suddenly he turned and his eyes looked directly into Alison's. She was startled but not frightened. She might not have withdrawn except for the additional worry she would cause Morgan.

The coach door swung open and Morgan appeared, his eyes assessing first Alison, then their prisoner.

"How is 'e?" Morgan's head nodded to indicate the Marquis.

"Sound asleep, though he frets as though he's uncomfortable."

"'e'll be more comfortable tonight when we're at the cottage. I'll leave ye to ride in 'ere for a few more 'ours, then ye'll ride 'oney. Jon's inside, fetchin' sommat for us to eat. I'm sorry but ye'll have to eat in 'ere, not inside the inn. I don't want anyone seein' ye in those breeches. Ye won't fool a soul into thinkin' ye're a lad."

Alison nodded in understanding.

Jon arrived, his hands full of delicacies wrapped in brightly checkered cloth. "Pasties!" he announced to his interested audience. "Lamb, pork and cheese. And for dessert . . . ," he tossed Alison an apple.

Jon decided to ride Morgan's horse rather than drive the carriage for this last leg of the journey. Morgan reminded Alison to call him the moment the Marquis stirred. Alison rued that her brother and Morgan had so little trust in her, then sighed in relief at Morgan's more gentle handling of the reins. The ride was smooth and she reclined comfortably against the dried leather squabs, the remnants of her last, uneaten pasty in its checkered cloth still in her hand.

Finding that the fingers holding the pasty were clenched tightly, Alison loosened her grip. This one pasty had to last her until tonight. Carefully she inspected it and found just a bit of the crust to be broken. Alison daintily picked the broken bits with her fingers and tossed them into her mouth. They tasted so good she could not help but take another bite. She was chewing happily and contemplating just one more bite when she chanced to look up and found two black, angry eyes on her. That last bite was swallowed hastily.

The Marquis was stretched on the opposite seat, his arms held taut and away from him. His head no longer hung senselessly, but was upright, and his black eyes bore into her with every semblance of loathing the lowest snake in Eden must have endured.

His eyes wandered insolently over her person, beginning with the poor woolen cap perched on her head, traveling over the worn peajacket which had seen far better days, over her breeches, which were ill-fitting for they had been Jonathan's as a child. For them to fit in length, they were a good deal too wide. Finally, his gaze came to rest on her scruffy boots. Apparently he found her person to be somewhat lacking for his mouth curved into a mocking, twisted grin.

Alison was suddenly thankful for the secure bonds which held him. She knew from the hatred in his eyes that he would strangle her if he could.

His eyes dismissed her and his attention turned to the coach. Cautiously, she melted against the cushions, as if she could disappear and he would forget she was here with him. Almost imperceptibly the Marquis began to test his bonds. The longer he pulled the ropes taut and the less he accomplished, the more impatient and angry he became. Finally, he grew exasperated and strained fiercely against them, his chest heaving with the effort, and let out a furious growl as he did so.

Alison quietly watched as the Marquis used his

whole body for this test of strength, crouching on his bound feet and threatening to take the whole side of the coach with him. The more he strained, the blacker his rage grew.

As it became more and more obvious that the Marquis could not escape his bonds, Alison grew increasingly brave. She should let Jon and Morgan know he was fully awake and alert, she thought reluctantly. But she might never have a chance such as this again, a little voice niggled in her ear. He needed his comeuppance sorely and she should be the one to give it to him.

Weary of fighting the ropes, the Marquis turned granite eyes on his kidnapper.

The lad's demeanor was a contradiction to his appearance. Slender hands were primly folded into his lap, almost like a girl. His legs were too thin for a sturdy lad and dangled to the floorboards. The worn black boots practically fell from too small feet. Sea-green eyes wavered from fear to a sort of schooled bravado. The mouth was beautifully shaped and the long, black sooty eyelashes were sorely out of place on this crude lad. For the moment though, Chatham had other thoughts than this incomprehensible and strange boy. The first one of which was murdering the oaf who knocked him cold and tied him like this.

The black eyes bit into Alison terrifyingly and his upper lip curled thinly. "Where's your master, you gawking, squint-eyed toad?" he bit out harshly.

Alison swallowed at the tone of voice. Then she reminded herself she had nothing to fear. He was thoroughly tied. Escape would be impossible. She and Jon had changed so much over the years, the Marquis

31

would never recognize them as members of the family he once visited. Morgan had changed, too. A bit more girth, more grey. His was the greater risk perhaps, but if he covered the bottom portion of his face with a kerchief, the Marquis would never recognize any of them.

Green eyes flickered over him. The confidence was soaring through her body. They had bested him. She, Jon, and Morgan won the day over this man. A smile spread across her lips.

The square jaw tightened as her gaze roamed freely. Chatham swore to wipe that smile from that gloating expression one day—and soon.

Alison was disappointed to find the only signs of dissipation and age on him were the crow's feet nestled just beside the eyes. She expected him to look more like a sinner.

Standing, he would be as tall as Geoffrey, but his shoulders were thicker, his thighs stouter. Heavy black brows framed the eyes, black lashes fringed them. The swarthy coloring and bridged nose were reminders of the child he had been. That same unfeeling youth who had beaten her years ago.

His black breeches and boots were stained and dusty after being dragged across the road. His buckskin coat and white silk shirt were creased and he badly needed a shave.

Not quite feeling as nonchalant as she appeared, she brought the pasty to her mouth and bit into it, chewing contentedly and continuing her scrutiny of him. His hold on the ropes tightened.

"I thought you'd be much better looking, a man with your reputation," she scoffed in her deepest voice.

32

"Perhaps looks don't matter, not with your wealth."

"I can buy you," he stated flatly. "How much do you want?"

A deliciously wicked sensation assailed her. "We haven't decided yet."

"We?"

She nodded, her mouth full of dry pasty.

"When you do decide," he bit out savagely, "let me know. But I promise you, right now, you'd best leave the country, for if I ever get my hands on you, I'll take my retribution out on your hide."

She wished heartily she had not tried to take refuge behind the pasty. It tasted like sawdust. With an effort she managed to swallow that last bite. "You're in no position to make threats, my lord."

"I never threaten," he sneered coldly.

Her skin grew clammy at the tone in his voice. Thoughts of torture and death, her own, convoluted in her mind. She gave him a smile so as to betray none of these fears and held the pasty out to him, "Would you care for a bite? We don't plan to starve you."

"I prefer to starve than to share with vermin such as yourself."

Alison shrugged her shoulders casually and carefully returned the pasty to its checkered cloth. "Are you very wealthy?" she inquired, wanting to wipe that smirk from his face. "We might be able to ask for more than we realized."

"Instant wealth?" he mocked.

"I imagine yours was instant, too, instant from the moment you were born.

"At least I came by my wealth honestly and am not a parasite like you. And not a very successful parasite, it

33

seems. That coat looks as though it's at least twenty years old, and your toes should break through that leather in the next five leagues. Are your cohorts as poor as you? Or as young? I'm beginning to shiver in my boots with the likes of you as my adversaries. I admit you make a most unlikely bandit. You're too slight to be dangerous, and our conversation indicates that you're anything but the brains behind this band. And while I'd like to wipe that smile from your face with the back of my hand, I'll admit it's more reminiscent of a puppy than a dangerous brigand."

The puppy statement was more than Alison could bear. Her eyes flashed angrily while she demanded, "Perhaps you would like to see just how dangerous I can be?"

The Marquis guffawed. Her weakness was too apparent. "What will you do? Bite me or lick me to death?"

Alison actually snarled. The truth of the matter was she didn't know how she was going to prove she was dangerous when she didn't think she was. Tossing her head in the air, she turned from him. All he could see was her profile. His gaze lowered to the gentle rounding of her bosom and a glimmer of surprise lit his eyes. No wonder he'd thought she made such a strange lad. His gaze hardened.

"You'll find out how dangerous I am. We'll be spending quite a bit of time together."

"How much time?"

Her brows lifted and she inclined her head to regard him better. "As long as it takes to receive the ransom. Unless you think your minions might not pay the ransom? If they think as highly of you as I do, they might decide good riddance."

"You insufferable puppy! When I get my hands on you, I'll teach you respect for your betters!"

"The trick is getting your hands on me. They're occupied by a stout length of cord at the moment."

"Not for lone, whelp!" he roared, the tethered arms coming forward powerfully in an attempt to break free. Alison held her breath while his straining filled the coach with more tension.

Breathing heavily he finally admitted his efforts to be useless. He sat and allowed his dark gaze to torment his abductor at length. The silence was unbroken until he rasped, "Would it be possible for me to have something to drink?"

"I have a flagon of ale. But alas, I have drunk from it. Are you not worried about my fleas?"

"Are you waiting for an apology? You'll wait forever," he responded haughtily.

Alison shrugged indifferently, retrieving the flask from beneath the cushion. "I haven't a glass."

"Your fleas won't drink much. Give me what is left."

There was only one way for the Marquis to drink and that was for Alison to stand and pour the liquid down his throat. The movement of the coach made standing difficult. Finally, she placed a hand against the door and with the other hand lifted the bottle to the Marquis' lips while he drank deeply. Her stance grew more difficult as the coach swayed and she had to shuffle her feet to keep her balance. The hand on the door wavered and lost its grip and Alison flailed around, seeking something solid to balance herself against. What she found was the Marquis. His hands might have been bound, but his fingers were free. At the first contact, they gripped her flailing hand so tightly she thought it would break. When she finally managed to free the hand, his grip slipped down to her wrist. The pain was excruciating.

Alison raised the flagon of ale she held in her other hand and brought it sharply down on his head. That and a few well placed kicks to his shins soon had her freed. Collapsing against the squabs opposite him, she fought to gain her breath.

"Had that been your neck I held, you'd be dead," the Marquis rasped.

His action stunned her. He was right, she would be dead. She'd never considered herself in mortal danger and was now realizing that she was. She glanced at the empty bottle. "I hit you hard enough it should have broken. Next time, it will."

She glared at him a moment longer, then lifted the curtain and called for Morgan. It was time she rode Honey instead of trying to keep this madman company.

Chapter Two

The view from the road was of a small cottage tucked neatly into the hillside, all but obscured by the snow covered tangle of woody growth surrounding it. A barely discernible path led the way to the front door and from there wended its way around to the rear of the cottage.

Honey responded to the clucking of her mistress' tongue with a smooth gait and the riders approached closer. There the dilapidated condition of the cottage became even more apparent. Peeling paint, splintered and askew shutters, and a dubious thatched roof cried out in neglect. Alison, whose only conscious thought in the last three hours had been for a bed with no bugs in it, looked askance at her brother.

"Nary a word, Alison. Not 'til we've seen the inside."

"I don't know that I've the courage," she answered drily.

"I told the agent it was privacy we wanted, and 'tis privacy we've here, in abundance."

"We?" she questioned in a censurious tone. "As I

recall, at no time have I been consulted about this venture—other than coming up with the scheme, that is. I could have found better than this."

Jon turned in his saddle, about to retort hotly when Morgan brought the coach to a clamorous standstill. The old servant glared at his two young charges. His mood had not been improved by the long drive or the uncomfortable seat and cold weather. "No more arguments. Remember, this is no May game. Jon, take the 'orses out back and see what sort of shelter ye can find for them. Feed and water them, then come back 'ere."

"Morgan," Alison began as she pulled brightly colored cloth left from the pasties from her pockets and proffered it to him. "I thought you might . . ."

The old man's expression grew grimmer, if possible. "Aye, lassie. 'Tis a good thought." He took the cloth and separated the two kerchiefs, one of which he handed to Jon. "Under no circumstances are ye to allow the Marquis to see yer pretty face." He held up a hand to Jon's impending protest. "I will do likewise. I may 'ave nearly fifteen years and a face full of wrinkles since he last clapped eyes on me, but I'm no one to be taking chances. And neither will ye, not as long as I have a say so. And lass, be careful. 'e may not know ye now, but if 'e ever sees ye again . . . and learns who ye be, we may all swing from Tyburn tree. No matter 'ow many breeches ye wear, ye still look like a demmed female. Do ye understand?"

Alison nodded. Just how dangerous their quarry was had been made known to her earlier this afternoon. Her fingers and wrist still tingled from the recollection.

Jon was less agreeable, however. Morgan was taking

over his role as leader of this arrangement, the lad fumed inwardly. No one was willing to give him the credit due for the implementation of this ingenious plan. Well, he would not spend the whole of the next week playing servant to Morgan or Alison. No, he had a taste for pleasure and freedom. If they thought to take over, let them. He'd show them. He'd go his merry way. Just as soon as he was done with the horses.

Alison rummaged a path through the brush, uprooting whatever would easily give way with her gloves hands. Unlocking the door and pressing it open, she found the inside of the cottage a pleasant surprise. Though it was cold, it seemed tight against the elements at least. The furnishings were shabby and old, but with a spot of work the cottage could be made habitable. She moved quickly through the rooms and found the kitchen on the other side of the parlor. Both rooms shared the same chimney. Her fond wish for warmth and a cup of tea seemed finally within reach. Alison began the onerous task of clearing the hearth.

Footsteps shuffled across the floor as Jon set an armful of dried wood on the raised hearth. The digust he felt was thick in his voice. "I'm weary and I'm famished. We should have spent the night in an inn."

"And left our prisoner tied in the coach one more night?" Her tone of voice chided him for his thoughtlessness.

Jon sighed greatly. "I suppose not. I don't mind caring for the horses or chopping the wood or doing any number of small tasks, but who among us can cook? If I don't get something to eat and soon, I'll waste away to nothing."

"You won't," Alison responded cheerfully. "I'll

39

cook." At the look of horror dawning on his face, Alison tried earnestly to reason with him. "No, really, Jon. I've been watching Emily for the past few days. I know I can cook every bit as well. It seems so . . . simple!"

Jon blinked at her words, the realization that she was serious already gnawing at his belly. So much for his peace of mind. So much for his physical well being. He knew better than to argue with her, the expression on her face was one he'd often seen before. He quit the room, his every instinct tumultuous, attributing to her all the traits she had in abundance: determined, stubborn, obstinate . . . girl!

When the fire burned briskly and the room began to warm, Alison decided to tackle her next task, that of finding water. Swinging open the door to the parlor, she looked around for Jon, intending to ask him where the nearest well could be found. He was not there so she crossed the room and opened the front door, seeking him outside. Instead she found Morgan who stood very still beside the coach, the checkered kerchief hiding his face, pressing a pistol at the Marquis' heart.

The Marquis was stretching himself beside the coach. The grooves at the corners of his mouth tightened when she appeared and the black eyes leveled themselves on her.

"Get back inside," Morgan growled to Alison.

The Marquis was even more intimidating in full height. Hastily, she complied.

The staircase was loose and battered, creaking dreadfully even under her slight weight. Upstairs she found the bedrooms, a large one which stretched across the front of the house and two smaller ones across the back. Jonathan and Morgan could share the large bedroom, one of the smaller ones would serve as a prison for the Marquis, the third one would be hers. The feather ticks looked to be almost, if not, new, so perhaps Jon's agent earned his fee after all. In a small cupboard in the back bedroom, Alison found clean bedding and, to her great surprise bedwarming pans. As she dragged the crisp, cool sheets over the ticks Alison thought how well they would all rest tonight.

The kettle was whistling as she scurried swiftly down the stairs. Morgan or Jon must have filled it and placed it on the hearth. Already she was so hungry she could practically taste hot, strong tea and biscuits. Her belly protested loudly its emptiness.

Her feet slid to an abrupt stop as she came to the parlor. The Marquis was alone in the room, a length of rope around his torso binding him to a large chair from which he faced the roaring fire. His feet were tied together and bound to the legs of the chair. His wrists were each bound to the arms of the chair.

He turned to look at her, his expression still foul.

A rush of pity swept through her for this man who was, yet again, bound hand and foot. She almost spoke to reassure him, stopping herself barely in time.

Derisive eyes scanned her briefly before he turned them from her. Clearly he did not think the "puppy" worthy of his concern. Alison wondered if he was always this unpleasant.

The front door blew open and Morgan followed, another bundle of wood held in his hands. Alison hastened to the door and shut it behind him, noticing how strong the wind had grown in the last few minutes. She followed Morgan into the parlor and watched as the wood tumbled from his arms and he knelt to toss more pieces onto the fire.

Obsidian eyes were fixed on Morgan and anger emanated from the Marquis. He seemed to be studying, assessing his opponent. The cords in his neck pulsed and his fingers drummed a staccato rhythm on the armchair.

Alison remembered the strength of those fingers around her own and realized he was already plotting his escape. He didn't even seem frightened! And when he did escape, he'd level his own form of punishment on Morgan, Jon, and her. Why should she waste sympathy on a man who would do much worse to them if the situation were reversed?

A thought came to mind and her eyes lit expectantly and she placed her hands akimbo, her head nodding toward their prisoner. "I've been thinking, Morgan. Perhaps we should keep him in the cellar. He can't possibly escape from there and he'd feel right at home . . . with the other rats."

Morgan chuckled as he stood and saw Alison's belligerent stance. The Marquis turned his eyes to glare at her, his brows lowering ominously. Just the fact that he now took notice of her sent her spirits reeling upward. She could relish every moment, as long as he was bound to a chair. "We could chain him to the wall like they used to do and let the rats nibble on his toes. Of course they'd have to chew through his boots first . . . Or do you suppose Jon could wear them?"

"Enough's enough. Don' ye go baiting the poor man any further." Morgan ordered though he was clearly amused. Turning to the Marquis, he said, "In spite of what my young companion says we mean ye no harm. I

42

apologize for the knock on the head I give ye, but it seemed the only thing to do at the time. Ye'll be made as comfortable as possible over the next few days, and we'll release ye as soon as we can. As long as ye cause no trouble, ye should bear no further discomfort."

Alison grinned mischievously, perhaps Morgan was right and she had gone too far. But it did feel wonderful to put this arrogant man in his place. "Oh, yes. You mustn't be too frightened of me," she said airily. "Morgan wouldn't allow me to do anything to harm you, no matter how much I might be tempted. So, you'll have a bedroom upstairs, the same as the rest of us."

The dark head lifted haughtily and thin lips curled, baring straight, white teeth. For the first time since he entered the cottage the Marquis spoke. And his words were very unpleasant. "I promise to deal with you personally. I'll strip the hide off your back and enjoy doing so."

Alison sighed in resignation. "You have the world's worst temper, my lord. Perhaps after a meal and a good night's rest, you'll be cheerier. Really, we mean you no harm, so there's no reason to behave like a blunderbuss."

The black head jerked upright. The word seemed like a challenge to the Marquis. "Your language is as lacking as your manners. I promise I will enjoy educating you in both. I trust whatever demand you sent my man is enough to see your loathesome hides from this shore for all time. Even so, I promise to find you! And when I do, you will sorely regret ever tangling with me!"

Alison's eyes met Morgan's. "Oh, I don't know that

43

our demand was as great as that. How much was it, Morgan?"

"Not enough." The words were gruffly spoken and the smile was gone from the old man's face. "Fetch some cups so we can 'ave tea and get this man to 'is room. I've had enough of 'is temper and threats. Well, get along lad. We've wasted enough time with words."

The lad, Alison, returned moments later bearing a platter full of cheeses, meats, and bread. By now, Morgan was sprawled in one of the most comfortable chairs, facing the heat of the fire, his boots off and his feet resting on the stone hearth. The tea was brewing and sending out a temptingly strong aroma.

"I have to go back for the cups. Where's Jon?"

"Putting that sorry excuse of a coach in the barn," Morgan answered with a scowl. "I'm getting too old for this sort of work. My poor body can't get itself up the stairs tonight."

Alison's eyes twinkled as she dared a glance at the taut face of the Marquis. "But this line of work pays so well."

The black eyes flickered, but it seemed the Marquis was done with threats for the moment.

"Another storm's brewing. We got here none too soon." Jon's voice sounded from the kitchen long before he appeared through the swinging doors. And when he did, Morgan's kerchief had been discarded in favor of a black domino.

"Oh, Jon," Alison said admiringly, "that's much more the thing. I wish I had one just like it!"

"I found it beneath the seat of that damned coach."

"Watch yer mouth!" snarled Morgan bitterly. "What would yer poor mother say if she heard ye now?"

The Marquis' mouth gaped open. The lad had a mother who would worry about his language? What about his criminal tendencies? And what about the flogging he had planned for each and every one of them?

"I knew that carriage had to be good for something." As Jon spoke, his eyes searched the room for their captive. The fair, soft texture of his skin and the gleaming blue of his eyes gave away his youthfulness. "Don't think I don't appreciate the offer of your kerchief, Ally, but I think this is much more what I need. Not quite so tawdry as a solid kerchief. Besides I can eat and wear it at the same time. Fair luck, eh? Too bad there wasn't another for you, Morgan."

At that moment he spied the platter of food. The hunger which had plagued him all afternoon leapt into the youthful eyes. The domino and the Marquis were quickly forgotten. He reached for a slice of bread and crammed it into his mouth, only then remembering their prisoner. A guilty flush rushed up his neck and face. "He can't eat tied like that, Morgan. Don't you think . . ."

"I don't trust his attitude or his threats. He's not been civil since we took 'im."

"Of course he hasn't," Jon proffered reasonably. "Nor would you be civil if you'd had to ride inside that monstrosity of a carriage all day, tied as he was. I imagine he'd like to slit our throats at the moment. Hold a pistol on him if you like, but untie him and let the poor man eat some food."

Morgan contemplated the poor man. If murder was ever on a man's mind, this was the man.

"Jon's right," Alison announced brightly. "It's only

civil to allow him to eat in comfort. He'll be tied long enough."

Morgan's brows furrowed impatiently. Grey eyes lowered onto the Marquis. "If I untie ye, will ye keep yer threats to yourself? I don't want my only decent meal in two days ruined by yer temper."

No one had ever dared speak to Chatham as these low creatures were doing. But he knew the foolishness of empty threats, just as he knew his time to seek revenge would come. He would bide his time, though the little one made that difficult. He'd like to get his hands on that neck and . . . There was time for that later. He nodded his head stiffly.

Alison rose, with the clear intention of untying him, but Morgan bellowed loudly at her to sit down. "I'm the only one wot touches these bonds. Neither of ye goes near 'im. Is that understood?" He waited for a spoken answer before loosening the ropes.

Tea was a morosely silent affair. Conversation was difficult when one had murder on his mind, another was practically asleep in his chair, and Jon was too busy eating to converse properly.

Afterwards, Alison and Jon cleared the table while Morgan took the Marquis outside for air. They returned and Morgan ushered him up the stairs and into the room designated for his use. Jon followed with a hammer and nails to board the windows closed, just in case the Marquis was tempted to try anything. Not that there was much chance of the Marquis escaping, not when his right ankle was chained to the bottom leg of the heavy cast iron bed.

"'e'll sleep tonight, as we all will," Morgan assured the others when he returned to the parlor. "'is head probably pains 'im from the blow I give 'im last night. Perhaps by morning 'e'll be in a better frame of mind. I hope 'e never claps eyes on any of us again, I wouldn't give a farthing for our chances against 'im."

"He does have a foul temper," Alison agreed.

"I belong in bedlam for agreeing to this madness," Morgan growled.

"I was hoping for a game of piquet or faro."

The others looked at him as though he'd lost his mind, so Jon defended himself stoutly. "Well, he is supposed to be a master of the game, and we all know I could stand a few tips."

"Maybe we should all get a good night's rest," Alison spoke through a barely stifled yawn. "Don't look for breakfast too early."

But the following morning proved no brighter. The storm had risen and was leaving cold sleet in its wake. The day promised to be miserable and the first task to be faced was water. There was no maid here who automatically brought it, so Alison would have to fetch it herself. She wrapped her woolen robe about her and pulled on her slippers. Her hair was still in the plait she wore to bed each night. She was just leaving the kitchen, carrying a heavy pail full of the liquid when the front door opened. The Marquis stepped in, his wrists bound in front of him, followed by Morgan who held a pistol high against his head. Alison quickly stepped back.

When the way upstairs was clear again, Alison hurried to her room, donning her disreputable breeches and shirt. She pulled her woolen cap firmly over her curls and returned to the kitchen. As she passed the Marquis' room she was tempted, only for a moment, to

47

see if he was in a better frame of mind this morning.

Last night the kitchen had looked merely dirty. This morning it was filthy. Two hours later, the walls were spotless, the cupboards wiped out and filled with provisions, the stove and tables gleaming. The floor would take longer and a stronger arm than she possessed. Breakfast first, she decided, then she would use what remained of her energy to turn Jon into a willing kitchen maid.

One glance at Morgan's face when he entered the kitchen and she understood this was not the best of mornings for him either. He stoked the oven without speaking a word, poured warm water into a basin, and glared at Alison as though expecting her to question his actions. "The man can wash, can't he?"

"I never said he couldn't." Alison muttered at Morgan's disappearing back. Shrugging her shoulders, she returned to her task. Later, she carried a tray of ham, kidneys, biscuits and tea up the stairs. She was proud of her first efforts at cooking. This should put both men in better moods.

The tray was snatched from her before the door was barely opened. At the firm closing of it, she did catch a glimpse of the Marquis, washing. He was demanding impatiently, "How much?"

From his tone she knew his temper had not improved a whit.

Between her and Jon, the kitchen floor was cleaned and headway was made with the remainder of the house. "A splash of paint, clean windows, some decent drapes and this could be cozy, just like a home."

"For heaven's sake, Alison, we're only here for a few days, not a lifetime."

"A few days, that's all?" she feigned disappointment. "Oh, well, if that's all the time you can spare . . ." She removed her woolen cap and scratched her head. "I do hope his temper improves. Keep an eye out for me, will you, Jon? I want to take a bath."

She'd had enough of dressing like a grubby, beggar boy. After her bath, she donned a simple gown of light green and wore a matching ribbon in her hair to hold the unruly curls at her nape.

The ribbon was loosening and the curls hanging in wisps about her cheeks when Morgan walked into the kitchen hours later.

His brows raised as he peered into the pot she was stirring. Alison grinned and announced proudly, "Jam."

"Next you'll be telling me that you're baking bread."

"Who else?" She couldn't resist laughing at the expression on his face.

"You've never cooked a thing in your life."

"I cooked breakfast this morning. Have you any complaints about that? Or perhaps you'd like to try your hand at the cooking?"

"No, no, no. I'm willing to try anything once, even your . . . talents."

"And what do you intend for him?" The hand holding the stir spoon gestured upwards, indicating the Marquis. "Will he eat in his room, or do you trust him to dine with us?"

"I ain't decided. I dislike keepin' 'im so confined but 'e leaves little choice. 'e's still 'otter'en a wounded bear this morning. In spite of anything I say I know 'e'd rather face me pistol than agree to a compromise. Unless 'e chooses to be more amenable there is no way

49

to alleviate 'is boredom."

The Marquis had his hands clasped behind his back and was staring out the window when Morgan returned. He turned, presenting a picture of careless elegance. A dark brow rose. "It doesn't appear the ransom demand will be answered any too soon. This storm could become waist-high drifts."

"We 'ave time. Seven, eight days. What difference will one day more or less make?" Morgan answered.

"Damn you! And damn those two urchins you connive with!" What little patience the Marquis possessed was long gone.

"'Ere, now. Calm yourself," Morgan placated. "It's too bad but ye've no choice. In fact, none of us 'ave a choice. Take a look 'ere. I've brought some good books to read, to wile away the time. You and I can play cards, ye'd like that, wouldn't ye?" His eyes lit eagerly as he watched the Marquis for some sign that he was interested. The black eyes never wavered. "No wagering, mind ye. I've not as much of the blunt as ye lords 'ave, but we can pass the time, amiably. That is, if ye've a mind to. Try one of these." Reaching in his inner coat pocket, Morgan withdrew two cigars. "They're from the colonies and I'm glad now I thought to bring 'em along. 'Ere, give one a try." Morgan shuffled across the room with the proffered gift in his hand, eager to please.

With a curt expletive, the Marquis knocked them away. "I want none of your pap. I want out of here, you filthy swine! What do you expect from me? If you get any of my fortune, you'll not hear the last of me until I've seen you hanging from my barn, you and those two swine who run with you." His eyes narrowed. "You want money? Let me go, and let me take those two bastards with me and I'll give you enough to keep you in luxury the rest of your days. I especially want the ragamuggin. I'll teach that one some manners."

Morgan's head drooped and he moved to the door, but the Marquis would not let the subject end. "Well, man? How much do you want for them? What's a bit of treachery among thieves? How much?"

Morgan's eyes met the angry gaze squarely. "I'll let ye out twice a day, once in the morning and again just before retiring. Yer meals will be served here, ye'll stay chained to the bed. We cannot afford to take chances with ye. Ye might decide to keep yer threats—"

"My promises you mean! Not mere threats!"

"Ye'll have no freedom as long as ye're here . . ."

"You'll be found. I promise you, I will find you. And then I will see you swing from the gallows."

"A few days from now, we'll have seen the last of each other." Morgan's expression was grim. "I 'ad 'oped to reach a better understanding, but so be it. Let me know if ye be wanting the books. They'd be better than staring out the window all day."

No answer came.

"Suit yourself."

Morgan quit the room in a fierce temper which dissipated as soon as he entered the kitchen. The first thing he saw was Alison perched on a stool, concentrating on the book spread out before her. She presented a pretty picture, sitting high, her honeyed curls filtering finely over her shoulders, her green gown hanging gracefully in folds from her waist. Her slippers were barely visible beneath the hem of her gown. She looked up at Morgan's entrance and gave him a

51

beaming smile.

"Cooking is so simple," she enthused. "I don't know why I never bothered to learn before. I borrowed Emily's cookbook, I don't think she'll notice it missing, do you? It has some of the most heavenly sounding recipes in it. I wonder if she's ever served some of them. They don't sound familiar to me. Have you ever heard of 'Cailles aux raisins en timbale,' or 'Sucre File'? I'm sure I'd remember if I ever ate anything as good as they sound. I wonder what they look like? Hmmm . . ."

Morgan moved to the stove, his eyes lighting on a congealed mass of green and white on a platter. A wary frown encompassed his face. "What on earth is that?"

"My version of 'Filet de Sole a la Florentine'."

"That's not what it's supposed to look like," the frown deepened. "That, I'd remember."

Alison lifted her spoon to her chin and considered carefully. "Well, I don't suppose it ever looked exactly like that, but we didn't have any spinach so I used broccoli, and instead of white wine, I used port. That's the red stuff on it." Her eyes met Morgan's appalled gaze and she immediately became defensive. "Port was all Jon brought, and who can have a good sole without wine?"

Morgan took another look at their dinner and groaned.

When all was said and done, Alison was proud of her creation. Her sole might not be too delightful to look at but it was perfectly edible. And she was certain she possessed a talent for cooking, all she needed was a bit of practice. Even Morgan couldn't expect perfection on her first try. Her bread was a bit questionable, doughy inside, the bottom turned black and the top slightly less burned. Butter and jam would improve its appearance, if not its taste, so she heaped that on the platter she sent up to the Marquis.

Morgan took one look at the tray, grabbed two glasses and what remained of the bottle of port and hauled all up the stairs with him to their prisoner's chamber.

The Marquis had relinquished his brooding for the moment and was now seated comfortably in a large chair, reading one from the stack of books. His mood seemed to have improved until he glanced at the tray and sneered, "My good man, I assure you my corpse is not so valuable as my alive and kicking body. So get rid of that poison and offer me something decent."

"Sorry, guv," Morgan replied honestly, setting the tray on the small table beside the Marquis, "Ye're eating the same as the rest of us and I sincerely 'ope you don't die from it, for if you do, we all do."

"If the problem is money, I do carry some on my person. Unless you have already removed it?"

"Oh, no, milord. We're not petty thieves, we're waiting for bigger game." Morgan chuckled good naturedly, taking a seat opposite the Marquis. "Just how much blunt have ye?"

A haughty brow rose and the lines around his mouth deepened as milord replied chillingly, "A great deal. More than the lot of you thieves can imagine. I'm not a man to forget my enemies. You'll be hunted down the rest of your lives."

"Well, if all ye're going to do is make more threats, I'll leave," Morgan said, rising. "I'd thought to keep ye company but . . ."

"Oh, sit down!" Chatham snapped. "I'm as tired of

making threats as you are of hearing them, and a waste of time and effort they are. You're the damndest bunch of brigands I've even run across in my life. We both know where we stand by now. And I've been alone with my thoughts enough, even if they are black ones, ending with your slow and painful demise."

"I'm quaking in my boots, guv." But this was patently untrue. Morgan's hand steadily poured the port. "'ere," he breathed deeply, offering the Marquis a full glass, "drink this. Ye'll need it to face that meal."

For once they seemed to agree on something. The Marquis had a couple of glasses before he braved his dinner. One bite of the sole and he dropped the fork onto the tray. "I cannot eat this pap. Take it back to the kitchen and fire the cook." His elegant lip curled as he took a sip of lukewarm tea. "Weak." He spat as though it were an evil thing. "Can your cook not even brew a decent cup? You did last night."

Morgan was still chuckling over the Marquis' order to fire the cook, as though it could be done. "'ere, 'ave another glass of port. I'll 'ave to eat the pap, the cook sits down to dine beside me. Maybe a few more sips wouldn't come amiss for myself," he added as an afterthought.

"I fervently pray you do not die from poisoning before I do, or my fate might be starvation. It's certain one or the other is bound to befall me."

Morgan was still laughing when he returned the tray to the kitchen, the port bottle remained with the Marquis. Sole and bread lay nearly untouched on the plate. "His lordship said if the bread was to be served with tea later, don't bother sending any up. 'e described yer cooking in unusual terms, lass. I don't think I'll repeat them. It would suffice to say ye don't compare with his chef."

Alison bristled. "Perhaps he'd like to try his hand at the cooking?"

Morgan's voice boomed with laughter. "'e offered. 'e does 'ave the advantage of at least knowing 'ow most of the dishes should look and taste. Ye should 'ave 'eard 'im ask if ye were trying to ransom a corpse rather than an alive, kicking body. I 'ad to refuse 'is offer to cook, I don't dare remove 'is chains. But for the prospect of something decent to eat, I was tempted."

"Well," Alison remarked nastily, "you can always polish off a bottle of port between you every night before dinner if your appetite needs the stimulation."

"Aye, lass. That's just what 'e said. A bit of port numbs the palate."

Alison's temper took a long time to cool. Jon's remarks throughout dinner did not help, nor did the amount of untouched food. So when it was tea time, the Marquis received the barest of trays. It held tea and one meager spoonful of jelly. "Tell him there's nothing to put it on but my bread and he's already given his opinion of that."

Morgan grabbed an apple on his way out of the kitchen. His conscience bothered him that such a large man should go hungry.

His lordship was undaunted. While eating the apple he let slip to Morgan that the tea was barely tolerable. "It's more like tepid water than tea. Perhaps if the cook boiled the water first. . . ." The Marquis spoke in a soft voice. "I like my tea, as I like all my drinks, strongly flavored."

Morning tea was considerably weaker. Alison did

not take criticism very well. In a burst of sympathy for her prisoner, she placed some of the doughy bread on the tray. And, in an answering spurt of hunger, milord ate it.

The days settled into a routine. Morgan cared for the Marquis; the only glimpse Alison might catch of the prisoner was in the early evening or morning when Morgan allowed him to stretch outside.

Jon did all the necessary shopping since he was already a familiar face in the village. In addition, he fetched water, chopped wood, tended the animals, and did most of the heavy work Alison was unable to do. There was not enough to keep him occupied, and soon he was riding far distances for a bit of fun and gone most of the night.

Alison spent most of her time in the kitchen doing her best to learn to cook. The second night she served a brioche loaf with salmon, mushrooms and onions. Alison only had to envision Emily's in her mind for her mouth to water, so she decided to try her hand once more at Emily's elaborate style of cooking. The dough fell apart and the salmon filling overflowed the pan. When she finally decided to remove it from the oven, the bottom was burnt to a crisp and the top still doughy. Thinking a sauce might help she searched the book for one, but hers lacked all flavor of Emily's, and the lumps were chewy.

Morgan took one look at the concoction and said warily, "What is it this time?"

"Oh, I know it's not so pretty yet, but just wait!" She set a colorful napkin, bright silver utensils and a vase of evergreen pine on the tray. The salmon was definitely a detraction to an otherwise attractive setting.

Morgan grumbled when she offered him a bite. "It's a good thing 'is lordship is 'ere or we'd 'ave to 'ire a taster. With your cooking, it'd be difficult to keep one." Grabbing a bottle of port he escaped just as she was about to vent her wrath at his rudeness.

The bottle was empty when he returned, the plate of salmon untouched. Morgan chuckled at the disappointed expression on Alison's face. "'e claimed 'e wasn't man enough to taste it. 'e'd rather die the slow death of starvation than the quicker, more painful one of food poisoning."

Alison's shoulders fell and she said sadly, "He could at least have tried it. How will I ever get any better if I don't know what I'm doing wrong?"

"Lass, I'm of the opinion that it takes a natural talent for cooking. You haven't shown any of that talent. Why not learn to do something else? Something less 'armful to us others? Why ruin everyone's appetite?"

Tapping the long, serrated knife with which she was slicing bread against the table, Alison snapped angrily, "Oh, bother! I'll learn, just you wait. Here, get the ham from the larder and use this knife to slice it. Then, you and his highness can take your second bottle of port and the two of you can go to oblivion for all I care. You're almost there anyway."

Morgan chuckled. "'e's worse. 'e kept drinking, thinking it might give 'im the courage to take a bite. Heh, heh, heh! I can still see 'is face when 'e took a whiff of it. Ooh, you'd have been truly insulted."

"Go, get drunk with your . . . your friend."

"Not my friend, too toplofty. But I can appreciate a good sense of humor in a man. Besides, I'm only trying to keep 'im entertained, though yer cooking does most of that. This bread isn't so bad. It actually slices . . ."

"Morgan, don't try my temper any further."

Morgan chuckled loudly, his palms raised in a supplicating gesture. Taking the threatening knife from her fingers he began to slice the ham and filled the platter with a generous helping. As he turned to leave, he said soulfully, "Five more days of this. I 'ope we all survive."

After that her cooking remained as simple as possible. She could not compete with Emily's expertise for sauces and spices, so she no longer tried. At least she now had the satisfaction of seeing the plates returned empty. Either plain cooking was her forte, or the others were hungry enough to eat almost anything.

As the week lengthened, the excitement of the kidnapping palled. The extra workload was becoming as boring as her lessons in Wiltonshire.

Jon tried to talk Morgan into allowing the Marquis downstairs in the evenings. "He's got a reputation for the cards, Morgan. Just think what I could learn from him. Why, if I went to London and won a fortune, Geoffrey wouldn't have to worry about my future. I could buy my own commission and dower Alison."

"Just 'ow much do ye plan to win?"

"Fortunes are won and lost everyday in London."

"And ye plan to win one?" Morgan demanded hotly. "Did it ever occur to ye more people 'ave to lose than win? And as for playing with 'is 'ighness, are ye out of yer mind? If 'e's with ye every night, nothing will stop 'im from recognizing ye or yer voice next time 'e sees ye, not even that demmed dominoe 'ides enough. And don't let 'is silence make a cudden of ye, 'e's still after our 'ides. Give 'im 'alf a chance and 'e'll slit yer throat so fast, ye won't be able to pip first. 'e's an angry man, I've never seen one angrier. 'e's all the more frightening when 'e's quiet about it. Being 'is lordship's brother won't save ye."

"You're right, of course, but if I could just learn some of his tricks . . ."

"Pick 'is mind when 'e's not yer prisoner."

"But I'm bored."

"So? Think of 'im. 'e's tied to the leg of the bed by a length of chain. 'e cannot move freely beyond the rug area. I've given 'im books, the same ones to which ye 'ave access. Ye 'ave freedom of the 'ouse and grounds and yet ye chafe. What of 'im? 'is temper grows worse, though I did not think that possible."

"I wish this was over," Alison said fervently.

"Two days yet," Morgan replied grimly. "And when we release 'im, we'd better be on our way fast. 'e's not going to waste any time before searching for us."

The plans were already made for releasing the Marquis. He and his horse would be returned to Oxford where they had been taken. Alison would remain behind in an inn where a hired chaise awaited them. Jon and Morgan would join her as soon as they could. They would all continue on to Wiltonshire, and no one would be the wiser concerning this last week.

As the time neared its end, the tension mounted. His lordship's temper crackled with every word or movement and Morgan had to be doubly on guard whenever he entered the room. There were no more congenially shared bottles of port or cigars, no more teasing remarks about the food. They were again on the footing of bitter enemies.

One evening, when Morgan was outside for a smoke and Jon already gone, Alison heard a commotion from his lordship's chamber. She washed the last of the dishes and still the noise did not abate. Donning her breeches, she carefully opened his door and saw him strain against the chains holding him to the bed post. Guilt swept through her at this first sight of him as a chained prisoner. The week was boring to her, it must have been intolerable to him.

His hands were bound firmly together and in the crook of one finger was the book he had been beating against the wall. The black hair was awry, as though he had been rifling through it with his fingers. Black eyes bore into her angrily.

"Where's Morgan?"

"Outside. He can't hear you."

"And the lad?"

"Gone."

"So there's just you." He spat the words, his distaste for her lingering long on his lips. "Untie my hands. There's a blister on my wrist from the rope and it pains me."

He held out his hands to her.

She was clearly tempted but too accustomed to heeding Morgan's orders, even if she might argue about them. The Marquis shook his hands demandingly and repeated, "They pain me."

Alison frowned. If he was truly in pain she wanted to help him. Never had her intention been to cause him pain. Cautiously she stepped nearer, taking his clenched hands into her own to study.

With an abrupt movement the long fingers grasped at her shirt and clenched tightly, dragging her forward and against his solid body. His fingers moved to her neck and found a soft spot there. Alison barely heard his satisfied grunt for she was too petrified at his hold. Squealing with fear, she kicked furiously against his shins. His hands groped around her neck. One strong forefinger clasped her chin tightly between it and his thumb. Instinctively Alison opened her mouth, his finger found its way in and Alison bit down savagely. With an oath the Marquis threw her from her.

"You cur!" he bellowed, rubbing his finger.

Alison picked herself up from the floor, looked sharply at him and swept grandly from the room. All her hauteur was undone though, for her breeches hung loosely around her bottom. She dared not admit the escapade to Morgan.

Jonathan's boredom became even more troublesome. He developed the habit of leaving each evening and not returning until the early hours of the next morning. He never told them where he was going, he laughed and said he would be back in time for his chores and that was all they needed to know. Morgan commented sourly how his lordship was easier to handle than Jon, at least he was bound and forced to behave.

The afternoon before their scheduled departure, Jon again disappeared. Alison packed and straightened the cottage, wanting to leave no sign of their occupation or hints of their identities behind. Morgan readied the coach. It would remain behind at Oxford, with the Marquis inside and his horse tied to the back.

The day lengthened into night and still Jon did not

return. Morgan paced nervously before the hearth until the wee hours of the next morning. Finally, he decided to look for the lad.

"Lock the door behind me, Alison. Don't let anyone in unless it's myself or Jon." His eyes went toward the staircase and darkened. "And don't go near 'im for any reason, any reason at all."

Alison nodded and watched from the window as Morgan rode off. A chill, black night was upon them and she did not envy Morgan his task.

Taking the ribbon from her hair, she shook her head and loosened the curls. Perhaps if she washed and prepared herself for a few hours of sleep the time would pass quickly.

Again she checked for a sign of Morgan. There was none so she dropped the curtain into place and settled down to wait.

Her head was resting against the arm of the overstuffed chair and a blanket was carelessly thrown over her when she heard the strident banging on the front door. The commotion awakened her instantly. She followed Morgan's instructions implicitly, demanding to know who was there before opening it.

"It's me, Ally, Jon. Open the door."

She pulled back the bolt. "Where's Morgan?"

"Here of course. Where else would he be?"

"He went looking for you hours ago!" she cried in disgust. "Oh Jon, look at you, you're foxed! Seventeen years old and drunk as a lord. And we were supposed to leave in the morning!"

"We'll leave. Just let me get a couple hours sleep, then I'll be fine . . ."

"Oh, certainly," she responded drily. "Up half the

62

night, bosky, you'll be sick as a hound by morning. Morgan's been out looking for you all night. Why, I'll be the only one of us fully alert tomorrow and I know I can't control the Marquis."

"Ally, I don't feel like arguing, do you mind? I just want to crawl in bed and go to sleep." These good intentions took him as far as the sofa, where he stretched full length on his back, put an arm over his head and immediately slept.

Alison turned to lock the door, but another rider was fast approaching. From the window all she could see of him was his size and his black greatcoat. A tricorne covered his familiar head. Morgan. Quickly, he reined in and leaped from the back of his animal. Alison opened wide the door for him. His temper was high and grew worse at the sight of Jon sleeping so peacefully on the sofa.

"'e was at a cock fight," Morgan announced grimly. "The butt of every joker in the place. Wagers were made over 'ow many drinks 'e could 'andle. 'e fought three different men and more wagers were placed on who would win. There's not a soul in this valley who won't know we're here by morning and wonder just who we are. The worst of it is, I don't know 'ow much 'e talked, and there was someone there asking questions about the Marquis."

"But this is so far from London. I thought surely it would be weeks before anyone might think to look for him here."

"We've kidnapped a powerful man and 'e 'as many friends. Since we've been here, we've managed to forget all that. Jon's brought the real world crashing about our ears again. We can't afford to wait. We're leaving right now. This fool," he spared Jon a contemptuous glance, "can wait for the moment. I'll see to 'arnessing the carriage and that the Marquis is secured inside it. You get dressed, but first go through the 'ouse again and make certain we've left nothing behind."

Alison did as she was told, but her earlier work had been thorough. The only room she needed to go through was the Marquis' and that would have to wait until he was gone from there. The stairs creaked as the two men descended to the front door. Alison remained in the kitchen, watching through the slightly parted door as Morgan, his pistol aimed at the Marquis' head, gave orders. "Walk slowly and don't move except as I tell you. I'd hate to put a bullet in yer 'ide just as ye're about to be released. But I will if necessary, so be warned."

The Marquis' hands were bound tightly across his chest. He seemed more disarrayed than usual, as though abruptly wakened. Already his temper was roused and Alison wondered if he even fretted in his sleep. "So I'm to be released," his lordship stated with icy hauteur. "You've finally received the ransom. I trust it was a goodly amount."

"Not as much as ye think ye're worth, but I grow weary of dickering."

"I'll find you, no matter where you go or what you do. I'll find you and those two bantlings . . ." His eyes lit on Jon. "So, that's the hurry." The Marquis said softly, a sort of grim humor twitching about his mouth. "You should never trust anyone other than yourself, Morgan. That is a lesson I learned many years ago."

Morgan waved the pistol in the Marquis' face. "Just move. Let yerself into the carriage. I'll bind ye in there.

Remember, I 'ave a gun."

Alison watched them leave before she mounted the steps to the Marquis' room. There was not much to clear out of there, just a few books and other odds and ends. When she was done she went to her room to change into her clothing.

Chapter Three

Morgan stumbled, his attention shifting briefly before he caught himself. The blunt pistol wavered momentarily as the old man's eyes grew accustomed to the darkness. "Go on, ye. Get out there," he snapped menacingly to the Marquis, following him into the black night.

The chill in the air hit the groggy Marquis and his body stiffened as he inhaled the scent of the cold winter night. Slowly his senses were coming fully awake and alert. His indolent stance was belied by the intent gleam in those black eyes.

The pistol jutted impatiently against his ribs. "Go on."

The Marquis' stride slowed, and with a lazy glance the black eyes took in his surroundings. "You certainly picked a remote spot," he drawled. "No one could ever guess this was my prison. I usually make it a point to frequent reputable establishments. One never knows what vermin may be found in a place such as this."

"Shut up!" growled the old man, waving the pistol.

66

The Marquis laughed unpleasantly. "Perhaps it was all you could afford? I offered you whatever coin I carried on me."

The coach loomed before them.

"Climb in."

The horses jerked nervously, whinnying and breaking the eerie silence. The wind rustled through the trees and Morgan shivered, tugging the collar of his coat around his ears, his attention wavering as he considered the impending storm.

The Marquis reached tethered hands to the strap on the side of the coach and lifted his leg to the bottom step. Morgan sidled nearer, the pistol's barrel slipping lower as the old man waited for the Marquis to ascend. In the next instant, Chatham lifted himself and turned, swinging his leg high, catching Morgan squarely on the belly and knocking the pistol from his hand. Morgan staggered and groaned with the pain but did not fall. His breath caught and he lowered his head, charging valiantly at the Marquis' chest, his fists reverberating desperately as he tried in vain to pummel and subdue him.

His lordship was too strong and quick. He stood aside and watched as Morgan's round body barreled toward him once more. Cupping the bound hands, he seemed to relent and moved within Morgan's sphere, only to bring the wicked fist up, to Morgan's chin. The fierceness of the blow stunned Morgan for only a second, but long enough for the Marquis to gain total advantage. Once more his hands made a fist and unerringly found their mark, the side of Morgan's face. The Marquis' next blow carried the brunt of the barely controlled anger he'd felt all week and Morgan crumpled to the ground in a heap.

The Marquis grasped the body carelessly and tossed it inside the carriage. Rifling through Morgan's pockets, he found a knife and, though it was awkward, managed to cut free of his bonds. A grim smile settled on the Marquis' austere features as he bound Morgan in the same manner he had once been tied. At least there was some justice this night.

His attention returned to the cottage and the black eyes deepened. The decision was easily made. Several long strides returned him to the cottage where he eyed a still unconscious Jon. The lad was dismissed instantly from his thoughts. Dark eyes slid to the stairs.

His lips curled grimly. She thought she was so clever, pretending to be a lad. No genius was necessary to see her soft hands, the curves she thought so cleverly hidden beneath the jacket and breeches. He made certain of her femininity during that first struggle between them. Even now, when he remembered the softness of her breasts as they pressed against him, he knew he would hold that softness in his hands and torment it. He meant to torment all of her.

By rights he should simply turn them over to the law. More than justice, however, he wanted sweet revenge. And he wanted his ransom. No one stole from the Marquis of Chatham and kept the ill-gotten gains. Morgan could not interfere, the lad was incapacitated also. Both would suffer in the morning for his part in this fiasco. But the chit! She would not escape unscathed. He would see her pay for those saucy manners and lack of respect for her betters. She might be lacking in birth and breeding, but, before this night was done, she would learn just how far above her he was. Let her laugh at him then!

He mounted the stairs, uncaring how they creaked. There would be no escape for her now, the Marquis gloated inwardly.

A slight scuffling sounded from inside the room as he gently turned the doorknob. The door swung open silently.

His gaze found not the dirty little chit he had been expecting, but a young woman in the process of disrobing. She did not see him for she was turned from him. She drew her nightgown upwards, uncovering trim ankles and thighs. Very lovely, he thought, his face expressionless, his eyes intent. The flannel gown rose higher and more creamy flesh was exposed. The lines of her legs were long and slender, the curves of her back and buttocks tantalizing him with thoughts of how revenge might be better combined with pleasure. The gown was peeled away and she turned slightly, bringing soft mounds into his view.

Hunger shuddered through him as he remembered how those full breasts felt against his chest.

Honey gold tresses tumbled free of the last of the gown.

The time had come to confront his quarry. This time he held the upper hand.

At the sound of the door closing, Alison's head jerked forward. She gasped with a mingling of surprise and fear when she saw who entered, and hastily grabbed for the gown, tugging it around her to cover her nakedness. It did a poor job. Her clinging hold on the gown only emphasized the fullness of the breasts she tired so desperately to hide. Little of her face could be seen through the mass of hair tumbling about it. He watched as she pressed her lips together in an effort to prevent their trembling. The sight soothed his ruffled feelings somewhat.

Dark eyes probed every soft curve for more of her. She was young, but not a child as he first thought. Those breeches hid the woman very well. She was small and that was most deceptive. She was no child merely to be punished, she was a cheating, scheming woman. Perhaps she was not the victim of Morgan's greed after all. Perhaps Morgan was her victim. His own kidnapping might even have been her idea. Anger beat through his brain at the thought.

"Get out of here!"

Scant heed was given her words. Too many thoughts tumbled about in his brain.

She was a scheming woman, he was certain of it. He knew many of her ilk. With her sort of beauty there was no doubt as to how she used it. Or would use it. She was probably just beginning in the business, but he did not doubt that with her lack of moral scruples she would quickly learn to use that beauty to its fullest advantage. As he watched her seeming indignation, he considered how easy his escape had been. Bitterness etched his mouth into a thin line as he wondered if she plotted the way she held the gown against herself, luring his eyes to her breasts. Her thighs were more revealed than concealed by the gown, enticing him with their softness also.

From the way she looked at him, dared him, he knew she had little experience of men. Not enough. Not yet. Tempting and tormenting a man seemed instinctive within her. All she needed for perfection as a whore was a bit of practice at giving a man pleasure. The idea of

70

being the man to give her that experience appealed greatly. And while he taught her, she would learn more about him than she ever bargained for.

His brow furrowed as unwelcome thoughts came to mind. So what was Morgan to her? And Jon?

"Where's Morgan?" she demanded, echoing his thoughts. Wary eyes flitted rapidly between him and the door.

"How old are you?"

Green eyes wavered between fear and anger. Bravado came to her rescue. "That's none of your concern," she snapped bravely, her courage faltering as he moved toward her. Quickly her footsteps retreated. "What do you want? Where's Morgan?"

His movements did not stop.

"Get out!" she squeaked in desperation. Morgan should have been here by now. He would not have allowed the Marquis his freedom, not willingly. Alison didn't like this man's mocking expression, or the way his eyes were so boldly raking her. "You'd better leave here now! If Morgan comes in and finds you, he'll . . ." The last words shuddered from her as she was backed against the wall. Fear spread, taking her breath with it. She was beginning to understand she was alone in facing him.

His hand closed around her wrist. "I asked your age."

Terror clutched at her throat, robbing her of the power of speech. Swallowing frantically, she barely managed to croak, "Nineteen."

The black eyes lowered and intimately probed the soft swell of her breasts.

She tugged the gown higher and the mound of flesh

rose fuller. Alison saw something in his eyes which had her stammering uncertainly, "You'd better leave now. When Morgan finds you with me, he will be so angry . . ."

The jeering laughter which answered her threat sent shivers through her body. "Not Morgan, lass. He won't know a thing until morning and then his bonds will maintain his helplessness. No, your only hope is the lad, and he's in worse shape yet. Not of my doing, of course. Much to my regret."

The touch of his hands on her bare shoulders was foreign to her and she tried to shrug them off, only to feel the hold grow bolder. The Marquis pulled her to him, depriving her of the flimsy protection of the wall. His hand reached for the one of hers which held the gown and forced the palm open. To Alison's horror, the gown slid slowly to the floor. A taut appeal sounded deep within her throat and was ignored as the Marquis tugged her close and brought the tantalizing breasts against his coat. The hand holding her wrist loosened and tipped her head back while the other roamed freely along her side, stopping to rest on the curve of her breast. Alison gasped and strained away from him, but his hold moved to her hair, pulling the strands taut to keep her still and forcing her to look up at him.

Mocking devil, she fumed silently, her eyes flashing fury at his jeering expression. Only the shuddering of her body gave away the trepidation she wished to hide.

His smile was predatory while his thumb brushed lightly along the pale pink tip of one delightful breast. His eyes watched as several differing emotions crossed her face. How clever she was, he considered, and so

72

adept at pretending to an innocence she did not possess. She almost convinced him that his hands on her were shameful.

His hold gentled as her frantic movements stilled, his fingers brushing through her hair and caressing her scalp. "You're frightened of me," he remarked silkily, "that's good. You've reason to be."

"Please . . . stop . . . stop touching me . . . like that . . ." Alison stammered, loathing that begging note in her voice. "Please, tell me . . . Where's Morgan?"

My lord gave a taunting twist of his lips before bringing them to lightly brush along the curve of her neck. She shivered violently as words were whispered intimately in her ear. "Don't worry, lass. He'll not be bothering us."

In desperation she held herself very still, not wanting to add to the anger this man felt for her. Perhaps if she allowed him to touch her he would be reasonable and tell her where Morgan was. "Don't hurt Morgan. He's an old man and wanted no part of this. Blame me, not him."

"Oh, I blame you, lass," came the softly spoken answer. "I blame all of you, but you the most. You've caused me a great deal of discomfort." His lips did not cease their moist travels across her neck as he spoke but his words held more menace than before. His head lifted and hard eyes intimately probed her body. She was too near for him to see all of her as he wanted to. She shivered at the hand again brushing her breast and turned her face into his coat.

"I deserve compensation for all the trouble you've caused, lass. I'd no idea you were so comely. It must

73

have been the dirt which hid the fact."

"Please . . . if you'll give me privacy, I'll dress. You can turn us over to the magistrate then."

Laughter mocked her and the hateful voice drawled, "I choose the when. And the time has not come. Not yet. I can't handle the three of you, not by myself. And not as incapable as your friends are at the moment. I have no intention of dragging prone bodies around, let alone carting them through a cold winter's night." He paused as though giving the matter weighty consideration, but Alison was not fooled. He wanted to frighten her all the more and he was succeeding. "And, as I have you, I have the game well in hand. I can easily find your friends through you.

"Of course, when I do turn you and your friends over to the magistrate, you will all hang. Kidnapping is a mortal offense."

Alison's face paled at his words, until she recognized the scorn in his eyes. Her arms came up to push him away. Immediately she was thrust between him and the wall. His body was a solid and heavy weight, reducing her struggles to nothing. His leg pressed against her intimately, sending a scalding heat surging through her.

"Or, you could consider ways to placate me," he continued thoughtfully. "With the right sort of persuasion, I might see my way to being more lenient."

As his words and their meaning were slowly comprehended, Alison's fear dissipated and her ire began to boil. Angrily she lashed out at him with her fists and bare feet, bringing a steady stream of grunts and barely understood oaths from him. "You . . . you . . . oaf! Who do you think you are . . ."

She found herself released abruptly and flew from him, crouching for the battle yet to come.

Her gaze slid to the floor and to her gown which was trampled beneath his boots. Slowly she straightened, her hands lifting strategically. They failed to provide any but the flimsiest of protection. Her bareness rendered her more vulnerable than before. Chatham smiled wickedly, stepping back to better ogle his prey.

"You . . . you wouldn't . . . We never thought when we . . . took you . . . that you were less than a gentleman . . ."

"No, my girl, you didn't think or you would never have tangled with me." The soft voice swiftly changed to cold anger. "Be in no doubt, I have the upper hand now and as I've undoubtedly paid very well for the honor, whatever I decide to do with you, I will do. Your act of innocence is very convincing but I'm not fool enough to be deceived by it. I know a whore when I see one."

His thighs were spread wide, his arms folded across his chest, the black eyes raking insolently over her. "You've caused me a great deal of trouble, and now, because I am a generous fellow, I'm giving you the chance to atone, to save your friends for a while longer. You've given me nothing but misery, now you may give me pleasure. I've not had a woman to compare with you in a long time, and you've thrown youself at my head." His laughter, soft and mocking, grated on her nerves. "Perhaps, if you give as much pleasure as your body promises I may consider the ransom well spent."

"But we don't have your money!" she cried, desperately wanting to reason with him, already knowing the effort was futile.

"Oh, no?" he jeered. "I was being released out of your generosity?"

"I can explain," she began eagerly.

"Not now you can't. We don't have time." His eyes left her to gaze about the room until he spied what he sought. Reaching across the bed for her breeches and tattered shirt, he tossed them to her. "Get dressed."

She gaped at the worn breeches in her hand, momentarily filled with hope.

"No, girl," he taunted softly. "When I take my pleasure with you, it will not be here where I must hurry, but in a place where I can thoroughly savour you."

"Please, don't do this . . ."

"You'd best wait with your pleas. I promise, you'll speak your fill of them before I'm done with you."

Alison's eyes were huge in her pale face. She believed every horrible threat he threw at her. Her shoulders slumped resignedly. "If I wore my dress, then, when . . . when you're done with me . . . ," her voice trailed off, she was having difficulty keeping her thoughts coherent. "It would be more seemly for a magistrate if I were to appear in a dress," she ended lamely.

"No, wear the breeches. The only matter on which we agree is that you'll travel safer in the guise of a lad. And perhaps when I do turn you over to the magistrate, I may feel generous toward you and purchase you suitable clothing." He allowed his words to penetrate and watched as her eyes blinked at the humiliating prospect before her. "Shall I help you?"

"No," she shook her head slowly. "I can dress myself."

76

"Then do it. And don't play such a martyr! Even my advances must be preferable to dancing at the end of a Tyburn rope!"

"I don't know if they are," she retorted gruffly, a semblance of her old spirit returning.

"Then just remember, if you hang, so do Morgan and the cub. How would that rest on your conscience?"

Eager eyes lifted to him. "We could take them with us. I will help you. It will not be so diffi . . ."

"Three against one? I'm not such a fool! I've faced those odds before. Besides, as long as I have you, it's as good as having them." His eyebrows arched, the black points of his eyes peering down on her. "Now, do I have to dress you?"

"No, I'll do it," she answered gruffly, turning from him. She stepped into her chemise, knowing he watched her every move. Once she glanced over her shoulder and found his gaze low and intent on her. She hurried into the rest of her clothing but her fingers were clumsy and slow.

The shirt was enormous for her size and the breeches hung more loosely than before. The boots caused her to look like a puppy which had not yet grown to match his feet. Only honey gold tresses remained to remind him she was very much a woman. The Marquis shook his head ruefully. "Come here," he ordered softly.

For only a moment she debated the wisdom of defying him—only a moment. Feeling very much a craven coward, she stood before him docilely as he straightened the buttons of her shirt. His fingers brushed the full side of a breast gently and she stiffened. "You don't fool anyone in that guise. Up close there's no doubt but that you're a female. I want

77

you to remain at my side the whole time you're with me, understand? At least I'm a known danger."

Alison nodded.

His hand went to her chin and lifted it. "Where's your cap?"

Alison gripped the cap tightly. His eyes never left her face as she tucked the golden curls inside and patted it into place. She stood still as his hand caressed the nape of her neck, struggling only momentarily when he pulled her into his embrace and his mouth descended on hers. His lips burned across her mouth and cheeks, moist and demanding. The taste and feel of him was not unpleasant, however much she might have thought they would be. His body surged around hers possessively, his legs wide as he held her tightly against him. He smelled of Morgan's cigars and tasted of brandy.

"I don't know how I'm supposed to spend the rest of the night in the saddle when my mind's on only one thing, you," he groaned in her ear.

When his hands slid to her hips and tugged her closer to his, she gasped a protest. But it was the surging heat of him that shocked her into beating across his chest with her fists and demanding her release. Chatham lifted his head and shook it, wanting to clear the fog of unsteady desire from his brain. "You have much to learn if you think to please a man."

"I don't want to please any man, especially you!" she retorted angrily, her fist delivering a hearty blow to his belly.

To her amazement, she caught him unawares and found herself instantly released. Chatham coughed and sputtered as he gasped for air, but when she would have turned and fled, the heavy hand came down on her arm and forced her to face him.

No woman had ever so much as tried to hit him, let alone land the blow! The women he knew wanted something from him, so much so that they catered to his moods, his wants, his desires. And he, of course, rewarded them very well for their patience. This one was too much of a fool to realize just how generous he could be. Or maybe she had enough of his fortune already.

He bared his teeth.

Alison clenched hers, squinted her eyes, squared her shoulders, and waited bravely for his blow to descend.

And as much as she deserved it, he found he could not lift a hand to her. She reminded him more of a frightened doe at the moment than of any other woman he knew.

He released her, his eyes narrowing. "As I said, you have much to learn about pleasing a man."

"And as I said . . ."

He held up a hand. "Spare me, please. And fix your cap."

His hand enveloped hers as he pulled her behind him down the stairs, past the soundly sleeping Jon and out the back door.

The barn seemed curiously empty without the old coach. But Honey was there and snorted as they entered. Alison shook her hand free and ran over to the mare, crooning soothing words as she lifted the saddle from its wooden perch.

Chatham shook his head, an unwilling smile tugging at his lips. "We're only taking one horse, mine. You don't think I trust you on your own, do you?"

In spite of his anger he had to stifle a laugh at her

forlorn expression. Did she really expect to escape him so easily?

He saddled the large black and led him from the barn. Mounted, he held his hand out to Alison.

She stood by the door, clearly tempted to run. A moment's consideration told her she could not possibly get far, not with that huge animal and this vengeful man after her. She bit her lip and accepted his hand, mounting behind the Marquis.

They rode at a fast steady pace all night. By the time the sun deigned to rise, Alison was weary, her bones jarred beyond recognition from the length of time spent in the Marquis' saddle. The snow covered landscape they traversed was melding into one huge blur when he finally reined the animal in. They stood before a wayside inn and the Marquis gave her grim warning, "If you cause one scene, it's you who'll pay."

Alison nodded. She knew he would keep his threats. By now her shoulders and wrists were surely covered with the bruises he caused.

Following behind him, she was silent as he spoke to the innkeeper. When the man demanded advance payment, she chortled inwardly, wondering how often the Marquis of Chatham had been treated with such little regard to his consequence. She knew she appeared disreputable but, peeping a glance at him, could find nothing wrong with his appearance. His clothing might be a bit rumpled and he might be in need of a shave, but surely no one could miss that arrogant demeanor which bespoke a nobleman. No one could mistake the quality of his clothing or the hawk nose which must be descended from some arrogant ancestor.

But someone had. The smirk was quickly wiped

from her face when the man at her side peered down on her.

The parlor was cheered and warmed by a roaring fire in the hearth. Thick beams of English oak stretched across the ceiling and walls. A long trestle table and benches stood in the center of the room, and several large comfortable chairs surrounded the blazing hearth. Alison removed the worn peacoat and was stretching her hands before the fire when the Marquis joined her. The door closed behind the landlord.

The Marquis spoke softly. "It was kind of you and your friends to leave my money in my coat, especially after I offered it. Perhaps it was not enough to tempt you?"

"I tried to tell you we were not thieves."

"Not petty thieves, as I recall." Milord straightened and swept his cloak from his large frame, tossing it idly onto one of the benches. He chose one of the large chairs which faced the fire to sit in, stretching his booted feet on the stone hearth. Alison grew increasingly uncomfortable beneath his scrutiny as she warmed herself.

"Come here," he ordered softly.

As quickly as the words were uttered, she was across the room, as far from him as possible. Taking a deep breath, she managed to bravely squeak, "No. And I don't think you'd like a scene enacted here anymore than I would."

Milord laughed grimly. "You'll pay for that."

"I'm sure I will," she responded, taking the nearest chair and folding her hands primly in her lap. "There is much I must pay for, in your mind. You want your revenge and nothing else matters. Well, you can't do

81

any worse to me than you're already planning. But you'll not terrorize me further."

"Oh, won't I?" he queried nastily, rising from his chair and advancing on her.

Alison knew she was nothing but bravado, that fact had piqued her all morning. Determined to be more courageous now, she watched his approach and was reminded of just how frightening he could be.

A knock sounded on the door. Alison sighed audibly. Milord scowled and slowed his steps, retreated to the fire and bellowed for entry. A serving maid entered with their meal.

The Marquis accepted the glass of port proffered by the maid and tossed it off in one swallow. The girl laid the platters on the table and curtsied, asking if anything else was needed. Bold eyes raked the Marquis and the "anything else" was made perfectly plain to all of them. The Marquis turned from her, casually dismissing her, and poured another hefty measure of the port.

As the door slammed behind the maid, Alison rose to the table and eyed the huge repast. She was starving. After all, she tried to live off her own cooking no more successfully than anyone else this past week. She sliced a piece of bread and buttered it, taking the first of many bites. She was chewing contentedly when the thought occurred to her. "I think you should have taken her up on it, my lord. Look at the trouble it would have saved both of us."

"What are you talking about? Your clothing must affect your manners as well as your intellect. You even eat like a schoolboy."

Alison ignored this. She was growing accustomed to his nasty temper. "The serving maid, of course. She was sending out lures."

His dark brows rose. "And you're an expert on such matters? Where did you acquire your . . . experience?"

"Jon keeps me informed."

"Of course."

Alison took another bite of the bread and looked curiously at the Marquis. "If you took the maid up on her offer, you could satiate your baser instincts and I . . ."

"You could go free, I suppose."

"Well, that was my original thought," Alison responded cheerfully. The food was making her feel much better. "Do you want some of this bread? It's delicious."

"Anything is better than the slop we've been eating all week," he answered fulsomely, taking a seat across from her. "Would you like some of my port?"

"Slop!" Alison echoed, aghast.

"Oh, was it you who did the cooking?" he questioned blandly. "It's a wonder any of us survived." His fingers snitched Alison's slice of bread and tossed it into his mouth before she could utter a protest. "What's under that cover?" he mumbled. "Mutton! Thank God, it's not ham. I've eaten enough of it these last days to last a lifetime!"

Alison forgot his insults, the snitched piece of bread, everything, at this news. "Not ham? Oh, how wonderful!" she said, tucking into her meal.

She fully enjoyed each and every bite. The Marquis was sipping brandy, very relaxed and contented from his meal before he spoke again. "Am I to assume you don't normally do the cooking for the three of you?"

She shook her head ruefully. "Probably never again.

83

Though I thought I did very well for a beginner."

He watched her relax against the stiff backed chair and wondered that she was a mass of contradictions. Her use of language was very fine for her to have come from too low a class, and she was definitely unaccustomed to hard work. Morgan, of all of them, was the only one who spoke within his station, his language and accent broadly announcing his northern rearing. He was definitely more accustomed to manual labor. The Marquis had not seen much of the lad, but his impression was much the same as with this girl, he was educated beyond his station. The Marquis would wager the whole of the ransom that the lad had done very little, if any, of the work. They were three unlikely companions.

"I heard Morgan call you Ally. A nickname, I presume?" He spoke casually and Alison nodded her head. "What's your full name?"

Alison hesitated, popping a comfit into her mouth. "Alline Jurot." She lifted wide, innocent eyes to him. "I'm a quarter French."

A smile tugged at the corners of his mouth. Baggage! "More port? Another comfit?"

"I'd really like a cup of tea."

"Whatever you wish, sweet. Your strength must be maintained," he jeered softly.

Instead of the coy reaction he was expecting, she murmured her thanks and relaxed weary shoulders against the chair. "Must we travel any further today? I'm so tired."

Chatham crossed to the fireplace and pulled the bellrope to order tea. His prisoner was very good at this act of innocence.

Alison poured. Milord grinned rakishly as she gave him his cup, his fingers brushing against her palm even as she pulled away.

"I shall dress you in satins and laces," he said huskily, "when I dress you at all. No more breeches for you, sweet."

The mocking lips curved upwards and dark eyes crinkled at the corners as he watched her reaction to his words. A slow flush spread across her clear features and she struggled in vain to seem indifferent to his goading. The tea burned its way down her throat. Somehow she found the courage to ask, "How long do you plan to keep me with you?"

"As long as it takes to weary of you. And to get my money's worth, of course."

"Of course." Her gaze dropped to her lap and the teacup she held in her fingers. "Would it make any difference if I told you none of this was done for money?"

The Marquis laughed. "And, of course, you would tell me now, when the truth cannot be verified?"

Alison raised her eyes. "I tried to tell you earlier. You would not listen."

"No, I had my mind on other things. It seems my mind has been elsewhere all night. Come here and give me a moment's peace."

Tears sparkled in her eyes. "Please, I know you have reason to dislike me, but I meant you no harm. The mischief you plan is more bitter than I deserve. Won't you let me go?"

"By God, you have a short memory!" he roared, rising from his seat and moving steadily toward her. "I have spent seven days manacled to the end of a bed, my

85

head was near split open and a pistol has been aimed at my heart! You would call that harmless?"

Her answer came with difficulty she was shaking so badly. "No, but our intention was only to keep you out of London, not harm you."

"And the ransom? That was a gratuity for your consideration?" he questioned angrily. "I am no man's fool! Be warned now, girl, I find your tongue and this arguing tiresome. If you think to make our . . . liaison unpleasant, remember what you have to lose. Seeing you as you are now in those garments, I question the reason I brought you along. Yet, the memory of how you looked bare tempts me, yet. You should be praying that beauty brings the satisfaction it promises, for as long as you please me, you, Morgan and the cub are safe from justice."

His face lowered and neared hers to give emphasis to his next words. "But this I swear. No matter what game you play, tonight you will be mine. You will earn that ransom which seemed so important to you, and you will earn it well. I have thought of nothing other than that delectable little body of yours all night and all morning. Whether you come willingly or not matters little to me. I paid for you and by God I will take you!

"It's obvious how little experience you have of men," he spoke scornfully, "or you never would have handled me so clumsily. You'd best pray that you have enough experience to give me pleasure. Perhaps you're clever enough to learn quickly how to please me so I will keep you for a long time. For just as soon as I'm bored with you, I turn you and your cohorts over to justice.

"The tables are neatly turned, my girl, and you are in my power now. Remember that. It is what I want that matters."

He tugged the woolen cap from her head, allowing the tresses to tumble down her back. Her fingers gripped the rim of the tea cup, but the telltale knocking of cup against saucer caused the Marquis to laugh grimly. Taking the cup from her hands, he set both it and the saucer on the table. His hands grasped her shoulders and pulled her to stand before him.

"Please . . ."

"Cease your prattle, girl. This small appeasement is all that's saving you from hanging. Give me a reason to keep you alive the rest of the day."

Fingers groped at her top button. Alison tried pitiably to stop him but her hands were ruthlessly captured and held taut behind her back, rendering her helpless. He tugged her against him so that her breasts met the iron hardness of his chest. His head bent and his mouth captured hers, the hot, moist tongue darting against her lips, coaxing them to open so he might taste her sweetness. Alison shivered, not wholly with fear, finding the flickering of his tongue teasing and tempting and very pleasurable.

Until this moment, she had always disdained sins of the flesh, certain she could easily avoid them. As sweet torment swept through her body, she learned how wrong she was, and how easy it would be to fall into temptation.

"Open your mouth," he ordered gruffly, his impatience coming to the fore. Alison complied, the feel of him against her too pleasurable to be denied. She was totally unprepared for the onslaught of senses which enveloped her as his tongue snaked inside her mouth, filling her, demanding more of her. She was pressed full

87

length against him and it was this pressure which must have caused the tips of her breasts to ache, the center of her loins to tingle.

Her lower lip trembled and he caught it between his teeth.

Her hands were freed as his lowered to her hips and her buttocks, pressing them intimately against him. Feeling very much the sinner, Alison curved her hands around his neck, pulling him closer. How could she have thought the smell and taste of him merely pleasant? The ache growing inside her could only be assuaged by his hands, his mouth, his touch . . .

His hands swept her side, tormenting ruthlessly as they rested on her rib cage, circling her being with a savage demand for satiation. One rose and gently cupped a breast, sending heated desire through her belly . . . and lower.

The kiss reluctantly ended, milord pressing his forehead against Alison's. His breath was harsh and erratic.

Alison's eyes followed the path of his gaze to her breasts, watching in awe as he gently unfurled her soft chemise and bared her full breasts to him. His hands rose and cupped each in turn, fingers gently teasing the pink tips. He spoke thickly, the words long and slow in coming, "How strange it is, to be removing a lad's shirt and finding a woman beneath. And no lad's shirt should ever cover these."

A shuddering breath eased from Alison. His head lowered. The first touch of his moist mouth on her heated flesh sent waves of desire surging through her. His mouth locked on a nipple and suckled, driving her to deeper torment. She whimpered, weak with her need for him. His mouth and lips suckled the other breast, his arms steadying her as her knees threatened to give way. Nuzzling her lips to his neck, she offered them to him in mute invitation. With a harsh groan he pulled her against him and hungrily took her shy offering, his tongue seeking all the secret places of her mouth, playing a game of temptation and torment within her.

As abruptly as this began, she found herself set away from him. The staccato rhythm of his breathing fanned against her hair as he struggled for control. The time was not now, not yet. Not until he could have a full night with her. Her wild response brought him near to losing control, something he never did. And something he would never do. And this one still had a lesson or two to learn from him.

"Sorry, sweet," the mocking tone was back in his voice, "but I must not lose my head or else Morgan and the pup will be breathing down our backs. I'm afraid you'll have to wait until tonight, though it is a strain."

A deep rush of shame crept up her entire body. How could she have responded to him like that? And how could something so earth shattering be so mocked by him? The sea-green eyes filled with moisture and she turned awkwardly away.

At the sight of her stricken face, he regretted the words. Her response was so sweet and trusting and he had to destroy it. His arms pulled her back into their circle. "I promise to try to control myself." The words were whispered through her hair. "Though, when you're behind me in the saddle and your breasts press against my back, it takes all my control not to lay you right there!"

Alison was disgusted with herself and with him. The

hot flood of desire was gone, replaced by a sick loathing. Her tears were dry without ever being shed. Abruptly she pulled from his embrace and turned from him, her hands busy righting her clothing. "You may be an educated nobleman, but someone, anyone, should have taught you manners! You're not a gentleman, you're nothing but . . . a . . . blackguard!"

Her outburst only amused the blackguard. A smile played around his mouth as he watched her fumble with her lacy chemise and the ragged boy's shirt. When she was done, he took her hand. "Let's go. The faster we travel, the sooner I can take my time with you."

"My cap!" she wailed as they reached the door.

He released her hand. "Then get it, and hurry!"

The rest of the day was long and wearisome. Alison lost all sense of direction as they traveled first west, then south, then west again. They traveled narrow lanes rather than roads, and Alison wondered how Jon or Morgan would ever find her.

Their pace was brisk, and their positions on the horse rendered conversation impossible. Her hands were around the Marquis' waist, loosening both times she fell asleep against his back. He felt her threatening to fall and jerked her into wakefulness by grabbing them tightly about him.

Weariness seemed to settle in her bones.

Daylight waned early this time of year. Her eyes were again closing as the huge black was reined in to stop. Alison slid wearily from the animal's back, her hand gripped by the steadying one of the Marquis' as she dismounted.

A sign high overhead boasted the Cock Crow's Inn, obviously a much neater inn than the one they

90

breakfasted at earlier. The Marquis followed closely behind her as she entered, not letting her out of his sight or out of his reach. Again he ordered a private room, again he had to pay in advance.

As they followed the landlord to the private parlor, he jeered for her alone, "I'm glad that gives you such satisfaction. We both appear disreputable."

"You could always tell them you're a Marquis."

"What? And have them laugh me out of this place? I need food and rest too badly."

Though the inn appeared unpretentious, neither the service nor the food could have been better. Supper was roast fowl and baron of beef, well cooked and soaking in their own juices. The vegetables were well seasoned, the biscuits light to the touch and golden brown on top. A pudding completed the meal.

Throughout it, Alison kept the Marquis' glass filled with claret. Her own glass was refilled only once. Already she felt the effect of the potent wine though it didn't seem to bother him a bit. No matter how much he drank. She was pouring yet another glass of wine for him when she lifted her eyes and saw unholy amusement in his. She realized her little ploy was not working. He was no nearer to being drunk than when they first sat down.

Before she left the table she slipped a small carving knife into her coat pocket.

The Marquis settled himself in a comfortable chair and faced the fire, his feet propped on the hearth, a full bottle of brandy on the floor beside him. Alison sat stiffly against the far wall, wondering if she might escape through the door before he reached her. She was under no illusion that he meant to take her tonight and she was woefully unprepared to fight him. Her response this morning taught her how weak her flesh was. She was no better than the lowest sinner who reveled in the sins of the flesh.

Green eyes measured the distance between the door and his lordship.

Tipping the bottle to his mouth, he spoke without so much as glancing at her. "I wouldn't if I were you. I would be very angry, especially now that I am so comfortable."

She forced herself to wait. She was drowsing when the landlord returned and informed the Marquis their room was ready. His lordship stood and looked severely down the long length of his nose at her. "Come along, Alvin." He spoke for the landlord's benefit, shaking his head as they passed through the door. "He ran away from school and his mother leaves it up to me to see to him. I think he deserves a sound beating, but if I take the strap to him when we get home, there the good lady will be, begging me not to be too harsh on the boy."

Alison winced for the children the Marquis might have, and that thought opened a whole new vista to her.

The small room was as neat as the rest of the inn. A bed was set beneath a wide window, fresh blankets and pillows covering it. A cot was stretched beside the bed and Alison supposed this was for her use, as the son. A washstand and basin of water were in the corner, a chiffonier stood against the far wall, a tray of glasses and a bottle of brandy stood atop it.

The innkeeper inquired if there was anything else his guests needed and when he was informed there was not, nodded, wished them a good night and took his leave.

Alison stood very still in the center of the room, mutely staring at her surroundings.

His lordship stood in the doorway, his hands folded across his chest. "Now, what's on that little mind of yours, besides wondering if you've gotten me so drunk I'll fall asleep and leave you alone?" There was rich humor in his voice.

"Are you married?"

The elegant body of the Marquis straightened and those black eyes deepened in intensity. "And that is no concern of yours," he sneered softly.

She rounded on him then, furious. "This was sordid enough before, when I assumed you were not, but if you are, and if you have children . . ."

"Sordid or not," he interrupted coldly, "I've bought and paid for you. And now, I'm done with words. I want something more." He moved quickly, his hand snaking out to reach for her, but all he captured was the cap which he tossed negligently onto the bed. Black eyes followed her fleeing figure and his fingers moved to his cravat and began untying the knot.

She stood across the room from him, only then realizing he stood between her and the door. Her eyes widened as he began to disrobe.

"You may as well face it, sweet. We will be sharing that bed tonight."

"I wish you would listen," she begged earnestly, growing more desperate as his shirt joined the cravat on a chair. "I am not what you think, nor am I bought and paid for!"

"Oh, not enough money? Well, as soon as I've learned how much you cozened out of my man, I'll decide that. If I decide to keep you, you'll undoubtedly be like the rest of your kind and grow more demanding. Jewels, carriages and clothing are not exactly cheap, and you'll probably want your own house. As a matter of fact, I might insist upon it. I treasure my privacy. No, I don't think you'll come cheaply."

She shook her head slowly, her mind whirling as she desperately sought words with which to convince him. Her head creeped steadily to her pocket. "You'll regret this. I am not that sort of woman . . ."

He stilled his movements, his eyes narrowing on her. "Stop this now," he ordered coolly. "From this time there will be honesty between us, that means from you as well as me. I would remind you, when you foolishly think to drive up the price with your protestations, that I might weary of arguing with you. And then where would you, Jon, and your Morgan be?"

Hope lit her features. "Do you mean you might weary of me tonight?"

The anger drained from him at the sincerity of her words. This act of hers was very convincing. Against his will, his voice softened. "No, not tonight. I think it will be a long time before you bore me."

"Oh." The disappointment she felt was easy to read in her eyes. Her hand clenched tightly inside her pocket. The other hand lifted to her cheek and she brushed away a tear. He knew the heated urge to kiss away all her tears, to tell her how little she had to fear from him. He had no wish to hurt her, but he had to have her tonight. His need had been growing like wildfire. If he waited much longer, his desire would be too fierce and he had to avoid that at all costs. He wanted to pleasure her also.

Breeches joined the shirt and cravat.

He stood before her naked. Alison lifted her head, her hair swirling wildly about her face. With fluid grace he came toward her. She felt distanced from the moment, as though she were in the midst of a nightmare, watching these happenings from afar. His greater strength was apparent in the corded muscles of his arms and chest, in the lean agility of his hips and thighs.

She backed away, her fingers still on the weapon in her pocket, her eyes glazed with moisture. The wall stopped her. Only now did she speak again, her voice low. "Please, don't do this."

He shook his head. "I won't hurt you."

A frustrated sob escaped her as she swiftly brought the knife from her pocket and held it menacingly toward him.

His movements slowed. "Where did you get that thing?"

"At supper," she replied, her eyes carefully avoiding him. "Don't come near me. I'll use it. I swear I will."

"You'll have to, if you think to stop me," he answered coldly.

He did not make idle threats, nor did she. He advanced further, his ire crackling in the stillness of the night. She feared his temper but the sight of him near was even more threatening. In clothing he looked dangerous, in his bare state his strength was more obvious. Sinewy muscles filled his shoulders and crossed his chest, tapering to a narrow waist and belly. Black hair tapered with his frame . . .

His mouth was twisted into a half-smile which seemed to dare her to strike. Still his stride did not slow. Swallowing convulsively, she lifted her arm high. One more step and he would be in front of her, within striking range. He took the last step. Pressing her eyes closed, she swung the knife with as much force as she could gather. The knife hit flesh and sank, but it was Alison's voice which groaned with pain. Her fingers released their hold on the knife as she struggled desperately for air.

The knife clattered to the floor and she felt strong hands on her shoulders, keeping her upright. Her eyes fluttered open and found his lordship holding her tightly. Something hot and frightening was in his eyes. His fingers slid to the buttons of her shirt and loosened them. She hadn't the strength to push him away. "You fainted," he said blandly.

"No, no. I didn't," she stammered, her whole body shaking in reaction. Whether she was relieved or anguished that he survived, she didn't know. "How . . . how badly did I hurt you?"

He lifted one of her hands and touched the fingers to his chest. A red sticky substance oozed onto her fingers.

Black anger was in his eyes. "See, it's not a bad wound, not too deep. Nothing to be too proud of." His voice was silky and cold, "But it gives you another sin to pay for."

Alison's eyelids drooped forlornly. "I am sorry!"

"Why? Was it not your intention to strike me?"

Her eyes opened wide and deep. "Yes . . . No! Not like that. I was aiming for your throat. . . ."

Alison gasped as she realized what she'd said. All she wanted was to keep him away from her.

The black rage on his face told her there would be no

96

mercy now.

His hand went to her throat, the fingers slowly twining into a vise. Blood rushed to her head and beat unmercifully against her brain. She was starved for breath when his fingers finally relented and only gripped tightly. His rough voice rasped in her ears, "So young and lovely, yet so bloodthirsty." The pressure of his hand forced her head up and her eyes to meet his. The brilliance of his gaze mesmerized her. His other hand tugged the shirt over her shoulders and pulled it low, his voice rough while it continued to jeer, "Though, you might remember in the future that you have better odds of hitting your target if you keep your eyes open and watch him. Does wonders for accuracy." The shirt was stripped from her and his fingers impatiently tugged on her chemise. The garment lay in shreds at her feet. Chatham lowered his eyes and she glimpsed the wild hunger in them. The knowledge of his desire for her was heady and titillating, more so as his fingers loosened and stroked along her slender neck.

"Your breasts are beautiful," he muttered thickly, a tic jerking erratically along his cheekbone. His head lowered to her and she thought he meant to kiss her. His motions were slow and sure, experienced. She was caught in a web of forbidden desire and did not know enough to break away. Instead of his mouth meeting hers, his face buried itself in her hair and he sought the sweet fragrance of her. Alison reached a hand out and touched his chest, the dark hair there thick and curling. His hot groan encouraged her touch and her fingers melted into the thick pelt, making him achingly aware of her inviting warmth.

"I prefer you bare to ribbons and lace," he rasped in her ear. The breeches fell to her feet, startling her out of her desire fuddled state. Her eyes widened and she bent down, intent on retrieving them, but his arms stopped her, circling and pulling her against him. His mouth took hers finally, hotly and wildly.

His hands were in her hair and around her face, cupping it as aching lips met sweetly. He was careful not to frighten or bruise her. At the moment his own need was foremost in his mind, closely behind that was giving her pleasure. Never had it seemed so important to please a woman before. His tongue delved hotly inside her mouth, filling it, tasting it, feasting on the sweetness of her. Her body quivered at the deepening intimacy of his kiss and she pressed against him, unaware of her unspoken invitation.

Chatham gasped for air, the raspy sound emitted from his throat testifying to his arousal. His mouth tasted her neck, depositing moist kisses along her nape. She shivered at the heated pleasure his lips aroused. His hands cupped her breasts, lifting their fullness, testing their weight and substance within his palms. Thumbs and forefingers lightly teased her nipples, arousing them to peak hardness, rendering her weak with wanting more of his touch, more of him. He brought his dark chest to the mounds, his hair lightly tickling the crests. Alison watched in fascination as he gently rubbed against her, his skin so dark and rough, so contrasting to her creamy, hot flesh. A groan of pleasure shuddered from her at this torrent of sensation he caused. Her hands lifted to his shoulders and neck, the aching need within threatening to shatter her into a million tiny pieces.

His mouth opened and locked over hers, his hands coming to cup her buttocks and bring her fully against him. The long sinewy thighs were wide spread, the heated center of him burning into her as she touched him with her nest. Her body jolted from the impact, her senses spinning until reality set in.

"No!" she cried wildly, pulling away from him.

"Oh, no, my sweet," he rasped at her, his hands tightening around her waist. In one swoop she was in his arms, his long strides heading toward the bed. "'Tis too late to play your tormenting games any longer. You've made me want you, and badly. What more do you expect of me?"

At his cold-blooded words sanity washed over her. She struggled to be free and found herself so when he tossed her onto the bed. Her freedom was short lived for, like a predator, he followed her and trapped her beneath him, his body boldly declaring his passion. Her thighs were scorched at the intimate clenching of his body.

Like a trapped animal she fought, but his hands wound around the wild strands of hair, tightening until her head was taut and the creamy lines of her neck, throat and breasts were brought into his range of vision. Hungry eyes found impudent nipples rising for his taste. And so he feasted. When she whimpered with her torment and tried to buck him off, the hands tightened and his mouth traveled leisurely up her shoulders and neck, nuzzling, sending tender torment through her. His tongue thrust inside her mouth, demanding every drop of sweetness within her.

He was slow and tender in demanding her response. The tormenting fingers swept her hips and thighs, nestling between them. Alison stiffened, knowing the sin she committed in wanting this man. Even if she found the strength to deny him, he would refuse to be denied.

The fingers dipped and found her moisture. Alison whimpered, her body heaving at this intimate touch. With his mouth he stopped her protestations, and his hand in her hair ceased her struggles.

His tormenting fingers ceased their probing. Lean hips lifted and settled over her. The hand at her nape tightened, bringing her head back so she arched toward him. Her breasts were offered to his gaze, to his touch, to his lips.

A hard thigh slipped between her own. His eyes were glazed with desire, his face and neck dark and perspiring with molten need. A grim smile settled on his lips. "And now my bloodthirsty little vixen . . ." A ragged breath shuddered from him as his hardness met the joining of her thighs. The hand on her nape tightened. "Now, spread your thighs, little one. I don't want to hurt you . . . just a bit will do. Ah . . . ," he groaned deeply as her thighs slackened and parted. "Yes, little one, that's it."

His hardness probed insistently. When he entered that first little bit she again gave that breathless gasp he eagerly anticipated. Like an experienced seducer he savored the moment, his fiery lips tasting the rosy tips of her breasts, his tongue sliding seductively over them. He wanted her dripping with need for him before he began the slow, tormenting process of assuaging that need. The heated pleasure of her moisture had him throbbing with desire. He found himself the one tormented, the one shuddering with aching need. His

100

hips thrust, his manhood penetrating, filling her womb with his strength and passion.

A cry of pain rose and pierced the night. His body tensed and his movements ceased. He released her hair and pressed his weight on the arms surrounding her, the corded muscles contracting as he lifted himself and gazed down on her.

The pain she suffered was apparent in the face she tried to turn from him. Moisture trickled down her cheeks, running into her mouth, tangling with her hair. Like the tormented man he was, he could not resist her. His lips tasted salty tears, his tongue licking along her cheekbone and darting between her lips. His sweet caresses sent wildfire spiraling through her veins. His hungry tongue probed and prodded until she was burning with need.

The pain receded. A creamy moisture brought on by molten need comforted her and enticed him further.

Lean hips thrust, filling her again, and again . . . and again. Alison arched against him, reluctantly giving in to his demands, craving the pressure of his thrusting body against hers. Rhythmically their bodies met. The ache pitted so deep in her belly threatened to consume her. He tormented her need rather than comforting her with each new thrust. The torment was at fever pitch. His words haunted her ears. "You are so sweet . . . so beautiful. Ah, yes, just like that . . . you move so sweetly . . . Do you like this? And this? And this?"

She gasped at each tormenting thrust, the pleasure bittersweet, her eyes and womb filling with moisture. She could bear no more. The tormenting pleasure he gave her threatened to shatter her into small bits of sweet pain. And he drove deep, deeper. Her body shivered as sensations swamped through her. Pleasure exploded within her as she arched one final time, the bittersweet sensations of the moment overwhelming her.

His mouth locked onto hers as though to taste of her pleasure. His body heaved within the circle of her arms, his throat against her ear, his nostrils inhaling the fragrance of her. His body erupted, filling her with his seed, the intense sensations streaming through his body.

"I'm too heavy for you," he said much later, rolling from her. The dark gaze watched broodingly as her face colored and she pulled a blanket up to try and hide her slender, bare limbs.

His hand stopped her in midair. "Why didn't you tell me?"

Her tear-streaked face would haunt him forever, he thought. Confused, her eyes were troubled and her mouth quivered with pain. "What?"

"Why didn't you tell me you were a virgin?" He raked a hand through his thick head of hair. "That's not the way I would have made love to a virgin." His voice lowered intimately but regret was threaded through his words. "I would have been more gentle. I never meant to hurt you . . ." The words trailed off. They were an echo of her earlier words.

Alison's mouth trembled. "What else would I have been? I'm not married!" she wailed innocently.

He released her, watching as she pulled the blanket over her, curling into a tight ball and scooting as far from him as possible. Her stifled sobs tormented him until she fell into a troubled sleep.

The decanter of brandy waited him on the chiffonier.

He rose and poured a hefty measure of the brew, his gaze on the slender lines of his captive.

So she's not married? Was she really so innocent that she thought marriage was required for the loss of one's virginity? No, not any longer she wasn't, he thought ruefully, downing the first of many glasses. He had taught her much of what she needed to learn, just as he promised himself he would. The thought brought him little pleasure.

She was an innocent, an innocent who gave him more pleasure than any woman before her. Already he was rousing. By morning he would be eager for her again.

And he would take her. By damn he would! His conscience might be troubled at treating an innocent girl so roughly, but he had to remember what she had done to him. She kidnapped him, held him for ransom, and to top that off, she tried to murder him. How could he ever have suspected her of innocence?

She still owed him. And she would pay.

All he had to do was become accustomed to what he'd done to the little brigand. The bitter taste of which he could wash away with brandy.

Tilting the bottle, he drank deeply. Tomorrow he'd show her he was not an animal.

Bah! Why should he worry what she thought? She was his, bought and paid for. But when he closed his eyes, all he could see was her stricken face, tears streaming down beautiful green eyes, eyes made to hold laughter, not tears.

The morning sun beat through the window panes,

sending rays of warmth across the bed. Alison stirred, the heavy aching of her limbs waking her fully. She opened her eyes, closing them as memories of the night before flooded through her mind. Her head drooped back onto the pillow. Inwardly she groaned.

The mattress shifted and a weight rolled toward her. Alison stiffened as the Marquis' arm instinctively came around her. Through it all, he slept soundly.

For several moments she lay there. Then, realizing he was not about to waken, she removed the offensive appendage and slipped from the bed.

Scurrying so she might be dressed before he wakened, she hurriedly tossed her clothing on and pulled her hair away from her eyes. When she was done and still he hadn't moved, she steeled herself and moved nearer the bed to watch him. He slept on, soundly, innocently. A long time passed and still he had not moved. Her eyes searched the room, spying several bottles empty of the brandy they once held. Her lips twisted scornfully as she realized he must have drunk the one left by the landlord and gone to fetch several more.

Apparently her idea had been a good one. She miscalculated in that she didn't pour the drink down him.

And then she saw the knife. It was still where she dropped it the previous night. Crossing the room, she retrieved it and studied it intently while thoughts rumbled around her mind.

No, she barely found the courage to strike at him last night. She could never strike him when he was so defenseless. She was no murderer! Her brows arched as a thought came to mind. But a little bit of vengeance for

104

her pain and humiliation . . . that was a normal inclination, surely?

Her prey shifted on the bed and Alison jerked away, prepared to run for her life if need be. He didn't waken. He was on his back now, spread-eagled and shameless.

Devious thoughts came to mind and a smile spread across her lips. He thought to humiliate her, did he? Well, perhaps he needed some of his own back! The thoughts became embellished in her mind and it was all she could do not to laugh aloud.

He would sleep soundly most of the day. At least he should if he drank as many bottles of brandy as were on the floor. Perfect. She only wished she would still be here when he wakened, but her freedom was more important than seeing her retribution.

Taking the knife in hand she set to work cutting the top sheet into strips. These she used to bind his legs to the bottom bed posts and his hands to either side of the headboard. His knees were bent so he could fit his full length on the bed but the drink had him so sodden, he muttered no protest.

She stood back to enjoy her handiwork and had to laugh aloud. My lord Marquis was quite a sight. She would relish this moment forever.

His clothing, she thought cunningly, they would be the perfect final touch. She made strips of these also, all the while imagining his furious reaction and laughing to herself. She left his boots in case he had far to walk, telling herself how generous she was being. The thought of him crossing the breadth of England in nothing but boots made her laugh again. But he would be walking. She would have his horse.

Her need for his money was greater than his, she

decided, rifling through his jacket for any coin before destroying it also. Stuffing her hair in the woolen cap she decided to forgo breakfast, just in case. She turned back for one more triumphant look and decided one last touch was needed—one which would protect his modesty. The last strip of tattered sheet she tied into a bow and placed in a most strategic spot. To see the look on his face when he found this was almost worth staying around for. Almost.

She sailed gaily through the door, to her freedom.

The landlord and his wife were in the kitchen, discussing their unusual guests. The genial landlord remarked casually, "I've never seen a man drink so much in one night. It's not strange at all he's sleeping so long. Still, he seemed in a hurry to get back to the wife."

"I'm relieved you took their money in advance," his wife answered shrewdly. "I don't trust them. They look scurrilous to me."

"They do. But as you say, there's no need to worry they'll not pay."

The wife was roused to the window by the commotion sounding from the barn. She watched for a moment before remarking to her husband, "How strange. The lad is up before his father, saddling the horse. I don't think the father's awake."

The landlord joined her musing. "Why doesn't he wait for breakfast? Now, where do you suppose he's going?"

The woman gasped. "You don't suppose . . ."

"I do," her husband replied firmly. "The man said the lad likes to run away. He should take a strap to his hide!"

"And the boy is traveling at such a fast pace. Do you

suppose you . . ."

"Aye, I think I should waken the father. Oooh, I pity that lad when he finds him. He didn't seem to be too patient a man, he has cruel eyes."

"Oooh, poor lad."

"The lad deserves it!" The landlord turned on his heels and mounted the staircase. He knocked curtly on the door but received no answer. Knocking again, he cried aloud, "Sir, Sir! I think your son has run off and taken yer horse!" Unintelligible mumbling answered this. The fist boomed louder. He turned the handle of the door but it was locked from inside. "Sir, Sir! I think—"

"Damnation!" came the cry from inside the room. The Marquis was well roused by now and struggling to break his bonds. "When I get my hands on that vixen, I'll . . ."

The landlord was worried. This was his house, after all, and there was obviously something very shady going on beneath his roof. Setting his shoulders against the door he shoved, and shoved again. He bellowed down the stairs, "Maude! Fetch Ben and send him up here. I need some help!"

And so it was that the landlord, his wife, Ben, their son, Harriett, their daughter-in-law, Toby, the stable boy, and one or two other guests were present when the door was broken down and the Marquis was first seen in all his regalia. The landlord's wife was aghast. Harriett fluttered her lashes. Toby said, "Blimey!" The landlord shook his head over what a son would do to his father, and threw Ben a darkling look. The Marquis was cursing and impatiently awaiting the moment he could get his hands about a certain lovely neck.

One of the guests pushed through the crowd and chuckled loudly at the sight. Henry Mordaunt had been in his lordship's service for fifteen years. Though not as a servant. He was much too irreverent for that. The balding, thick set man was the man who handled whatever was too difficult for any other to do. As a past master criminal, he was a genius when it came to tracking down information or hiding information, if that be the case, or seeking lost noblemen. Chatham knew who would find him. He just wished Henry had gotten here earlier.

"So there ye are, guv! I might'a know ye'd appear in a most unu'sal manner. And here we've been looking high and low for ye!" Laughter boomed again, loud and raucous. "This promises to be a most entertaining story!"

"Get those demented persons away from my door and cut these damned bonds!" snapped the Marquis, in the world's worst temper. "And Henry, get me a horse!"

"Aye, guv! What'ere ye say!" Henry beamed genially.

Chapter Four

Gay lanterns beckoned the city dwellers of London to the pleasure gardens of Vauxhall. The flickering lights lent a soft glow of illumination to the mysterious depths of the island. Boats bobbed their way through the murky waters, picking up fares among wise persons who refused to wade through the throngs of people crossing by the bridge.

Patiently the Marquis of Chatham waited at the landingsgate for the arrival of one of the small crafts which would take him across the river and to the pleasures of Vauxhall. A beringed hand idly tossed the ends of a brown velvet cloak over his shoulder, revealing beneath it a gold brocade coat with Mechlin lace foaming at the neck and cuffs. As always, he refused to wear a powdered wig; instead he tied black locks to his nape with a black riband. A trace of white powder on his face was his only concession to the current fashion. On the little finger of his right hand was the shining gold ring which bore the family crest of Chatham. Across his eyes was tied a black, satin mask.

By contrast, his lanky companion was garbed in full court dress. His periwig was tightly curled around his face and neck and heavily powdered. A lone black patch adorned the tender spot at the corner of his mouth and his lips bore a trace of red color which seemed as unnatural as the whiteness of his face. His black coat was adorned with elaborate silver buttons and deep cuffs from which flowed white lace. A grey westcot and tightly fitting breeches completed this ensemble. White stockings were embroidered with white satin clocks, and silver buckles embellished high heeled shoes. A wide brimmed tricorne bearing a simple cockade flowed from his head. Again, the face was hidden by a black mask.

The small craft hovered by the pier. Chatham turned to the coach which waited a few steps behind the men and opened its door. From within the dark bowels rose two exquisites. Not that much of them could be seen. Long, thick cloaks covered each from head to toe, protecting them from the chill of the evening. Only the bright color of their masks announced their status as fashionable ladies. Petticoats of bright lace rose and dipped as the ladies climbed onto one of the small crafts, each woman on the arm of one of the gentlemen.

The trip to Vauxhall was swiftly undertaken and accomplished. From the shore to the gardens was but a short walk, the pavillion only a bit further. Chatham led his guests to his box and, once there, assisted his lady in the removal of her cloak.

His eyes widened in pleasure as her emerald satin gown was revealed. The gown dipped low over white shoulders and bosom, the material clinging temptingly to every curve. Light wisps of lace would draw any man's attention to the mounds so displayed. This sloe-eyed nymph was a small woman, impatient too, for her toes tapped a staccato rhythm as Chatham studied her. His gaze took in her twinkling eyes, her mouth curving in a suggestive smile. Neither coy nor innocent, she was a woman experienced in pleasuring a man.

The comparison brought a fleeting memory of another moment and another woman, one not so experienced. . . . As had happened all too often of late, some of the pleasure of the evening began to fade.

Impatient now, Chatham lifted a glass of port to his lips and his eyes went to the floor of the pavillion and the many dancers in their bright, clever masks. A tug on his arm had his attention returning to his companion and he determinedly put thoughts of the little brigand from his mind.

"What?" Peter Dunraven questioned boldly of the Marquis, "have you no sense of decency? Four glasses, my lord. We each need a drink after that lengthy journey." The powder was beginning to wear off and a swarthy complexion was revealed.

Dunraven was filled with good humor this night, Chatham thought enviously. He filled the glasses and as they each received their drink, Dunraven lifted his glass and proffered a toast. "To what promises to be a most interesting evening!"

Chatham drank heartily to the toast. His thoughts had been elsewhere for too long. It had taken Dunraven and some good natured jesting to make him realize that since his return to London he had not joined in any of the entertainments the city had to offer. His mind had been elsewhere. Between attending Parliament and plotting with Henry to find his kidnappers, he had been very unlike himself. Always a serious man, a man who took his responsibilities to heart, he had still found time to play, and time for the ladies. For the last three months he had done neither. He was beginning to believe he would not find her. Apparently the time had come to set the saucy wench from his mind, if it could be done. He had willed it often enough these past months.

Sliding closer to his beautiful companion, he nodded and whispered seductively in her ear, "A most interesting evening, indeed." He only wished he could mean it.

Dunraven's companion laughed. She was built on more queenly proportions, her tall figure garbed in rose silk. Thick hair was piled on her head, loose curls dangled around bare shoulders and neck in the Grecian style. She leaned nearer to Dunraven and placed a hand on his arm, whispering words for his ears alone. Dunraven's brows raised and his eyes slid to Justin, to glare provocatively. The Marquis' attention was again waning.

A smirk thinned his lips. "Forgive my friend, Miss Denville. My lord's mind is on heavier matters."

At the words, Chatham's attention was indeed captured. He turned to his companions and gave a stiff nod. "Peter is right, there is much on my mind. Forgive me," he cajoled softly, "and I will promise to behave."

"You've no need to apologize, my lord," Miss Denville answered. "I understand that men have weightier matters on their minds than mere women." She lifted her fan below her eyes and waved it softly. The coy action made him recall twinkling green eyes and a woman who would have scoffed at such

112

pretentious words.

Damn! If the woman didn't leave his mind, he would go mad.

Supper was light, the conversation forced. The dark of the night slowly and steadily crawled into the gardens. As the other boxes filled, the ladies were more than happy to entertain the Marquis and Dunraven with gossip about many of the other persons attending Vauxhall this night. The light from the lanterns brightened and the men rose, offering each lady a dance. Jennifer Denville's small figure flowed with the music, taking the Marquis' thoughts from the green-eyed wench who had taunted him for so long.

During a country dance much later in the evening, Chatham noticed the Earl of Wilton dancing with a fair cyprian. He would prefer not to acknowledge the acquaintance, an acquaintance which had twice led to disaster. At least Wilton was not with his wife, Chatham thought, relieved. Anyone was better than Eileen, as he had experience to know.

Another turn of the dance brought into view the very woman he considered such a shrew. Eileen Belden, Countess of Wilton, stood aside in the rotunda next to her brother and another man, a man Chatham struggled to recall. The red mask she wore confirmed her identity rather than hid it. Tiny, encrusted jewels outlined the velvet mask, setting off the collar of diamonds which encircled her neck and dipped low between her breasts. Chatham recognized the Belden family jewels, jewels he had not seen since the Earl's mother wore them. His belly churned at the remembrance.

The Countess' eyes scanned the throng of dancers.

A premonition swept over the Marquis as he finally rememberd the young man with Eileen and David Belden. The dance caused him to turn. They were lost from his sight.

Later he saw the Countess again, dancing with the younger man Chatham knew as Stacey Fielding. The red satin of her gown followed every intimate curve of her slim body. Petticoats of white and silver flashed with each gay movement, beneath these peeped silver shod feet, diamond buckles glistening brightly.

Eileen preened prettily for the partner whose eyes were only for her. Stacy Fielding smiled and bowed deeply, his hands lifting hers to his lips. A veritable youngster, Chatham thought, with the reputation of a monster. An idiot who was so besotted with beauty that he failed to look beneath the surface and see what a cruel, greedy woman she was. Women of her ilk were charming, as long as they had their way. And she was definitely charming the young Stacey Fielding. There was only one thing the youth could offer her, Chatham thought, his movements slowing as it dawned on him what was to happen next. And it was his own actions which put this in Eileen's devious mind.

Since his arrival in London a scant half year before, Stacey Fielding had dueled and won on the field of honor. Gossip held that he was the quickest and most accurate duelist of his generation. Chatham's feet ceased dancing. His partner watched him in puzzlement, standing silently beside him.

Murmured whispers wafted through the rotunda as the other dancers slowed and ceased whirling. All attention was for the Earl and his wife. News spread quickly that they were together in public for the first

114

time in many years, and that they were each with other partners.

The Earl still whirled as Stacey Fielding moved to stand before the Countess, waiting with a threatening stance as the music stilled, and the Earl finally noticed his wife and her latest lover. David watched from a safe distance. Wilton's expression carried the arrogance Chatham remembered from childhood, when as a lad he was near to losing his temper. And as a lad, he'd often lost it. Now, he was in no danger of that, he was coldly insulting with only his eyes and lips. Fielding spoke low and unintelligible words, his expression growing ugly at the curt retort from the Earl. Chatham could not hear what passed between the two men, but could easily imagine.

The word "whore" rang about the pavillion, the Earl's lips curling over the pronunciation of it.

Very deliberately, the young man lifted a gloved hand and brought it against the Earl's face. Fielding's own face was flushed, his eyes bright with anger.

Chatham watched this interplay closely, remembering what he had heard of Fielding. A hothead, yes. Fresh from the country, certainly, but not stupid.

"I believe the choice of weapons is mine," the Earl said coolly. A foolish onlooker could almost believe it was he who had manipulated this moment. "I choose pistols."

"Name your second!" Stacey spat. "Mine will call on yours tomorrow."

The Earl lifted his gaze about the room, his eyes meeting Chatham's. A sardonic twist altered his lips. Both men must have been thinking the same thing.

Chatham moved forward through the thick crowd.

"I'll stand second."

The situation was ironic, he realized. He had not seen Geoffrey Belden since that fateful night the Earl returned from the colonies. How long had he been gone to America, Chatham wondered. Was it seven or eight years? And before that he was elsewhere in the world. He married young, a couple of years after the deaths of his mother and stepfather and left England before he had time to settle into his marriage. Chatham had often wondered if he was gone from England for so long so as to forget his marriage and his disastrous wife. Why he married Eileen, Chatham would never understand. As a lad he held nothing but disdain for her.

The years had brought bitter hardness to Geoffrey. His hair was still the deep golden brown of his youth and his brows so thick and black they met in the center of his forehead. Traces of the youth well still there, all of them deepened and intensified.

That night he returned from the colonies, he found the Countess in Chatham's arms. Admittedly, they were barely through the front door and the matter was not quite as it appeared, but Geoffrey was not to be reasoned with. When he challenged a duel, he did not do so with a tame glove, he used an iron fist. Chatham's jaw was sore for days afterward.

It was the next morning before Chatham's own temper cooled down enough to tell Geoffrey the truth, and the truth was spat at the thick-headed man.

"You may wish to give your wife the satisfaction of a duel being fought over her, but I refuse. If you think I would touch her, then more fool you. I have nothing but loathing for her. I saw her home from Madame Ledoux' gambling club for one reason only, she was

116

too drunk to stand. And it was not the first time, as you would know, if you ever bothered with your own wife. Fool that I am, I couldn't bear to watch her one moment longer. Why I interfered, I don't know. I've been asking myself that question for hours now and still find no answer. Perhaps I was momentarily deranged! All I know is I couldn't bear to watch her tear your reputation to shreds anymore. Even dead friendships have their moments of good memories. All I know is I did it, I interfered and brought her home. The compulsion was momentary and I deeply regret it. I should have let her drag your name further into the mud. It would have served you both right."

Oh, yes, he and Geoffrey together put this in Eileen's mind. And Stacey Fielding was simpleton enough to fall for her persuasions.

"And your second, Mr. Fielding?"

"David Belden will be my second."

The Earl's lips curled. "Ah, my esteemed brother-in-law! I might have guessed. Until tomorrow, then?" He nodded curtly to his opponent, nonchalantly to Chatham and offered his arm to the fair cyprian. With a motion of his hand, he ordered the music to resume.

Henry Mordaunt was proud of himself. Balding, aging and with an enormous girth, he still managed to find the stamina to spend days at a time in the saddle searching for those culprits. All to no avail. The three culprits had disappeared without a trace.

He'd found the house and the coach, just like the Marquis said. He even traced two of the criminals as far as the first inn. There, all trace of them ended.

The thought of telling his lordship once again of his failure did not appeal to Henry. The Marquis didn't seem to be in a decent frame of mind these days. Henry had never seen him so angry. And now he hadn't the least idea where to begin looking for them next. Not that the culprits had done the Marquis any real harm, not unless one counts the blow to his pride. A grin flashed across Henry's face as he recalled that fateful morning. If his lordship ever got his hands on that girl . . .

Henry dismounted outside the mews. His back ached, his knees took sweet time to lock together properly these days, and his rear felt as though he'd been strapped. Moreover, it was a cold, black night and he was hungry, tired, and miserable. Maybe it was time his lordship found someone younger to do this strenuous work. Henry gave a thought to his widowed sister and realized she would expect him to abide with her if he did not remain with the Marquis. All dreams of fishing and drinking to while away the days disappeared. He'd stay on a while longer.

Henry met one of the maids as he slipped into the house by the back door. He ordered a glass of cold brew brought to him in the parlor. There, he stretched his corpulent frame in one of the chairs facing the hearth and raised his weary feet to the stool, drink in hand. This was how the Marquis found him in the wee hours of the morning, when he returned from Vauxhall.

"Good ale, yer worship! Best I've had in ages!"

"I am happy you can appreciate it," milord commented drily.

"I always appreciate a good drink, though, I'll wager

ye won't appreciate me much when I give ye me news."

"You did not find them."

"Not a trace of 'em after the Owlshead Inn."

"They can't have disappeared! Did you mention there was a girl? She might have changed into a dress when she met up with them."

"She never made it as far as Owlshead. Just the two of 'em 'ere. 'ey left after asking about ye. I think 'ey followed ye, met up with 'er shortly 'ereafter and skipped off to another part of the country. It's all wot could have 'appened. 'ey did not stay at a local inn, I asked everywhere. I felt a demmed fool, too, asking about two men and a boy, or mebbee two men and a girl. One woman asked me why I couldn't make up me mind!"

The Marquis laughed in spite of himself. "That's why I sent you! I hadn't sufficient courage!"

Henry drained the tankard. "The things I do for ye." Mournfully, he shook his head.

"I'll see to it you're well compensated. Here, let me offer you another glass of ale." Milord pulled the bellrope, his mouth curving into a grin as Henry made himself more comfortable.

"Don't mind if'n I do, guv! This whole business boggles me mind. Have ye learned anymore?"

"No ransom demand was ever received."

"Never?" At the Marquis' negative answer, he removed his cap and scratched the balding head. "Well, I'll be . . . 'en why do 'is thing? I dun unnerstand."

"I've been asking myself that same question. They were such a ragamuffin bunch of criminals. I don't believe they did it just for sport."

"Well, I expect we'll find out. Everything's done with

some motive." His eyes closed contentedly as he sipped of the cold ale. A moment later, the eyes peeped open, glaring at the Marquis speculatively. "Blackmail?"

"How could that pathetic week lead to blackmail?"

"Mebbee 'ey thought to embarrass ye, bein' kidnapped by a female. Mebbee that's why she tied ye to thet bed and left ye in thet ribbon . . ."

"Get that moment out of your mind, Henry," his lordship sneered impatiently. "It's good I'm a rich man or I could not afford to keep you in brew."

"Thet's why I first came to work for yer father. 'e kept the best stock in the county. Now, wot do we do?"

"Watch the dockets for one thing, though I don't suppose they'll land there too soon. They'll lay low for a time. We send a man to watch the Owlshead and another to watch the cottage. I want them found, Henry."

"I know ye do, guv, and I'm doing me best. The cottage was hired."

"Yes, to one Alf Dougherty. They have imagination, I give them that."

Henry was chuckling. "I'd like to clap me eyes on 'er just once. The bottom thet gal must 'ave . . . Why, who'd ever 'ave thought . . ." At the sight of his lordship's irate expression he quickly shut up. If those culprits were wise they'd lie low the rest of their miserable lives.

"Maybe they wanted me out of London? But why?"

"I dunno, guv."

"Go to bed, Henry. I work you too hard."

The door closed behind the old man. Chatham stood by the hearth, the toe of one foot idly kicking at the fire, ignoring the flying sparks. Three months had passed

120

and not a trace of them. He considered the possibility of not finding them. The thought was unpalatable and unacceptable. He'd find them if he had to go through England bit by bit.

He could still see her in his mind, the way she moved and turned, the haughty manner she used in tilting her head. What business did a low creature like that have with such arrogance?

She'd pay for laughing at him, and pay dearly.

Chapter Five

The ormolu clock struck the quarter hour. Chatham spread wide heavy velvet drapes and peered out onto the darkened street. A fog hung low over the cobblestones, creeping through nooks and crannies to spread the early morning chill. In the distance, an approaching carriage could be heard. As it rounded the corner, he recognized it as belonging to Peter Dunraven.

Sweeping from the house, he met the carriage and tucked his head low as he climbed aboard. Dunraven and the Earl sat facing each other. The Earl nodded briefly as the Marquis took the seat beside Dunraven.

Peter Dunraven greeted Chatham easily. "Fine morning, ain't it, for madness?" The horses were sprung.

The Earl studied his second carefully, his mouth twisting mockingly. In spite of the early hour, the Marquis of Chatham was finely garbed in black smallcoat and breeches of grey superfine. Lace trailed at his wrists and neck, a small diamond studded his cravat.

"Still playing the dandy, eh, Justin?"

Black brows rose at the Earl's scrutiny and a softly mocking voice jibed, "I can recommend my tailor, Geoff. He would put some dash in your appearance."

The Earl shook his head ruefully. "Even as a child, you were overly concerned with your dress."

"You were, too, once, and now you look as though you still lived in the wilds of America. You are home now. You can take some effort with yourself."

"Why? To fit London's opinion of an Earl? No. I have come home to settle some matters for my brother and sister. As soon as that's done, I'm leaving again."

"Anything's better than being too near your wife? I always wondered what ever possessed you to marry her. You loathed her as a child. Damme, we both loathed her greedy mind and selfish manners." Geoffrey opened his mouth to protest and Justin lifted a ringed hand to gesture silence. "Never mind! It seems your destiny to duel over your wife, Geoffrey, and mine to be there when you do."

Geoffrey relaxed against the squabs, his eyes never leaving the Marquis. A rueful smile settled over his features. "Even as a child, you had to be in the thick of everything. That trait has not changed."

"How can you say so?" protested the Marquis glibly. "I am here only because I feel culpable in this. Had you and I not put the idea in the minds of your wife and her brother, I think Stacey Fielding would be home sleeping safely between his sheets this very moment."

Geoffrey's jaws tightened. "He will regret his foolishness."

"I believe you."

123

The Earl turned to Dunraven. "The pistols?"

Lean fingers stroked the fine wood of the box he held and tightened. "Geoffrey, forget this. . . ."

"These are the beauties which belonged to your father."

"Yes, they are. And my father died with one in his hand. Think about that. You could be killed."

"Dying is not in my plans, Peter. My wife and her brother will learn a sorely needed lesson today. I am not so easy to be rid of."

The Marquis rested languidly against the cushions. "Last month, this Stacey Fielding killed Anthony Tessier." The Earl paid strict attention as Chatham continued, "Oh, it was a fair fight, but 'tis said there has not been his like as a marksman in years. He is young and a hothead, not always gauging his opponent precisely, but he is accurate with his aim. The day he learns to control his temper is the day he becomes truly deadly. Until then, you only need to anger him to find victory within your grasp."

"That answers the nagging question of what my wife saw in the youth."

"However," Chatham continued gently, "from what little I have heard of your reputation," he referred to the Earl's well known victories against the French and the Indians in the colonies, "I do not believe he is your real threat. Watch your brother-in-law. He would dearly love to be rid of you so his father might step into your shoes, leaving them available for him at Naylor's death. What a pit of vipers you married into, Geoffrey."

Much of the bitterness left Geoffrey's face and his

mouth curled into its first real smile in some time. He laughed. "I owe you an apology. I was angry the night I returned home. I should have apologized the next morning, but I was too proud to do so."

"I don't need an apology from you. I have watched your wife and her brother for a long time. They were selfish, greedy children, as adults they are more so, and they lack all moral fiber."

"They were raised solely by Naylor. What more could you expect?"

"Very little. But remember these words. This duel will take place on a field of honor, and I believe Fielding possesses that honor. David does not know the meaning of the word."

Chatham turned from the other occupants of the coach, lifted a gloved hand to the window and pulled the curtain aside. Fingers of light were barely discernible over the horizon as the carriage pulled to a stop.

"Maybe they won't show up," grumbled Dunraven hopefully.

"They'll come," Chatham answered.

A moment later, he was proven correct. The newly arriving carriage pulled to a stop and Chatham descended, Geoffrey following. The entire width of the park separated the two carriages. Stacey Fielding and David met them half the distance across the park.

The men nodded curtly, but no one was inclined to delay. Chatham removed the lid of the box which held the pistols. "Our weapons, your choice between them."

David tested each for weight and balance, finally settling on the one he considered the finest.

The Earl spoke softly as he watched Stacey Fielding.

"Are you sure you want to do this?"

Stacey nodded stiffly. "Shall we proceed, gentlemen?"

The men faced each other, each man clad only in black breeches and white shirt, pistols in hand. The Marquis addressed them. "Have you anything to say to each other?"

At the negative reply, David spoke impatiently. He was much like his sister, fair of hair and complexion. In society they were often referred to as the Belden twins for they resembled each other so very much. They were not twins, David was the older by three years. He stood on Stacey's side of the field now and was eager to finish this business. "Then before we waste the whole of the day, let us begin. You will turn from each other and as I count, you will move apart by ten steps. On that count of ten, you will turn, lower your pistols and take aim. I then begin another count. At the count of three, you will fire. One shot is all to which either of you will be entitled. Make the most of your aim."

Fielding nodded stiffly, looking so young that pain shot through Wilton as he was reminded of his younger brother, Jon. Ignoring this, he flashed his opponent a mocking grin and held the pistol against his nose. "For my wife's honor!"

Proud anger stiffened Fielding's body as he turned, his back against the Earl's. Geoffrey could feel the tension within his opponent though they barely touched. For a lad who'd killed a man on the field of honor, he behaved with naivete. "One, two . . ." the count began. At ten, the men faced each other. David again crooned, "One, two . . ." But before the final count was made, the pistol jerked in Fielding's hand

126

and flashed with the fire inside it.

"Damn you!" Chatham roared, crossing to Fielding and grabbing the heated pistol from him. "The count wasn't finished."

"I'm sorry!" Fielding stammered. "The pin went off accidentally. I did not mean to fire!"

"Obviously," retorted the Marquis, "or the Earl would not still be standing. You do know what this means? You have taken your shot!"

Fielding swallowed. His voice came low. "The Earl still has his ball."

"And you must remain standing while he fires."

"He will kill me." The words were gritted.

"He probably will! Don't prove yourself a coward as well as a careless bastard!"

Fielding glanced at the Earl, all color draining from his face.

"At least make yourself the smallest possible target." Chatham snapped.

Fielding closed his eyes and turned his body to the side, only his shoulder facing forward. The Earl leveled the pistol at his opponent's head.

Chaos erupted as more than one bullet was fired. The Earl dropped to the ground, blood spewing from his shoulder. When the smoke cleared, Stacey Fielding was down, clutching his bloodied knee, keening with his pain.

"Dammit, I aimed to miss!" the Earl bellowed as he rose. "What fool shot at me?"

"That fool." Dunraven, who had not troubled to alight at the beginning of the duel now stood beside the coach, the butt of his still smoking pistol pointing toward the far end of the field where a stranger's body lay beside a spent pistol. "After listening to Justin's words, I thought it wise to simply watch. Good thing. He remained in their coach, not showing himself until the end. They wanted to ensure your death, no matter what."

Chatham grabbed David by the neck and slapped him across the face. "Don't you ever weary of your cunning?"

David Belden's hands spread wide. "I had nothing to do with this! Mawson claimed to be a friend of Fielding's."

"Liar!" groaned the injured man from his crouched position. Speaking was difficult. Fielding had to force the words through tight lips. "You introduced me to him. I would never cheat at a duel."

"Who will you believe, Cousin? A stranger or me?"

The Earl's attention was for Fielding who was gasping with the wracking pain. He tried vainly to stem the flow of blood from his knee with his fingers. From the amount of bloody bodily tissue on the wet morning grass Wilton knew he'd done much damage. He ignored his cousin. "You are a fool, Mister Fielding. I am not certain you deserve to live, not after the dishonor you perpetrated here. You would not have been harmed but for your plotting. Killing a man in cold blood is not to my taste. I aimed to miss."

Stacey drew a taut breath and peered up at the Earl through pain ridden eyes. "You may not believe me, but I repeat, I plotted none of this. I thought this would be an honorable duel, not the farce it has become."

The Marquis approached Fielding and would have helped him to the carriage, but the younger man gasped aloud, "I don't need your help!"

Chatham ignored the words and lifted him bodily. "Don't be more of a fool than you can help. Do you wish to live? You need a physician, and quickly. At least I believe your words. Given the choice of either you or David as the liar, I choose David. Be grateful for that."

"Damn . . . you." Fielding roared weakly, before passing out from the pain as he was placed inside Dunraven's carriage.

"David," the Earl spoke softly. His blonde cousin was all attention. "This is my only warning. Another of these fiascos and it is you who will be buried. Don't look at me with such innocence. I am not so easily fooled." His eyes followed the morning frost still on the grass, across the park and to where the stranger lay. "You will see to your friend's body. We will see to Fielding."

They waited until the physician arrived at Fielding's lodgings before continuing to the Marquis' home.

"They plotted cold-blooded murder!" Dunraven finally exploded. "Had Fielding taken better aim that first time, you would be dead!"

"No," answered the Earl. "Fielding's hand was shaking so badly the gun went off before he meant it to. Justin spoke the truth. He's a young fool with more courage and brawn than wits. He was a perfect tool for my wife and her brother."

"And what do you plan for your wife, now?" Dunraven sneered.

"I shall take her to the country, lock her in her room and give her nothing but bread and water for the next twenty years. Oh, and beat her nightly for good measure."

Dunraven grunted. "I wish you luck."

"Short of killing her myself, there's nothing else I can do with her, nor am I inclined to do much with her. She's no part of my life. In other circumstances I might have sent her to Wiltonshire and buried her there, but I did not want Alison and Jon near her influence. Dammit! I still don't want them around her! That's why I'm home. She and Naylor have been hinting at a marriage between Alison and David. They insinuate my sister is deeply in love with the man. If she's so much as set eyes on him, I'll strangle him! I absolutely forbade any contact between them. I don't want my brother and sister ruined by my relatives."

Black eyes flashed at the names mentioned. Alison and Jon? . . . Alison, Ally . . . Thoughts whirled about the Marquis' mind. He felt a complete dolt, but, of course, it could be them. Everything fit. Ages, names . . . and Morgan! Yes, they had a servant with that name. He worked in the stables. And Geoffrey's little sister had been very attached to the man even then. But nothing made sense. Why? My God, why?

"What's with you, Justin? You look as though you're the one with the hole in him instead of me."

Chatham sat upright. "We ought to see about a physician for you," he answered absent-mindedly. He was running to madness, he had to be. Just because the chit's been on his mind for so long, he's seeing her everywhere. She won't be found through the Earl. The thought was sheer lunacy.

Eyes pressed on him curiously. Chatham tossed the ridiculous thought aside. "What you ought to do is shoot her and her brother, just like the dogs they are." He spoke harshly, trying to gather his wits. The coach slowed and he searched his mind feverishly for a way to extend the morning. He had to know more of Geoffrey's family. "I have arranged for a victory breakfast at my home."

"Victory? You had such faith in me?"

"I've never thought you a fool, Geoffrey. If you had not stood a chance against the man, you would not have faced him," Justin answered drily, alighting from the coach.

"My chances were better than good. I survived the colonies, and that meant facing men on the battlefields. My marksmanship is well proven, though I don't know if killing a man is something to boast of."

A physician was summoned to tend Geoffrey's wound. He pronounced it to be a mere scratch, though he insisted his patient be blooded. The Earl bluntly refused before sending the man on his way.

They had hearty appetites and were served their breakfast in the small dining room. The conversation took a political direction and was often heated, but thought provoking. Dunraven thrived on arguing against the opinions of his peers, and the Marquis enjoyed baiting his controversial beliefs. The Earl relaxed in his seat, his eyes half closed as he sipped the dark brandy slowly, offering a dry comment whenever Dunraven's pragmatic conclusions seemed to be weakening. Dunraven was particularly opinionated concerning the American colonies and that was when the Earl joined in the heated conversation.

The morning was half gone before they moved into the study, leaving the dining room so the servants might have a chance to clear it. The men were comfortably settled in heavy leather chairs, the brandy well filled in their glasses on the table between them, and a silent moment shared for the first time that morning. Dunraven nodded off in his chair. Chatham sipped of his glass and remarked very casually, "Tell me more of your brother and sister. I haven't seen them since they were small children."

Geoffrey gave an uneasy shrug. "Jon is in his second year at Oxford. He talks of buying a commission in the Royal Navy and joining his big brother." The smile which lit Geoffrey's face was filled with fondness. Clearly, he loved this young brother. "We shall see. Alison remains at Wiltonshire manor. She should have made her come-out last year, but, as you witnessed this morning, I cannot bring her to London to mingle with my wife and her brother, and I have no other female relative to whom I can turn to sponsor Alison. She should be married and in a home of her own. I dread returning to the colonies and trying to arrange her future from such a distance, but if she waits for my return, she will be an old maid." He gave Justin a sheepish grin. "As you can probably tell, I was not prepared for the changes I found in her this time. When I was last home, she was a child. Now she is a grown woman. And as a woman she needs a life, a home of her own." His expression grew more determined. "She deserves a home of her own. A happy home, like the one my mother and stepfather provided for her."

"When were you last here?"

"My last leave was four years ago. Alison and Jon rode the wilds of Wiltonshire like two lads reveling in their freedom. It was good for a boy, but I shuddered even then to think of Alison in society, straining to please the matrons. I was gratified to see how well she'd grown up. Four years ago all she cared about was her horse, me, Jon and how to placate Morgan."

Morgan.

Morgan. The more Chatham considered, the more decided he was that in spite of the kerchief which covered the lower half of his face, the belly was the one telling trait. Yes, the Morgan of his kidnapping was this same Morgan.

Chatham wanted to appear relaxed, but every nerve in his lithe body jangled. He should have remembered the name himself, eventually. He recalled the time before the accident. The three were inseparable culprits even then.

Hooded eyes turned to the Earl. Geoffrey knows nothing of the kidnapping or he would not have bandied their names about so carelessly. "She has never complained of boredom, living in the country year round?"

"I don't imagine Alison is ever bored," Geoffrey laughed. "She's too busy involving herself in everything and everyone in Wiltonshire. From the lowest stable lad to her brothers, everyone comes under her wings for protection, in her mind. She's fierce about it, too. There was some talk of a match between her and the squire's son, but the boy flapped his tongue too much about the state of my marriage, angering Alison. She hasn't spoken to him since. 'Twas just as well. Her heart wasn't with him, and she's a woman who needs to marry where her heart is. She will be fiercely loving with her family. I have been thinking that perhaps I ought to stay in England for the season. She's a beauty. She'll have her choice of husbands when she does make her come-out."

"She sounds a veritable paragon," came the dry response.

Geoffrey looked at him sharply. "Not a paragon, she's too spirited for that. It will take a good man to handle her. Still, she's beautiful and wealthy, many a man's dream."

"Are you extolling her virtues, my friend?"

"To you?" Geoffrey looked shocked. "Good Lord, no! She's just a child, not in your league at all."

"You relieve my mind."

"I want to see her married to some nice young man who'll love her as much as Jon and I do, who'll give her a passel of children, each of whom will give her as much trouble as she's given me." He grinned conspiratorially at Justin.

"That should be sufficient retribution."

Geoffrey shook his head sadly. "You mock everything, Justin. I knew you would not understand, you've never had a brother or sister to love."

"I've had few to love, but there is my grandmother." The words were unnecessary between them. Both men remembered the lonely child whose grandmother had not wanted to be bothered with him, not even during the holidays.

Chatham chose not to remember those years, nor the holidays, nor the friendship with Geoffrey, nor the accident. He wanted information from the Earl, information he was willingly given. Wilton was easy with names and facts. Most assuredly he knew nothing of the kidnapping. And if he ever learned of it, or of the night spent with his sister, Chatham knew it would be himself facing the Earl on the field of honor.

The Marquis spoke lightly, those hooded eyes intent

on the Earl. "A few months ago I feared for my life. I was kidnapped by three of the lowest creatures it was ever my curse to meet. They kept me for a week. At the time, I thought the motive must be ransom, but no note was ever received."

"Did they harm you?"

"They taunted me mercilessly, fed me the most vile food I have ever eaten and still, I do not know why." The Marquis spoke grimly and Geoffrey felt a twinge of pity for the culprits. He did not doubt they would be caught. "I have just found them and when my man brings them to me, I will have my answers."

"I don't envy them. You're cold-blooded about this. What will you do with them?"

"Many tortures have crossed my mind, the rack, thumbscrews, beheading. I have even thought of making them suffer their own cooking for a solid month. That would be enough to kill anyone."

Geoffrey laughed as he rose to take his leave. His gaze leveled onto Dunraven who still slept soundly in the chair. "If you need help, I owe you for this morning. I imagine I can learn to apply thumbscrews."

"I may call on you. You could have two of the criminals at any rate. The third is mine."

"Scruffy, were they? I'm surprised you wish to soil your hands on them. Turn them over to the magistrate."

"Oh, no. This pleasure is mine."

"They aren't by any chance related to my wife's family?"

"If that proves to be the case, you'll be the first to know."

Geoffrey was still laughing as he nudged the sleeping Dunraven to his feet and both men took their leave.

135

They were gone when Chatham crossed the room to the bellrope and pulled it. His eyes were alight with anticipation as he poured himself another good measure of brandy and tossed it off, almost in a congratulatory fashion. "Send Henry Mordaunt to me," he ordered of the servant who answered the summons.

So, Geoffrey knows nothing of this, Chatham thought, but he confirmed that his brother, sister, and their servant were all involved. And money was not the reason. There remained only one other alternative . . .

So that was her game, was it? The thought was enough to wipe the satisfaction from his face. She thought to compromise herself into marriage. And he'd fallen into the trap like a simpleton.

He remembered her as a child, a headstrong, stubborn bit who taunted him even then. She'd run off with his shoes when he left them outside the door for cleaning and taken pieces of his clothing, and then she'd lie and say that she'd never seen them at all. And there was that last time, when she threatened to tell her parents of the Christmas sleigh if she didn't have the first ride. It was his sleigh, his and Geoffrey's. They'd worked and planned it for months, and that little brat was threatening to ruin the surprise. That was the final straw. That was when he gave in to temptation and treated her as a cunning brat should be treated, with a spanking. He could still see the gloating grin on her face when Morgan found them and took her side. She reminded him of a whinnying horse.

He should have recognized that taunting female immediately.

So her game was to compromise him into marriage?

136

He would not have thought her so desperately bored. In spite of Geoffrey's words, she must be bored in the country. And why him? He knew so little of her anymore. After their day together, he would have thought she would be wary of him. But of course they made their plans before she learned how dangerous he was. Marry her he would. He relished the thought. That would give him her lifetime for retribution. She still played her little games, though as he could testify first hand, she was grown up now.

As Geoffrey's sister, he would be forced to marry her. Marriage suited him just fine. She needed taming and teaching. Her first lesson would be learned through shock. She could think he meant to refuse her. Where would her precious reputation be then? Let her worry over that awhile. Then, when the truth might nearly come out, he would arrange a wedding ceremony worthy of her. And later, much later, she would still be paying for her deviousness.

"You can cease searching for our culprits, Henry. I have found them!" the Marquis announced gleefully as the servant entered.

Henry grinned broadly, peeping curiously about the room, as though the culprits would be found there. "'at's wonderful, but where are 'ey?"

"In Wiltonshire." The Marquis brought his hands together and rubbed expectantly. "Now here's what I want you to do . . ." For the next few moments he outlined a plan in which Henry would go to Wiltonshire and kidnap the kidnappers.

"Are you sure about 'is, guv? I never kidnapped an Earl's sister afore. I never kidnapped enyone afore! Besides, why'd she want to go and kidnap ye? Her brother's rich as . . . as . . . 'at feller . . ."

"Croessus," finished the Marquis, his mind elsewhere. "She always was a spoiled brat, demanding and getting whatever she wanted. Apparently she hasn't outgrown that trait. But she will, she will! You just get her for me, Henry. I look forward to taking that young woman in hand."

Six days later, a weary Henry returned without their quarry. "Sorry guv, but by 'he time I got 'ere, she were gone. I quizzed around 'e stables and scuttlebutt has it she's come to London to visit her brother. Mebbee she's gettin' ready to make her move!"

A light shone in the Marquis' eyes. His smile was positively jeering. "Perhaps she is, Henry. Yes, perhaps she is."

Chapter Six

Morgan Hull leaned wearily against the wrought-iron fence which surrounded Chatham House. Shadows loomed about him, cast by the bright moonlight against the multi-turretted house and outbuildings. The chill of the winter wind whipped through him and across the park which separated the wrought-iron fence and the opulent London residence. Morgan lifted his eyes and gazed hopefully at the Marquis' home, praying the Marquis would be returning soon.

Since late afternoon Morgan had been here, and in another hour the sun would be rising over the horizon. It was no wonder he nearly fell asleep against the hard bars. Morgan felt a keen sense of sympathy for those in the Marquis' service who had to keep these late hours on a regular basis. At least he had the task only this once. Twice, he amended, if he counted the night of the kidnapping. At least it was not snowing tonight, not like the last time he waited for the Marquis.

The old man stifled a yawn. At first, he'd been entertained by the many persons who passed him on their way to unknown destinations. Morgan studied the mixture of the normal and the strange with blatant curiosity. As the evening lengthened into night, the eerie silence of London captured his imagination, but even that entertainment wore off. Now, he was simply bored and weary, wishing this onerous task was done.

He had no idea how the Marquis would react to seeing him here, let alone to the news he brought. All he knew for certain was that he could not approach the front door and simply ask to speak with the Marquis. That would see him thrown out on his ear.

So he waited.

He was dozing against the fence when a rush of wheels had him jerking into wakefulness. As his eyes opened, he realized he'd nearly slept through the arrival of the Marquis. The carriage was already stopped in front of the house, its passenger alighting.

Morgan crept steathily around the fence, toward the front of the house, and through the gate which he found slightly ajar. Across the shadowy blackness of the park he scurried, toward the house, his feet whispering as they pattered across the frosted lawn.

The coach continued to the stables. The Marquis and his footman were alone, ambling slowly toward the front door. Morgan glanced around furtively, decided there was no one else present so he would never find the odds better. Sprinting from the shadows, he gave a muted shout, "Milord! Milord! I must speak with ye!"

The Marquis turned to Morgan. The harshness of his expression might have daunted a less stout person, though Morgan wondered at it. Hadn't the man had time to recover from the kidnapping? No harm was done, none was intended. The real harm was perpetrated by the Marquis himself.

The footman gave instant chase, his body moving between Morgan and the Marquis to protect his master from the pursuing madman. Facing Morgan, his arms were akimbo as he made clear his intent of throwing the intruder from the grounds.

With a softly spoken command, the Marquis intervened and the footman backed away.

Justin Sarrett had anticipated this moment. His hand raised to his waistcoat pocket.

"Ye've no need for a pistol, I've come unarmed!" Morgan wheezed emphatically, desperately trying to catch his breath. He was too old for this sort of chase. "I've a letter for ye, 'at's all!"

Gradually, the Marquis lowered his hand from his coat pocket. He'd been a victim of this man before and was reluctant to trust him too far. Not that he thought of Morgan as dangerous, just foolish. Black eyes slowly appraised the older man, mockery in their depths. Morgan looked exactly what he was, untidy, unkempt and tired. "Very brave you are, Morgan Hull, to confront me in my own home. Very brave and very foolish."

Morgan stiffened at the use of his surname.

"Ah, it surprises you, does it, that I know who you are? I know everything, all about you, your mistress and her brother. I have been expecting you for some days now."

Morgan's brows lowered. "I knew we were bein' followed! So it was yer man?"

Chatham bowed low from the waist in acknowledgement. "I find my memory constantly stirring with tidbits I thought forgotten," he rasped softly. "I

141

promised you I would find you, only I did not need to come for you. Like a fool, you came to me. I only wonder that you waited so long. You left Wiltonshire eight days ago. I expected you before this. You have much to answer for, you and your cohorts."

"'Tis time we 'ad a truce, milord," Morgan spoke earnestly. "This letter will make everything clear to ye. I'd not be 'ere, if not for . . . for wot's in the letter. I thought to spend the rest of me life avoiding ye."

"It would have done you little good. I promised to find you, and I meant it." The softness of the tone accentuated the threat in the words. Only thoughts of Alison kept Morgan standing as still as he was. "You said you had a missive for me? From . . . Ally, I presume?"

Morgan nodded and took a wary step toward the Marquis. The footman intervened, remarking dourly, "I'll take the note. Put it in me 'and."

Morgan hesitated. He promised he'd deliver this directly to the Marquis. On further consideration, this seemed to be as near the man as he would get.

The Marquis took the note and ambled to the front porch with it. There, beneath the light of a candle, he unfolded it and scanned the missive quickly. Black eyes lifted and met Morgan's. The candle added harshness to the features. That taunting jeer was again there when he spoke. "This will explain everything? 'I must see you,' signed 'Alison'? What sort of fool do you think I am?"

"Is that all she wrote?" demanded Morgan incredulously, climbing the front steps and taking the paper from his hand to study it himself. The footman followed closely behind him, his body still acting as a buffer between Morgan and the Marquis. That was all it said, Morgan had to admit, thinking sourly of the two days she spent over the paper, quill in hand. Apparently, Alison spoke the truth when she said she didn't know how to write her news. Biting his lip to keep the anger from spilling over, Morgan glared at the Marquis. "Well, wot she says is true. She must see ye."

"She must? Am I to take that as a Royal Command?" the Marquis jeered. His expression feigned disappointment. "I am busy for the next several days. I cannot think when I can possibly see her again."

"Ye don' unnerstand . . ."

"Oh? Is there so much in either of your minds that is difficult to understand?"

Morgan's ire rose hotly at the insult. "She didn't want to come to ye at all. I brought 'er 'ere. She told me as 'ow ye raped her. . . ."

"Raped her? My memory of that night is somewhat different. By the time the act was completed, there was no rape involved."

Morgan's fists clenched tightly, but he was determined to hold his temper. "'Twas a matter of force, 'at I know. I don't care to 'ear the filthy details."

"You won't," the Marquis jeered softly, enjoying Morgan's defensive stance. Chatham had been at this man's mercy once and the feeling still sat uncomfortably on him. Let the old man suffer for a while. "What is it you came for now? The ransom you neglected to collect at our last meeting? Or to clear her 'good name'? Does she consider herself compromised? As far as money is concerned I taught her a manner in which to earn some. And as for her so called good name . . ."

Morgan had had enough insults, enough indifference to Alison's desperation. Pressing past the foot-man, he leveled his thick-set body at the Marquis. A second thought had him stopping just short of his target. He'd been weeks recovering from the Marquis' last blow. Why invite another? His poor, old body couldn't take much more.

A swift glance at Chatham's face told him the words were bait for a blow from the man. Chatham's fists were doubled and his eyes alight with anticipation. Morgan cleared his throat and stood upright. Clearly any threat of battle was done.

Roughly, the envelope was shredded and the bits tossed at Morgan's head. "Come back in a week. Perhaps by then I'll have tired of my present mistress and be seeking a new one. Your Alison wasn't too unpleasant, though she needs tutoring desperately. I can probably manage that. I might even offer her my protection, if she can curb her tongue long enough to please me."

Morgan watched his back retreat into the privacy of the grand manor house. To the footman was left the task of watching Morgan vacate the grounds.

"I had a feeling this was all a waste of time. We should have done what I wanted from the first!"

"No," Morgan grumbled, seeking warmth from the hot cup of tea he held in his hand. "Yer child deserves a name, and I mean to see 'e gets one. Marquis or no Marquis!"

"Well, without the Marquis' cooperation, I'm afraid the baby won't have a legitimate name." Alison reasoned quietly. "I was hoping this could be handled peacefully. I wish you would have kept your fists to yourself. I don't imagine the Marquis took kindly to having his nose bloodied and being given a shiner anymore than you would."

Morgan flushed at her reminder of his little white lie. Servant or no, he had his pride too. He simply embellished the mad thoughts which were foremost in his mind. "Well, 'e took the first swing, lass."

"Yes, well, I can't blame him for being so angry. We weren't very nice to him. We couldn't expect a better reception than he gave, and I'm not sure what I have to tell him will make his attitude toward us any better."

"We weren't nice to 'im?" Morgan repeated in disbelieving tones. "My God! Look wot 'e's done to you!"

Alison took a deep breath and struggled to control the queasiness in her belly. All it seemed to take was the mere mention of the Marquis for her to feel herself turning green. The wave of nausea passed and the color crept slowly back into her face.

"Not purposely, Morgan. I doubt he knows what he's done. I didn't, not at first." Silence stretched between them as each remembered the waiting and worrying. Alison took a deep breath and spoke her next words haltingly.

"Don't you think it would be easier if I just disappeared? It wouldn't be difficult. We could return to Wiltonshire and pack my things. I have the jewelry Mama left me . . ."

"She'd turn over in 'er grave!" Morgan pronounced heavily. "If she was 'ere, she'd insist 'at blackguard marry ye and give 'is babe a name. And if 'e was an 'onorable gentleman, 'at's just wot 'e'd do!"

145

Alison sighed greatly. "You don't know everything, Morgan. That . . . that morning I escaped . . . well, I left the Marquis in a bad way. You see, I never thought I'd have to see him again . . . and I . . . I . . ."

Morgan's frown deepened. He knew there was more to what happened than she had told him. "Go on, girl. Get it off your chest. I want to know everything."

So she told him. About the knife, the brandy, the ribbons. About *everything*.

The silence stretched and lengthened. Finally Morgan rasped, "No wonder 'e's so angry."

"Yes. It's no wonder."

"I still won't let ye run away. 'at baby's coming whether ye run or stay."

"I suppose you're right, Morgan," Alison agreed on a sigh. "Perhaps I should go see the Marquis myself."

"Ye'll not go to 'is 'ouse, Alison! I forbid it."

"No, of course not. I can see where that wouldn't do at all," she admitted softly, raising a curious gaze to him. "How's your eye?"

Morgan reddened. To give credence to the lie, the Marquis had to get in one blow. "'e don't 'it 'ard enuf to leave a bruise." Morgan's head jerked as he caught the jist of her thoughts and he turned to glare at her. "Ye needn't worry about 'at. Even 'e blackguard 'e is, 'e wouldn't dare lay a finger on ye."

"I wouldn't be so sure of that, not when I say my piece." She was seated comfortably on the sofa, her knees tucked beneath her. The night had grown long and cold as she waited for Morgan in her nightgown and robe. Everyone else was sound asleep. She waited up because she had to know what Morgan learned. She was the one to let him in the front door when

146

he returned.

"We don't have much longer. I may have waited too long as it is. Eileen was looking at me queerly all afternoon. I think she suspects something." Alison spoke wearily, the seriousness of her problems weighing down her spirits. "Perhaps if we went to a hotel and waited until the Marquis answered my summons . . . A week, you think?"

"Yer brother don' mind us stayin' 'ere a little longer."

"He kept asking when I would be returning to Wiltonshire."

"Don' ye go pityin' yerself," Morgan snarled roughly. "Geoffrey's got 'is 'ands full, wot with 'at woman 'e married and 'er brother. 'e just wants ye out of their way. 'e don' think they're any better for ye than I do."

Alison gave him a sheepish grin. "What trouble I am for you, Morgan. I don't know why you've stayed all these years, or why you're dealing with this right now. It's not your problem. It's all my fault and would serve me right if I had to face it on my own."

Morgan frowned heavily as he sat beside her on the sofa. His huge paw tightened around her smaller one. "We're in 'is together, lass, whatever 'appens."

Watery eyes lifted and met his, and Morgan enveloped her in his huge bear hug. "Ye're not alone, lass, never."

Alison was too ill in the morning to think of leaving or of anything else. The attack of nausea left her weak and trembling and she crawled back into bed.

Mistress Mobley, the housekeeper, insisted Alison was suffering from a simple cold and a bit of rest would see her well. The housekeeper insisted on personally caring for Alison. By the second day, Mistress Mobley was proven correct in her diagnosis. The nausea did not abate, but was accompanied by fever and aching.

Three days later, Alison was feeling much stronger. She rose in time to join her brother for lunch, but as she entered the dining room, she wished she had not. Eileen and Geoffrey were both at the table. Their being together for so much as a meal was a rare and usually unpleasant occurrence. Neither could hide their dislike for the other.

Eileen greeted Alison with more simpering warmth than usual. Alison took the seat beside Geoffrey and was surprised to hear him say, "Gad, but you're white! Are you sure you're well enough to be up from your bed?"

Eileen's gaze was curious on her and she replied carefully, "I'm still unsettled from my cold. It will pass." But the sight of the kippers and liver caused her stomach to churn more. She settled for toast and tea.

"You should heed Mistress Mobley carefully," Geoffrey remarked over the meal. "She is gifted at curing all sorts of upsets. Eat only what she prepares, nothing else."

"Geoffrey, how can you be so cold to your own sister? I would die of shame were I to treat David in like manner." Eileen spoke in a cajoling voice which made Alison want to cringe. She did not want to be the source of a new argument between them. "Your harsh words lack all sympathy. Alison so seldom comes to London, and yet you are barely civil to her. Of course you trust Mistress Mobley, but cannot you trust Alison's judgement also? Or do you think she's young and foolish? Why, Alison probably holds me accountable for your coldness to her."

Eileen's beautiful mouth formed a pout and she placed her hand over her young sister-in-law's. "My dear, I assure you, I welcome you and would have had you here years ago but for Geoffrey's objections. I would be shocked to think I might come between brother and sister, especially since I am so close to my own. I have often suggested he invite both you and Jon, but he has refused."

Eileen turned to her husband and pleaded, "Can you not find it in your heart this once to have her near? You needn't trouble yourself with her. I'll see to her entertainment myself."

"You've said enough, Eileen!" Geoffrey rasped as he tossed his napkin on the table and rose. His face was pinched and white, there were fine lines about his mouth. His relationship with his sister and brother was the most bitterly regretted thing about this marriage. Above all he did not want to lose their regard, but to have his motives twisted like this was intolerable. He could not keep either of them here, not where she, David, or Naylor might reach them.

"Tonight we are invited to a ridotto. I can think of no entertainment more suited to a young girl."

"And I say she is not well enough!" Geoffrey snapped coldly, his lips thinning as he glared at his wife. Turning to Alison, his expression softened slightly. "If you're done with your meal, you should go back to bed until you're completely well."

Sleep eluded her that night. Her presence seemed to be causing more trouble for Geoffrey. It was time she was leaving London.

In the morning she sent another note to the Marquis' home, by a footman this time, imploring him to call on her. If only this matter could be settled quickly so she would know what to do for the future. Then she could leave Geoffrey's home and let him come to terms with his marriage. Alison was hurt by his attitude, she felt herself an encumbrance to him.

All morning she waited for the Marquis to come.

As was Eileen's usual habit, she rose from bed just before lunch and missed another meal with her husband and Alison. Later, Alison sat in the library, reading a book, hoping it might take her mind off her troubles.

She was settled comfortably in a chair when Eileen entered in a flurry of lace and velvet. She was dressed for riding in a habit of blue superfine, the finely cut lines displaying her trim figure to its fullest advantage. The smile she bestowed was sweetly beckoning.

"I think it's time we had a confidential chat, my dear," Eileen began as she perched herself daintily on the arm of Alison's chair. "I don't know why the thought only just occurred to me. I suppose it's because you're a vicar's daughter, and of course, this sort of thing never happens to vicar's daughters, or so I thought. Of course, your father did die when you were so very young. Perhaps that's how you went wrong. And you've spent so much time cooped up in the country, but still, I did not think it possible."

Eileen gave Alison a considering scrutiny. "You're not too unattractive, but don't you think sending notes to the Marquis of Chatham might be just a bit presumptive? No, no, no, no need to get so upset by all this," she soothed as Alison started to rise. "Of course I realize what's happened. The rogue seduced you! And I thought the country was so boring! But, my dear, if you think you can induce him to marry you, you'd better think again. More sophisticated women than you have tried and failed. I don't think your interesting condition will mean a great deal to him. He'll just claim that brat was sired by someone else."

"You're wrong!"

"Oh, no. I am anything but wrong. Your . . . your illness proved very interesting, as did your disinclination to leave your room in the mornings, your waistline . . ."

Alison was shaking her head feverishly, knowing all the while how futile her denial would be. Eileen's knowledge could only lead to disaster.

Eileen clicked her tongue impatiently. "You really are an innocent, aren't you? To be caught like this. Oh, it happens often enough. Why, several of my friends have been in the exact same position, only they were married. It's so much more respectable then. You really should have waited until after you were married to get involved with a man like Justin Sarrett, my dear. It makes bearing a child so much more acceptable."

"Eileen . . ."

"No," she held her hand up in a silencing gesture. "Don't interrupt me, my dear. As I was saying, several of my friends have been in this position and the fathers of their babes could not possibly have been their spouses. Do you follow me? That could prove very embarrassing, no? Especially when trying to explain to one's spouse. Well, I have an open mind about such matters, but your brother does not. He would be greatly disappointed in you."

151

Alison hung her head. Listening to Eileen made this nightmare even more sordid and ugly than it was before.

"Don't bother denying it. The signs are unmistakeable. I am only surprised it took me so long to recognize them. You have the air of a desperate woman, my dear. But," her tongue clicked almost gaily, "I have only come to help. I have a name and address . . ." Feeling about in her reticule, she found what she wanted. "Ah, here it is." To Alison she handed a slip of paper on which were scribbled several words. "This is the name and address of a physician. His office is on Harley Street and he is well qualified to help you. I know several ladies for whom he has performed this intimate service. It was such a relief afterwards, or so they told me."

Eileen rose and spoke more briskly now. "I do wish I knew how you enticed the elusive Marquis to your bed, my dear. I've been trying for years with no success. And here I thought you led such a rustic existence in Wiltonshire."

Alison was staring dumbly at the small slip of paper in her hand. "You mean this physician . . ." she faltered.

"Yes, this physician will get rid of the child for you. It is the only possible solution in your case, is it not?" Eileen pulled on her gloves. "Believe me, our Marquis will not marry you. If marriage were in the offing, you would not be writing to him now. He would be here. Geoffrey will not be pleased to hear of this predicament. I suggest you take care of it." Slender fingers raised to her hair and patted it in place. "I am going for a drive with Crispin Matthews. Ah, you wouldn't know

152

him, would you? Or perhaps you do? It seems you have more forms of entertainment in Wiltonshire than I ever dared dream." The skirt of her riding habit flared as she moved to the door. Hand on the knob, she turned to Alison. "I would hate to have Geoffrey discover this little problem, not when you have the solution in your hands."

The book fell to Alison's lap and vaguely she heard the door close behind Eileen.

The Marquis did not make an appearance that afternoon, nor that evening. Perhaps Eileen was right and he would not come at all.

"I've a confession, lass." Morgan said ruefully, later in the evening. "I delivered four more notes to the Marquis which were supposedly from ye. 'at's five 'e's received."

"Six. I sent him one by a footman."

Morgan cleared his throat gruffly. "'e must be detained. 'e'll be 'ere on the morrow."

Alison shook her head. "I don't think so. Lying to ourselves is no use, Morgan. This is not his lordship's concern."

"It damn well better be 'is concern!" Morgan snarled. "We'll tell the Earl! 'e'll see to it 'at 'e Marquis does right by ye."

"Oh, Morgan, what will that accomplish besides another duel? And that's what landed us here in the first place. I wanted the Marquis to help me on his own accord, not because Geoffrey forced him into it. I can't think of a worse future than being tied to a man who hates me as much as he does. No, I think I must do as I wanted to originally."

Exasperation tinged Morgan's voice as he said, "If ye

disappear, ye will only 'urt Geoffrey and Jon."

"I will hurt them more if I must share my humiliation with them. Besides, I don't want my child known as . . . as a," she had to whisper the horrible word, ". . . a bastard." Her hands were clenched tightly in the pockets of the apron she wore and one of them touched paper inside. Pulling it out, she was vaguely surprised to find the slip of paper Eileen gave her. The thought of that visit shook her still. "Eileen gave me this. It has a name . . . "

"Eileen? Don't tell me she knows of this!"

Alison sighed. "She says I'm very transparent."

"Ye didn't admit enything?"

"I didn't say a word." Alison's eyes raised to Morgan's. "She gave me the name of a physician she said would help me . . ."

"No!" Morgan's voice boomed. "A physician! More like a murderer, ye mean! Ye'll die, the child will die! 'at's wot 'appens to women who go to those butchers! Ye canna do such a thing! 'Tis a monstrous thought and monstrous of her to even suggest it!"

"Yes," Alison said softly. "I thought so, too." She rose from her chair and walked stiffly to the door, stuffing the piece of paper back inside her pocket. "That's one solution we don't need to consider. But Morgan, I think we should leave in the morning."

Geoffrey had the final say in that, refusing to allow her to leave until she had more color in her pale face. "Are you sure you've only a cold?"

Alison smiled at his concern. "I need to go home. I'd be more comfortable in familiar surroundings."

"Rest today. Tomorrow I'll accompany you. When we're back in Wiltonshire we'll see Dr. Simmons. He'll fix you up."

"Oh, Geoffrey, it's not necessary that you come with me. I'm homesick, that's all."

"I'm going with you. I want to speak with the doctor."

A sigh escaped her as she realized she had yet another problem. Geoffrey would be terribly disappointed in her when he learned the truth about her sinful nature. She should have done as she wanted from the first. She'd be settled in a cottage by now and she wouldn't have to see Geoffrey's face when he learned the truth.

She didn't think she could bear his disappointment.

Chapter Seven

The morning sun streamed through the bedroom windows, promising a day of some warmth. Alison sat on the bed and gazed outside, wishing herself at home in Wiltonshire and on the back of Honey. She longed for the freedom of familiar countryside and amiable friends. The boredom of her confinement in London was withering her spirits. She had thought to be gone from here yesterday but Geoffrey delayed them again. He was intent on traveling to Wiltonshire with them and said he had a few business matters to tend to before he could go. At the very latest they would leave on the morrow.

She rose and donned a dress of pale lilac wool. White ribbons were woven through her hair and tied around her waist. The thick outside walls of the house allowed little of the sun's warmth to penetrate and Alison threw a crocheted shawl over her shoulders.

Anticipating their departure on the morrow, she gathered her belongings and packed what she could. She had little enough. She'd not expected to remain this long and was sorely wishing she'd never bothered to come to London. Geoffrey's company would only complicate matters on her return. How could she disappear when he was right there? And how would she overcome the awkwardness of the doctor's visit? Deceit only seemed to embroil her into further deceit.

She was tempted to go downstairs but wanted to avoid her sister-in-law. Geoffrey was already gone for the day. She waited until she could stand her growling stomach no longer, then crept stealthily down the stairs.

Her spirits rose when she learned Eileen was out, only to fall again as she considered the ominous future over her meal. At this moment, everything seemed so hopeless. After eating Alison rose, intending to hide herself in the library.

The brass knocker sounded as her feet touched the landing, and she paused. Willis, the Earl's aging butler, ambled across the foyer, tugging on his sleeves and his neckcloth as he did so. He opened the door and in a voice devoid of all feeling, announced in formal tones, "Yes, milord. I will see if Miss Alison is in. Please allow me to present your card."

Alison would know the low tones which answered him anywhere. For the first time in days hope surged through her. She stood, transfixed on the sight of the Marquis moving through the door to the foyer below. He was dressed much as he had been during the kidnapping, in black topboots, buckskin breeches, and black riding coat. In the folds of his cravat was a diamond stud. His eyes lifted and darkened as they found her, his quirt slashing impatiently against his legs.

Alison had forgotten how large he was. Her cheeks burned furiously as his intent eyes studied her. His scowl deepened and his eyes harsher and blacker as they roamed over her warmly clad form, lingering on the tight fit of her bosom. The sight of him reminded her of the torment his touch aroused. For months now she had been so certain seeing him again would bring only nightmares, she was not prepared for the sudden eagerness swamping her. Her eyes took in the shape and form of him, he was handsomer than she remembered. He was also very angry.

Alison blinked, her hope dwindling. He would not make this easy for her, she realized dismally. "Good afternoon, my lord," she spoke softly, trying desperately to sound normal.

An angry glitter entered his lordship's eyes. "I believe I was summoned, Miss Asher. I am not a man to be at the beck and call of another, but when I am bombarded with such demands, I answer. If only to be certain the haranguing ceases."

With difficulty she swallowed. "I will receive his lordship in the yellow salon, Willis," she spoke carefully. "Oh, and please bring us some . . . sherry."

Once inside the room, conversation lagged. My lord watched her discomfort assessingly as Alison wondered how to begin. Her palms ran down the length of her thighs and some of the woolen material twisted between her fingers.

"I hoped you would come before this. Tomorrow I return to Wiltonshire," she said gruffly.

The black eyes glimmered in surprise. "I think not. You would not have returned until you had seen me. You have too carefully calculated your moves. I repeat,

I am not at your beck and call. I did not choose to call on you before this."

"This is difficult enough. Must you . . ."

"I hope it is impossible for you. Blackmail should always be carefully considered."

"Blackmail?"

"Yes, an ugly word, is it not? There is only one natural result from the night we spent together, Mistress Asher, and, of course, I am the one to take the blame. You must consider me a veritable fool, ma'am!"

"Natural . . . ? Oh!" she echoed faintly, flushing deeply as she thought she understood the meaning behind his words.

At that moment, Willis bore a tray of sherry and glasses into the room. "Shall I pour, milady?" he inquired.

"Yes, would you please? No, don't bother with any for me."

The Marquis accepted the glass and as soon as Willis left the room, downed it. The glass was slammed onto the tray and black eyes followed to where Alison stood very still.

"In this case, my lady, your cunning has trapped only yourself."

Alison's face paled with every word he spoke. "I am sorry. I know you don't believe me, but blackmail was not my intention. We are both at fault in this. I had hoped you would help me . . ."

"How generous of you to share the blame!" sneered the Marquis. "I enjoy being absolved by a woman little better than a streetwise whore. You kidnapped me and tempted me with that lithe, little body of yours. My judgement is not always the best and when I've been in the situation you forced on me for so long, I am even less judicious. Your planned seduction went very well for a beginner, did it not? Have you and Morgan congratulated yourselves for your success?"

Drawing a deep breath at the horrible name he threw at her, Alison clenched her hand for control and shook her head frantically. "I planned nothing of what happened. Please, don't make this any uglier than it is."

"Ugly? What a word for you to use. You look so innocent, yet you behave like the veriest trollop who sells herself on any street corner."

Alison's hand lifted to her throat as she stammered in a strangled voice, "No, it was nothing like you say . . . You forced me to go with you, I never dreamed such a thing would happen . . ."

Chatham had had enough. He'd come here with every intention of behaving just as he was, though as he faced her now, the implementation of the cruel plan was difficult. She looked so very young, and so very fragile. He could crush her with one palm, break her if he chose to. But she was not so tender, he well knew how her cunning had brought them both here.

Everything he intended was happening. She was frightened out of her wits, but she could, and would, learn respect for him at last. By tomorrow, he would return, claiming to have calmed down and admitting marriage was the only solution to this compromising position. And with the marriage would come many more lessons. Oh, yes, he would marry her. He wanted nothing more than to marry her and refine the halting responses he had from her that night. But the marriage would be on his terms, not hers.

He forced a mocking twist to his lips though the urge

to touch her comfortingly nearly won out. "You never dreamed I would say you nay? You should have been denied your own spoiled way long ago. You were very clever, the way you manipulated to make me feel obliged to offer marriage to you." His eyes peeled from her every bit of pride and dignity she possessed. "I am not so easily coerced, milady. Oh, you played your game well, withholding the ransom demand, pretending such endearing innocence," he broke off quickly and looked away from the anguish in her eyes as she paid close attention to his every word. "I suggest you think before you take this charade any further, unless you wish to see one of your brothers and Morgan Hull hanging from Newgate. I will not be forced into marriage! When I wed, it will be my choice."

Never in her wildest imaginings had Alison envisioned a scene such as this. "No," she whispered quietly, defeat bowing her head. Abruptly she sat on the small settee behind her. Her legs threatened to give way beneath her.

She seemed almost prim now, with her hands neatly folded in her lap. The Marquis knew she was on the verge of crying and he had to remind himself this was merely another ploy. "I advise you to remain silent about this to Geoffrey. You would not like the repercussions."

Alison nodded jerkily. She wanted him to leave before she humiliated herself further. A horrible numbness spread through her as she suddenly realized how much she had been counting on his help. Now, she never wanted to set eyes on him again. Never had she regretted anything so much as turning to him. He was a cruel devil!

"Do you understand me?" He repeated the words, his dark shape looming over her. He wanted an audible admission, a quick shaking of the head was not good enough. Alison was impaired by the lump in her throat. "Do you understand me?" he repeated once more, more fiercely. His hand reached for her chin and forced it up. Tears sparkled in her eyes and he abruptly released her. "Yes, I see you do." The quirt slashed against his legs as he crossed to the door. "Next time, I suggest you choose your victim with more care, someone more pliable than I."

The moments passed slowly after the door slammed behind him. Pain and humiliation spread through her body, threatening to suffocate her, they beat so fiercely within her chest. She tasted salty tears and lifted her hand to her mouth, wondering when she began to cry. How she hated him!

Suddenly she thought of the child and that it was part of him and she hated it, too. She wanted nothing of Justin Sarrett. Standing abruptly, she wiped the moisture from her eyes with the back of her hand. Only more humiliation would follow if she carried his child. His child! His child! The thought beat in her brain . . . she didn't want his child! The thought of carrying it even one more hour was unbearable.

Choking back sobs, she ran through the door, leaving it ajar in her wake, and climbed the steps to her room. Rummaging through the pockets of the apron she wore yesterday, she found the small slip of paper with the name and address on it. Crushing it in tightly clenched hands, she skittered down the stairs and out the front door, onto the street, never noticing or caring that Willis called after her. All she knew was how fresh

162

and clean the air felt on her face. Her run increased in tempo, as a sudden sense of freedom assailed her.

Harley Street was not far from here. She remembered seeing it as she first journeyed to Geoffrey's home. No great distance for a healthy country girl. That was all she was, and to the Marquis, not even that.

Everything she passed as she ran was a blur, even the many persons who stopped and watched curiously as the distraught young girl flew by them. Her life had become a nightmare in these last months, and somehow she had to go back in time. There seemed only one way to do that.

She skirted several streets and ran past many shops. Fine carriages passed her in a blur. Alison was oblivious of them all. She bumped into a man heavily laden with packages and caused them to spill over the walkway. His fist raised threateningly toward her, lowering as he saw her real fear and pain. She backed away from him, turned and broke into a swifter run.

Harley Street was just ahead. Slowing now, she made an attempt to breathe normally as her fingers unclenched the slip of paper so she might read the number scribbled on it. Her eyes carefully studied each office and shop, searching until she stood before the correct one.

The office appeared neat from the outside, a bit more ostentatious than the others. Alison bit her lower lip as she gazed on the heavily carved door which invited her inside. This was what she wanted, the solution to her troubles. She could wipe out the past and begin anew as though nothing had ever happened.

And as suddenly as it left, sanity returned.

How could she have thought, even for a moment, she

could do such a thing? Nothing would erase what was happening to her, nothing could make things as they were three months ago. This baby was part of her, too. More her than him. Destroying the child would destroy her.

She shivered as it dawned on her how close she had come to committing folly. This might be Eileen's solution, it was not hers.

Justin Sarrett wanted nothing of them. She accepted that now. But he was not the beginning nor the end of the world.

Her expression softened and the tears ceased. Curious eyes watched her and she began to feel very foolish. Turning, she walked slowly in the direction of Geoffrey's home.

She had to make her plans now. The Marquis would not help and she could not turn to Geoffrey, not when he had enough on his mind with his wife and her family. Alison swore she would suffer no further humiliation beyond this horrible day.

She had the money left by her mother, not a great deal but, with careful handling, it could support her and the child for a long time to come. She could manage alone, but she would not have to. Morgan would stand by her.

But they had to leave now, before Geoffrey joined them. They had to be gone before morning, even though that meant leaving surreptitiously in the middle of the night. She would leave Geoffrey a note and pray her words would be adequate to comfort him in this added worry.

Reality quickly descended as a filthy hand tugged at her skirt. "Tuppence, milady! Tuppence so's I c'n get a bit of summat for mesself to et!"

Alison looked down and saw a small, very grubby child hanging onto her. He was so pitifully thin and dirty that her heart melted. At this moment she could not help him. She had run from Geoffrey's home in such a hurry and with so little thought that she had no money, no reticule, not even a cloak with her. The child could be no more than six or seven years of age, she thought. Probably illegitimate. The word threatened to choke her.

"I have no money with me, I'm sorry." The boy released her skirts and uttered an oath which would have been more in keeping with a full grown man. He was about to run off in pure disgust when she said, "But if you'd like to come with me, I can promise you a good meal."

Large, fringed eyes looked askance at her. "How fer be 'is place ye'd take me to?"

"A good walk . . ."

"Wall," he drawled, "I has to be back afere nightfall. 'at's wen 'e morts wot 'as coin com' out."

"You will be," she promised.

The child scrutinized her once more, quickly, and then nodded. Her spirits must be recovering, she thought as she felt a laugh build within her. She must not look too fearsome. The child was probably worrying more about what she would feed him than what she would do with him.

He walked beside her, his eyes sliding over to her curiously time and time again. "Wot're ye doin' out alone? Don'e ye ken Lunnon is a danger fer ladies wot are alone?"

"Dangerous for me, but not for you?"

"No, not fer me! 'Tis me 'ome. Coursen' I knows 'ow to be careful."

"Then I wish you'd teach me," Alison said drily. "What's your name?"

"Thomas."

"Well, Thomas, do you think you can teach me to be more careful?"

The youngster's head nodded sagely. "First, ye gotta learn where to 'ide and where not. Tekes a long time to learn. Lunnon is a mighty big place."

Willis tried to stop Alison as she ran from the house. He blamed himself for not being more cautious. He would have had to be deaf not to have heard the Marquis tear into her like that. His place was not to interfere and he doubted he would have been able to handle the Marquis alone, anyway. But he would have liked to have tried. Miss Asher was too nice a young lady to be treated like that.

His thoughts turned to Morgan and one of the younger footmen was quickly dispatched to go after him. Morgan came as soon as he heard Alison was involved. Willis wasted no time in telling Morgan what had occurred.

Morgan listened to this tale with increasing anger. So, the scoundrel wanted nothing to do with her, he thought grimly.

But where would she have gone?

And then he remembered last night and the name and address Eileen had given her. He should have taken the paper from her then. "Where's Lady Eileen?" he questioned grimly.

"She left late this morning and hasn't returned. Probably a good thing, too. If she'd been here, all of London would know about this by now." Willis spoke bitterly. Lady Eileen was no better liked among the servants than among her husband's family.

Morgan tried to remember the address of the physician, but all he had of the paper was a swift glance. She couldn't have gone far, not on foot. His horse was saddled and brought to the front of the house. From there, Morgan began the most desperate ride he'd ever made. There was no sign of her on the busy streets of London. His search spread wider afield, to lesser known streets and alleys, growing more urgent as he rode longer and swifter. Still he found no sign of her.

Then came the moment when he realized there was nowhere else to search, at least not that he knew of. Slowing his horse, he thought how desperate she would have to be to even consider such an act. His Alison was probably in some quack's back room, right at this moment, stretched out on a bed. If she died . . .

And it was *his* words that drove her to this, Morgan thought grimly. He reined in the mare and turned her, riding hard and fast to Chatham House. By God, Sarrett would answer for this!

The Marquis was in the library, downing several glasses of port. He wanted to be senseless, maybe that would rid his mind of the expression on her face as he left. What had she to look so pained about? He was the one harassed! So why did he feel guilty? She was the one who needed this lesson.

For months she'd been on his mind, and all on hers was blackmail. The thought angered him anew. What

167

more did he expect from a cunning female? And why did he feel so absurdly let down? She had earned his anger today. And the more he drank, the more he convinced himself it was so.

A tremendous commotion at his front door dragged the Marquis' attention from his liquor. A familiar voice shouting "son of a bitch Marquis" had him opening the double doors which led to the library and striding through them, to watch as the front door was crashed through by Morgan Hull, a force which sent several of his servants flying.

At that moment, his own thoughts turned to murder.

Morgan's head jerked up at the sight of the Marquis and, without pausing for breath, he went for the man. It took three footmen and a butler to pull Morgan's fingers from around his throat. While he was being held back by the four men, Morgan still managed to jeer nastily at the Marquis, "Ye're a brave man when you 'ide behind so many! Or when ye face a lone girl! But ye turn and run like the coward ye are when ye 'ave to face a man! Ye may be 'ighborn and wealthy, but ye're lower'n a mongrel cur in 'onor!"

The Marquis eyed this entire scene with acute distaste. He had lost his composure once today and did not relish the thought of doing so again, especially in front of his servants. But this Morgan had been asking for trouble, he and that chit he connived with. At the moment nothing seemed more pleasurable than to give one of them the thrashing they deserved.

"So, you've come to add your persuasion for me to marry her? How faithful you are!" the Marquis drawled mockingly.

"Nay!" Morgan bellowed, his body straining to be

168

free of the Marquis' men. "'Tis too late. By the time the day is done, there will no longer be reason for ye to marry 'er. The child will be gone, and so, probably, will she! I've come to make damned sure ye send no more young girls to abortion 'ouses!"

Justin Sarrett felt as though he'd just been kicked in the belly. All he could see was red before his eyes. "You lying bastard!" he rasped savagely. "She would have told me!"

"Wot in 'ell do ye think she was trying to say? Ye don't think she would'a come near ye agin for any other reason? Did ye ever give 'er the chance to speak? No, ye were too damned busy calling 'er foul names. And as soon as ye left, so did she. And the Countess, bless 'er soul, did us all the favor of giving 'er the name of a physician wot could take care of 'er little problem! I wonder if ye supplied the name to the Countess just for that purpose!" Morgan bellowed savagely. He didn't care that he no longer made sense. He wanted to get his hands on the Marquis.

The realization of what Morgan was saying enraged the Marquis and his face twisted savagely as his hands formed fists. "Release him!" he spat at the men holding Morgan. He was done playing games with this old man.

Morgan was released and Justin lunged at him, knocking him to the floor. An angry fist pummeled a blow to the old man's face, bringing a rush of blood from the servant's nose, smearing it onto his face and clothing. Morgan tried to hit back but the Marquis was too powerful, too young.

"Get up, damn you! Fight back! You're her champion, the least you can do is land a blow!"

169

Morgan tried valiantly to rise but his body was too heavy and sore. He knew he was too old for this sort of fight. He should have found a younger man to handle the Marquis, only he'd been too angry to think properly at the time. He'd make up for that now. His head lolled and the Marquis grabbed the material at his neck and pulled him up to face him.

"If she's done anything like you suggest, I'll kill you both!"

Morgan gasped breathlessly at the man's boldness. "Ye think yerself blameless? 'Twas ye wot forced the child on her. Wot was she to do if not come to ye first? I wanted to make damned sure she never set eyes on ye again, only, ye gave us little choice, did ye not?"

The Marquis was barely winded as he rose and allowed Morgan to stand.

With feigned difficulty, Morgan found his feet. He breathed heavily as he stood, his knees knocking together weakly. His opponent seemed virtually unscathed, except for a creased coat and tousled cravat. The sight angered Morgan anew. He clenched a fist, intending to land a blow on Sarrett's face, only to have the Marquis easily catch the fist in the palm of one hand.

"Old man," the Marquis spoke scathingly, "another blow could kill you. Much as I detest you, I'm no murderer!" With a savage growl, he lifted Morgan's winded body and tossed the man over his shoulders.

Many prying eyes watched from the front windows of the house as the Marquis tossed Morgan over the saddle of the old man's mare and lithely swung himself up behind. Morgan was too stunned to protest. Kicking the flanks of the mare, Sarrett swung her around and set a relentless pace through the streets of London. They did not stop until the Earl's townhouse was reached. Sarrett jumped down and hauled Morgan Hull with him. Literally, he dragged the old man through the walk and up the steps.

Willis opened the front door and his mouth gaped wide at the sight which met his eyes. The Earl stood just behind him on the landing of the staircase, curious as to the cause of so much perturbation. Sarrett hauled Morgan Hull through the hall and dropped him before the stupefied Earl.

Morgan decided it behooved him to play senseless. It was one thing to take on the Marquis physically, another to face the Earl and his anger.

"Where's your sister?" Sarrett demanded viciously.

The Earl was stunned by the fiercely uttered question. "Alison? What do you want with her?"

Justin threw him an impatient glance, stepped over the prone body by his feet and headed for the staircase. Geoffrey recognized the high temper the Marquis was in and thought it best to appease him. "She's in the kitchen. I was just going there myself. I understand she's been upset most of the day."

The Marquis' eyes darkened and his lips thinned at the understatement of these words. "The kitchen? My God, you have no idea what folly you're committing, even allowing her in the room!" His tone was curt, his steps quick and sure. He walked on and on, poking his head in corners it did not belong, until he found the room for which he searched.

Alison was there, and in perfect health. Relief flowed through him as he saw she seemed very calm now, very much herself. She was speaking with a filthy, beggar

171

brat, laughter punctuating her words. He loomed in the doorway, large and menacing, and for a moment Alison was too surprised to speak. She thought never to see him again. Fear surfaced and she retreated as he came toward her.

"What are you doing here? Get out! Get out . . ."

The Marquis grabbed her wrist and pulled her behind him, through the many rooms of the house and to the staircase where Geoffrey last stood. From there, they moved on to the parlor where, Willis informed him in stern tones, "milord" now awaited them. Morgan's body had been removed from the hall and was reclining there on the sofa.

The Marquis dragged Alison into the room, threw her bodily at Geoffrey and rasped harshly, "I have come to request the hand of your sister in marriage. And no is a word I refuse to accept!"

As soon as Alison saw Morgan's prone body, she gave a smothered cry and ran to him. Morgan was more bloody than in pain but he dared not open so much as an eye. Let the Earl handle this, he thought.

"Willis," she ordered shakily, "I need some water and bandages, quickly." Her hand lifted to Morgan's head and brushed back the thinning, grey hair to inspect the damages. A bleeding nose seemed to be the cause of most of the bleeding. The mass of dried blood made the wound appear worse than it was. Morgan would be fine once he was cleaned up and had some rest. No thanks to the Marquis, Alison thought bitterly. But with such a slight wound, why wasn't Morgan conscious?

Alison turned angry eyes to the Marquis and demanded, "Are you responsible for this?"

"It is my pleasure to announce I most certainly am. My only regret is that he did not last longer. I relished the meager single blow."

Alison stood at his words, hatred spilling from her eyes, her hands clenched tightly as though that were the only way she could keep from hitting out at him. She suffered from no loss of words now. "You devil! If I were a man, I'd kill you for this!"

"If you were a man, my dear, you would be lying there instead of Morgan. And I would not be here now, forced into a marriage because you carry my child!"

"What?" roared Geoffrey.

Willis chose that moment to enter the room. At the harsh words of the Marquis, he dropped the bandages but managed to salvage the water. He set the ointments on the small table beside Alison who was crouched again beside the ailing Morgan.

"Thank you, Willis," she said earnestly. "Morgan's been mishandled dreadfully, but I expect he'll recover fully, in spite of certain vicious attempts to kill him," she ended tartly.

Very gingerly Willis removed himself from the room.

"What the devil do you mean, Justin?" Geoffrey's eyes were blazing.

"Just what I said. Morgan informed me your sister and I are expecting a surprise bundle sometime in the future. Your sister is remarkably silent on the issue." The last words were leveled accusingly at Alison's bent head.

"What? How the devil did you two . . ." his eyes swung to his sister. "Alison, is this true?"

Ceasing her cleansing motions, Alison rose and turned, barely able to meet her brother's gaze. "I would prefer to speak of this alone." She looked askance at the Marquis, her whole body bristling with anger. "And when he's not around. It's none of his affair."

"None of my affair?" echoed the Marquis. "Morgan claims the child to be mine, he also claims you were seeking a way to be rid of it!"

Alison flushed guiltily at that and the Marquis uttered an oath at the unspoken admission. She was ashamed that such a thought should be common knowledge. Lifting her chin she replied coldly, "Only for a moment. But you, milord, you were the one who refused to acknowledge the child. I repeat, since that is your decision, this is none of your affair!"

"I never denied my responsibility! I never even knew of it!" Sarrett roared angrily.

"Would you both shut up? I want an answer to my question. Alison," Geoffrey repeated, "are you with child?"

The stillness in the room was most unwelcome. Alison could hide behind chaos and confusion and avoid answering, but this silence was unnerving. Her shoulders drooped as she turned to face her brother. Her courage was only beginning to surface when the Marquis sneered softly, "Yes, please give us an answer! We are positively agog with curiosity!"

Alison's temper snapped. Rising to her feet, she rounded on the Marquis, her skirts swinging and her fists in tight balls. She drew back and swung as hard as she could, hitting him square on the eye. "You've said enough!" she cried, choking on her anger. Then, as though she just realized what she had done, she gasped and raised the back of her hand to her mouth. Her expression mirrored the Marquis' shock and she

174

stepped away quickly. "I've never hit anyone before in my life! Look what you've made me do!"

"I might have known that would be my fault, too!"

"I am sorry," she uttered in mortified tones. "I should not have hit you!"

His fingers gingerly felt the eye. By morning it would be black. He let out an angry snarl and any compassion she felt for him fled.

The Marquis eyed her distastefully. "No soothing pack for me?" he queried.

"Later," she replied sweetly, "when Morgan no longer has use for it."

A throaty laugh sounded from the doorway. "Well, it seems your afternoon was more entertaining than mine," Eileen drawled. Her eyes lit on the sofa, sliding over Geoffrey, and onto the Marquis. Blonde brows lifted when she saw Alison. "Well, well, it seems you've snared a Marquis, no less, and the elusive one. I didn't think you had it in you. Congratulations. Better women than you have tried and failed."

A statement which had Alison wishing she were alone so she could give in to the luxury of a well deserved cry.

The subject of their conversation gave a sudden yelp. With one hand he rubbed a sore shin and with the other he held fast onto a flailing, grubby, beggar boy.

"Ye jest leave her allone, unnerstan? Morts like ye done 'ave no use fer dessent wimmen!" Thomas cried belligerently as he hung in the air by his seatpants. He was still trying to sink his teeth one more time into some effectively painful spot.

Justin Sarrett lifted the child higher to take a closer look at him. Instantly he dismissed the child by tossing

175

him carelessly onto the floor. "I am constantly astounded by the quality of your champions, madame!" He gave Alison a mock bow, which tempted her to give him a blow for the other eye.

"Justin," Geoffrey bellowed, "you've insulted my sister enough for one day." He took a deep breath and muttered loudly, "We're getting nowhere and I need a brandy."

"That's the first thing I've heard that makes sense," the Marquis stated.

"I think so, too!" Eileen added, tossing her hat onto the nearby desk and smiling broadly.

"I don't drink brandy, and even if I did, I'm not sure I could keep one down," Alison choked, her face turning a dull shade of green.

"Oh, Lord!" Geoffrey said, giving the Marquis an angry glare. "You filthy bastard! How could you have done this to my sister?"

"Brandy?" Thomas' eyes opened wide. "I'se used to gin, but I'll give brandy a snort!" He grinned broadly and revealed several missing front teeth.

"I wonder how many it would take to get him foxed," Eileen speculated.

"You're not experimenting with Thomas," Alison snapped. The beggar boy's face fell. "Thomas, did you eat the meal Cook prepared for you?"

"Didna 'ave time, not after 'is mort 'ere grabbed ye like so. I thought ye mite be needin' me," Thomas responded proudly.

Alison smiled at him. "I did and I thank you for your help . . ."

Thomas moved closer to her and whispered in a confiding tone. "If'n ye want to be red of 'im, I knows a mort wot'll do it fer a schilling."

Her eyes followed the Marquis and she commented speculatively, "A schilling? Isn't that rather expensive, for him?"

Geoffrey smothered a laugh in spite of himself. The Marquis snickered loudly. Eileen giggled.

"I tenk so, too, but one schilling et be!" Thomas confided.

"Hmmm, well, I'll think about it."

The black brows rose haughtily.

Alison straightened. "Come, now, Thomas. Cook will have fixed a bag of food to take with you. You did say you had to return by dark, didn't you?"

"Aye, mum," he sighed. "'Tis a long walk."

"Would you rather ride in the carriage?"

Thomas' eyes gleamed. "Yes'm."

Alison pulled the bell rope and gave several instructions to Willis. "Oh, and Willis, we'll need some brandy and glasses." Thomas' expectant face fell. He was looking forward to trying a new drink, especially one of which only the rich imbibed. Alison knelt next to him. "I thank you for your help, Thomas. If you ever need my help, all you have to do is ask."

He smiled broadly. "Yes'm, I'll dismember 'at!"

"And come see me again. Cook will always have a meal waiting for you."

Willis returned with the brandy and glasses, setting them on the table. He motioned for Thomas to follow him out the door.

Alison felt uncomfortable as all eyes turned to her. She poured the brandy in an attempt to hide her nervousness.

"What? I thought you daren't brave anything other

than a glass of milk," the Marquis jeered.

Alison shook her head. "I'm having tea. A pity since brandy might possibly fortify me into enduring your company," she answered sweetly.

"Can't you put that body somewhere else?" demanded the Marquis. "It's unsightly."

"Morgan stays right where he is!" Alison responded, a fighting gleam in her eye. He might have intimidated her earlier, but not now. Not again. Especially not with Geoffrey here.

Justin considered her for a moment. "Even as a child you were strong willed and domineering, two traits I abhor in a woman. However, if you want to sit on his knees, that's fine. I'll take the chair." He promptly shook out his coat and sat on the one remaining chair in the room.

Geoffrey frowned and summoned a footman. "Take Morgan to his room. He'll recover there more quickly anyway."

Morgan hated to pass up the brandy, Geoffrey's selection was second to none, but he wasn't going to open his eyes and get involved in what was to come for any amount of the stuff.

"Now," Geoffrey began when the room was empty of all but the four of them. "What the devil is this about?"

Taking a deep breath, Alison spoke quickly, wanting this torment done with. "When I learned I was with child, I could not think of what to do. So Morgan and I came to London to find the Marquis. I was hoping he would help and I would not need to involve you. It was our sin, after all. Only he refused to see me. And when he did . . . he . . ."

178

Geoffrey cleared his throat. "Yes, I've heard all about his temper. What I want to know is how this happened. How the devil did you meet him again, after all this time? I would have thought the two of you would have avoided the other like the plague!"

Alison bit her lip. "I . . . I . . ." Desperately she searched her mind for a plausible explanation. She couldn't tell him she kidnapped the Marquis or she'd have to tell him why. And then what would happen? Another duel. Geoffrey and the Marquis have hated each other since the accident, this would only fan that hatred. No, any explanation had to be avoided at all costs. "I did try to avoid him, this happened anyway. So we came to London to find the Marquis, only he wouldn't see us right away. He said later, only I didn't know how long later was. I needed to get back to Wiltonshire and couldn't wait so I wrote him again. Only he still didn't come. And then this afternoon, he did come . . ." she gasped for a breath.

All eyes followed her slim hand as it lowered protectively to her belly. Geoffrey said drily, "I think I begin to understand."

"I hoped he would help me, but all he did was accuse me of blackmail."

The Marquis was slowly sipping at his brandy as she spoke. Geoffrey turned on him and demanded angrily, "And what's your explanation? I couldn't fathom any sense from hers."

"I was kidnapped," Sarrett stated flatly. "I told you about it. Your sister was one of the gang, the most deadly, I might add. She demmed near poisoned me."

"You're a liar, Chatham! My sister would not be

179

involved in such a thing," Geoffrey stated in a deadly tone, rising to his feet.

The anger had gone quite far enough. "He's speaking the truth, Geoffrey." All eyes turned to Alison. "We did kidnap him. This . . ." her eyes lowered to her belly, "this happened when he escaped."

"We? Who else was involved?" Geoffrey demanded.

"Who do you think?" Justin answered sardonically. "Morgan and Jonathan, who else?"

"Alison, why?"

She swallowed with difficulty. "I admit it was the three of us," she said hesitantly, wanting to tell him all, but knowing she could not. None of this was Geoffrey's fault and he would think it was. Frantically her eyes searched the room, only to find the Marquis comfortable in his seat, a self-satisfied smirk on his face. Her head lifted challengingly. "Be that as it may, I didn't ask to be taken from Morgan and Jon by him. And we did nothing to harm him. He took me along, then he . . . he took me to an inn and we . . . we . . . he . . ."

"I seduced her," Justin Sarrett snarled. "I should have throttled her. It would have been less dangerous." He tossed off the last of his brandy and rose to pour another.

"What right have you to judge?" Alison ranted. "Even in Wiltonshire I heard the gossip about you! I may have been caught, but I don't make a habit of such . . . such immoral acts! How many times have you tempted fate?"

The Marquis lifted his glass in toast. "More than I can count, milady."

"Alison, I think you've said enough."

Violet eyes widened as other thoughts came to mind. He was no novice, for that she could vouch. The thought that she was not alone in the predicament, and perhaps caused by him, threatened to make her ill again. She stammered, "Has this happened to you before? Is that why this seemed so 'natural' to you?"

The Marquis' eyes darkened. "How dare you?"

"You're right," she admitted, blinking rapidly and taking his words as admission. "I don't want to know. I don't want to know anything about you." She pushed away the cup of tea and felt tears burning in the back of her eyes. Unsteadily she found her feet. "I don't feel at all well. I need to go to my room."

"We haven't settled this yet!" the Marquis retorted harshly.

She rose from the sofa and headed for the door. "Later," she muttered. "I . . . I . . . I don't . . ." Her fingers flew to her mouth and she ran from the room.

"Damn you, Justin!" Geoffrey roared, closing the door behind her. The servants had enough to talk about as it was, without them hearing of this conversation too. "I won't have my sister giving birth to a bastard!"

"And I won't have my child born a bastard!"

"Then you'll marry her?"

"Oh, I'll marry her. In spite of your sister's obvious opinion, I am not in the habit of seducing respectable young ladies and deserting them. Though I begin to wonder if that harridan you call a sister has ever been or ever will be respectable!"

Geoffrey bristled. Eileen questioned curiously, "Oh? Then she was not a virgin when you took her?"

Sarrett turned to her and gave a mock bow. "She was. And that's the only reason I'm prepared to marry her."

"There's no need to be so insulting!" Geoffrey snapped.

"No?" Justin sneered. "And you do not consider her attitude toward me insulting? No one has ever spoken to me in such an insolent manner without learning to regret it, as will this ignorant sister of yours. Don't look as though she's the one wronged, I'm the one kidnapped, remember?" His expression was hard as he spoke. He rose and poured himself another healthy draught of brandy.

"Yes, that's another thing. Why on earth would she kidnap you?"

Justin was returning to his seat and paused at the Earl's words. "Why, to trap me into marriage, of course! Even Eileen said so. How did you phrase it, Eileen? She 'snared the elusive Marquis'?" His upper lip curled at the repetition of the words.

"If you really believe that then you're a bigger fool than I took you for!"

"Have you another explanation?"

"No, but I'll damn well get one! I'll get to the bottom of this yet!"

The Marquis shrugged his shoulders indifferently. He was beginning to realize how these latest events played right into his hands. He wanted revenge. And now he had a great deal of time to extract that revenge. The rest of their lives.

"This marriage is not what I wanted for her, but it seems too late for a choice," Geoffrey admitted softly. "At least her name and the child's can be protected this way. She does not need to be a burden to you financially, I am prepared to see to all her needs. If she lives with you until the birth, just for appearances' sake, that will suffice. You can both go your separate ways then."

"I think you misunderstand," Justin answered swiftly. "We will marry and she will be my wife, in all ways. Make no mistake about that. And as my wife, her needs will no longer be your concern. You need not interfere in matters between us. You are accustomed to looking on Alison as a child. It is time she grew up." He was hard as granite.

"If you harm her . . ."

"I will not harm her, but I will teach her to be a proper wife."

"She's no meek maid to be kept under your thumb."

"She will do what I expect of her."

Geoffrey was becoming more uncomfortable by the moment at the thought of this marriage. Maybe when the anger was gone, Sarrett would be more approachable. "There's the matter of the dowry . . ."

"Settle any amount you would give her upon the child. She'll need nothing more than what I provide."

"That places her at your mercy!"

"She has already placed herself there. That will be her first lesson. Her second lesson will be to learn to curb that tongue of hers. I will not tolerate her insults!"

Geoffrey set his glass on the table which separated the two men. He spoke softly, "She is very special to me, Justin. All my life, especially in the troubled times, when I wanted to think of more pleasant times, she came to my mind. Her laughter, her gentleness, her openness, thoughts of those traits soothed me, even at a great distance. I have always envisioned her future as filled with love, laughter, children. She does not deserve your harshness. You would break her."

Justin smiled grimly. "She will learn."

"I will be watching you, Justin."

The Marquis gave him a mocking bow, set his empty glass on the table and quit the room.

Chapter Eight

Alison was wakened during the night by one of the maids and told to hurry, her lord awaited her in the den. Assisted by the maid, she garbed herself in a morning gown of blue dimity and hurried down the stairs, into the room where she found Geoffrey reclining in a comfortable chair, a cup of morning tea in his hand. The Marquis stood by the window, his hands clasped behind his back and glaring out into the darkness of the early morning. He did not turn until the door closed behind her.

Alison was relieved to see the eye which took her blow last night was only slightly discolored and not a black bruise as she had feared. The Marquis did not seem pleased, however. His eyes took in her freshly scrubbed complexion and the childish gown she wore and he scowled deeply.

"Alison, have you nothing finer to wear?" Geoffrey inquired softly.

"She's fine as she is," the Marquis hastened to assure him, his eyes on Alison. "Since our need to marry is of such immediacy, I saw no reason to delay. Between the servants in this house and my own home, all of London should know our business shortly and I prefer to be legally wed when the gossip spreads and you begin to show your . . . your condition. The ceremony is arranged. It only needs us to be complete."

"But I have not agreed to marry you!"

"Of course you will marry me, my lady. Was that not the point of this farce? I choose not to waste more time on pretense, so you shall have to forgo the imitation of a courtship. You shall have the marriage, after all, and that child you carry will have my name. I have accepted the inevitable, must you insist on a traditional proposal? Do you demand I go down on my knees?"

"No!"

"Then, come," he held out his arm to her. "The minister awaits us. This is why you came to London and sought me, is it not?"

She dared not meet the challenge in his eyes, and so quickly dropped her gaze. He was right, she had no choice. Her thoughts of running away and setting up a home by herself were not so sensible, not when the option of giving her child a father such as he was available. She accepted his arm, and on doing so, missed the bitter twist of his lips.

Geoffrey gave one of the maids a curt order as they left the room and the girl quickly ascended the stairs, returning later with a cloak for Alison's shoulders.

Once inside the carriage, Alison felt brave enough to break the silent tension. "Why are we doing this so early?"

"I would like privacy in this, my dear," the Marquis drawled, as though some inner thought delighted him.

"The minister agreed to perform the early service. Perhaps we can avoid some of the scandal attached to this situation. With luck, we can be back at the house before most of London stirs."

Alison moved to the corner of the carriage and lifted the curtain to peer out. Light barely peeped over the horizon. Another hour would pass before anyone stirred. She dropped the curtain and relaxed against the squabs, her gaze finding the derisive eyes of the Marquis on her. With an abrupt movement, she turned from him.

The wheels of the carriage droned rhythmically against the cobblestones and Alison's thoughts wandered to the fine old church at Wiltonshire where her father was once vicar. Built during the reign of Edward III, ransacked during the years of turmoil under Henry VIII and, later, Cromwell, it was finally restored during the reign of Queen Anne. No longer as ornate as it was originally, it was the most beautiful church Alison had ever seen.

Always, in her dreams of the vague future, she thought it would be there she was married, there her children would be baptized, and there she would one day be buried. The dream seemed to have died long ago, with her father.

Black lashes dropped to her cheeks as Alison coped with the haunting spectre of disgrace. She supposed one day she would grow accustomed to her husband's contempt and anger. The thought of the years ahead had her trembling with dread. Chatham saw the slight movement and leaned forward to tug the ends of her cloak together. His hands burned. She could not avoid him. There was nowhere to turn to run from him. She was forced to sit quiescently until the cloak was snug and the Marquis had resumed his seat. She could not bear to look at him. She knew what mockery she would see on his face.

The carriage pulled to a halt. The Marquis was the first to alight and he held out his hand for Alison. The nearby creek let off an offensive stench of sour water and sewage which assailed her the moment her feet touched the cobbled stones. Even a newcomer to London such as she had heard of the large brick building at the end of the street which housed debtors. She knew she was on Fleet Street.

Geoffrey moved beside them, his voice deepening. "There was no need for such haste as this . . ."

"Here is our destination," the Marquis remarked genially, moving forward toward a large building and taking Alison with him.

"Another day or two would not have mattered!" Geoffrey spoke bluntly. "This is a blight on your marriage."

The Marquis tightened his hold on Alison's hand. "But Alison is in such a hurry. Aren't you, my dear? You're anxious to see this marriage a fact, admit it."

The color ebbed from her face as she gazed at this part of London. The smell, the poverty, the filth, all were part of this reality of her marriage. The surroundings symbolized desperation and despair. Geoffrey was right, the marriage was already blighted.

Geoffrey's temper was rousing. "I must have been mad to think you capable . . ."

"It's nearly done, Geoffrey. And the necessity for haste precludes the many niceties a woman likes. Alison doesn't mind, do you, my dear? After all, you've

188

gotten your way. That's the most important item, as always."

"Justin . . ."

"No," Alison protested shortly. "Let him have his pound of flesh. I want this marriage over and done with."

"Oh, not the marriage, my dear. Perhaps the ceremony, but certainly not the marriage."

She wanted to withdraw her hand, she couldn't bear his touch but he would not release her. "So anxious to hurry inside and tie the knot?" he jeered softly, tucking her hand in his and clasping her tightly, as he moved with her toward the building.

This was a hideous nightmare, growing worse with each passing moment.

The Marquis lifted the brass knocker and allowed it to fall against the door. The woman who answered bobbed a curtsy and led them into the hall and up the landing. "Ye be the newlyweds, eh?" she questioned, her smile displaying missing and blackened teeth. The once white apron was splattered with remnants of an ancient meal, her skirt was torn and filthy where it dragged against the floor. She did not wait for an answer before grinning again and speaking. "This way, then. Reverend Daunton be ready for ye. I be Mistress Daunton, yer witness."

Once garish furniture was now shabby and thread-bare, the gold paint on the walls peeling. Poverty might have been acceptable, such filth was not. Alison stifled an urge to lift up her dress and cloak so the hems would not reach the floor.

Mocking eyes watched her expression carefully. He was enjoying this, she thought wildly. Like the

189

ceremony, her marriage would be a constant humiliation.

Reverend Daunton carried a protruding belly which swept everything from before him. His long-tailed black coat groped about his belly, ill fitting and puckering where silver buttons fastened. Tight breeches strained with the bulk of the man, tapering down from knees and meeting tattered lace of once fine stockings. The leather boots were cracked and worn. His wide brimmed hat carried a sprig of herbal greenery in the band, his grey hair flowing from beneath the brim. His face was plump and red cheeked, and when he smiled a gap appeared between his two front teeth. His shabby appearance faded in importance as Alison met his expression. Small, greedy eyes lowered to her form, lingering over her bosom. Alison restrained the urge to pull her cloak more tightly about her and she moved closer to Geoffrey, but it was the Marquis who stood between them and spoke curtly to the insolent one. "Get about your business, man!"

Reverend Daunton lifted his eyes solemnly and began to speak in a soft, cajoling voice. The alcohol on his breath made it foul. "So you wish to be married?"

Alison trembled, uncaring how much satisfaction that would give the Marquis. Nothing ever again would hurt quite so much. She sought Geoffrey's comfort but it was the Marquis' arm which held her tightly against him.

Mercifully, the words were quickly spoken and the deed done. The grip on her waist tightened as Reverend Daunton said genially, "I've some fine brandy to toast the newlyweds . . ."

"No!" rasped Geoffrey.

Alison could stand this farce no longer. She pulled free of her husband and ran from the foul room, onto the street. The air was little better here but she breathed deeply. The sun was risen, making the street brighter and cleaner than that oppressive house. People were beginning to stir and several of them looked her way. Alison climbed into the carriage, unable to face the curious expressions which told her they knew what would have prompted such a hasty wedding. Geoffrey followed her.

"It's over now, Alison."

Her dismay was too apparent in the white face raised to him. Geoffrey moved beside her, taking her hand in his. "Justin will regret this, Alison. I think he does already. He wanted to hurt and humiliate you, but even he couldn't have realized how bad it would be.

"Alison, this marriage is not what I would have chosen for you, but it is the best I have to offer. You and Justin took the matter from my hands. Of all of us, you are most like your father, straight and true. You would not have survived the scandal of bearing a child alone. This is the best solution for you. I, too, am angry at the way Justin arranged the wedding, but it is done. You are married to him and you must make the best of your marriage. I could interfere now and demand he apologize for this day, but I fear that would make him even angrier than he is.

"God knows I am no authority on marriage, but I can assure you of this, Justin will not harm you. He seems fierce and angry now, he wants to frighten you. He thinks you trapped him into this and he wants his vengeance. But he will not harm you. Surely you can forgive him this day. In time he will come to love you."

191

Tears streamed down her cheeks as Alison carefully considered his words. He wanted her to make the best of this and she would try. But what good could come of a marriage begun this way and with the bitterness between spouses as was between her and the Marquis? She could not add to Geoffrey's burdens any further and so kept quiet. All she wanted was to run and hide. The thought of seeing that arrogant man day after day, for the rest of her life, was unbearable.

The Marquis swung himself into the carriage and it began to ramble on its way. Alison could not look at him, she knew the gloating expression she would see in his eyes. Leaning her head against the squabs, she closed her eyes and wondered what horrors the rest of this day might bring.

The first stop was Geoffrey's townhouse. He alighted and turned, proffering a hand to assist Alison in joining him. She rose to accept, but a tug on her waist caused her to pause. Her eyes grew puzzled as they rested on her husband. Chatham watched her but his words were for her brother. "I am sorry, Geoffrey, but it is time your sister was introduced to her new home. She will see you some time later."

He moved quickly, pulling the door shut and rapping at the driver to continue on their way. Alison watched in horror as Geoffrey was callously left behind, his expression scowling.

"Why did you do that? Have you no decency at all?" she demanded.

"None," the Marquis retorted blandly. "You're a married woman now and it's time you learned to behave like one. Your brother's home is no longer yours, you both needed reminding of the fact." He rested his head against the cushions, his black eyes on his wife. "Mrs. Land, my housekeeper, has planned a very nice luncheon, a sort of celebration to welcome you to your new home."

"Please, let's not add hypocrisy to this day."

His hand snaked out and grabbed hers, jerking her against him. "Perhaps you need the rules of behavior made clear to you. You share my name and fortune. I wish you great joy of them. I, in return, own all of you, from your lovely tresses to your dainty toes. The only drawback is your tongue, but with time, I can curb even that." He pulled her forward, ignoring her resistance, until her chest reclined against him and his face was next to hers. "I expect a dutiful wife, a mother to my children, note the plural, a mistress for my homes and servants. You will have little room for complaint, unless you demand too much of my time or attention . . ."

Alison had enough. She was tired, her head ached and she hated this polished, jeering ass with a passion. She lifted her chin challengingly. "Do you use the plural, children? I believe that might take some of your time."

"Not as much as you might think." The Marquis flashed a humorless smile. "As I recall, I was patient with you. I wanted to give as much pleasure as I was receiving. It need not be like that again. I can take you as I please and there will be no one to stop me, no threats of being followed by Morgan or the lad, no brother with the right to interfere. And as I do have a desire for posterity and as I'm saddled with you, I'll make the best of you. Be warned, wife, it will not do to defy me. If it becomes necessary to use more than

193

words to enforce my will, I shall not hesitate. You've trapped me finely, chit, but I'll not suffer one moment beyond this morning and the meaningless vows we spoke."

"You spoke. I said not one word at that fiasco," she retorted bitterly.

"No matter. You are as tied to me as I am to you. I'll feed you, I'll dress you, I'll even take you in bed, but I'll be damned if you will ever be more than a brash chit to me! One who took advantage to gain for herself a title and wealth. For a whore, you set a high price on yourself." His face delved closer to hers and she watched the fine lines around his mouth deepen. "I swear, you'll repay me for every farthing you cost!"

His hands bit into her shoulders as though he would shake her. She tried to push him away but that only had the effect of making the hands tighten. How had Geoffrey thought he would not physically abuse her? Weariness and fear joined within her to cause tears to gather in her eyes and she stilled her movements, barely managing to gasp, "Please, you're hurting me!"

The hold loosened, but the black eyes glared their contempt at her. "I want to be sure we understand each other," he drawled hatefully. "Provoking my temper is unwise. Or must I offer you further proof?"

She shook her head. Her shoulders ached where he manhandled her and she was certain that took little effort on his part. If he chose to, he could be very painful. "Yes, I understand."

"Good." He smiled grimly as he released her, his eyes hard on her. She turned from him to stare out the window.

The carriage rolled through the gate. The lawns of

Chatham House were spread before her as the house and its mullioned windows came into view. The Marquis alighted and turned to assist his bride. Alison took a deep breath as she placed her hand in his and accepted his help. Her feet touched the ground and she tried gently to free herself from his hold. Her eyes were unseeing as the Marquis tightened his grasp and led her into his home. All she wanted was solitude so she might regain her lost composure.

Many servants were there to greet them, but Alison remembered clearly the words of the Marquis early that morning. Too many of them knew of her condition and the thought humiliated her greatly. The Marquis was speaking. She realized he was introducing her to some of the servants and tried to concentrate, but her mind was feverishly wondering how she would get through the rest of her life with this man.

"Alison," the Marquis interrupted her thoughts. "Mrs. Land has kindly offered to show you the house."

"Oh, I'm sorry!" Alison responded, her face flaming at her seeming rudeness. She held a trembling hand out to the housekeeper and found it firmly clasped. "My mind was wandering. It's been such a long day and . . ."

"Of course, milady," Mrs. Land responded quickly. The trembling was not wasted on her. The harsh expression on her master's face told Mrs. Land something more than haste was very much amiss with the marriage. But the housekeeper was relieved too, after all the wild gossip belowstairs, to discover her new mistress to be so young and so personable. Even if a certain part of the stories was true, she was just a child. Mrs. Land knew her Marquis and knew it would be more his doings than this child's which were to blame.

195

"Perhaps I should show you to your room and you can rest? Later you can see the house. You have ample time ahead of you." Mrs. Land smiled kindly at her.

"Oh, yes, please!" Alison replied eagerly. "If I can take time to freshen up . . ."

"Take all the time you want, Alison. The celebration will have to wait until this evening. I am engaged for luncheon and will not return until late."

Mrs. Land frowned, but Alison sighed in relief as she realized she was free of his presence for the rest of the morning. The Marquis watched grimly as she followed the housekeeper up the stairs.

The chamber set aside for her was spacious and bright, but Alison took little notice of it. With Mrs. Land's help, her gown was removed and her hair unpinned. She slid between cool sheets. Her entire body ached and she felt only a nagging urge to cry. For the first time, she felt heavy and burdened with this child. She needed time to gather her strength before she faced her husband again.

Just before she fell asleep, she climbed from the bed and locked the door.

The room was in darkness when she wakened. She must have slept for hours and now she found she was ravenously hungry. She rose, intending to don her blue dimity gown, but could not find it. Glancing around the room, she saw her toiletries neatly set on the dresser. Crossing to the bureau, she opened one drawer and then another and found all the clothing she brought from Wiltonshire to London here. Someone had gone to Geoffrey's house, fetched her things and brought them here, while she slept.

All she could think was there was another key to

her chamber.

As she mulled over the matter, a young maid arrived and offered to help her dress. The girl found Alison's white satin dinner gown in the closet and helped Alison step into it. The bodice was stiff in front with a lace ruching accentuating her bosom. The satin skirt was covered with a fine lace overskirt, both widening from waist to feet. Her shoulders were bare except for the long curls of blond hair clinging there.

The maid left and Alison waited as long as she dared. Peering cautiously out into the hall, she found no one there, so she grew braver and slowly descended the stairs. Her feet barely touched the lower landing when a door below and to her left opened.

"In here, Alison." The Marquis watched as she walked toward him, moving aside to allow her to enter. As she passed him, his nostrils caught the fresh scent of her hair. She paused just inside the room. A half step would take him to her. The lace on her bosom drew his eyes to the creamy skin. The sleeves of her dress clung low on her arms. When she turned her head a lone curl traveled the length of her flesh, coming to rest in the cranny between the tempting mounds.

Chatham turned abruptly and moved a distance from her. "I trust you slept well?" At her nod, he sipped of an amber liquid in the crystal glass he held. His words sounded gruff. "You slept all day. Mrs. Land was concerned you had nothing to eat. Have you an appetite now?"

She was wary of him, yet she could detect none of his usual mockery. "A ravenous appetite, milord."

"Then we must not keep you waiting. Mrs. Land has been patiently keeping dinner for us." He held out his arm and when she took it, seemed unable to resist a jeer. "We can't starve the child at this stage of the game."

Alison jerked clumsily away from him. Would every moment of the rest of her life be filled with discord? A scant second seemed to go by between insults. He appeared not to have noticed the awkwardness. His fingers tightened on hers and he made innocuous small talk as they crossed to the dining room.

The first course of capon and salmon was served with champagne. Alison would die rather than admit the drink was never served at Wiltonshire, not to her anyway, but she truly didn't think she could keep down such a bitter drink. She played with the stem of her glass until, with a slight crook of his finger, the Marquis summoned a footman and lemonade miraculously appeared beside her plate.

Conversation lagged. The Marquis made several references to mutual acquaintances and inquired if she had seen any of the sights of which London boasted so proudly. Alison confessed she had not, and was so brave as to admit she would like to see the tower. Beneath his lordship's guidance, the conversation veered to horses. Alison's eyes lighted up and she regaled him with questions about races and curricles and betting, laughing pleasantly after he imparted the tale of one worthy race.

"We had a curricle race once, in Wiltonshire," said she, for the first time at ease with him. "Billy John Stockwell and Emery Dart raced through the village in their father's curricles. Only imagine, when they were done, both fathers hauled them off to their homes and I heard Billy was whipped and locked in his room for three days. His father is a local magistrate and he was appalled that his son would endanger lives like that." Alison laughed gaily as she spoke. "Everyone in the village knew about the race and so the lane was emptied. The worst part of it was, no one was able to collect their bets. Mister Stockwell declared all bets forfeit and took the monies for the orphanage. Morgan lost a day's pay. I always thought it would be great fun to bet on a race and be able to watch them cross the finish line."

"Dessert in the parlor, Daniel," Milord ordered as he rose from the table.

"This is delicious, my lord," Alison pronounced when she tasted the trifle. "Nothing like Emily's. I tried to make this once," she began wistfully.

"I remember," the Marquis replied, laughter in his voice. In spite of his anger over the kidnapping, he recalled momentary fragments which still made him laugh. "The pudding ran and the cake nearly caught it. I ate the fruit though. Not much you can do to ruin fruit."

"No, my fruit was delicious, even if I say so myself," she answered with a touch of arrogance, laughing at his answering expression. She declined a second serving of dessert, though milord was not so shy. The tones he spoke in were low, his humor dry and witty. Alison found herself laughing and very comfortable in his company, until her loosened tongue veered the conversation to topics still dangerous between them.

"Was it Geoffrey who brought my things? Is he still angry with you for leaving him standing in the road as you did?"

"I fetched your belongings, and it doesn't concern

199

me whether your brother is angry or not."

"He looked ready to murder you," she answered lightly, missing all the tell-tale signs of impending anger. "I would have been trembling in my shoes. I wish I'd seen Morgan this morning. Has he recovered from the blows you dealt him?"

"Blow, singular. One measly one to the nose. He was not nearly as wounded as you seem to think. Morgan is a master of feigning injuries. You might have shown such concern about my wound. And when I arrived this morning, before dawn, Morgan was being given his walking-papers by your brother. A more fitting end I have never seen. The man's nothing but a damned incompetent, letting you run loose like you have been. That will change, I can promise you, my girl."

"Geoffrey fired Morgan?" Alison cried, aghast. "How could he do such a thing? Morgan's part of the family."

"No, he's not, he's a servant who has outgrown his usefulness. The man deserved his rewards, just as he deserved more of a pummeling than the one I gave him last night."

"He did not!" The light of battle sprang to her eyes. "You are cruel in your assessments. I would hate to be your servant if that is how you behave to every one of them!"

Milord held up a beringed hand in a gesture of silence. "Spare me your reading of my character. How I treat my servants is none of your business. I imagine they prefer working for me for a wage to working for you for nothing more than an odd laugh now and then."

Alison gasped at his words. "I have always considered you cold and hard, unfeeling where another person is concerned. You're too concerned with yourself . . ." her voice trailed lamely as she realized they were arguing, again. Besides, the black anger she hated so much was again on his face.

The Marquis tensed with anger as he rose to stand over her. "Will you never learn the wisdom of silence?" he roared. His hand tugged at her wrist and pulled her to her feet, his arms snaking about her trembling body. "I know one method of silencing you, my lady."

His mouth lowered and angrily plundered hers. Alison struggled only briefly as the iron hardness of his chest and arms imprisoned her. Struggling would be useless, as she should well know by now. Her whole body was racked with a final shudder and her fingers were pressed into his coat. His head lifted at the reluctant quiver and he could see the misery in her eyes. Her mouth trembled.

His hold loosened and she thought herself released. A groan sounded as his mouth returned to claim hers, more gently this time. The soft touch of his lips was offering comfort. The flame of his tongue licked at her lips and when she parted them, it inveigled its way into the tender parts of her mouth.

He smelled of soap and hay, horses and tack. The warmth of him drew her and all caution was tossed to the ends of the earth. Niggling in the back of her mind was that she should not be accepting him like this. Hadn't one sin been enough? The thought was pushed aside by his heat and fire, by the fierce hunger she felt surging through him. He held her impaled and breathless with his need. The long buried memory of the feel of his length against her and the touch of his long, lean fingers was reawakened.

His head lifted and she barely managed to whisper an unconvincing, "No." Ignoring her feeble protest he lowered his mouth to the skin he had ached to touch throughout dinner. Her arms crept around him and she arched in invitation. So much for her resistance to sin. Fingers dipped below the lace and cupped her breasts, freeing them from their confines and for more of the warm, moist kisses he bestowed. Hot blood surged through her veins as his tongue tasted one rosy nipple. All coherent reason fled.

The insistent knocking on the door penetrated. The Marquis' breathing was harsh as he lifted his head. Alison's hands reached for him, to stop him from leaving her, but his voice came gruffly to her ears. "Cover yourself. Have you no shame?"

Her face flamed at his words and, with a gasp, she jerked from him. Turning, she put clumsy fingers to her bodice, fumbling anxiously, until she righted her gown.

Never could she face him again, she thought dismally. Why did she do it? Again! How could she have been so lost to all decency to behave as she did? Her sinful tendencies seemed to be overtaking her life. Never again, never again, she vowed repeatedly.

What kind of a person was she, to give way so easily to sins of the flesh? She'd always been God fearing and Church going. She was a good girl, she knew she was. Until she was near him, her conscience cried.

His voice came, seemingly from a great distance, but he was only as far away as the hearth. "Come in," he ordered.

202

Mrs. Land entered and Alison took the coward's way out. Scurrying past the housekeeper, she fled up the stairs and into her room.

Her face flamed as she stared at herself in the mirror. This was a stranger, not someone she knew so intimately. She must be the weakest person on this earth, she thought. Her mother and father would be as ashamed of her as Geoffrey was. Why couldn't she be stronger? Then a more level head spoke within her mind. But in many ways she was strong. She was strong in her beliefs of right and wrong. She never told a lie. She was a true friend. And these strange things she wanted to do with the Marquis, no one had ever tempted her with before.

Would he come to her tonight? And could she resist him? He was physically stronger than she was, true, but did she have to encourage him? Why wasn't she stronger when it came to sins of the flesh? Would it ever be possible for him to touch her and for her not go up in flames?

No, she didn't think so. Oh why did her husband tempt her so? She didn't need his help to heap humiliation and disgrace on her. He did plenty by himself.

His opinion of her was so low that he actually thought she planned the child and the marriage. What was he thinking right now? That she plotted only to tempt him more?

He promised to treat her as a whore. Was this the fulfillment of that threat? Oh, why did she have to rush eagerly into his arms every time he held her? Hot palms pressed against her flushed cheeks as she remorselessly flailed herself with words.

If only she were less of a coward and more resolute. If only he weren't so experienced . . . and his caresses weren't so arousing . . . If only, if only . . .

She moved to the window and pressed her nose against a chill pane. A sob escaped her and she raised a knuckle to her mouth to stifle the noise. Through her tears, a movement in the rose garden caught her attention. She sniffled and wiped her eyes with the back of her hand. A man stood there, a big, burly man with a tricorne.

Morgan. She shuddered at the sight. His hands were deep in his pockets as he watched the house.

She had a choice now, she realized. She could remain here, here with the Marquis and her own uncontrollably sinful nature, or she could go with Morgan. Was there much choice? The Marquis left her in no doubt what he thought of her. And she did this to herself. If only she had controlled her lust . . .

She hadn't much time, she truly expected the Marquis to come to her. Why not, when she was such easy prey? Why should he deny himself the pleasure of humiliating her again?

Hurriedly, she changed from her satin gown into a green traveling dress and boots. A pillowcase was stuffed with personal items and this she took to the window and propped on the sill. Another thought came to mind—her mother's jewels. She would have need of those. They were in the upper drawer of the secretary, still in their velvet lined boxes. Tucking these inside the pillowcase also, she opened the window and tossed the neat bundle onto the ground. With a thud it landed.

A large oak tree stood beyond the window, just

within reach, if she were very careful. She glanced down and realized the fall would be painful if she was not. But if she crept carefully along the ledge, she could grab one of the sturdy branches and swing herself into the vee two branches made. Suddenly she wished for her breeches. A gown made a poor climbing companion. But once in the center, she considered, she would have an easy descent.

As she stood on the ledge, the distance between her and the tree and her and the ground seemed to have grown. She placed one leg in front of the other, carefully creeping along the building's narrow ledge. Her fingers grew sore from the abrasion of the bricks but she dared not loosen her grasp. The toes of her boots had to be carefully placed in the building's niches. She could not relinquish her previous position until the next one was securely tested with her boots. Twice she fumbled, when her skirts got in the way. She heard a door open and close but did not dare look down to see.

One more step and she would be within reach of the tree. From here she could jump . . .

Her balance was not what it used to be. For a moment she stilled her movements and waited for queasiness to pass. Her fingers grew more tender until she could wait no longer. So she closed her eyes and took the plunge. Her hands flailed wildly before capturing one of the branches. When she opened her eyes she found she was within easy reach of the main trunk. Taking a deep breath she swung this last distance, sighing greatly when she found the secure niche in the nest of the tree. As she examined herself, she found even her reticule intact. Quickly she made her descent, falling the final steps to the ground. Relief and exhaustion shook her body as she crumpled to the solid earth and dropped her face into her hands.

Approaching footsteps had her jerking upright. She expected to see Morgan, and paled at the sight of her husband bearing down on her, his face every bit as white as she imagined her own to be. He must have witnessed the entire scene.

"What the hell are you trying to do?" he bellowed, once he found his voice. "Kill yourself?"

Her legs refused to cooperate as she tried to stand. His hands bit into her arms as he pulled her to her feet. "Are you all right? My God! I've never seen anything so foolish! You could have been killed, and it would have been my fault . . . ." His body gave a jerk and he fell to the ground, Alison on top of him. Hands came to her waist to help her to stand.

The butt of a pistol was still in Morgan's hand.

"I'm always 'itting 'im over 'e 'ead with somethin'." Morgan said reflectively once he had Alison on her feet. "But 'e was right! Wot in 'ell were you doin' up there, girl? Ye're not a cat!"

"I have to get away, Morgan. I can't stay here."

"Of course ye canna," he responded gruffly. "Not after 'at bogus ceremony today. I'm surprised Geoffrey allowed it," Morgan grumbled. "Well, 'urry. As much noise as the two of ye made is certain to wake someone." He pulled her by the hand behind him. "'urry!"

"My knapsack! I dropped it over there."

"I have it. I saw ye throw it from the window."

"You did? Oh, Morgan, it's so good to see you again! But how . . . ?"

206

"I'll explain, all in good time. First, let's get out of 'ere." They raced along the house and across the park, keeping to the dark shadows made by the huge trees. Frantic voices followed their retreat and Alison realized the Marquis had been found. Guilt swept over her and she thought she might burst into tears. She did not want him hurt, not again, and not at her hands.

Morgan helped her onto an open wagon and clambered up beside her, reaching for the reins and snapping them. They were well on their way before either of them spoke another word.

"Ye 'eard I was fired this mornin'?" Morgan looked down on his fair companion as he spoke. At her nod, he continued, "Well, I wanted to make sure everything would be fine for ye, I thought I might even be able to speak with ye for a moment or two. Lass, I wouldn't have felt right just leaving ye in the lurch with that man. I followed when ye left with Geoffrey and that Marquis. I admit, my curiosity got the best of me. But it was Fleet Street I followed ye to, lass. Why, yer marriage may not even be legal. Not a marriage dont 'ere. I couldn't leave ye, not like 'at."

"I'm so glad you came, Morgan," she confided, tucking her arm through his. Tears lodged in her throat as she considered the risk they both took this night. The image of her husband, concern etched on his face as he found her on the ground tortured her. "Are we doing the right thing, do you think?"

"Course'n we are. That was no wedding, pshaw. That minister was nothing more'n a drunken sot, not worthy of yer father's big toe."

"You're right, Morgan," she answered softly, still doubtful in her mind. His lordship would be angrier

207

than ever after this last escapade. And it was too late to turn back.

"I am. I knew what ye'd be thinking, and if either the Marquis or the Earl knew ye better, they'd 'ave barred the windows. Once yer mind is made up, there's no stopping ye. I'd put nothing past ye, not even shimmying down the side of a 'ouse. I knew you'd be taking off on yer own. Which is why I'm 'ere. I'm not going to let ye, ye're too damn young to be on yer own.

"So it seems our lots have been thrown together again, ye might say, and we'll make the best of 'em. Though wot we'll live off of is beyond me ken. Ye've a name for the child, for the time being, until that Marquis decides he wants the marriage declared illegal. An' he damn well may, or why the shabby ceremony on the Fleet? Ye don' 'ave to live with those doubts. Marriage, bah!" Morgan clicked his tongue and shook out the reins. A time later, he peered ruefully at his slight companion. "Hmm, one pregnant vicar's daughter and an old stable 'and no one else wants. I canna see the Earl extending me pension for this."

"I've been considering the money, Morgan. I've brought my mother's jewels . . ."

"Not yer mama's jewels, lassie!"

Chapter Nine

Lord Chatham thrust wide the double doors to his study and strode resolutely through, leaving the paneled oak ajar in his wake. His face was lined with impatience and worry as he crossed the room to his desk and sorted briefly through the stack of correspondence there. The scowl on his face made it clear that whatever he searched for was missing. The frown deepened and he tossed the morning's bills and invitations onto the desk with a barely uttered deprecation.

Nothing, again. No word from Henry, nothing from his secretary nor his solicitor, nothing from Geoffrey, and nothing from her. His errant wife had been gone for little over two months. Common decency demanded she make some form of communication with him. Apparently there was little common decency in her.

If he hadn't seen with his own eyes how she'd made that treacherous descent safely, he might have that on his conscience, too. For all she cared.

He turned and, abruptly, the dark brows lifted and

the scowl disappeared. In spite of his somber mood, Chatham was hard put not to laugh as he watched Henry sleeping soundly in his own favorite chair. Folding his arms and crossing well shod feet, he leaned negligently against the mantel. He simply must find Henry tasks which could be accomplished more easily and during the day. He would, just as soon as his wife was safe at home, just as a proper wife should be.

Henry yawned, his thick body stretching and turning, seeking a more comfortable position in the overstuffed chair. On the table beside him stood an empty pitcher and glass, telling their own tale of the previous night.

The smile hovered as milord tugged the bell rope. A maid entered and curtsied, her eyes mirroring her surprise at finding Henry asleep in milord's presence.

Lord Chatham ordered a hearty breakfast brought into the study, "For two."

Henry wakened at the softly spoken words and his sleepy eyes focused gradually on the Marquis. A yawn escaped through tautly held lips and Henry blinked rapidly. Suddenly he jerked upright and eagerness lit his eyes. "I been waitin' for ye, guv! Though I donna' ken how ye tolerate these long 'ours. 'ey'll make an old man of ye afer yer time," he admonished.

Milord silently reflected on his late night of gambling and heavy drinking and agreed with his servant. "You should not have waited up for me, Henry."

"Oh? Will ye think the same when ye take a gander at 'is?" Henry's fingers fumbled about his coat pocket and pulled out a square of soft material. Emerald green glittered as it unfurled and a small piece of jewelry

210

rolled out onto the table beside him. "I guessed ye'd think 'is more important than me beauty sleep."

Black eyes cast off all semblance of boredom and deepened in color as Chatham crossed the room and accepted the intricately wrought bracelet to study it. He nodded in satisfaction, "It's hers."

"Course'n 'tis," Henry grumbled. "Do ye think I'd be this excited if'n it wasn't? See? It matches the sketch perfectly, and aboot time, too. I donna mind telling ye, guv, I was getting worried at all 'is silence. I didna know iffen we'd ever find 'em. But ye were right, she's down to selling off her jewelry and chose the city to do et in. Foxborough's." A triumphant smile lit the old man's face. "And of course Mr. Maurman gave her a good price, or I should say gave 'im a good price. 'Twas Morgan Hull who brought it to London and sold it, guv. Foxborough's give him twenty percent over what he could have gotten anywhere else in town, just like ye told 'em to."

"Of course you will see to their reimbursement, Henry." Chatham held the bracelet to the window and the sunlight danced through the facets of the gems. "Well worth the price, would you not agree?"

"I donna know about 'at. Jest a trinket. Coursen, et will lead to that lass ye want so bad." Henry's eyes bulged with curiosity but the Marquis said nothing more. "I ain't watched ye go after someone so neck and neck ever. I donna unnerstand. If 'tis already yer jewelry, why . . ."

"What gave you the idea this was my jewelry, Henry? It's hers, all legal and tight and traceable." Satisfaction oozed from the voice. It little mattered whose jewelry this was. Not now that it was in his possession. This little piece of jewelry would gain him the full prize. And soon.

"Wot? Wot?" Henry was incensed. "Do ye mean I been wastin' me time lookin' fer sommone as didna pinch yer jewels? How's ye know wot the bracelet looks like?"

"Her brother drew the sketch. Very simple when you think about it." The teardrop shaped gems tinkled and glimmered brightly as Chatham studied them with a gloating expression on his face. "Ah, revenge is mine, and soon, Henry. She'll rue the day she ever tangled with me."

"She probably already does that, guv."

"And Rand Maurman made certain Morgan Hull would not take the jewelry anywhere else?"

"Maurman paid the price ye said." Henry replied tartly. "Coursen, if this Morgan Hull has more brains than ye give 'im credit fer, 'e'll already be suspicious and will lie low . . ."

"He won't. His lack of sense is his overriding characteristic. He'll be right back to Foxborough's, just as soon as they need more blunt."

Breakfast was announced and the men moved to the dining room. Henry nibbled on a biscuit. "I thought as we'd play cautious, get Willie to watch Foxborough's, get some more men to watch the other jewelers in town. No matter who 'e goes to, we'll nab 'im."

"Do as you think best, but I see no reason for much concern. Morgan Hull is a fool and his mistress is no better." Chatham spoke almost indifferently. "He'll return to Foxborough's to sell the rest of the jewelry, and soon. She is not the sort to suffer poverty for long."

"Mebbee 'ey'll kidnap some'un else and 'is time,

make sure 'ey collect ramson," Henry quipped good-naturedly. "Sooner or later, even 'ey've got to get it right."

The Marquis' air of indifference evaporated and was replaced by a fierce scowl. The knife clattered as it hit the plate. Chatham glared into the distance. The sudden change of mood surprised Henry. His eyes widened and his ears perked up. He knew all along there was more to this than the Marquis was telling him and was curious to find out what.

Chatham pushed his plate aside and spoke tersely. "No, they've learned their lesson about that, I promise!"

Henry was eating heartily a moment later when he remembered his other piece of news. "Some'un else 'as makin' inquiries into the girl and Morgan Hull. Mr. Maurman tol' me the man was tall and thin, a blonde man. 'e tried to bribe one of 'is men for information."

Chatham's attention was suddenly riveted on the aging servant. "Oh?"

"'at's one reason I be so late. Mr. Maurman 'as tellin' me as 'ow thet sam mon returns ev'ry day askin' questions. So," Henry tossed the last bit of ham in his mouth and chewed. "I parked meself around the side of the buildin' and waited. And waited. Blasted man didna come until 'ey were closin'." Grey brows lifted expectantly. "Guess who?"

Chatham turned so only his profile was visible to Henry. Henry was not deceived. The muscle in the Marquis' lower jaw ticked dangerously. "David Belden."

Henry's mouth snapped shut in irritation. This was his story, he waited for hours for the man. What blasted business did the Marquis have, guessing the truth? "Aye," Henry grumbled. "And 'e 'as keepin' mighty dangerous company last night. Morts as I wouldna wanna tangle 'ith unless I 'ad good men aside me." Henry pursed his lips and lifted his gaze. The eyes were clear and serious. "Ain't he next in line to the Earl of Wilton?"

"No, second, after his father."

"Wall, 'e ain't up to no good. And I'd like to know wot 'e 'as to do with the girl. I think yer not tellin' me all wot I need to know, guv. Mebbee something which might be useful in the future, like by saving me neck? I donna wanna be used against any Earl . . ."

"Don't fret so, Henry. Have I ever asked you to do anything immoral or illegal?"

"Ye've come pritty demmed close."

"No crime in that, is there? Am I to assume you did more than identify David Belden?"

"Coursen I did. 'at's why I was so late. I followed the bloke. 'e met men I swear I've seen on posters offerin' big, tidy rewards.

"I followed 'em to the White Horse Inn and sat behind 'em at a table. I couldn't see much as 'ey spoke, but I could 'ear a bit. Two words were Earl and Cheltenham. If a man does business with thieves and murderers, 'at must be 'is goal, thievin' and murderin'. I 'eard enuff so's I came 'ere. Cheltenham road leads to Wiltonshire, the Earl must be their target."

"He certainly seems to be one of the targets. I think the girl is probably the other. You're certain Belden does not know Morgan Hull was at Foxborough's, pawning the bracelet?"

Henry shook his head. "Maurman 'as no reason

to lie. 'e knows ye're good for a lot more blunt 'en David Belden. No, 'e'll not betray ye."

"Good. Set two men outside Foxborough's and let them understand how important it is to find the girl and Morgan. If Belden gets his hands on them first, you can wager his intentions are much less honorable than mine."

"What does he want with the girl?"

"I'm not sure. It would behoove him to get rid of the Earl," Chatham mused. "And you're right, the inheritance is a powerful motive. Geoffrey may have been safe when he was gone from England, but here? No, I think he's David's main target. Maybe the girl's his guarantee."

"Why? Wot's she got to do with the Beldens?"

"Did you not know she is the Earl's sister?"

Henry stood on his feet, horror in his eyes. "'is sister? I thought she was something to do with Morgan, his daughter mebbee. But the Earl's sister? And she kidnapped you? My Gawd! If the Earl hears of this . . ."

"He has heard all of this." Henry's stupefaction was dismissed with a negligent shake of the head. "But I think you're right, Henry, David must know the Earl plans a trip to Wiltonshire, and he must be planning something very nasty. Something which requires the assistance of murderers and cutthroats. Perhaps soon." Chatham's thoughts seemed to gain him a great satisfaction for when his gaze returned to Henry, the black eyes were sparked with amusement. "Perhaps I should warn the Earl and put him in my debt. He has been cold as ice to me since his little sister's escapade."

"Well, a'coursen ye should warn 'im, I wouldn't 'a

tole ye aboot it otherwise. I swear, ye're gettin' hobbilled in yer ol' age! 'at demmed kidnappin' must'a mottled yer brain," Henry snapped in irritation.

"Calm yourself, Henry. I would rush to the Earl's side instantly if I thought his life were in imminent danger. However, I believe he is quite capable of handling his own problems, his wife and her brother among them."

Chatham rose and crossed to the door, leaving Henry standing in the middle of the dining room. "Finish your meal, Henry. You've earned it and more. When you're done is soon enough to put more men at Foxborough's. You might have someone follow David Belden." He was nearly out the door when a final thought occurred to him and he turned. "Let me know immediately when Morgan Hull surfaces. I can have the girl safely away from David Belden in a few hours' time. I may have faith in the Earl, but not in his hen-witted sister."

"Are ye sure ye donna want me to nab 'em for ye, guv?" Henry was eager for real action. "I'd like to tussle with thet Morgan bloke, 'specially after the knock on the 'ead 'e gave ye. And it'd be quicker'n followin' em."

"No, Henry, I want to do this nabbing myself."

"I never 'armed a woman," Henry warned, "an' I ain't gonna start now."

"Don't be a fool," the Marquis spoke curtly. "I don't plan to murder her, merely to give her an eye for an eye. Let her taste the joys of being kidnapped and tied to a bedpost for days at a time."

Henry winced in sympathy for the girl.

"I'll warn her brother about David," Chatham continued, "and even offer to help him. But when

216

Morgan shows his face again, Geoffrey will be on his own. I plan to give his sister my undivided attention."

The Earl was just finishing his morning meal when Willis entered and announced the arrival of the Marquis. The Earl's expression hardened at the news and he tossed his napkin to the table and rose. "I'll receive him in the den, Willis."

No words of greeting were exchanged. Chatham simply opened the velvet material in the palm of his hand and the bracelet was revealed.

Wilton recognized it immediately and nodded. "It was my mother's."

"Morgan sold it at Foxborough's. I made sure he received a more than fair price. He'll return there when he needs more money. And then I will have the both of them."

The Earl's lips thinned. "You make it sound so simple, but you lost her once."

"Ah, but now I know to tread more carefully where she's concerned. And to make certain there is no avenue of escape open to her, no matter how far fetched it may seem."

The sardonic expression disappeared and Chatham said simply, "Actually I came because I knew you would be relieved to have word of her. At least we know she is safe."

"I knew that last evening, when this was delivered." Geoffrey searched the top of his desk until he found the missive he sought.

Chatham accepted the letter and briefly scanned it. A scowl settled on his face. If she contacted anyone, it should have been him. "Decent of her to finally communicate. And decent of you to let me know."

"Did you care? As you can see she says she is fine, so is Morgan. The letter is full of trifling news."

Geoffrey was right, there was little information in the missive. Chatham tossed the letter back at him. "You should have notified me immediately. Not have waited until the next day. Or would you have contacted me at all?"

"I'd planned to see you this morning. I hope this letter means she has relented and wants to return home. I'd like her to feel she can do so without worrying about you playing the heavy handed spouse. Why don't you let her return to Wiltonshire with me? You wouldn't have to bother with her anymore and I could sleep at night. You treat her as though she were the enemy whom you must conquer, instead of your wife . . ."

"She didn't stay around long enough to become my wife."

Wilton sighed. "You're hard, Justin, and making mistake after mistake with Alison. If you harm her . . ."

"What? Harm my wife and my precious child? What sort of monster do you take me for?"

Wilton's ire was rising and his eyes flashed his anger. "I take you for a man with a devilish temper. You want everything your way, and if it's not, pity the poor folk standing between you and your goal. This time, my sister is the impediment, and I'll be damned . . ."

"Undoubtedly. However, you needn't worry, I won't harm a hair on her pretty, little, vacant head. She needs to learn being a wife, my wife, means more than running off when her schemes backfire."

The Marquis made an irritated gesture with his hand. "She's not the only reason I came this morning.

Henry had some information I thought you might be interested in, that is, if you plan to be around long enough to save Alison from her tyrant of a husband."

"I'll be around long enough," Geoffrey answered drily.

"David Belden has been inquiring about Alison. Henry learned this from Rand Maurman and so followed him. David went to the White Horse Inn where he met with several rapscallions. Henry heard very little. Two words were easily recognizable. Earl and Cheltenham."

"Oh."

"Oh? So does that mean what I think it means? That you are planning a trip to Wiltonshire and to go by Cheltenham road?"

"Cheltenham is one of the main roads to and from London."

"The number of Earls inhabiting London is not large. This is too coincidental. Do you mean to tell me you do not plan a trip to Wiltonshire?"

Geoffrey shrugged his shoulders negligently. "Of course I'm going to Wiltonshire, and I must be David's target. He has much to gain if a mishap occurred to me. Don't look so shocked by David's plotting. I've been in London five months now and it's been two since the Stacey Fielding fiasco. I'm only surprised they waited so long.

"I have cut Naylor and David loose of my purse strings and from what I understand they are growing desperate. They might even end up in the Fleet for their debts. A worthy thought, no?" The day was early yet but whenever Wilton spoke of his wife or her family, he felt the urge for a drink. He held the cut glass aloft in an offering gesture, but Chatham shook his head. Wilton tossed off the drink quickly.

"Eileen has been brought to heel, somewhat. With little money she has lost her attraction for the young men. I am forcing her to accompany me to Wiltonshire and you know how loudly she proclaims to hate my country estate. I must expect repercussions for my ruthlessness, so perhaps this is time. And frankly, I am eager for the battle to begin. I grow bored with the city and I detest waiting. I am not a patient man."

"I've heard rumors that David and Naylor are in debt," Chatham spoke. "I did not realize the debt was so large."

"I was always a generous fellow. They cannot accustom themselves to any less than they have had for the last ten years."

"Geoffrey," Chatham obviously considered that the Earl had gone mad. "Do you understand what I'm telling you? David means to kill you, and you seem unconcerned."

Wilton stared long at the Marquis before giving a self-deprecating laugh. "Oh, Justin, this is not the first time, not even the second I have been a target for their greed. I can see to them. After all, they are my family and no one knows them better than I."

"Your family? You consider them your family? How can you live like this?" Justin demanded hotly.

"I have lived like this only for the past few months. Why do you suppose I was in the colonies so long? At the tender age of eighteen, one does not think horrible blood curdling thoughts about beheading and quartering one's wife. At eighteen one is too noble and upstanding," he spoke sneeringly. "'Tis a good thing

I did not realize what a bloodcurdling monster I would become or I might have shocked myself."

Geoffrey's mouth tightened and the lines around it multiplied. "But I don't like him looking for Alison. I don't want him near her." Lean fingers crushed the paper which had once been her letter and Geoffrey lifted his eyes. "It seems I need you again, Justin. You must find my sister and quickly. You must make certain he does not get near her."

"You need not ask. She is my wife and I will protect her."

"I must get word to Jon. I'd send a man to protect him, but he'd accuse me of not trusting him. And I don't. I tore him to bits for his part in your kidnapping."

"Oh? And what did he say?"

"He said it was Alison's idea," came the dry reply. "Every time he's in trouble in his life, it's been Alison's idea."

"I can imagine. When do you leave for Wiltonshire?"

"In two days. I've made no secret of my plans, Eileen knows the whole."

"So, what will you do?"

"I'll have some men follow the coach. A greater number than David can afford. In my experience, greater strength comes from greater numbers."

"And are you as careful not to turn your back when you are in the same bedroom as your wife?" the Marquis sneered impatiently.

A rueful smile crossed Geoffrey's lips. "I am never in the same bedroom with my wife. She is at her most dangerous there."

"I need that drink now."

Geoffrey poured and handed the glass to the Marquis. "Don't look so disgusted, Justin. I have earned every bit of my wife's and her family's contempt. I was an idealistic fool, too young and stupid to follow my instincts. So I believed Naylor's words when he said my duty was to marry within the family. I married Eileen, even though I knew at the time I disliked her.

"But you, you're the enigma. Why did you bother to warn me? I weakly allowed you to take the blame for my parents' deaths. And if that wasn't enough, later I accused you of seducing Eileen." A grin lit his eyes. "Actually, when my sister turned out to be the one seduced, I was almost relieved that your tastes were not as bad as I feared. That is after I recovered from the urge to kill you with my bare hands for daring to touch Alison. Though that caused yet another problem for you. You have been forced into a loveless marriage. I take no responsibility for that, you accomplished that on your own. But, offhand, I would say you would be well rid of me. At least you would have a free hand with Alison. I could not object to anything you would do."

"Object all you like, it makes no difference. Understand this, what is between Alison and myself is not your concern. You'll have little cause for complaint, I do not physically abuse those less strong than myself. This marriage is not one made in love and its beginning has precluded any possibility of love between us. Alison has manipulated this marriage and I wish her joy of it. But if I am to be saddled with her as my wife, she will learn to behave as a wife. I will not suffer the likes of your marriage, Geoffrey."

"You know so little of my sister." Geoffrey shook his

head sadly. "You have created a vision of her in your mind, seeing her as some conniving, clever woman. You are determined she pay for the marriage. Your game of vengeance will stir repercussions you may not like. Remember that, Justin. Perhaps when your little charade has begun to pall in its humor, you will find in her something precious. I hope for your sake it will not be too late."

Every day Alison and Thomas walked to the small village near the cottage she and Morgan occupied. Before leaving London, Alison insisted on finding and bringing the boy with them. They would need help and she preferred someone she knew. Thomas was more than happy to go, he was glad of the regular meals. In the two months they had been here, both he and Alison and grown stouter.

The cottage was situated in the north, in a tiny valley where the winter rolled in and stayed for a good many months. Alison felt buried by the cold and snow, anxious for the first sign of spring. She could imagine this fertile valley in bloom, the fields bursting with their carefully planted and cultivated crops. A small stream trickled behind the cottage and Alison pictured it in her mind as it increased its flow to brisk. Spring and summer could not come quickly enough.

The cottage was small and built of brick, a tiny replica of a Tudor mansion. Remnants of ivy vines reached lean, nimble fingers to upper story windows. By summer the cottage would be a thick mass of green leaves. Behind the cottage stood a small barn, barely big enough for the chickens and one mare. Thomas'

223

daily chores included cleaning the barn and feeding the livestock.

The early afternoon sun was bright and warming. A straw basket in Alison's arm swung as she plodded along the road, Thomas beside her. A gust of wind came up and blew her thick woolen coat between her legs and the hood from her head. Hastily she grabbed the hood. The fluttering of the cloak brought her rounding belly into view and the hood was swept from her fingers as she reached for the billowing cloak. After the days spent in London as the victim of the Marquis' taunts, she was very shy of her body's changes. Only when the cloak was held securely against her, did she continue walking.

This was her daily excursion from the confines of the house. The walk was more for pleasure than business though her basket was filled with eggs for trading. The grocers accepted the eggs against their bill and Alison continued on her walk, pausing by the milliner's shop. She needed a ribbon for the baby gown she was sewing and that dainty white lace cap displayed in the window was tempting. The ribbon was duly purchased, but she shied away from the cap. Perhaps she shouldn't spend too much money today. Morgan was still worried that they needed to sell her jewelry in order to live. He had been a bear ever since he returned from London last week. She crossed the road and entered the clothier's shop. She ordered a length of wool to fit Thomas, he needed a new coat, and some fine muslin for the baby.

"So many clothes for a babe, Mrs. Afton?" the curious shopkeeper clucked briskly. "Yours will be the most finely dressed in Earthmore."

Alison laughed easily. "Babies do need many clothes."

"Not so many."

"Mine does," Alison responded quietly, confidently. Money would not be spared where the child was concerned.

As Mrs. Afton, Alison had woven an entire history around the tragic widow who was expecting her first child. So far, and to her great disappointment, she had not needed to use it. Morgan purported himself as Morgan Wade, her father. And no one could understand Thomas well enough to ask him who he was.

"Thomas," Alison called to him. "What color would you like your new coat to be? The navy blue is nice and so is the brown."

Thomas stood beside her, his eyes growing big as he gazed on the two pieces of material from which he would select. "Blue, wit big, brass buttens!" he answered without a moment's hesitation. "Me pa had'un once, looked a regl'ar prickmedainty, 'e did! 'en some mort talked 'im into pawning it fer two bob. Well, it paggled on'em and a retturken claimed it be snaggled from em!" Thomas shook his head regretfully. "Never seen the likes of thet coat agin, ma'am."

The shopkeeper opened her mouth and stared at Thomas in utmost fascination.

Alison clucked her tongue sympathetically. "Well, you must have a coat exactly like your father's," she said reasonably. "Six brass buttons or eight?"

"Eit, mum, a dubble row!"

"Then a double row it shall be. I'll need thread and lining material to go with that also," she informed the shopkeeper. Thomas carried the package as they left.

225

A frosty wind came up during the return trip to the cottage. "We'd best hurry, mum," Thomas coaxed. About halfway to the cottage Alison felt, rather than saw, the movement along the side of the road. Stopping, she turned and carefully peered at the trees and through the darkening pine forest, but could see nothing. A chill crept along her spine. Everything seemed so unnaturally quiet and still that she was unnerved. Turning, she resumed her walk at a much swifter pace. Stealing a glance at Thomas she saw he was impervious to any such premonitions and she felt slightly ridiculous. Shaking her head, she laughed hollowly to herself. But she urged Thomas to an even faster gait.

As they reached the front door of the cottage, the prickly sensation was back, crawling along her spine to the nape of her neck. She spun around quickly, again there was nothing to see. Alison scooted Thomas inside and bolted the door behind them just as Morgan entered the room from the kitchen.

"It's about time ye returned. I was ready to 'arness the 'orse and wagon and come after ye. It 'pears like we're in fer a storm."

"I think so, too," Alison spoke breathlessly, unraveling her cloak from her shoulders. "What's that I smell? I'm so hungry."

Morgan knew Alison well, and he had not seen her so perturbed in a long time. "Wot's wrong? Did somethin' 'appen in the village?"

"No, of course not." She gave a brittle laugh. "It's my imagination again, just as you always say. Really, there's nothing."

"Is that why ye rushed inside and bolted the door?"

Alison smiled ruefully. "Foolish, aren't I? I saw nothing, it was just a feeling I had, probably caused by the wind. I'm full of eerie thoughts today, Morgan."

"Now, don't ye go gettin' nervous on me. The last thing I need is female hysterics."

"I've never been hysterical in my life," she retorted hotly.

"Don't start now," Morgan warned.

The chaise and four took the bend smoothly, swaying with every deep pitch and springing back into upright position effortlessly. The coachman cracked his whip in the air and the speed of the four matched bays increased. They were a splendid team, their movements rhythmic with each other, even to the harmonious bobbing of their heads.

The Countess was seated across from her husband, her body stretched awkwardly against the squabs of the coach. Her refusal to accompany Geoffrey to Wiltonshire met with the quietly spoken information that if she had any need for an allowance, she should reconsider. She did. The full red lips pouted as she remembered how Geoffrey had cut off the allowances of her father and brother. The meager amount of funds she sent them was all they lived on. She no longer doubted he would do the same to her. He was a changed man from the gangly youth she'd married. Her shoulder was turned to him in an arrogant pose. Inside she bubbled with fear. She did not know this Geoffrey.

Once they were at Wiltonshire, she mused angrily, Geoffrey would leave her alone. He would spend his time astride his horse, seeing to his estate while she would have to remain alone in that huge barn of a house. If he thought to keep her there long in the winter, he would have to think again. She might possibly see her husband at dinner. Might, that is, unless some of the equally rustic neighbors invited him to share theirs. Geoffrey never refused an invitation. And no, she would not go with him to dine at some country bumpkin's residence. She would be bored to flinders.

So why the insistence that she come with him? The answer to that was what she feared most. Covertly she glanced at him. He was relaxed, his head against the squabs, his eyes shuttered in a semblance of sleep. Geoffrey was a very attractive man, with that shock of white blond hair mingling with the gold. Why had she never noticed this before? Perhaps because she'd always seen him as a fool, just as her father wanted her to. All her life she, David, and their father had been close. Whatever she had was theirs, whatever they had was theirs. She accepted their behavior as normal and not until lately had she questioned it. She listened to them in everything, yet she was unhappy. She took the lovers her father decided might be useful to them, she ridiculed everyone who was not her father or brother. She manipulated and plotted for them, for their gain. She gave them everything she had, her possessions, her love, her loyalty. Yet Naylor threatened her when they lost their allowances and she could not regain them.

For the first time in her life she wondered about her family and their so-called love for her. Perhaps all those years ago when she chose them over her husband, she'd been wrong. During those early days of their marriage she might have gained his love. Instead she chose to plot with her father and David against him and lost any chance of ever having that love.

He would never trust her now. He hadn't touched her intimately since the first week of their marriage so she could never reach him that way. All she knew was that she couldn't bear the look of hatred in his eyes when he saw her.

He appeared indifferent to his surroundings, except for the arms crossed against his chest. He was not asleep, she knew that. She recalled their last argument, the night Chatham delivered her to her home and the last time Geoffrey laid hands on her. He could be brutal if he chose. So what if he suspected their plans? A white, finely boned hand rose to her throat. If he knew of their plans and was prepared for them . . .

The Earl grew bored of the incessant traveling. He should have ridden his horse. At least the physical effort would give him some release. The grey eyes opened and rested on Eileen. Not such a pleasant or reassuring sight, he mused. He reached across the seat and lifted the window curtain to peer at the surrounding countryside. There was not much to see, not from a chaise traveling at such a rapid pace. The Earl seldom wasted time, and if some of his wealth could ensure a quick and comfortable journey, he considered it money well spent.

He carried no outriders, as was his usual custom. This journey must appear as normal as possible to everyone. His eyes slid to his wife and he considered the word everyone. She watched him with an expression he had never seen on her face before. He turned away, unable to bear the sight. If only he could be rid of her as easily as he would be of her brother. But it seemed he

229

must wait. Sometime in the future she would receive what she deserved, just as today David would.

Last night was spent at a posting inn. Eileen grumbled about the food, the sheets, and the service. This morning she complained of the breakfast, the handling of the horses, and the weariness of her body. They were on the road shortly before dawn. Again she complained. Presently, they were passing through the long, lonely stretch of road between villages where the distance seemed to crawl—and where Geoffrey expected David's treachery.

The first of the shots rang out and Geoffrey could not prevent his eyes from turning to her. She bit her lips and stared at him, as though she were afraid. So she was in this with them. Why was he feeling disappointment? He always knew she would be. His lean body turned and he reached for the loaded pistol kept in the side pocket of the coach. Geoffrey lowered the gun to the window.

What fools she and David were. What did they think he had been doing in the colonies all these years, if not fighting? Indians were far more dangerous than his pampered and primped brother-in-law.

His aim was deadly accurate as he pulled the trigger. A man cried out and a horse's hooves beat into the ground as the animal passed the window, free of its rider. Geoffrey pulled the pistol inside the coach and began to reload. A small muscle twitched at the corner of his mouth.

"'at's it, buckos! Stan' and deliver!" An ill bred gloating sounded from just outside the chaise. Another shot rang out, this one echoing from a distance. The same voice grunted once with pain as the man was hit by a ball. "Wot 'e bloody 'ell?" the man roared furiously.

"'ey, Jack! 'ere be a dozen of 'em comin' after us!"

The hills reverberated with the fury of pounding hooves as the highwaymen rode beside the chaise and another group of men rode toward them from the forest, a dark and secret hiding place for honest men as well as highwaymen.

Geoffrey's fingers nimbly worked the patch and ball, his eyes guarded as he glanced often to Eileen. For once in her life, her own actions seemed to stun her.

He returned to the window and leaned through it to get a better aim. His body jerked with the impact of the shot as the pistol fired. Pulling his body inside he reloaded for the next round. Again he straddled the window with his form and his arms reached far to shoot one of the men retreating. A stray bullet hit him and tore a hot, searing path through his shoulder, jerking him against the side of the coach. Gingerly he pulled his body through the window and sought solace against the squabs. His breath came in gasps of pain but he clearly heard David's voice shouting triumphantly.

Eileen sat rigidly in her seat, watching as he lifted a kerchief to the wound in an attempt to control the bleeding, only there was so much blood. The blood oozed onto his fingers and over the palm of his hand, dripping onto his black breeches.

Usually she was full of fire and spit and arrogance. He had never seen her so pale. A sardonic smile spread across his features. "Don't look so downcast, my dear. I'm not dead yet, and I've always been a tough man to kill. It would take a better man than your brother to bury me."

David's voice came again, desperation threading it, "No, don't run! I shot him! We can finish him off this time! There's six of us, we're a match for them!"

Geoffrey began the pain filled process of reloading.

"You pigs! You'll not get one coin for this night's work! Come back here, you cowards!"

"David's friends seem to be running. Perhaps they're brighter than he and realize they've already lost the fight." Geoffrey spoke softly. "What do you think? Will he stay and fight alone or will he run with the rest of the brigands? Personally, I think he'll run. Only a coward strikes a man from behind, and David is a coward."

Eileen watched dumbly as Geoffrey leaned to the window, his bloody shoulder pressing against the door of the coach. His wound ached as he lifted his arm and carefully sighted the pistol. "It seems I was right, he runs, but his back makes a fine target."

"No!" Eileen screamed, her body thrusting forward to dislodge the pistol. Geoffrey's arm jerked and the ball roamed wild. Clenching his teeth against the incredible pain, and with perspiration trickling down his forehead, he struggled to get the searing ache under control.

His voice, when he found it, was raspy and deep. "Next time, I'll kill him. And you won't be near enough to stop me."

"Geoffrey, I couldn't let you kill him." Her fingers clutched at his lapel and her eyes begged him to understand. "He's my brother."

"I can't bear your touch. Get your hands off me. You may look beautiful on the outside, but inside you are a poor shell of a woman. Inside you're everything tainted and ugly. You have a small mind, a smaller heart. You seek and grab, you want all for yourself. There is nothing within you which is generous and beautiful. I have never known such ugliness as you possess. You make a man feel dirty just being around you."

"Don't say that!"

"Why? Why the tears? Does the truth hurt so much?" When she did not release him he tore her fingers from his lapel and threw them from him. With a contemptuous glance his eyes raked her. "I won this round and the victory tastes like bitter gall. Sit back and compose yourself. Your tears should be saved for someone whom they would affect, not for me.

"I find I cannot bear the thought of you being in my home after all. You may go back to London and find your joy in your filthy little affairs."

"I don't want to go back to London. I want to be with you."

"But I don't want you."

The coach was pulled to a stop when the robbers were turned away. Voices of the outriders could be heard as they approached. Without a backward glance Geoffrey opened the door and swung himself down. He would ride on to Wiltonshire. The chaise would return its baggage to London. And Geoffrey would have nothing more to do with her.

Chapter Ten

Alison yawned as she rose from the chair and stretched muscles rendered stiff from a full evening of sewing. The strain caused by the dull candlelight was beginning to tell in her eyes. Morgan was in the kitchen, preparing a cup of hot tea and Thomas was spread out on his belly before the fire, practicing his one-handed shuffle with cards.

The fragrance of pine burning in the fireplace was in her nostrils as she moved to the window and drew aside the curtain. Cautiously, she peered outside, her eyes seeking each dark niche and cranny in the trees surrounding the cottage. The sensation of being watched was still with her though many days had passed since that trip into the village. The belief that the Marquis would one day appear and cause more turmoil in her life was firmly entrenched in her mind.

Morgan claimed it was guilty conscience playing on her mind.

But nothing was there. Drawing the drapes wider, she pressed her nose against the chill panes of glass and watched her breath spread a fine mist over them. Idly, she wrote various names through the fog, names which disappeared as quickly as they were written.

Alexander, Fitzgerald, Marella, Samantha. Naming a baby was more difficult than she'd ever thought.

The game palled and she drew the curtains closed. Morgan had returned to his chair and sat sipping a cup of hot tea. Gently she touched his shoulder and said, "Morgan, I'm going to bed now."

"Go on with ye. I'll be comin' up shortly meself."

"Goodnight then. Goodnight, Thomas."

"G'nite, mum."

Alison climbed the staircase to her room and found it to be almost as cold as the winter outside. Brief experience as mistress of her home taught her early that a warming pan, filled with hot rocks and placed beneath the sheets an hour before retiring, made bed much more appealing. But first, she had to undress in this cold. As quickly as she could, she donned her long, flannel nightgown and scrambled into the bed's deep warmth. The door to Thomas' room opened and closed behind him, just as she was beginning to drift off to sleep.

Morgan remained in the chair, sipping from the teacup and nodding off for another half hour. When the fire died out so completely that the room began to chill, Morgan decided it was time he was in bed, also. Stretching his tired muscles, he rose from the chair and banked the fire. As he stood, he noticed the front drapes were ajar. He was tugging the two ends together when a brief movement outside caught his attention. His body tensed with alarm and he followed his first instinct, that of hurrying to the kitchen to find the pistol he always kept in the pantry. Just as his hand reached upward for the pistol, both arms were grabbed and drawn tightly behind his back. He opened his mouth to cry a warning and a thick, foul tasting cloth was stuffed inside. He tried to spit it out, struggling valiantly all the while, but the man holding his arms was much stronger than he. Another fellow, his face obscured by the tricorne he wore, tied a cloth around the first one and wound it about his head so none of his curses sounded any louder than a muffle. The hold on his arms tightened and a familiar, menacing voice came to his ears. "I owe you this one, Morgan Hull." Roughly he was dragged to a chair and forced to sit. "Bind his legs and arms tightly, Henry."

As the older man was completing this task, the Marquis couldn't resist another jeer in his prisoner's ear, "I should have knocked you cold. I owe you one, remember?"

Morgan growled an unintelligible answer but the Marquis wasted no further attention on the man. "Don't forget the lad, Henry."

"I'll jest lock 'im in 'is room for the night."

"Not him you won't. He'll scramble out the window quicker than his mistress. Tie him to the bed post."

Henry lifted the tricorne from his head and scratched the balding pate beneath. "I been watchin' this bunch for days, beats me wot ye'd want with 'em. 'ey might 'ave abducted ye, or so's I believe, fer ye're not a mon to lie, but I canna unnerstand 'ow they kept ye. They're as 'armless a bunch as I've ever seen."

The laden chair rocked heavily against the wooden floor and the volume of Morgan's curses increased.

"'Tis their ineptness which makes them dangerous,"

236

Chatham replied, his eyes resting distastefully on their prisoner. "I don't want the whole bunch, just the girl. Morgan and the boy can remain here."

Henry's jaw dropped. "Why 'er? She might be comely, I've never seen 'er up close, but she 'as the funniest demm walk I've ever seen."

"You should cultivate better powers of observation," Chatham said wryly. "Once you've taken care of the boy, bring the carriage round. I'll fetch the girl."

"Wot'ere ye say, guv. Though, I still think ye're daft to want a woman wot waddles, but ye pays well, so who am I to question?"

"Quite true," the Marquis answered absently, his mind already elsewhere in the house. Bounding up the stairs two at a time, he was anticipating the moment he would have his hands around a lovely, white neck.

From Henry's men, Lord Chatham was well aware which room was hers. A good deal of self control was required just so he could open the door without bleating out the unalloyed delight spreading through him at the thought of having her in his power. The door knob turned noiselessly. He paced careful steps across the wooden floor and stood at the foot of her bed. In the center slept his prey, blankets pulled up to her chin. She was barely visible but for the hump she made. A satisfied smirk tingled its way to the Marquis' lips. All these months and here it was, so simple. She was sleeping like a baby, suspecting nothing of what was to happen next.

She was due for a shock, and he was more than willing to be the one to give it to her. So far she'd had everything her own way. From this moment on, everything would be far different.

Deciding he'd have to wait for the long anticipated moment when she first recognized him, Chatham pulled the corners of the blankets from the top of the mattress and tossed them over her head. Alison stirred briefly. The moment for resolute action had come and Chatham swept her over his shoulder and headed toward the staircase. The blankets obscured her vision and acted as a binding for her hands.

Her first reaction was to sleepily protest. As she wakened more thoroughly, outraged cries sounded through the blankets and her feet lashed out furiously, threatening to dislodge her from his hold. Lord Chatham clenched his teeth as a foot mangled his nose, halting her protests by grabbing both her feet and holding them firmly. Paying little attention to her objections, he bounded down the stairs. The boy, Thomas, could be heard yelling and cursing through his bedroom door. For the moment, Morgan was still harmlessly tied in the kitchen.

Chatham's bundle suddenly gave a furious shove with her entire body and nearly tumbled free of him, but the hasty save of the Marquis' heavy hands prevented her falling down the stairs. This time he soundly thwacked her bottom. She groaned loudly, but for the moment, her opposition was stilled.

She was bundled quickly inside the waiting coach. Henry gave the four horses their lead just as Chatham was settling her on the seat. The force of the abrupt movement sent the Marquis flying backward and Alison's body onto the hard floor.

The horses smoothed their gait momentarily and the coach settled into well-modulated movements. The pile of blankets on the floor shuddered and moaned in

238

discomfort. Chatham set her again on the seat, his hands working around the many blankets, searching for her face. Tousled hair was touched and his hand moved to cup her face, forcing it above the blankets and to look at him. His moment of triumph was here and he was clearly gloating.

He was totally unprepared for the sickly, white face gasping desperately for air. Her eyes were barely opened, all her concentration was on garnering her breath. Alison's body shook with the effort as she took one deep breath and another, and another. As her breathing steadied, her eyes lifted warily to her captor. Though they were moist with tears, her gaze was steady, and Chatham realized his arrival did not come as the abrupt shock he hoped for.

The lines around his mouth tightened and Alison quickly understood something more was expected of her. Her chest trembled with the effort of forming words and uncertainly she stammered, "Oh, it's you."

The moment was deflating for the Marquis. He wanted her afraid of him, not so prosaic about her own kidnapping.

His mouth grim, he set about the task of loosening the blankets and freeing her hands. Gradually, her white pallor was replaced by healthy pink and her breathing became normal. She drew as far from him as possible in the closed carriage.

Elbows on his knees, he relaxed and allowed her to study him. They had all the time in the world. Vengeance would wait a moment or two longer. The black eyes mocked her and long, lean fingers dangled loosely between his thighs.

If she thought to feign illness again, too bad. He was

not such a fool. She was healthy enough when he was the victim. And this was not so rigorous. Alison Asher was going to get exactly what she deserved.

Her mouth trembled, and the sight pleased him greatly. "What . . . what do you plan for me now?"

Chatham smiled, humorlessly. It was more a vindictive twist of his lips. "I should tie your hands to either side of the coach and your legs together. It's a most uncomfortable way to ride."

The green eyes disappeared behind swiftly closing lids. She'd had enough tumbling about for one night. Her body was beginning to ache, and that uncomfortable, sickly sensation was spreading through her again. She tried to think of several reasons why he would not harm her, but her mind's eye saw him as her prisoner, tied in the carriage, bound to a bed. Slowly her eyes opened and she watched his mood closely, before daring to offer hesitantly, "You wouldn't do that."

"Oh, wouldn't I? I would relish doing just that. I suggest you change your haughty tone, or I might be more tempted."

Swallowing was difficult. This madman was capable of doing anything he threatened. Desperately she tried to keep the fear from her voice but could not prevent the note of pleading entering her words, "We meant you no harm. Truly."

"Your repetitions grow tedious. Don't worry, I have no intention of tying you to the carriage like that. You might become truly ill and ruin my plans for the future. I intend to have a good deal of entertainment at your expense." Leaning forward in his seat he watched her expressions closely. Soon, he thought, she would understand the meaning of the word misery. So, she thought she was clever? She was certainly clever enough to wear a wounded expression and appeal to his protective instincts. Her eyes were dark and wide in her pale face, and she was biting her lips as though to keep from crying. Chatham stiffened his resolve. He knew better than to soften toward her. The night she ran away was proof of that. But she'd learn, even if he had to spend the rest of his life teaching her. "You've caused me a great deal of trouble, my girl. You created this unpalatable situation and when it became too much for you, you ran. Like the coward you are. There's nowhere for you to run now, nowhere that I won't find you. You have no choice but to stay and pay the piper."

Alison curved her head deeper into the pillows, but her shoulders sagged wearily and she spoke with resignation, "I've been expecting you. You're a blight on my conscience."

"Are you apologizing for abducting me in the first place? Or begging me not to be too harsh on you?"

Shaking her head, she answered slowly. "I don't think you want me to beg."

"I do. I want you to beg. I want you on your hands and knees crawling to me. But first, you'll understand what it is like to be confined for days at a time, to be fearful for your life, to be forced into marriage . . ."

"I did not plan the marriage. That was more your doing than mine. I grant you have the right to satisfaction for my abduction of you . . ."

"Thank you."

"And I suppose this sort of turnabout is fair play," she admitted grudgingly. "If you keep me your prisoner for a week your pride should be satisfied, should it

241

not?" Vainly she waited for some sign of agreement before continuing in a low, hopeful voice, ". . . and I should be free to go."

The Marquis stared at her as though she were some rare and deadly species of insect. He never dealt with a woman who considered fair play and patently did not believe it to be a serious consideration with her. She was in no position to dictate terms, not to him, she wasn't. That loathsome smile spread over his features and he queried coolly, "Don't you think you should know what I have in mind for you, before you give your . . . er . . . your permission to proceed?"

"If you are a fair man, you will keep me in my room for a week . . ."

The Marquis chortled loudly. "That might have sufficed, once, but since then I have added another bruise to my collection suffered at your hands. Remember, the night you ran away? No, now, I require something not quite so short and simple and sweet. You've caused me a great deal of inconvenience, far beyond one mere week. That's no longer enough."

The warmth of the carriage threatened to stifle her so she loosened the blankets and freed her arms and shoulders to the chill night air. She took another deep breath to keep her gorge from rising, wanting no further humiliation this night. By the light of the moon she could see his face and knew pleading with this mocking stranger would bring her no peace. He wanted his pound of flesh, and he would have it. Her fingers clenched at the binding on the blankets as she sought to divert her thoughts from her discomfort. "Not a week? How long, then?"

"Perhaps a lifetime, the same as you have trapped

me." His shoulders shrugged indifferently.

Another deep breath stiffened her resolve. "Two weeks, that is all I will give you. After that time I consider I will have paid for my crimes." Her brave words took more strength than she possessed. Swiftly closing her eyes, she prayed for control. The carriage hit a boulder in the road and lurched dangerously. The eyes flew open, the fear in them palpable. "Where are you taking me now?"

"Concerned for your plight? That's good." His smile was wicked as he relaxed fully against the squabs, taking his sweet time in answering. Her voice held almost the correct combination of fear and pleading. Almost. Just a few moments more.

"We will travel in the coach most of the night. I, too, have access to small hideaways in the country. Mine is more luxurious than the one you used, but I intend for myself to be comfortable. It will do for you as well." He noted the lightening of her worried brow and continued smoothly, "It is very private, perfect for my purpose. Of course, I let most of the servants go, the ones who remain are the ones I can trust to keep their mouths shut. You won't fare too badly. I'll have Henry set up a cot for you in the cellar."

Alison frowned. "The cellar?"

"Of course." The Marquis responded easily, relishing the reemergence of her wrinkled brow. She had a good deal of self control and it surprised him. "That's what you planned for me, was it not? Until fate stepped in and you discovered the cottage you hired did not have one."

"That's not true. I was joking. The cottage did have a cellar, but we would never have left you there."

243

"I'll never know that for certain, will I? And my plans are already made. I promise you, I never jest."

"A fortnight in your cellar?" she gasped, horrified.

"Or longer, should I decide. A cellar is not so easy to escape from. The more I think of it, the more advantages I see."

Her eyes grew wide. "Is it damp? Is . . . is there a window?"

"Plotting your escape already? Damp, I don't know. There is no window. Of course, you were jesting also when you likened me to a rat. I am afraid a few of the rodents use my cellar. They won't eat much, only a toe or two. I have on great authority that they prefer only the softest parts."

Alison's frown spread and her stomach churned rapidly. "Have you no sense of decency?" she rasped hoarsely. "That's going too far."

"Not where you're concerned, my dear." Chatham was so engrossed in his own thoughts that he missed the telling sign of her fingers whitening where they gripped the blanket. "The worst part of a confinement of this sort is when you need privacy, but must always have an audience. Very humiliating. I imagine you will like it even less than I did."

Alison swiftly averted her eyes. "I don't think I can stand this."

"Perhaps I did not make myself clear. You have no choice."

"You . . . ," deep pools of fear widened on him, ". . . you didn't bring any of my clothing."

"You won't need any."

Alison's hand lifted to the strap hanging by the window and clung tightly. The blankets stifled anew

244

and she pushed them away impatiently. "I don't know why you hate me so much," she said bitterly. "You were never harmed. And I never wanted the marriage, that was all your doing."

Her distress was finally becoming apparent, even to the Marquis. The labored breathing came deep and raspy, echoing throughout the small confines of the carriage. Color ebbed from her face as her mind pictured the next few weeks of torture.

She lifted the back of her free hand to her mouth as the realization swamped her that she was no longer in control. Dropping the strap, she plucked at the Marquis' sleeve in desperation. Alison could not speak, but her expression was much more eloquent than mere words.

"Good God!" the Marquis ejaculated. This was something he had not foreseen in all his imaginings. Leaning out the window, he bellowed at Henry to stop the carriage. "Immediately!" he cried, his glance returning briefly to Alison.

The carriage jolted once more in its effort to stop and she scrambled from the blankets to the opposite door, the one where the Marquis was not. He saw only a flash of slender, white ankle and thigh. The muslin gown clung to the swollen burden of her belly. A protective instinct swamped him at this proof of her fragility. Deliberately, he had set from his mind the changes his child would cause within her.

While the carriage still struggled to a stop, Alison flung the door wide and jumped out, unbalancing herself in the soft snow. Justin tried to reach her but before he could, she had risen, lifted her gown and exposed her bare feet as she hurried to find a more private spot.

"Are you trying to kill yourself, woman?" Chatham demanded loudly, watching her form as it disappeared into the night. Muttering an oath, he reached back inside the coach and grabbed the blanket. He went after her, but as her sobbing grew louder, he hesitated, not wanting to add any further to her distress. As the sobs lessened, he approached nearer. From a distance he watched as Alison tried to compose herself.

The night was too cold for much patience but he neared her cautiously. She heard his footfalls and cringed low, finally reduced to begging, "Please, give me my privacy in this. I promise you, I won't run away." Her voice caught on a sob.

The nausea returned, as did her humiliation, and she jerked from him. When she was done this time, she was near to collapsing. Her body huddled in a ball on the hard ground.

Justin spread the blanket about her shaking shoulders and gave her a moment before rasping softly, "Are you ready to return to the carriage now?"

His hand offered a handkerchief which she accepted gratefully. Justin tucked the blanket around her, lifting her gently into his arms. Her head lolled weakly against him, her sobs coming slow and muffled by this time.

Chatham felt like the most inane of fools as he carried his burden to the coach. What had he been expecting, he asked himself. Not until she'd thrown the blankets off and run from him had he bothered to be concerned with the physical changes in her. He hadn't even considered those when he tossed her so carelessly over his shoulder earlier.

When she jumped from the coach he thought for a

moment she would be unable to rise. Her arms and legs were so slender, and the burden of her belly touched him as nothing else had in his lifetime. How often had she said, 'I never meant you harm'? Now, he knew the meaning of those words.

In his arrogance, he thought he knew all he needed to know about women. For the first time he was beginning to understand what it meant for her to have a child, his child.

Henry's mouth gaped wide as the Marquis reappeared. Shuffling to the side of the coach, he opened the door for his master. "Guv . . ."

"She'll be fine once she's warm and has some rest. I think we might have been too rough on her, Henry."

"Ye didna tell me she was . . . she was . . . increasin'," Henry accused in a low whisper. "I don 'old with kidnappin' wimmen, let alone wimmen in 'er condition."

"Forget it, Henry. The necessity should never arise again." Chatham lifted Alison into the coach and she stumbled wearily into the seat. As he followed her, he remarked casually to his man, "Take it a little more carefully this time, will you, Henry?"

"Aye," he snapped angrily. "I'll walk the demmed 'orses! I don want 'er sickenin' on my conscience," Henry snarled in answer, pushing his tricorne forward on his head.

"Don't be too slow about it, Henry. We need to be at the lodge before daylight. She has no clothing." The door was pulled to a close as Henry stood gaping at him.

Alison was seated in the far corner of the carriage, her hands folded primly in her lap, bare feet just above the floor. Her face was pale, her body so slender and fragile, he couldn't understand how he had not seen the difference in her. Golden hair hung in unkempt strands around her face and neck while she lifted the back of her hand to wipe away remnants of tears. She watched him warily as he sat next to her and took a chilled hand in his. She tried to pull away, only to have his hold tighten and his fingers begin to rub lightly. "I must warm you, Alison. You're chilled to the bone."

Her hand and fingers tingled as sensation returned and spread. Chatham took her other hand and performed the same service. His mouth was curved into a thin, forbidding line and Alison realized she had angered him anew. She forced herself to remain very still as she accepted these ministrations.

"Lie back. Here." His lap robe was folded and set behind her. "Use this as a pillow, you'll be more comfortable. Try to sleep, we've hours yet to go."

This considerate man was no more trustworthy than that other who occupied the same body moments ago. Alison felt bruised, humiliated, and a far cry from sleep. She'd learned her lesson, however, and would do her utmost to keep him appeased. Leaning her head against the squabs, the lap robe beneath her shoulders, she closed her eyes.

They flared open the instant the Marquis lifted her legs to his lap. A protest rose to her lips and she struggled to sit up, but his fingers touched her shoulder comfortingly and motioned her to remain as she was. "No, don't worry. I'm not going to harm you. Your feet are colder than your hands and I'm going to help, that's all. Lay back."

Sleep was never farther from her mind. His hands

were warm and soothing on her feet as he rubbed the circulation back into them. Half closed eyes watched him, trying to reconcile this gentle man with the angry one she knew more intimately.

His sudden smile changed the hard look of him. "What a pair we make. I leave you everything but shoes, you leave me only my boots. After ripping my clothes to shreds . . ."

Her calm fled and her hand grasped the buttons around the neck of her nightgown, as though he'd just threatened to remove it. Tears burned the back of her eyes and she wondered wildly how she would stop him, how she could stand any more tonight.

"I was only teasing, just as you've done often enough. Don't look so frightened," he snarled, his good humor vanishing. With a lithe movement, he dropped her feet and took the seat across from her. "In spite of your obvious opinion, I'm not a monster. Lay back and go to sleep. I promise you, I will not leave you naked to the world."

Still unsure whether to trust him or not, a few moments passed before the tension eased from her body. Stretching onto the seat, she snuggled her chilly feet deeper into the blanket, rubbing them together to warm them. As she settled down, her eyes watched him. At the moment, his attention was elsewhere. He gazed unseeingly through the window, his face expressionless. When he turned to her, she hesitantly began to speak. "I am sorry about destroying your clothing. I was too angry to think properly. What . . . what happened?"

The mocking expression she so hated surfaced. She almost regretted asking the question but knew she

249

would do it again. Her fury of that early morning waned quickly and she spent many days after that conscience stricken about him. She shouldn't have shredded his clothing, taken his money, his horse nor left him as vulnerable as she had.

His eyes, angry and black, darkened at the remembrance. "Oh, I was found, in all my manly glory," he jeered softly, "by the innkeeper, his wife, son, daughter-in-law, countless numbers of their children, and guests . . ."

Alison moaned at his words. No wonder he was still so angry. Knowing she deserved every bit of that anger made it no less difficult to bear. If she had to face the world naked . . .

"Henry came to my rescue, of course. Fortunately, he was at the inn. If you'd waited around another hour, you could have met him earlier."

"Henry?"

"Our driver."

A dull flush spread across her face and she dropped her gaze. "I am so sorry. I didn't even stop to think what you would do. I don't think I was thinking of anything at the time, but myself."

She wasn't apologizing from fear, but because she meant the words. He found the act which enraged him so at the time dwindling in importance in his mind. In fact, it was now almost humorous. A half grin twitched at his mouth. He must have looked ridiculous.

"Well, perhaps I deserved it. I was a bit rough on you."

His words had her blinking. A bit rough? Tears welled. Just a bit. His roughness had changed her whole life. She would be married to him forever, and be miserable with it.

"That is not the way I would have taken a young virgin, had I known." Chatham spoke awkwardly, averting his eyes. Apologies did not come easily to him. No answer came from her and a sharp anger began to beat in his breast. If she thought to mock him for his apology . . . His glance lifted and found her wallowing in misery. The anger fled and he leaned over his knees, taking her fingers in his hands. "Perhaps we owe each other an apology. Neither of us used good judgement."

At his touch, her head nodded swift agreement and she jerked away, freeing her fingers.

"Are you warm now?"

"Yes, thank you."

"Your feet were like ice."

"They're fine."

Even as she spoke the words, he was leaning forward to learn for himself. "They're not fine. You should have told me." The lean fingers lifted her foot and stroked her toes first, gently, and moved to her arch. The blankets fell away from the soft, white calves and his palm moved upward to her ankles. He had an urge to stroke higher and touch the texture of her skin, but he felt her nervousness beneath his fingers. He'd frightened her enough for one night. "How does that feel? Can you wiggle your toes?"

Irrationally, a smile spread across her lips. "No matter what the occasion, I can always wiggle my toes."

"So I see. How about your other foot?"

His warmth soothed that, too. "You're very good at warming feet. Thank you, I feel much better now."

So prim and proper, his wife, he thought. But he was not fooled, she wanted none of his touches and less of

251

him. He decided to let the matter lie for now and tugged the blankets over her legs and feet.

The carriage jolted and threatened to dislodge her at the next bump, but Chatham was there to catch her around the waist and help her keep her seat. "I told Henry to be careful."

"It's difficult to drive at night. I don't know how he sees anything."

"Henry has many hidden talents," Chatham answered, watching as she snuggled deep and stretched her lower limbs. Soon she was asleep, one slim hand barely visible as it rested on the ruching of the woolen blanket. On her finger was the plain wedding band he gave her the day of their wedding.

In spite of the interruption, they made good time. Well before dawn, the chaise drew up in front of the Marquis' "cottage." In reality, it was a hunting lodge, large and fully equipped, but empty at this time of year, save for a very few servants.

Henry's wide-eyed visage appeared as the door was wrenched open. "'ow is she?"

"Sleeping like a baby," Chatham replied easily. "I find myself extremely loath to waken her."

"Does 'at 'appen offen?" Henry inquired bluntly.

"What?"

"Ye ken wot I mean, guv. Does she get sick very offen like 'at?"

"Henry," the Marquis responded in exasperated tones, "I've been asking myself the same question for hours. Would you believe I haven't the slightest idea." He straightened and lifted the sleeping form of his wife into his arms, his back to his man. "Now, get the doors for me, will you?"

Alison stirred as he settled her against his chest. The flurry of hair tickled his chin and her hands crept to his shirtfront. Comfort surrounded her, until he whispered softly in her ear, "Put your arms around my neck."

His words had her partially waking. She should not be in his arms, she remembered, but not exactly why. Contentment slurred her words, "I can walk."

"In your bare feet?"

She nodded and he had to laugh. Barely awake, she did not fight him. She felt like a soft kitten, all soft and pliable and sweet. Her fragrance was natural, like a breath of fresh air. "Put your arms around my neck. The steps will prove awkward and I don't want to drop you."

At his words her eyes opened and she jerked fully awake. The kitten was gone. Stammering, she pulled from his hold, "No, no . . . I can walk!"

His gentle mood dissipated at her obstinacy. "You're right, you can walk," he barked. "But you won't. What you will do is climb from the coach and into my arms. I'll be damned if you're walking through this snow to the house. I have no intention of turning my lodge into your sickbed."

He was angry, again. Alison sighed as she went into his arms and felt awkward as she placed hers about his neck. His back was stiff as he carried her to the house and up the front steps. A little lie, she thought, a white lie for peace. Surely that wasn't so sinful?

"I thought I might be too heavy for you." She spoke hesitantly, taking a deep breath and praying he believed her. Wearily her head dropped to his chest. The arms tightened their hold.

Inside the house, he set her on her feet. Her eyes took

in the lodge and its unexpectedly fine furnishings and she clasped her hands together nervously. This was no small cottage, she thought. More a fashionable, opulent residence, like the ones found in London. And it probably had a very large cellar.

"Are you hungry? Would you like something to drink?"

Without thinking, Alison shook her head and immediately wished the response retracted. If she spent time over food and drink, her trip to the cellar would be forestalled that much longer.

Chatham clasped her elbow and moved through the foyer with her. "Not even a brandy? Warm milk? I thought that was the preference for expectant mothers."

"I . . . I would like a cup of tea."

Chatham pushed open one of the set of double doors to the study for her and gestured for her to pass through. The room was large and masculine, obviously well used. Leather bound books lined the shelves on every wall. Overstuffed chairs flanked the fireplace. A desk stood against the far wall beneath a wide window.

The soft closing of the door sounded and Alison was once again alone with her husband. Every time she had been alone with him before this had led to disaster, she recalled nervously. He motioned her to a seat in one of the comfortable chairs. Crossing before the fireplace, she paused long enough to stretch her hands and warm them. The flickering flames of the fire silhouetted her form beneath the gown. Her shape was softly rounded, curving where it should. Her breasts were full and tempting, her waist narrow and her gently flaring hips beckoning. Chatham stood transfixed as she slid into one of the chairs.

He pulled the bellrope and poured a snifter of dark brew for himself. A moment later, a maid appeared and the Marquis ordered Alison a cup of tea and some biscuits for the two of them. As the maid bobbed a curtsey, her eyes glimmered with eager curiosity. The girl was an incongruous sight in her night clothes and cap. The door closed and the Marquis took a seat across from his wife. Alison's mouth gaped open. "Will your servants get up for you at any hour of the night?"

"Of course. Don't yours?" he responded easily, sipping from his glass.

"I don't know. I've never been later than they have."

"I imagine Morgan does anything you want of him."

"Morgan's hardly a typical servant," she scoffed lightly. "He chases me off to bed when he thinks I ought to be tired, whether I am or not."

"He's been taking good care of you, then?"

"Morgan? Of course, but I take care of him as well."

Tea and biscuits arrived and Alison busied herself pouring and making herself comfortable in the huge expanse of chair. As she sipped from the cup, warmth flowed through her throat and belly. She had not felt so relaxed since the early days at the cottage with Morgan. She scooted deeper in the chair, enjoying the warmth of her full belly. Weariness combined with the comfort to loosen her tongue.

"I . . . I have been thinking about our marriage, my lord. I found some old newspapers at the lending library. The courts have upheld that Fleet marriages are not legally binding. So, maybe the problem isn't as permanent as you think." Alison's tongue licked at her lips and her eyes watched him for a sign of encouragement. There was none. Haltingly, she continued, "We

255

could be free of each other." Her tongue was dry and she sipped of her drink, seeking solace there.

"You've been reading too many scandal sheets, my dear. Those marriages were set aside because coercion was used. Coercion was not used in our marriage, and your brother was the witness. We are well and truly married. The license is registered, it would take a full act of Parliament to declare that illegal. And I, for one, would not care for the notoriety. Sit down, please," he barked when she began to rise in agitation. "You have the most annoying tendency to run away whenever things become the tiniest bit uncomfortable for you. End that annoying habit right now. Morgan's no longer available to assist you, and I can easily outdistance you in your condition."

The cup clattered against the saucer, tepid tea threatening to spill over the rim and onto her gown. Alison lowered her eyes wondering desperately how to mollify him now. He was right, he could outrun her. He could outdistance her, he could do anything he liked with her. She wished it was morning and she'd had a full night's sleep. She might be able to handle him then. Right now, she was too weary and too worried about the cellar to think straight.

"Go to bed, Alison," he said softly, standing over her, his fingers removing the cup from her hand. "You're exhausted." He set the cup on the table and turned away. When he was far enough away that she thought he could not reach her, Alison rose jerkily and skittered to the door, her face pale and set with fear.

He was at her side in moments. "You're not running from me now," he muttered, exasperated. His hand snaked out and grabbed her by the wrist. "I'm too weary to give chase, and you're not a bit better to be leading me one."

"Please don't lock me in the cellar!"

He dropped her wrist as if the words burned him. The angry glare he turned on her frightened her anew and she dropped her eyes to the carpet. A fine trembling began in her hands and spread through her belly to her feet.

"The cellar is not ready for your use yet." He enunciated each word slowly as though she were too dimwitted to understand if he spoke more normally. As he turned from her he grabbed the brandy and took it with him to his chair. He did not look at her as he spoke. "Your room is the first door to your right, at the head of the stairs."

A few moments later he heard her soft footfalls as she mounted the stairs, hesitating as she searched for the right bedroom. She found it and closed the door behind her. She would soon be asleep, he thought, lifting the decanter and pouring himself more of the strong brandy. Angrily he tossed it off, staring at himself in the mirror above the mantelpiece as it burned a path down his throat.

So, she thought him enough of a monster to lock her in the cellar for weeks at a time? The scowl on his face deepened as he threw the fine brandy snifter into the hearth and watched it splinter into a thousand small pieces. "My lord?" Alison spoke hesitantly from the doorway.

Startled, he turned and saw her as a mere shadow. The candlelight did not penetrate as far as the door. The loosely fitting gown trailed about her bare feet.

"I thought you were asleep," he snapped, angry with

257

himself for not hearing her.

She flushed at this ungracious welcome, but steadily entered the room. The pieces of glass on the carpet drew her attention. "Did you have an accident?"

"Damn. I forgot about that. Stay where you are. Don't try to pick your way through this mess. All I need now is you cutting your feet badly and Geoffrey will slit my throat. He thinks I'm careless enough with you as it is." He was by her side in an instant, and easily carried her to the chair which faced the hearth.

She gazed curiously at him. "Have you seen Geoffrey?" Lines of weariness and worry etched themselves on her fair complexion.

A desire to place his hand on her cheek and soothe the worries away smote him. He straightened as he spoke. "Yes, in London. Did you not think I would go to him when you disappeared? He has been nearly as worried about you as I have."

"You've been worried about me? But you hate me . . ."

"Hate is a strong word, Alison. I do not hate you."

"I don't understand . . ."

"Of course you don't. You didn't stay around long enough to understand. You were never around long enough to discover what we might have made of a marriage between us, were you?" He drew his fingers through thick black hair. "It is too late tonight to go into that. I thought you were in bed by now. What do you need? Couldn't you find the bedroom?"

"Yes, but I couldn't sleep, not when I thought about Morgan and Thomas," Alison began hesitantly, settling herself in the chair. "I didn't see them when we left . . ."

"You were in no position to see much of anything."

"No, I wasn't." Her eyes implored his understanding in this. "But Morgan is getting too old to be in the middle of any more fights with you. That last battle you two had took so much out of him that he was a long time recovering. And Thomas is just a boy. I'm the one who planned your kidnapping, and I think I should be the one who pays for it. Morgan didn't even want to do it, and wouldn't have except Jon and I would have done it anyway, with or without his help . . ."

"You wouldn't have managed without his help."

"I would have. I am very stubborn when I think it necessary."

"How well I know that. But tell me, how would you have managed by yourself?"

"I could have hired someone."

"Oh? And henchmen are so readily available?" Chatham's expression hardened. "You would probably have ended up the victim. Don't you have any common sense?"

"I have common sense!"

"Where? Sensible women don't do stupid things like kidnapping perfect strangers."

Alison hated to admit the truth of what he said, especially to him. Lately, she'd been repeating the same words to herself over and over. She'd had these past several months in which to regret the actions of that week. Creeping to the edge of her chair, she folded her hands primly in her lap and admitted softly, "No, they don't. I am willing to pay the price for my actions. Thomas and Morgan shouldn't have to also."

Chatham sighed resignedly and stepped over the broken glass to reach the hearth where he pulled the bellrope. When he turned, she was standing before the chair, her hands reaching for the warmth of the fire. Her back was curved as she leaned forward, the folds of the gown pressing intimately against her hips and buttocks. When her fingers were warmed, she straightened and turned, toasting her backside.

The glow of the fire lit her cheeks with golden warmth. Tilting her head, she smiled at him and wondered where his intent thoughts were. A doubt entered her mind and she quickly glanced down to see herself. Gasping at the transparency of her gown, she gathered the extra folds and crushed them to her legs.

"Sit down," Chatham rasped as the knock on the door sounded. He moved to stand in front of her so Henry would see nothing but her face.

The old man entered hesitantly. "Ye rang fer me, milor'?"

"Watch out for the glass, Henry."

Henry picked his way daintily through the mess, his head shaking. "My gawd, wot ye get up to when I ain't aroun'. I 'eard the bell and as they've all gone to bed but me, I figured 'tis me ye wanted. But I ain't no maid to be cleanin' this up. 'Twill have to wait fer morning."

"I didn't call you for the glass. My wife is worried about Morgan and the boy. Will you set her mind at rest?"

"Yer wife?" Henry stammered, his mind boggling. "Yer wife? Then the child . . ."

"Is mine." The Marquis answered swiftly. "You have yet to congratulate me, Henry. My little family is expanding at an astounding rate."

"Couldn'a ye 'ave done a more conventional wooing?" Henry demanded when he found his voice. "I

260

don' like family squabbles."

"I do not squabble, Henry."

"Seems 'ike a squabble to me," Henry muttered beneath his breath, trying to peer around the Marquis, to get a glimpse of his new mistress. Alison was every bit as curious about this stranger.

Henry diffidently removed his tricorne. "Ye've caused a lot of trouble, milady. I'm 'enry Mordaunt, been in the Marquis' employ for years. I do all sorts of work for 'im, but this is the first time I've been called on to do kidnappin'. I'm sorry about the coach ride tonight, but coachman is not one of me reg'lar jobs!"

"You were the man following me!"

Henry's face fell. "You saw me?"

"Well, no," Alison hastened to reassure him. "You weren't noticeable, only . . . I have this intuition. Morgan thought I was losing my mind. So, you see, now that you're here and real, I'm relieved. And what a surprise you are, Mr. Mordaunt."

"Not as much of a surprise as ye be. Ye don' look much like a kidnapper to me, if I may say so."

"But I am! And a very successful one. Just ask him."

"Beginner's luck!" the Marquis retorted, a smile playing about his lips.

Alison laughed. "That too, but being more clever than my victim helped."

The smile instantly disappeared. "What?"

"Well, I am not such a slow top that I would have fallen for a poor ruse as you did. A drunken lad, indeed." Henry was nodding his head slowly, in full agreement with this statement.

Chatham knew he should be insulted, but the humor of the situation caught him by surprise. He replied evenly, "But you must remember, at the time I was half foxed myself. All my sympathies were with the lad. How was I to expect such underhanded play from someone I was merely trying to help?"

"Oh, I never thought of that. How could you ever trust anyone again, after what I did to you?"

"I know. You're sorry. You meant me no harm." In spite of his mocking words, his eyes held warmth and for the first time she did not fear his anger. Her mouth curved in an answering smile.

"Sounds like a family squabble to me," Henry muttered, silencing both other occupants of the room. "Aboot Morgan. I left 'im tied up in a nice, tidy, warm kitchen. The boy 'as locked in 'is room, tied not too tightly, and if I guess right, he 'as oot in a matter of moments. As a matter of fact, I'd wager Morgan's been free for 'ours now and 'e and the boy are plannin' yer rescue. But I'm ready for 'em."

"Then you didn't harm them. Oh, thank goodness! I do appreciate your telling me all this." Her eyes lit hopefully. "Er . . . do you suppose they really have a chance of finding me here?"

"Not a one," Chatham answered swiftly. "Thank you, Henry. I believe you have answered my wife's questions. Alison?"

"Oh, yes. I do appreciate your trouble, Mr. Mordaunt."

"Satisfied?"

"Yes, milord. Thank you."

"We are married, Alison. Do you not think you could call me by my name?"

She shook her head. "I don't know you that well."

"You've known me for months now. You've learned

some of my faults and we've shared intimate moments. Isn't that enough?"

"Our intimacy was long ago."

"I was referring to earlier tonight, when you were ill. That was certainly intimate. And I was not a monster then. I tried to help. I am not the monster you seem to think me."

Alison blushed furiously. "I was over that particular ailment until you burst into my life."

"I did not foresee your sickness . . . or a few other things. I might have handled this differently. Come, it's time you were in bed. You're tired."

"Don't you want me to help you clear away this glass?"

"Why do you suppose I pay so many servants?"

"You let most of them go."

"I have enough left to see to my needs, and yours. No, I don't need your help. Now, will you go to bed?"

What a temper he was in, over a simple offer to help. "Did you cut yourself?"

"What? No!"

"Well, most people have a reason for behaving so disagreeably. I thought you might, too."

With a strangled sound, he swept her in his arms and carried her across the room, depositing her outside the study door. "Go to bed, wife. This is one squabble we can finish in the morning."

Chapter Eleven

Eerie shadows flickered along floors and walls, cast by the candle he carried, as Chatham climbed the stairs and entered his bedroom. The soft glow from the taper captured the sight of his wife beneath the blankets in his bed, curled and warm. The light wavered and illuminated the windows and the opposite side of the room, dimming as it was set on the chest of drawers.

One brief tug loosened milord's cravat. Dark eyes wandered toward the bed and he wondered what he would tell her in the morning. That she had mistaken his directions and gone to the wrong room? No, she'd take herself off and he'd have to think of another lie tomorrow night. She must understand the way things were going to be between them.

They were married and so they would remain. That included sharing this bed. Breeches joined the coat where it was casually tossed onto the chair. The wick flickered and, as Chatham turned, he glimpsed the shadow of his body in the reflection of the mirror.

He was not such a bad looking fellow, he thought.

He admitted he'd known precious few innocents in his time; she was the first if he really counted them, and knew little of the way they thought. But what would make this one so different from other women, such as his mistresses? They were eager to please him. Why should this one spend her life running from him?

The mattress dipped with the weight of his body as he tugged the covers high. Alison was on her side, facing from him, her fingers curled against the pillow. Her warmth reached him through the mattress and blankets and he felt an almost irresistible urge to touch her.

No, he thought with a surge of disappointment. Not tonight. He couldn't take the chance of frightening her further. The decision was difficult to make, he was a man who denied little to himself. He rolled as far from her as possible, and slept.

Morning sun streamed through the windows, across the chair and bed. His first conscious thought was of the fragrance assailing him; his second was of the warmth so near. A hand lay across his breast and their thighs touched, hers soft and silky. Faint breathing tickled his shoulder. Turning his face, he studied her as she lay quietly sleeping. Her hair was tangled and spread over him, her mouth soft and pliable. She must have sought more warmth during the night and found him. The thought was infinitely pleasurable.

Stirring slightly, she nestled nearer, her hand lowering precariously. Chatham drew a deep breath and knew it was time to rise.

As he dressed he considered his next moves. She must come to trust him. The fear she felt was what he thought he wanted, but now he knew differently.

Suddenly she was more than the chit who abducted him. She'd become his wife, a woman he wanted to come to know.

He'd buy her some trinkets, that always worked with his other women. He and Alison had much to settle between them, his forgiveness had to be earned. But she could earn it, that much he decided. He might even let her off more lightly than she deserved.

He ate his breakfast, ordered the carriage brought round and informed Mrs. Banks he would return some time later in the morning.

He returned to find his lodge buzzing with activity and people. The aroma of freshly baked bread spread through the house, tantalizing him as he strode through the hall. Two new maids dusted and straightened his den, surprising him. The cleaning was normally done when he was not around. Henry waited him in the study.

The Marquis tossed several packages on the sofa and rummaged through his desk for paper and a quill. "Henry, I'd like you to take a message for me."

"Guv, I've been workin' so 'ard lately I thought I might take a rest. I'd like to stay 'ere for a while, just until I get me strength back. Me throat," he coughed roughly, "feels a bit scratchy, and me 'ead aches . . ."

Milord turned slowly in his chair and stared in surprise at him. The old man rested comfortably in an overstuffed chair, as though he'd been waiting some time for his master. For the first time ever, a guilty flush crossed his features and he could not meet milord's eyes. The Marquis did some rapid calculating. Henry loathed the country, he'd often complained when his work took him beyond the limits of the city. That was the second surprise of the morning. A houseful of new servants, and now this.

"How many other servants have you hired?"

"Oh, a few." Henry answered with a shrug. The Marquis' piercing stare caused him to mumble uncomfortably, "Seven."

"Seven." Chatham's brows raised and he accused softly, "Liar. I left this morning and have returned to find my home filled with scores of new servants—"

"Not scores, guv." His fingers splayed in an innocent gesture. "I told ye, seven."

". . . scores of new servants, and my faithful Henry, who grumbles about the shortest excursion from town, more than willing to put up with what is to him great inconvenience, and all to provide my wife some extra protection. And from me, her husband."

Henry's bushy brows lowered. "Not for that reason."

"You and Mrs. Banks are the only ones with enough authority to hire. Not that you have authority precisely, more like audacity."

"No, no, no," Henry soothed. "Ye don' understand. I know 'ow ye like to be comfortable when ye're in residence, and there was nowhere near enough servants. Why, ye'd be 'ollering down the 'all for a tipple afore ye knew it. Would ye be 'aving Mrs. Banks quit on ye? Overwork 'er and she will," Henry warned.

"You'll be damned in hell for your lies, Henry." The Marquis said darkly, adding almost thoughtfully, "Alison seems destined to draw the most unlikely champions."

"Well," Henry cried aloud in exasperation, "wot in 'ell did ye want to go and kidnap 'er fer anyway? She's not up to yer weight. And as I've 'ad a 'and in this, I'm not goin' anywhere until I'm certain she'll be safe from you."

"Spare me, Henry." The Marquis raised a hand in mock salute. "I give you my word she will be safe with me." His eyes narrowed suspiciously. "You do trust my word, don't you?"

Henry had to think about that for a moment before nodding his head. "Though I've never seen ye so ticked off at anybody before."

"And you never will again. She has a way of getting under my skin," Chatham answered drily. "Now, I want you to take this note to my grandmother, and go to my house in London . . ." He spent much time making sure Henry understood exactly what he wanted.

As Henry rose to leave, the old man gruffly questioned, "Are ye sure ye don' need me 'ere? She might run away again or . . ."

"Don't worry, Henry, you'll be back here before I have time to do much more than torture her."

Henry regarded the Marquis thoughtfully. "Ye know, guv, at first I couldn't blame ye for bein' so 'ateful, I mean gettin' kidnapped, and then tied to the bed in the inn. My Gawd, if I hadn't come along when I did, one of those other gawkers would 'ave 'ad to untie ye, and ye can bet it would'a taken 'im a long while, between snickers that is. But it seems to me ye got back at 'er a'right, as a matter of fact it strikes me now as 'ow she might'a been gettin' back at ye, at that inn."

"If that was her intention, she certainly accomplished it."

Henry couldn't resist a grin. "Ye would'a done much worse in 'er place."

Henry was gone when Chatham pulled the bellrope and summoned the housekeeper. "Has my wife wakened yet?"

Mrs. Banks blinked in surprise. Until this moment she had no idea just who was in the bed upstairs. "No, milord. She was still asleep when Katey looked in on her."

"Take her a tray, she's probably starving by now." He lifted the packages and questioned in afterthought, "Who's Katey?"

"Ooh, she's one of the new girls, milord. She does hair and Mr. Mordaunt thought we might be needing someone like that. Wasn't that clever of him?"

"Yes, very clever," Milord agreed, striding from the room. "Put something on that tray for me, too. Will you, Mrs. Banks?"

So, even faithful Henry had come under Alison's spell, Chatham thought as he mounted the stairs, the packages beneath his arm. Who next?

He strode through the bedroom door, determined to rout his wife from bed if necessary. The bed was empty "Not again!" he thought in exasperation, tossing the packages on the bed and turning from it. Then he saw her, seated in the chair beneath the window, eyeing him apprehensively.

Green eyes were large in her pale face and her hands played nervously on her lap. A drab gown of ugly brown material enveloped her, several sizes too large and hanging about her feet in folds. Chatham recognized the gown instantly as the one he brought for her use. She looked every bit as ridiculous in it as he knew she would.

"Take that ugly thing off." His eyes wandered over

her in unconcealed revulsion.

"It's all I could find. It was lying on the foot of the bed when I woke. I thought it was meant for me." She had difficulty keeping her voice steady. "I couldn't stay in my nightgown all day."

Alison felt hungry, dowdy, ill at ease, and she hadn't a clue as to this man's mood. The receiving end of his anger burned her more than once. Last night she might have thought herself capable of coping with him after a good rest, today she knew better.

"I won't have my wife wearing such a garment," he scorned, gesturing to the bed. "I purchased those for you. There's not much there, but the village shoppe is small and they had little. I bought some material, I thought you might be able to make use of it." He waited for her to say or do something to show how grateful she was. When she said nothing, he barked irritably, "Well, aren't you even tempted to see what I bought? And stop looking at me like you'd like to do nothing better than run. There's not a damned tree to shimmy down here." His glance raked her from head to foot. "You wouldn't get very far in that garment and no shoes."

Alison stood, lifted her chin bravely and said, "I wish you would stop ranting at me." Crossing over to the bed, she opened the first of the boxes. In it was a simple gown of green muslin which she held against herself. It was too large and the Marquis informed her coolly she would grow into it. Another box held black, leather boots which buckled up the front, and another box contained fine, leather slippers for day wear.

"There's a shawl, too, somewhere. I thought you might need it." Other boxes contained underwear, two more dresses and some material, ribbons and thread.

"Mrs. Banks sews and probably most of the maids do. You'll have more to wear in no time."

"I sew too," she said hesitantly. "I've made a few things for the baby . . ." Her voice trailed lamely at the expression on his face. "Thank you. I don't mean to be such trouble."

Chatham regarded her strangely. "I should have thought of clothing before this. I never considered shoes. And don't worry, Alison. We'll send for the clothing you made for the child long before he's born. He'll come into the world with all his mother's handiwork about him." Softly he mocked her. "And whether you mean to be or not, you are a great deal of trouble!"

"It serves you right."

He laughed. "So it does. Come, you don't have to change before we eat. Aren't your feet cold?"

"Yes," she smiled, "and that's as good an excuse as any to try on my new slippers." Pulling them onto her feet, she admired them and held her toes out so her husband might see how they fit, displaying a good deal of ankle. She dropped the dress into place and smoothed the skirt, not noticing how intently he watched her until she lifted her eyes.

Another new maid brought their meal. She set it on the table and curtsied low.

"You must be Katey." The girl nodded at his words. "Alison, you now have a proper lady's maid, thanks to Henry. I understand you do hair?"

"Yes, sir."

Alison greeted Katey, a girl few years older than herself. Katey acknowledged this shyly, her brown eyes dropping. "I'll do my best for ye, milady."

271

She was gone and Alison remarked, "I've never had my own maid before."

"You need one now. You're a child no longer, Alison. If Katey works well enough, she may go to Chatham House with us."

The food was delicious, which seemed to matter little as Alison was so hungry. The Marquis grinned as she took a large bite of bread and jam, teasing her at this display of unladylike appetite. "At least I don't make you suffer my cooking."

An irrepressible grin peeped out before Alison was able to stop it. "You didn't cook this? And you thought yourself good enough to give me advice."

He set his utensils beside his plate. "I can cook better than you, Alison. At first I thought you were planning to slowly poison me. It wasn't until I saw Morgan eating the same miserable meals that I realized what you were was just a rotten cook." His smile took the insult from his words. "We all lost weight during that venture. Even you. And if you've been eating your own cooking these last months, it's no wonder you're so thin."

"Morgan's been doing the cooking. He wouldn't let me near the kitchen," she admitted ruefully. "And in case you haven't noticed, I'm hardly thin."

"Not shimmying down any more trees, I trust?"

"No, that was my last one for a while." Her eyes wandered out the window, toward freedom.

The Marquis reached a hand across the table and touched hers. "It won't be so unpleasant, Alison."

She sighed. "As long as there are no rats. I've never been able to stand them."

Justin threw his napkin on the table as he rose.

"Must you continually harp on the cellar? That's not what I was referring to! I merely meant you might like being a married woman. You've never given it a chance."

Her eyes widened. "But I don't feel married."

"You most certainly are."

"Do you really think that sham of a ceremony makes any of this right? Why, I woke up this morning and found myself in your bedroom. And I don't even know how I got here, I mean I thought I followed your directions, and last night it looked just like any bedroom, not particularly yours. And then I realized how much more trouble I must have caused you, and I am sorry, it was not deliberate . . ." Her mouth compressed tightly. "Where did you sleep?"

His head shook in amazement. "How you rattle!"

"Yes," she hung her head, "Jonathan always ridiculed me for doing that."

"You begin with one topic, change it twice before I can even follow your reasoning. You make absolutely no sense, yet I understand you, that's what really frightens me. To answer your questions, yes, that sham of a ceremony, as you call it, was perfectly legal. We are married, we will remain married. And right? Of course this is right. Married people should live together. Gives them a better chance of staying married. And as for you sleeping in my bedroom, what's wrong with that? I intend to share a lot more than a bed with you. Oh, don't look so surprised, I—"

"I can't share a bed with you!"

His brows rose haughtily. "But as it's my room, and I don't intend to give it up to you or anyone, you have nothing to say in the matter. It's either me or the

273

cellar, remember?"

"I . . . I have to choose between sharing your bed and the cellar?"

"Don't look so abashed, my dear. There are all sorts of choices in the world. You must choose between me and the other rats." His fingers moved to her chin and pressed it gently, closing her mouth. His expression was hard but she had the feeling he was laughing at her. "Think it over. The choice shouldn't be so difficult."

Chatham quit the room, leaving Alison in a vortex of confusion. She stood and tried to find her bearings, her eyes encompassing the comfortable room which she longed to choose over the cellar. The room was large, brightened by the wide windows and the sunlight which streamed through. Blue brocade drapes hung to the floor and a matching brocade trimmed the ends of the four bedposts. A walnut chiffonier stood opposite the bed. A small, round table and chairs were set beneath the window and overlooked the forest beyond the house. The furniture was old, yet obviously well cared for. The room was comfortable and well used, just as was the whole of the house.

The cellar was probably every bit as neat.

She was curled in a chair in the library, her legs tucked beneath her when the Marquis returned. Her curly head was buried in an ancient book she'd found on witchcraft. So enrapt was she with her reading that she did not hear him enter. He spoke her name and she started, her hand flying to her belly.

"Oh! You startled me," she accused, wide eyed.

He grinned and turned the book over to read the cover. "Ah, I remember this one very well. It gave me nightmares as a child." He returned it carelessly to her

274

lap. "I recommend it highly."

"Isn't it gruesome?"

"Very." He liked the way her eyes sparkled and her head cocked to one side when she concentrated. "I have more gruesome news for you. I thought we would be able to leave soon for Chatham House, but it appears we're in for a major storm. I think we'll stay here rather than chance being snowbound in some inn."

"We were leaving here? But I thought—"

"We're not now." His eyes met hers, a distinct challenge in them. "So it seems we have the perfect opportunity to try out our marriage, to see if we can get along together for any length of time."

Alison digested this, setting the book on the small table beside her. "Then you had no intention of keeping me in the cellar?"

That hateful expression was again on his face, as though he found the subject of the cellar even more distasteful than she did.

"There's a cellar in each of my houses," milord shrugged casually. "I can lock you in anytime over the next forty or fifty years."

"But you won't now?" Alison felt as though a tremendous weight had been lifted from her shoulders and she smiled. "I can't thank you enough. You can't imagine what it does to my spirits to think of spending the night in some dank cellar. I may deserve it, but I couldn't look forward to it, not with the cold and the rats and all . . ."

"Will you stop that damned rambling?"

"Yes, milord."

"Justin is my name. You haven't used it since we met. Can't you say it? Justin."

His temper was rising. She would have liked nothing better than to jump from her chair and flee the room, but he stood over her like an angry devil waiting for the words. His eyes were hard, his mouth curved into a sneer.

"I'm waiting."

Her eyes studied the carpet beneath his boots. The word was barely audible. "Justin."

"That's better," he said calmly, straightening. "Brandy?"

"No, thank you." She didn't breath until he moved and no longer blocked her chair.

"No, thank you . . . ," he encouraged.

Alison swallowed. "No, thank you, Justin."

"Good. I didn't think my name was above your understanding."

Alison rose, her face flushing. "I don't think we'll get along at all well. We haven't been alone together five minutes without insults and arguments flying."

"I admit civility seems beyond us, but it's not civility I want from you."

"No, you want me frightened out of my wits most of the time."

He paused in the act of pouring himself a brandy. "Are you frightened of me? That's not the impression I have."

After consideration, Alison surprised herself by admitting, "No, I'm not frightened of you," and ruined the words by adding meekly, "Justin."

His grin was lopsided as he advanced on her. Alison's head came up and she retreated in as dignified a manner as she could. Only when he was very close did she turn to run, but a hand was clamped on her elbow

276

and pulled her to face him. "No? And yet you run?"

"I'm not stupid."

"You think I will hurt you?"

Alison felt the touch of his hand on her elbow, gentle, not likely that of a madman set on harming her. And certainly nothing like the angry man he had been last night, or during their earlier acquaintance. His grin was mocking, true, but only in a manner calculated to intimidate her, not to harm her. "No," she answered more strongly than before. "No, I'm not frightened of you. But I think you would like me to be."

Instantly the elbow was released and he returned to his drink, ignoring her. A moment later, he seemed surprised to see her still in the room. "Well, what do you want now?" He demanded in irritation.

"I thought I might make a suggestion."

"Oh, and what might that be?"

"Well, as it seems we are here together for the next few days, and we really should learn to get along better than we have been, perhaps if we did not talk too much . . ."

"How much is too much?"

"At the point you become nasty and sarcastic, we should stop talking at all. Perhaps we might rub along better if we did something together."

Milord's face was bland. "My thoughts exactly. Er, what exactly did you have in mind?"

"Cards," she answered bluntly. "We might pit our skills. That should keep us civil with each other. You do play?"

"Some games, as long as they are not too complicated."

"Jon claimed you were something of an expert, but

277

Morgan wouldn't let him play with you." Her eyes rested hopefully on him. "I would like to learn a game other than gin rummy or Earl of Coventry. Jon laughs at me because that's all I know, but he won't teach me. And if I could learn just enough to best him once in a while . . ."

Chatham shook his head sadly. "I don't know if we can. We can't hold a decent conversation without you worrying about the cellar or rats, and rambling on . . . and on . . . and on . . . I don't know if the idea is plausible."

"I promise to try harder," she promised eagerly. "I mean I always try, but sometimes things happen and nothing works out right . . ." She was rambling again and bit her lip. "I promise to try."

"Do you think you can become meek, mild, and sweet tempered?"

"Don't laugh at me."

Her sincerity touched him. "I don't want you making any promises you can't keep."

"I do so want to learn faro!"

Milord scrutinzed her carefully. "How good *are* you at Earl of Coventry?"

"Oh, I always win at that," she replied cheerily. "Morgan owes me so much he refuses to play with me anymore and poor Thomas is even more in debt to me. That's why he keeps playing, he hopes to win back his wages. Not that I play to keep the child's wages, but losing to me is much better than him spending it all at the pub, isn't it?"

Milord studied the glass in his hand. Alison thought she was forgotten and was at the door before he spoke again. "After dinner? Here?" She nodded eagerly and

278

Justin raised his glass to her, a half smile playing about his lips. She heard him softly laughing as she mounted the stairs.

"Mrs. Banks should be pleased with you. It's not often a guest of mine has a third helping."

Alison gasped and dropped her fork. It hit the Sèvres plate and clattered its way to the floor. Flushing, she stammered, "You're not supposed to count. That's what Jon does."

"Abominable, aren't we? No, no, I was teasing. After suffering your own and Morgan's cooking so long, it's no wonder you need to put on some weight. Have another helping."

"No, thank you. A succession of governesses taught me young ladies aren't supposed to eat their fill."

"That's right. Proper young ladies are supposed to stuff themselves before and after dinner, and during dinner pick at their food. Makes them seem cheaper to feed. Take care when we're in London. I wouldn't want my friends to talk about my wife's ravenous appetite."

"Are we going to London?"

"Not yet, not for a while after the child is born. But I thought you might enjoy the season once or twice. Have you ever been presented?"

She shook her head. "No, there was never the chance. Besides, I don't know that I would like it." The gaze she lifted to him was rueful. "I wasn't exactly a roaring success at the dances I attended in Wiltonshire. I can't see myself fitting in with some of Geoffrey's friends. They're so stiff."

"They would be a poor choice for your first evening

in London. You need a younger crowd, certainly a group less jaded than Geoffrey's friends.

"I think you would like the opera, the ballet, Shakespearean plays . . . Have you ever been to the Tower?" Alison shook her head, her eyes huge in her face as she listened to him. "There's much to see. You could attend a session of Parliament, perhaps hear me speak. You would need a wardrobe. With your looks you could set the style, not follow that set by some foppish dandy. I shan't stint as your husband, you can buy whatever you like." She was so enraptured in these dreams that he was encouraged to continue, "Perhaps one day we might travel to the Continent. You should see France and Italy, the city of Venice especially. You would love the waterways and the art. There is so much I could show you."

"Have you been abroad?"

"I had my grand tour as other young bucks do. But I thought of it as an adventure, only for sowing wild oats. There is much I missed."

"I would like Italy."

"And I'll see to it that you miss nothing," he said, rising from his seat and assisting Alison from hers. His hand lifted her fingers to his mouth and softly kissed the tips. Alison's eyes widened. No one quite like Justin Sarrett had ever come into her life before, and when he exerted himself to be charming, she was lost. "Now," he said softly, tucking her arm into his and leading her from the dining room. "We shall play a few hands of cards before tea. You wouldn't want to miss tea, would you?"

Chatham was stretched comfortably from the table from his wife, cards in hand as he shuffled them.

"Faro, it is." Alison nodded, her eyes bright. The skirt of her pale blue velvet gown brushed against the carpet and table. "But no game of cards is complete without a wager."

"Oh, I agree. Morgan and I even gambled on gin rummy. I warn you though, I am frightfully lucky. We've been playing gin ever since we escaped from London and Morgan says he'll be working for the next twenty years for only bed and board, that's how much he's lost to me."

"Is that how you see it? That you *escaped* from me? Just like a debtor does from prison?"

"Sort of . . ." Why couldn't she keep her mouth shut? Every time she opened it, she made him angry. Lifting her hand in a placating gesture, she tried to make him understand. "At the time, you didn't like me very much, and I didn't know you very well . . . , and nothing seemed to be going right . . . , and I knew a diet of bread and water would starve me to death . . ."

"I never threatened you with bread and water," milord roared, throwing the cards so they littered the table and floor, several of them clinging to the hem of Alison's gown. Milord poured himself a hefty measure of brandy and downed it.

"It seems I must reiterate my thoughts on this marriage. I have given you my name, a position in life of which you can be proud, and you will have all the money you could ever possibly crave. In return, I expect a child and a semblance of respect from you. We need not interfere with each other's lives. You can do much as you have always done, and so will I. I see no reason why this marriage should not work . . ."

"But you just spoke of the Continent . . ."

"We needn't go together, I was forgetting . . . other obligations."

A constriction lodged in her throat. "And London?"

"London will be happy to welcome you as my bride. We need not see much of each other there. A token appearance now and again will suffice."

Thoughts of a future such as he described chilled her to the bone. She thought of the miserable marriage Geoffrey and Eileen shared and knew she would smother in such a life. The thought of Eileen brought other concerns to mind.

Was there another woman? And why did the thought hurt her so?

The evening had gone so wrong so quickly. She wanted to apologize and begin anew, but he was pouring brandy down himself so rapidly she realized how dangerous one more word would be. Why couldn't she learn to keep her mouth shut? Feeling a hopeless failure, she rose.

"Bed already, my dear?" he sneered. "Shall I order the cellar made up for you?"

Violet eyes swam with remorseful tears.

Milord turned. "Go to bed, Alison," he spoke wearily. "Upstairs. Now."

She fled the room, barely making the top of the stairs before the sobs burst from her.

Chapter Twelve

Alison wakened to the scent of brandy and the feel of harsh stubble against her cheek. She was wrapped in a warm circle, too comfortable to move so she slept on, until the low rumbling of a man's snore sounded in her ears. She jolted fully awake at that, but a later, softer snore told her he was still sleeping soundly. A pulse beat in the hollow of the neck beneath her gaze.

Curiosity surfaced. She'd never had a chance to study her husband when he wasn't aware. Her head slipped back and she watched him, and thought how relaxed he looked in sleep. The tiny lines around his eyes and mouth were smoothed and his expression softened with slumber. The dark stubble on his jaw was thick and wiry, no wonder it scratched her tender skin. His breathing was deep and regular. The black hair which was normally pulled back from his face was loose and hung in straight strands around his head. She was tempted to lift her hand and brush it away from his eyes. In face, she would like to touch his mouth and eyes, and that little spot which pulsed so . . .

Temptation beckoned. She snuggled closer to him and lifted her hand to brush the errant strands away, when suddenly her thighs were touching very masculine ones. And very naked ones. The contact brought with it reality and she carefully crept away from him, moving his heavy arm to crawl beneath it.

Her feet grew cold as she stood beside the bed and studied him. He was a handsome man, maybe that was why she was tempted to crawl back in bed and get warm all over again. And he spoke of going separate ways and neither knowing what the other was doing . . . , and so on. The thought was dispiriting. She wasn't about to look the other way for him. And he'd throttle her if she put one wrong foot forward . . .

Of course he would. Her brow lifted and the eyes beneath glinted with sudden pleasure. He'd throttle her with his bare hands, muttering angry threats to her life all the while, his face an angry mask. A smile lit her features. No, he wasn't about to let her go her own way and the thought was infinitely pleasing.

Lured to the window by the brightness of the day, she saw the countryside blanketed with snow. It sparkled and glistened, dancing to the sun's rays. The hour was too early for anyone to be up and about, so no footprints as yet marred the whiteness of the snow.

Alison made up her mind quickly and chose the drab gown of brown wool and the black boots to don, topping all with the cloak her husband purchased yesterday. She was pulling a woolen cap over her hair and the mittens into place as she raced down the stairs and onto the front porch.

The sound of the door closing wakened the Marquis. He sat up sleepily and caught a glimpse of Alison's fingers reaching for the heavy wool cloak as she tugged it behind her and through the door. The sight had him awake and instantly rising. As he grabbed pieces of strewn clothing and donned them, he cursed loudly for all the trouble she was, for all the running she did. He raced down the stairs and onto the porch. There he stood and glanced around for his errant wife.

Alison kicked at the snow with the tips of her boots. Bending, she scooped up a handful, rolled it into a ball and let it fly as high in the air as she could. The next scoop was in her hand as the front door opened and she turned in its direction. Her husband stood on the threshold, his face grim. How could anyone be in such a temper on this beautiful morning?

The snow chilled her fingers and she suddenly thought of Jon, wishing he was here. She owed him a snowball to the top of the head since last winter and the urge to let her arm fly was hard to resist. As it was, the only target available still frowned heavily, though he seemed to have relaxed substantially since seeing her. Her mouth quirked and she wondered how long it would take her to run and hide in the barn. Oh, dear, it was tempting. Her eyes returned to her husband. Now, he half smiled. She gave a little smile herself, juggling the snowball once. Milord grinned and shook his head.

"You wouldn't dare!" he said softly.

The words were just what she needed. She was shocked at her own impetuosity the moment the cold clump of snow wiped the smile from milord's face. His expression was of such surprise that she could hardly keep from laughing aloud. Now was the time to make herself scarce.

The depth of the snow and Chatham's longer legs had not been given enough consideration, she realized as she trudged through to the barn and heard him rapidly advancing on her from behind. She lurched forward bravely but he still gained on her. Her bravado was now being regretted. Well, she'd just have to do what she always did with Jon. When in doubt, attack. Quickly she turned, gathered more snowballs and pelted them furiously at his head. Whenever one landed in a particularly good spot, she laughed outrageously.

Chatham must have decided he'd had enough, for he gave her a furious glare and began tossing snowballs of his own. His aim was more accurate than hers, also stronger. His laughter began to grate on her nerves when she wiped snow from her face for the umpteenth time. At least he laughed now for which she was grateful.

She turned and bent over to take advantage of the snow behind her. Chatham's well aimed ball caught her on the backside and knocked her face first into the snow. She sat up, covered with the cold, white snow and could hear more grating laughter. Clapping the wet mittens together to rid them of clinging snow, she pushed herself up and gathered more balls, tossing them in swift succession at his head. Chatham was not abashed in the least. Slowly it dawned on her that she was losing. She backed away gradually, but he noticed immediately and advanced steadily, in spite of the heavy onslaught of snowballs she heaped on him. When he was too close for comfort, she turned to run and was hampered by the snow and her skirts. Glancing behind her, she squeaked to find him within easy reach. Alison lengthened her stride, tripped over her feet and fell backward into the soft stuff. She opened her eyes and found her husband standing over her, hands on his hips.

"Running away again," he queried nastily.

"No, just retreating." Her mistrust of him shone in her wary eyes.

Justin's mouth quirked as he watched her. The woolen cap barely covered her head now, and strands of the blonde hair escaped it, reminding him of the urchin who licked her fingers after eating a pasty. The hot rage of those days was replaced by a gnawing feeling of foolishness. How did he ever consider her dangerous? His gaze lowered, her belly was no reminder of that child.

He offered his hand and her apprehension vanished. She laughed brightly and took the hand, brushing the snow from her skirts as she stood.

"I almost didn't throw that first snowball, thinking you'd be angry with me!" She cocked her head to one side as she peeped at him. "But you aren't, are you?"

"How can I be? I won."

"This time, but just you wait," she mumbled mischievously.

His hand stopped her when she would have moved to the house. All teasing was gone from his voice. "When I woke up and you were gone, I thought you'd run away."

Her smile faded. "No, I promise, I won't do that again."

His fingers became entangled in her hair, pulling her toward him as he thought how beautiful and gentle she was. His head bent and his lips touched hers. The woolen cap disappeared into the snow. Chatham's fingers relented, but he was breathing heavily as he spoke. "You go to my head, little one. Don't ever run away from me again. There's not much that frightens me, but the thought of that has me quaking in my boots!"

"Justin . . ."

Alison felt something cold and damp slide down the back of her gown. Justin had a silly grin on his face. She squeaked and pushed him so ferociously he fell backwards into the snow, cursing loudly. She was dancing around in her footprints, trying unsuccessfully to be rid of that cold, wet snowball. Slowly it melted, dripping moisture into her undergarments. When she was as uncomfortable as she could be, she glared at her husband. "How unsportsmanlike of you! Especially when I had already admitted defeat!" Angrily, she hauled more snow and, not even bothering to pat it into snowballs, tossing it at his head.

Justin held her cap up to protect himself and laughingly protested, "I couldn't resist it, Alison! You weren't expecting a thing. You should have seen your face!" He opened his mouth once too often and she got him.

Huffily she turned her back and began to trudge through to the house.

"Wait!" he called as she picked up speed. "Aren't you going to help a fellow up? I did as much for you!"

"Not for you, you're too unprincipled!"

"You're a coward, Alison!" he bellowed loudly, rising and chasing after her.

"No, just cautious!"

"Words, words words!" he taunted.

She barely reached the front porch before he did and was breathing heavily by that time. Justin reached for her waist and swung her around to face him.

"You win, Justin! I give!" she laughed breathlessly. "Until the next time and then we start all over again!"

"Not unless you've dried out by then," he retorted softly, pushing her into the house before him. Removing her wet cloak, he spoke sharply, "You're soaked through. Alison! And you're wearing that damned dress!"

"It's wool, Justin, and warm."

"Well, don't wear it again!"

"What? And wear my muslin next time you decide to throw a snowball down my back? I'm not such a dimwit, sir." Her teeth were chattering as she spoke.

"Come on!" He tugged at her hand and pulled her up the stairs after him. "You need something dry to wear."

"And a bath."

"That, too."

"I smell cinnamon rolls."

"You would."

"I'm starving."

"Bath first, then warm clothes, then the cinnamon rolls," he said firmly.

"I don't think I have the strength to do all that. I need food."

"Food, after your bath. And get rid of that damned cap!"

"It must be yours, I found it in the closet."

Once inside the bedroom, he led her to a chair. After tossing several small pieces of wood onto the fire and watching as they caught, he threw a larger log on top of all. He turned to Alison and she was still trying to tug the boots from her feet. The gown was up to her knees and displaying the thick, white stockings beneath. Justin knelt on the floor and gave his assistance in pulling the boots off.

"They're so tight," Alison said, grimacing.

The boots and stockings were removed. "Stand up, that gown's too wet to wear any longer. Here, move closer to the fire." His fingers roamed insistently over the buttons in the front of the gown until she brushed his hands away.

"I can do this," she said in a prim little voice. "You'd better see to yourself."

"Don't be coy, Alison. I'm not the one soaked through to the skin." His hand tugged the bodice of the gown free of her shoulders.

His tone of voice was so abrupt that she stood meekly before him, but she refused to allow him to go any further than the gown. "I've been undressing myself for years, milord."

He was furious with himself for getting her so wet, and with her for insisting on calling him "milord." An argument nearly ensued but for the convenient arrival of the maid, Katey.

Chatham knew it was futile to remain, however much he wished to be the one to assist. Long strides took him to the door. Alison called after him, "Be sure to save one of the cinnamon rolls for me!"

His gaze returned and wandered over her barely covered form. Thin straps of a lacy chemise dangled low over her shoulders. Her thighs were white and bare. "I imagine there's more than enough for the two of us, even with your appetite," he teased. His eyes were warm as they rested on her. "Are you sure you don't want my help scrubbing your back?" he queried hopefully.

The thought was tempting, but she shook her head. Justin sighed forlornly. "Perhaps another time?" His voice was gentle as he watched the confusion spread across her features. "I'll wait to breakfast with you."

He left and Alison wondered how many other backs he'd helped scrub. The women he knew would be sophisticated and beautiful. Most of all, *slender*. He was too good with mockery for her to risk any sort of back scrubbing.

As she dressed she wondered if, maybe, she tried harder not to irritate him so much, though she didn't really try to irritate him, and if she were nicer to him, he would make another lewd suggestion like scrubbing her back after the baby was born. She would say yes then and do her best to make him forget those other women.

Peering at herself in the mirror, she considered the possibility of becoming a sophisticated beauty, and admitted it was slim. Her brows didn't arch right, her hair was too light for powder. She'd look ridiculous in one of Eileen's fussy gowns, or with one of those black patches on her cheek. Alison cocked her head to one side and made a moue with her mouth. She narrowed her eyes to appear more seductive. All she looked was ghastly.

She hadn't heard the door open. Chatham's voice startled her. "I thought you were hungry?"

She straightened quickly, her face flushed. "I am."

"The cinnamon rolls are getting cold."

"No!" she objected vehemently to this shattering piece of news. She hurried down the stairs and missed

291

the broad grin on her husband's face as he watched her from the back.

For the remainder of the morning Mrs. Banks and Alison cut out material for dresses. Alison may have learned to ply the needle but she knew little about patterns. The housekeeper knew instinctively how to cut, as well as having in her possession several patterns. They worked until early afternoon when Mrs. Banks had to begin preparations for dinner. Alison labored alone a while longer.

Chatham watched from the doorway as she pinned together two pieces of the fabric. As he entered the room she smiled up at him.

"You look busy," he commented. "I'm going to the village and wondered if you needed anything."

"Nothing, thank you. You purchased enough material to keep me busy the rest of the winter, and spring and summer, too."

His eyes scanned her lovely face. "Geoffrey was right not to bring you to London," he murmured.

The frank words hurt. Alison dropped her sewing and rose. Her face was set, as though preparing for yet another insult. "Because I'm not quite a lady yet?"

"Because Eileen would have tried to destroy the best in you. Jealousy would have eaten her alive."

"Oh, pooh," Alison scorned lightly, suddenly loving every word he spoke, because he spoke them. "Why would she be jealous of me? Just this morning I was wondering how I could become more like her . . ."

"Don't you dare!"

"You're hurting my chin, Justin. Thank you for releasing it. I don't know why I always make you angry."

"You speak such nonsense! Why would you want to be like her?"

"Men admire her. *You* admire her."

"I? I do not!"

"Of course you do. You challenged a duel over her!"

"Oh, so you heard about that, did you? Well, I admit I lost my temper, as did your brother. When he slapped me I was so enraged I accepted the duel. By morning my sanity had returned and so I informed Geoffrey. For your information, little one, I cannot abide your brother's wife. She is shrewish and unfaithful, nothing like the sort of wife I need. I regret anything I have ever had to do with her. So rid yourself of that notion!" His finger gently rapped her chin.

"You weren't having an affair with her?"

Chatham frowned. "With Eileen? No. How could you even think such foolishness?"

Alison wasn't about to answer that, not truthfully, anyway. "Oh, I heard something a long time ago. It seems so silly now."

"Gossip is rampant in London and for some reason, I'm always in the midst of the most unsavory stories. Until now, I never cared. I can assure you, I have not so much as flirted with Eileen."

Alison stared longingly at her husband's retreating back. How could she ever tell him this was all one horrible mistake, all based on some silly gossip? She knew better than to listen to gossip, she certainly didn't spread it. But Jon was in the same room with them when the duel was challenged, for heaven's sake, and he didn't spread gossip either.

Oh dear, she thought, he should never have been kidnapped at all. Then she wouldn't be here, and he wouldn't be here. There wouldn't be a baby coming. He'd strangle her if he ever found out! And she ought to strangle Jon.

So, all the plotting and conniving she, Morgan, and Jon had done was for nothing. The worst of it was she couldn't tell Justin the truth. He'd dislike her more than ever. Her father was right, gossip is the worst of sins.

Too agitated to sit and sew, she donned the old woolen gown, her boots and cloak and went for a walk. The afternoon sun was bright and warming. Snow melted in the roads and from rooftops, leaving puddles about the house and barns. Alison paid scant attention to any of this, she was deep in her own dreary thoughts. She followed the road until Mrs. Banks grew worried and sent one of the stable boys to fetch her.

The large black belonging to the Marquis was tempermental and swift. Man and horse returned, both spattered with thick mud. Chatham left the black to be rubbed down by one of the stable lads and entered the house by the back door where he left his muddy boots. One of the new girls was ordered to fetch water to the Marquis' chamber and two of the men hauled the copper tub to the room.

He had just poured a sherry and lowered himself into the bath. The water was warm and soothing to his cramped muscles and he relaxed against the tub, allowing steamy heat to invade his body. Tension drained from him and the last thing he saw before he closed his eyes was the bathtub screen which assured his privacy.

He was wakened from his reverie by the sound of the bedroom door closing. He heard soft footsteps and a ferocious grunt. A pause ensued, as did the sound of clothing rustling against clothing and another grunt of disgust. A very muddied gown landed with a thud on the chair beside the tub. Justin raised his brows and grinned as he heard Alison speak in furious undertones. A stocking was added to the dress, then another stocking. A petticoat, another and another. This was becoming very interesting, Justin thought, keeping as still and quiet as a mouse. A chemise was carelessly tossed onto the pile. Justin's fingers tightened against the tub, but he bravely steeled himself not to make a sound.

Alison appeared around the screen, as bare as the day she was born. She moved to the commode and poured water from the pitcher into the small basin. Mud was spattered in her hair, on her face, her legs, and there was one little spot, on a trim and tantalizing buttock. Milord's gaze drank in the sight of her. There were many changes in her body. Her breasts were fuller and her waist not quite so narrow, but her hips were more womanly. Pride surged through him at the sight of her rounding belly. Her skin was as smooth and pink as he remembered. He couldn't help himself; his hand reached out and wiped the mud from her buttock. Alison spun around and a look of pure horror crossed her face. A hand raised to cover a breast, another lowered strategically. She gathered her wits and disappeared around the screen, out of his sight.

Justin laughed. "Where have you been? You've mud in the most peculiar places!" He chuckled again, more loudly this time.

An awkward, embarrassed silence answered him. Justin stood and wrapped a towel around his hips, and stepped out of the tub. He rounded the screen just in time to see Alison tie her wrap together. Her face was rosy with embarrassment. He grinned and dripped water all over the carpet as he advanced on her. His eyes probed the light covering for more of her and his hand reached for the tie to the robe. His grin faded quickly as his hand was smacked.

"I won't have you laughing at me, Justin. I already know how funny I must look."

His eyes widened. "Is that what you think? That you look funny to me?" he asked incredulously.

"Of course. I can see how round I am. I must look disgusting next to the other women you've known . . ."

"Be quiet!" he roared. "You are the damndest woman I've ever known. Come here."

His hand snaked around her wrist and tumbled her toward him, until they were nose to nose, chest to chest. Alison's courage faltered. Her gaze lowered and she bit her lip to stifle a gasp as his fingers went to her belt and slipped the gown from her shoulders.

"One little hand doesn't cover much, Alison." She heard the amusement in his voice and steeled herself to take more of his mockery. His hand slipped lower until the palm caressed the slight bulge of her abdomen. His lips went to her hair and he pulled her into the wide circle of his chest and other arm. "How could you think this would disgust me? For months I have wondered about the woman carrying my child. I longed to see, to touch all of you, yet you denied me that. You would still deny me that."

"I . . . I didn't realize . . ." The words were muffled against his chest.

His hands pressed to either side of her head and

tilted her face up to look at him. "I find you enchanting now, as I did months ago when we made this child."

"You hated me then."

"I have never hated you. I have been angry enough to murder you on occasion, but I have never hated you."

"But you want to lock me in a cellar . . ."

His hold tightened. "I do. I find the idea infinitely pleasurable . . . if I'm with you." His nostrils breathed in the scent of her hair and his hands moved to her buttocks, pressing her against his hard arousal. "How can you think I would find you disgusting, when I find you more beautiful than ever?" He shook his head as though her thinking was beyond his comprehension. His long fingers caressed teasingly below her breasts, threatening to move higher. Her breasts swelled and the nipples hardened in anticipation.

His face lowered, his mouth opening to taste of her lips when a slight movement fluttered in the abdomen pressed against him. The lean fingers stilled. His eyes met hers and he smiled. "He moves?"

Alison nodded. "She does, often."

He grinned broadly and lifted her in his arms and bore her to the bed. Her robe and his towel slipped to the floor. "So you want a girl?"

She loped her hands around his neck, loving the feel of his hair in her fingers, the strength of his neck. "I don't care which. I don't want you too adamant, though. You might be disappointed."

His body followed hers to the bed. He hunkered back on his heels to take a long look at her. When she flushed and lifted her hands to conceal some part of herself, his hands held hers still. "No, I want to see all of you," he spoke thickly.

Her embarrassment fled as she saw the eyes with which he studied her were not filled with mockery, but with something more akin to admiration. All she wanted was to be beautiful for him, and she was proud if he thought her so. Her breath caught as she realized the glint in his eyes was a well remembered desire. An answering heat spread through her body and loins. His eyes flickered to hers, the flame in them leaping brightly. "You're even more beautiful than you were," he whispered softly.

His hand reached out and the fingers gently stroked along the lines of her abdomen where the skin was drawn taut, to the navel and below. The fluttering came again and he smiled as he raised his eyes to hers. "I think he likes his home."

"She. And sometimes I think she wants her freedom."

His fingers were raising, stroking along her thickened waistline and to her breasts. "Your nipples are darker." The fingers circled the crests until they puckered for him. "I like the home you offer our child. Will you want more than one child?"

"Oh, yes," she spoke so low he barely heard her answer.

His mouth swooped over hers, his body lowering beside her. His tongue inserted itself hotly but his hands were infinitely gentle. His mouth moved to her nose, her eyes, her forehead. He kissed and caressed, teased and tantalized. His hands cupped and stroked. His thigh pressed against her and she felt the heat of his desire. Her hips rose and pressed in her own method of enticement.

Justin drew a deep breath and pulled away, his eyes dark as they watched her. Long, black lashes fluttered closed, her lips were swollen from his kisses and parted for more. "When you look as you do now, I want to bury myself in you and give you as much pleasure as I take. Does that sound like a man 'disgusted'?"

Alison was beyond thought. Her hands reached for his face and pulled him down to her. Their lips met and clung in a lengthy, loving caress. She wanted to remain as they were forever, sharing this warmth and tenderness. He tantalized her with his brandy taste and soapy smell. The arms embracing her were iron hard, yet oddly tender.

Taking a deep breath, Chatham summoned the strength to roll from her. It was now or never, he knew. Regret tore through him at the pain he heard from her barely stifled protest.

His voice came raspy to her ears. "Now, get in the tub before the water turns cold. Mrs. Banks will have dinner ready and we'll both still be naked." Alison winced at the words. She wanted more of him, so much more. Yet he had such control and she always seemed to make a fool of herself. As she turned from him, her legs quivered like jelly.

He was dressed and gone by the time she came around the privacy screen. Katey helped her into her dress and did her hair, declaring the blue voile to be the finest garment ever made in the village. The low neck was embellished with a fine, white lace, and stiffened at the shoulders to decorate Alison's slender neck. Velvet ribbons trimmed the ruching about the skirt and sleeves. Ribbons of the same material held her hair high on her head.

Alison peered at herself in the mirror, trying to see just what he would see. From the side there was a slight bulge, and from the front there was very little. Of her or the gown, she thought. Alison glanced down at the low cut of her bosom and wondered what her husband would think. Perhaps, this once, she should find out.

Chatham grinned as Alison entered the room. His eyes wandered over her appreciatively. "You must be clean, two baths in the same day. Are you sure you found all the mud? My offer to help still stands."

Smiling at his teasing, she shook her head.

Chatham clicked his tongue regretfully, holding up a bottle. "Sherry?"

"No, thank you."

"Mrs. Banks keeps apricot brandy somewhere. It's disgustingly sweet, but you'd probably like it."

"What I'd like most is dinner. I'm starved." As she took her seat, she allowed the lacy shawl she wore to fall gradually from her shoulders. Justin's eyes widened at the sight of the breasts threatening to spill over the confines of the gown. Alison was inwardly very thrilled with his reaction, outwardly she pretended not to notice and busied herself rearranging the shawl about her arms and waist. As they spoke, she fiddled with the shawl, allowing the lace to lay against one creamy mound until he noticed, and then she'd pretend to be chilled and tug it higher around her. Until the next time it gradually fell away.

She thought she must be learning the art of flirtation very well, judging from her husband's reaction. His eyes were right where they should be. The thought of the other women Justin had known was creeping to her mind too often for comfort and she determined to wear this gown much more frequently. At least it kept his thoughts where she considered they belonged.

Finally, setting his empty glass on the table, he sat beside his wife and took the ends of her shawl in his own hands. "If you really want dinner, love, then I suggest you leave off tempting me for the moment." As he spoke, he pulled the ends together and hid some of her bounty. His fingers went to her lace and stroked it lovingly.

Alison gave a contented sigh and rested her head on his shoulder. "All this time I thought I would be an abyssmal failure at flirting, but I'm not."

The warmth of his breath tickled her ear. "No, I would say you are an accomplished flirt."

"Good," her mouth quirked as she teased, "I must keep up with your reputation, my lord."

"Just as long as you remember to save all your flirtations for me, little hussy."

"All of them?" she spoke wistfully.

"Every one," he spoke firmly. "I did not think I would be a jealous husband until this moment. The thought of anyone else looking," his mouth lowered and he pressed a kiss on her creamy flesh, "tempts me to lock you away forever. I can personally tutor you in other vices you may desire, gambling, carousing until all hours. I'll even arrange an orgy . . . for two, in case you're ever bored."

"I hope Mrs. Banks knows what to serve at an orgy. I haven't the slightest idea."

His mouth nuzzled her ear. "Food again, love? The orgies I have in mind don't require refreshments. I was thinking more like . . ."

"Dinner is served, my lord."

Chatham rose to his feet, his eyes alight with amusement as he witnessed Alison's blushes. Mrs. Banks was much less embarrassed. "Thank you, Mrs. Banks. Alison?" He held out his arm and escorted her into the dining room.

Dinner was a full seven courses, and long before the last, Alison sighed, "I can't eat another bite."

"Until dessert," was the prompt reply.

Alison grinned and toyed with her glass as he finished his meal. "Tell me, Justin, what kind of cows do you raise?" Her chin was propped by the palms of her hands, her elbows rested on the table.

The fork paused in midair. He pushed his plate aside and set his utensils beside it, wiping at his mouth with a napkin. His expression was bland as he answered, "Holsteins and Herefords. Why?"

"Oh, Morgan and I were thinking of delving into the livestock business when you . . . you came along. I was learning much about livestock."

"Oh? Did you raise cattle?"

"We were thinking about it. Actually we had started our herd."

The devil in him had him inquiring, "What kind?"

The pause was lengthy before she answered. "Holstein."

"Oh? I suppose you had quite a few?"

Alison glanced at him sharply, wondering if it were possible he knew exactly how many she and Morgan had. No, he couldn't. "Oh, a few."

"How many is that, Alison?"

He was laughing openly now and she realized she was caught. "We had one Holstein. But we were just beginning in the business and concentrated our efforts on something smaller."

"How small?"

She sighed, wishing she had never started this conversation. "Chickens."

Chatham blinked in surprise. Henry never mentioned this. Perhaps it was two chickens. "You were raising a herd of chickens?"

Her eyes narrowed and her hands clenched into a fist. "You always laugh at me. Raising chickens is a perfectly honorable and serious occupation. If you don't stop laughing, I'm going to hit you!"

"I can't help it," he said between stifled bouts of laughter. "I can just see you cleaning the chicken coop—just as you did the stables when you were a baby. No wonder Morgan loved you so. You did all his work for him. What a grubby child you were, Alison."

"I remember you as a child, too," she answered feelingly. "No one ever laid a hand on me before you did. You hurt me!"

"I did not. You only pretended to get Morgan's sympathy. You shouldn't have gloated at me. Nothing ever gave me such satisfaction in my life as beating you did. You were a miserable, cocky brat. I should have known then I was mad for you." His eyes watched her thoughtfully. "Did you make any money on your livestock?"

"I really don't know. Morgan handled the accounts."

"From what I saw you lived comfortably, though not lavishly."

"I had some money."

"Geoffrey didn't think so. He said your allowance was usually gone the moment you received it and the

amount wouldn't have maintained you beyond frip-
peries anyway. It wasn't difficult to guess you'd resort
to pawning your mother's jewels."

Alison flushed guiltily. "So you and Geoffrey know
about that, do you? Was he very angry?"

"Very." Left unsaid was at whom Geoffrey was
angry. "I was relieved. It was through the jewels we
found you."

Her mouth gaped open. "How stupid of me!"

"Not stupid, not sensible either. I had the jewelers in
London watched. Morgan would have to go there to
fetch a decent price, even for jewelry as fine as yours."

"I'd still be free . . ." The moment the words were out
of her mouth, Alison realized she'd made another
mistake.

The silence which followed was lengthy. Milord
threw his napkin on the table and rose. His scowl made
Alison's stomach churn. "You were never free. You
were hiding from me because I'd find you if it took the
rest of our lives. That is not freedom."

Alison rose from the table, her fingers clutching the
napkin agitatedly. "I've done it again, haven't I? Just
when we seemed to be getting along, my cursed tongue
gets in the way. I am sorry. I do not mean to make you
angry, I can't seem to help myself."

"All your talk of escape and freedom. You make me
feel like a damned monster. Tell me, when have I ever
hurt you? When?"

"Never," she answered swiftly, but her gaze flickered
to the door.

"Stop being such a coward," he roared. "You
tremble and shake whenever I'm near . . ."

"No, only when you raise your voice. You are very

intimidating, my lord."

"You prefer a cellar to my bed . . ."

Alison blinked. "But you said . . . only this afternoon . . ." The words reminding him of this afternoon's intimacies would not come. Swallowing, she could only stammer uncertainly, "I never said that."

"You have been considering the choice for two days." He strode angrily to the door. "You may have your chaste bed, my dear faint heart. I do not want you so badly that I would force myself on you again. I have learned to regret that night as much as you have. If I had *escaped* then, I would be a *free* man now!"

Alison's face went white. Shaking her head, she could only repeat herself, "I am sorry."

"And I am weary of your apologies!"

For the third consecutive night, Chatham was closeted with only his brandy for company. Alison's footfalls could be heard ascending the stairs as he downed another brandy. His anger began to dissipate. He cursed her damned tongue, and his, too. She angered him. He hurt her. As if there were a devil within him, he said those horrible things and watched as she flinched with each word.

This would be another long night. He'd have to wait until she was asleep, then he'd sneak into his own bedroom and disrobe in the dark.

Damn! he felt little better than an outsider in his own home. He filled his glass and set the decanter of brandy down with a thud. Her shawl lay on the sofa and he was reminded of the way she looked in that blue gown tonight, the low decolletage she filled so womanly and the high sweep of her hair. His fingers touched the garment softly, much as he did when she filled it.

305

Earlier they'd been laughing, and she'd not fought him then. In fact she'd welcomed the touch of his hands. She'd been willing, very willing . . .

Chatham loosened his cravat as he mounted the stairs.

The room was in darkness except for the soft glow of the last lingering embers of the fireplace. Chatham bumped into a chair and cursed softly. He moved toward the bed and stubbed his toe on the bedpost. His curse came louder.

"I'll light a candle," Alison offered, scrambling from the bed and scurrying to the fireplace. A candle stood on the mantel and this she dipped into the fire to light. She straightened and turned, holding the taper high.

Her limbs were bare to his view, the gown shadowy in the soft glimmer of the fire. Her skin seemed to glow with the embers. He unbuttoned his shirt, shrugged it from his shoulders and tossed it onto the nearest chair. His eyes met and held hers. Alison was fleetingly tempted to run, but the memory of his touch this afternoon haunted her still. He wanted her then, just as much as she wanted him. The knowledge gave her courage. She squared her shoulders and faced him unflinchingly.

For her patience, she was rewarded with softly spoken words, words made all the more emphatic because of their very softness. "I was angry with you for kidnapping me, for humiliating me at the inn, and for the marriage." His fingers went to the waistband of his breeches and began unbuttoning. "I concede the marriage was not your fault, if anyone was at fault, 'twas me. What you don't know is that I welcomed the marriage. For months the taste of you lingered with me.

306

The night Morgan came to me in London elated me. I had you in my grasp at last. Yes, I admit 'twas all my doing which brought about the wedding. You had little to do with it." He tugged the breeches low, revealing the line of muscle encompassing his chest and abdomen. A sprinkling of black hair covered him, darkening where it disappeared into the breeches.

"And my humiliation at the inn was probably well deserved. I was not gentle with you that night, a fact which has haunted me since."

The dark head reared back and his eyes were hot on her. "My kidnapping? *You* must explain that to me. However, I know now it was not for ransom nor blackmail.

"For the ugly words I spoke to you in your brother's home, I owe you an apology. No," he raised a hand, "don't interrupt. I will apologize. 'Tis not an act which sits lightly on my soul and I doubt that I have apologized more than twice before in my life, but I will apologize to you now for the horrible things I said that day. And I thank you for not punishing me as you were tempted, by ridding both of us of the child." His voice lowered. "For that, I cannot thank you enough."

"I don't want your thanks—" she began, her face flushing brilliantly.

"I know you don't want my thanks. You've wanted little enough from me. To continue, I do not apologize for beating Morgan. He made his wounds seem worse than they were." Chatham sat on the chair and pulled his boots and stockings from his feet. As he stood, he continued, "And that horrible marriage ceremony cannot be regretted sufficiently enough. But, I remind you once again, it is legally binding."

307

His fingers tugged the breeches lower, until they fell from him and he kicked them aside. He stood before her bare and arrogant, openly aroused. At her shocked expression, he grimaced, wondering if she found him repellent and grabbed the first thing he found to wrap around his mid-section. Her robe barely fit, but it gave him a semblance of modesty. As she relaxed and her brow unfurrowed, he continued, "You have made me angrier than any woman ever has. You have humiliated me, made me laugh, made me swell with pride. For those many months I could not find you, every time I looked at another woman it was to seek you. When you were not the woman, I forgot her."

Black eyes watched Alison intently. "Tonight we argued again. I thought to remain downstairs until you were asleep. That way I could avoid you and keep my pride. But Alison, I must have enough pride for the whole village already. I do not need more. I cannot go on this way, being married to you, yet not married to you. I understand your wariness, your thoughts of freedom and escape. I hurt you badly when I took you that first time, but I can be gentle, too. You did not find my touch so distasteful today, did you? You were so sweet, calling my name, begging me not to stop."

Alison hung her head. "I behaved quite shamelessly, my lord. I think you should know, I have foresworn sins of the flesh."

"What?"

Alison sighed, knowing she would have to explain herself, yet not quite knowing how. "You didn't hurt me. In fact . . . in fact, I enjoyed what . . . you did . . . to me."

"Thank you." A familiar half smile played around his mouth.

"No, you don't understand." Her head was shaking vehemently. "My father was a good, God-fearing man."

"He was a vicar, Alison. He was God loving as much as he was God fearing."

"He would be so disappointed in me if he knew what I just told you. We weren't married, we barely knew each other, and yet . . . yet look what I let you do! Don't you understand? I must be punished! I committed a most grievous sin of the flesh."

Chatham stood halfway across the room, very nearly naked, a fist on one hip. He was very tempted to say, "but you make such an enchanting sinner." One look at her face told him how inappropriate the comment would be and he wisely bit his lip. Of course she would think it sinful, when he was still a child, so did he. Crossing the room, he took the taper from her fingers, blew it out and set it on the mantel. His breath fanned her hair as he pulled her into his arms. "The sin was mine, Alison. I forced you."

"I shouldn't have enjoyed it."

"Maybe you shouldn't have," laughter rumbled from his chest, "or not quite so much."

The stiffness went from her shoulders and she slumped in his arms. "I think I'm an incurable sinner."

"I hope so. The thought of committing sin after sin after sin with you leaves me breathless. Of course, to sin quite so badly we'll have to forget we're married. I'm willing, if you are."

"Don't mock me, Justin."

Immediately sobering, he said, "The most grievous sin we could commit now is to not fulfill our marriage vows."

As he swung her into his arms, Alison sighed and relaxed her head against his chest. "Justin, I don't think I could bear it if you regretted this in the morning. But in every article I read on Fleet marriages, once consummated, they were legal. Unless coercion was involved, of course."

"Hush, I've been trying to tell you for days how legally bound we are." The robe fell from his hips as his body melted like liquid fire with hers to the bed. His lips tasted of hers, his tongue teasing until she was shivery with desire, aching with a need to have more of him. He groaned with pleasure at the wildness of her response, his fingers cupping her breasts through the sheerness of the gown. His mouth lowered, nuzzling at the fabric to reach her bare skin. Fingers worked at the buttons of her gown, tearing the fine material in his eagerness, until the fabric spread for him and the nipples of her creamy breasts stood impudent and tempting, aching for the moist caress of his tongue.

Wearing a self-satisfied smirk on his face, he tore the gown to her toes. His brilliant black eyes roamed hungrily over her as though she were a feast and he had to decide where to begin tasting. A groan of pleasure came from him as he lifted himself over her and lowered until his chest barely touched her aroused, aching nipples. The black hairs whisked against her, up and down. Her breath came shivery, her hands glided over him to pull him nearer to her. His movements didn't cease until the passion filled her breasts, making them heavy and molten with need for his touch.

Her body heaved against him, and he lost all control. Groaning her name and muttering endearments, he crushed her to him, his arms and legs twining with the silken softness of hers. The effect was a heady jolt of passion. His mouth groped and found hers, the intimacy of the kiss deepening as he feverishly tried to absorb all of her into him.

His need burned into her. Alison wanted to learn more of this tactile heat and lowered a hand to him. He groaned with pained delight and wrapped his hand around hers to still any movements. His voice was rough and raspy as words were breathed into her ear, "Oh, sweet, I want you so badly, I hurt. But I want to be gentle, I promised you I would be gentle. If I lose control I'm not sure I can keep that promise."

"Please, Justin . . ."

"I know, sweetheart, you hurt, too. Does this help?" With sure and experienced movements, his fingers found her and stroked lovingly. "Do you like this, . . . and this?"

Alison tried desperately to answer but all she could form was a hungry groan. Her head reared against the pillow, the blond strands flying about her mouth and neck. His mouth suckled at her nipples until she thought she would die with wanting him.

And then he rose over her, his heat separating her thighs and slipping inside slowly, until she whimpered for more of him. He kept tight rein on the urge to thrust into her, riding her gently, taking great care for her softer flesh. Words of love poured from him, mingling with hers. Alison urged him deeper, accepting what he gave and stroking him with her moistness, wanting to give him the utmost in pleasure.

The muscles on his back and neck bunched beneath her caressing hands with the effort to restrain his wild hunger. The tempo of his thrusts increased to match hers. It was becoming more difficult by the moment to restrain from driving into her and taking satisfaction. And then her body heaved in his arms, her need exploding and he lost control, losing himself in the vortex of smoldering hunger and sensation which left them weak and panting.

Much later, Alison lay cradled in his arms and Justin lifted her fingers to his lips. "Had I known what awaited me, I would have apologized long ago."

"I owe you an apology, too."

"Later. I haven't the strength to fully appreciate it right now."

"I should not have run away. I especially apologize for Morgan hitting you on the head. Did it hurt badly?"

"What hurt badly was losing you again. I was livid for weeks afterward."

"I promise to reform."

Chatham chuckled at her words. "The reformed wife of the rake?"

"If you like," his wife said, smiling sleepily. "This is so much better than arguing."

"It is, isn't it?"

"We should do it every night."

"And every morning."

"Are you laughing at me again?"

"Yes, you make me laugh. Do you mind?"

"No. I don't think you ever laughed at any of those other women. Did . . . did you make love like that to them, too?"

"Oh, Alison," he groaned, rolling over to press a kiss against her temple, "I have never found such sweet pleasure with anyone else."

Her fingers tightened. "Thank you."

"Did I hurt you? I wanted to be gentle, but I was so hungry for you."

"Stop worrying about hurting me. I'm not made of china."

"No, you're made of soft, sweet skin and I don't want to bruise it." His lips touched her shoulders.

"You won't," Alison assured him, yawning, her eyes fluttering closed. She nuzzled against his neck and slept.

The morning sun barely peeped over the horizon and yet Chatham could have sworn he felt warm, sweet lips against his mouth. He opened one eye and peered at the curly head which now rested on his chest. Alison lifted her face and smiled at him and, being the brazen hussy she was, pressed several tiny kisses on the broad area.

Her husband smiled and a yawn overtook him. He stretched like a huge, comfortable cat. In a quick movement, he rolled onto his side and brought Alison's breasts against him. He grinned wickedly. "Early morning kisses? Don't stop now."

"I won't. But I was wondering, do you like this?" Her teeth nibbled on his chest. "And this?" Her lips licked at his nipples and her hand lowered. "And how about this?"

A rough, raspy voice groaned and pulled her beneath him. "Oh, yes. I like it all."

*   *   *

313

It was noon before they rose, and then only because my lord claimed his overworked libido demanded nourishment.

"You should blush, you hussy," he teased over breakfast, as Alison offered him nourishment for the fourth time. She burst out in laughter and he clasped her hand, teasing, "A vicar's daughter to boot. I'm shocked!"

Alison lowered her eyes. "You didn't fight me off."

"So demure you are, so sweet, so angelic. And such a devil in my bed."

"No more cellars for me?"

"I didn't say that. I'm a man of many peccadillos. I think a few nights in the cellar, with me and the brandy, would be great fun."

"No regrets this morning?"

"One. I didn't shut you up and attack you months ago."

"I have a confession to make. When we were living in the cottage I wished you had done just that. And I wondered about Geoffrey and Jon, and . . ."

"Me?" he queried hopefully.

She smiled. "Yes, you most of all. I wondered if you were still lying beneath that window and I hoped you weren't hurt too badly. I never meant you any harm."

"I know that now, Alison. But when you first kidnapped me, how could I have known? I was angry, I was out for vengeance. In London, with Morgan, I was still angry. I took my time answering your letters because of my perverted anger. I did not realize you were worrying about a baby, or I would never have tolerated your being so frightened." His fingers tightened their grasp. "And when Morgan told me you ran away, I was so ashamed of myself."

"I wasn't thinking. Believe me, I could never have done such a thing!"

"Alison . . ."

Whatever he was about to say was lost in the confusion of the next moments.

Chatham frowned at the distraction, wiped the corners of his mouth and tossed the napkin on his plate. Alison followed him into the hall. Immediately after the door was opened, a rough voice sounded.

"Where is she, you cur?"

"Morgan," Alison cried, appearing around the Marquis and tumbling into the old man's arms. "It's so good to see you!"

Morgan clasped her to him as though he feared for her life. Holding her before him, he scrutinized her carefully and found her smiling. She looked to be fine, but Morgan had felt the roughness of her captors, too. "Ar' ye alright, child? I came as soon as I could." His eyes lit on the Marquis, his bushy brows snapped together and his mouth frowned. "Jest stan' behin' me, girl. I'll take care of this'un." His fists bore upward threateningly. "Ye rogue! I'll murder ye if'n ye've 'urt 'er!"

"No, Morgan, I made a tremendous mistake. I should never have run away. But I panicked and ran and . . . and I'm such a coward!"

"Did ye forget the Fleet weddin'? I ain't. Get yer 'ands off'n 'er, ye demmed cur. As far as I'm concerned, ye ain't married!"

Chatham removed his wife from Morgan's clasp and held her to his side. "I admit the preacher was a poor choice, one I've learned to regret. However, it's done. I assure you we are legally married and will remain so. You are welcome to remain with your mistress, Mr. Hull. I know how she regards you. However, I do not see you in the same light. Around me you will guard your tongue . . . and your fists. We have no reason to like each other and I could very easily boot you from here, but I'm willing to tolerate your irritating presence for her sake. And provided you learn to be less irritating, of course."

Morgan scrutinized this arch enemy carefully. Apparently matters had undergone a change during the past two days. Still, it might be best if he were to remain here, for a little while at least. He lowered his fists. "I don't ken why the two of ye could'na tried to get along in London," he grumbled. "It would'a saved me a lot of trubble."

"If you had not chased after her . . ." Chatham began hotly. "Never mind. We will forget the past and begin anew. But watch your tongue, Mister Hull."

Morgan cleared his throat. "I ken wot ye were plannin' to say and I want ye to know I agree wit ye. I should'a stayed out of it. She demmed near killed 'erself climbing from 'at window!"

"So I saw," Chatham retorted drily. "Here, if you must vent your spleen, do it in the privacy of my den. I don't need anymore stories about me or my wife traveling across the country. We've enough to live down. I'm trying to lead a spotless life now that I have additional responsibilities, but my biggest responsibility makes that difficult, if not impossible. I think we both need a drink, Mister Hull."

"By Gawd, so do I! I've traveled 'ard this day and I'm dry as dust."

Chatham poured generous measures of brew. "I didn't expect you for another two days at the soonest. You surprise me."

Morgan smiled and hefted the glass in toast. "The snow 'eld me up or I'd 'ave been 'ere early this morn. Ye're not the only one with cunnin'. I ken ye 'ad this place when we went to London to fine ye. I made it me business to find out all I could about ye." Morgan drank deeply. "I thank the good Lord this business is settled."

"Good. The handling of my wife is best left to me."

"Gladly. She's young and full of juice. She's a good girl, but when she gets a certain glint in 'er eye, it means trubble . . ." The old man shivered as he gulped.

Chatham's eyes gleamed. He had experienced a few of those glints, himself. Just this morning.

". . . she rides like a boy, sometimes dresses like'un. That 'as fine when she was younger, but now that she's full growed . . . Well, ye can see the trubble she's landed us in!"

Alison listened to Morgan's speech with something akin to pain and shock on her features.

"I ken ye meant well, Ally, but we've not been doin' too well at all. We were runnin' out of money for one thing, and I couldn'a stand anymore of yer tears, or that Thomas' language. My Gawd, a body would think 'e didn'a speak the same tongue." Morgan drained another glass. "And then ye went and got yerself with babe. Wot was I gonna do with a babe? No, 'e did it to ye and 'tis 'e must 'andle it. Yer where ye belong. 'is lordship 'ere, 'e's a younger mon. Now, if ye need any help with the child, when she's older . . ."

"Thank you, but no." Chatham responded curtly.

"You may word for us, Mister Hull, I give full permission for that. I draw the line at allowing my child too near you. You belong in the stables and if we have a daughter, she'll stay in the house, where she belongs, and learn to behave as a female. I'll not have her cleaning out barns with the likes of you!"

Morgan grinned. "Ah, Ally was always overly fond of me company, but I unnerstand wot yer sayin'. Of course, I'd not trade my Ally fer ennyone, I'll do wotever she wants. Yer child 'ill not find a better friend, that I promise. 'owever, since ye'd not unnerstand me feelings about me girl, I'll let the matter lie. If ye've a job fer me, I'd appreciate it. I'd like to be around Ally as long as she wants me to be."

"Oh, Morgan, I'll always want you around me." Alison tucked the old man's hand in her own and smiled at him.

A spurt of jealousy flared within the Marquis, to die instantly. She earned this old man's love, he'd seen that when he was just a boy and watched the old servant hover over her like an angry bird. He refilled the glasses while Alison went to order a meal for the hungry traveler. She watched as he ate and asked questions about the boy, Thomas. "Ach," grunted Morgan, "'e went off in the opposite direction I took when we separated to search fer ye. 'e's un who'll 'ave to learn the 'ard way. A bit of thought would'a saved him a lot of trubble."

"I do hope he's not lost."

"Serve 'im right if 'e was. 'e might as well learn now as well as when 'e older."

Chatham wondered wearily if he would have to find a place for this Thomas as well. He supposed so.

318

Chatham left his wife and Morgan in the den arguing over the boy. When he returned, they were arguing over a card game. Bowing to the inevitable, he joined them.

"With Mrs. Banks we would have four for whist," Alison said eagerly. "I'll pit my skill against yours, my lord."

He grinned. "You do a lot of gambling and wagering for someone who's pawned her jewelry."

They were on the fourth set when another carriage arrived. Chatham shook his head but did not interrupt his deal. "All this tramping about in the mud. It's incomprehensible."

Mrs. Banks calmly informed them of the arrival of one Jonathan Asher, and "another person, rather sorry looking, my lord, who goes by the name of Thomas."

Justin turned to his wife and inquired drily, "What now, a game of canasta?"

Jon heard the mocking words as he strode into the room. "Don't be a dolt. I didn't come all this way and in these miserable conditions to play cards."

"I thought you kidnapped me to learn my secrets. If not, then please enlighten us as to why you are here."

"Yes, Jon, what are you doing here?"

Jon glared accusingly at his sister as he tossed his wet tricorne on an empty chair. He peeled off his wet gloves and dropped those as carelessly. "The trouble you have caused me, Alison. I can't tell you how I regret that damned kidnapping. Geoffrey's been on my tail for months now, thinking I'd had an inkling where you might be hiding. I tried to tell him the only thing I was stupid enough to do was get involved with you in that damned abduction. And I swore then, never again."

"Well, you were looking for a way to get Justin out of London."

"And you came up with one. The abduction was all your idea. Be honest once in your life and admit it. Was it or was it not your idea?"

Alison bit her lip "It was my idea."

Jon nodded his satisfaction. "Do you always have to cause such havoc in my life? Can you imagine trying to live a normal life while your older brother and guardian is breathing down your neck? And it's all your fault. I tried to tell him you could take care of yourself, better than anyone I know, but would he believe me? Not on your life."

Alison felt compassion stirring within her for her ill-used brother. Morgan could only stand and gape at him. Chatham said drily, "Appalling."

Jon turned to him and casually saluted. "Exactly. I couldn't do a thing for the monkeys he had tailing me around. I told him I didn't know where you were." Jon's nostrils flared and his mouth screwed into a painful grimace. "He kept repeating some of the most ridiculous things, like 'poor, innocent Alison' or 'the unwary child.' I swear it made me ill each time he spoke of you."

Alison clucked sympathetically.

Jon's eyes narrowed. "Ever since we were children you've gotten me into trouble, you've coerced me into doing exactly what you wanted me to do and this is the worst of the lot. It might have been my idea to help Geoffrey, but you came up with the kidnapping. And what a mess you made of it! Now, you leave me no choice. If I ever want Geoffrey to leave me alone, I've got to get you out of this mess."

"What mess? I'm not in trouble . . ."

"As long as you're with him," his thumb jerked toward the Marquis, "there's trouble for me." His gaze turned to his new brother-in-law and sized him up. Clearly, Jon didn't like what he saw. He stood, legs apart, thumbs hooked in his pockets and shook his head regretfully. "It seems there's only one thing to do now. Make you a widow."

Alison gasped. Morgan groaned. Thomas walked in at that moment and said blithely, "Gor!" The Marquis bit his lip and quietly said, "Do I take that as a challenge?"

"I wish you would! I'd feel ridiculous slapping you across the face with my wet gloves."

"I wouldn't take kindly to that myself."

"Jon, this is ridiculous. I won't have you challenging my husband simply because your nose is out of joint."

"And that's another thing," Jon rounded on her, his expression incredulous. "He's your husband. After all your fine talk about retribution and justice, about how he killed our parents, you married him? You married the blackguard?"

Alison gasped and clutched a fist to her mouth. "I did say that, didn't I? Oh," she turned to find Chatham's eyes blacker and angrier than ever on her. "I've done it again, haven't I? I'm so sorry! That was before I knew you . . ."

"If ye think to fight a duel, think agin, Master Jon," Morgan roared. "All this 'appened because of the last 'un."

"By last one, if you mean duel, may I remind you it never took place?" Jon queried nastily. "We kidnapped him to make sure it wouldn't."

321

"Well, wot d'ye want us to do now?" Morgan snarled. "Kidnap ye to stop this foolishness? Mayhaps we can lock ye in the cellar until ye cum to your senses."

Alison warily watched her husband. Summoning her courage she thought she could prove her husband's innocence on at least one score. "You were wrong, Jon. There was never going to be a duel. We kidnapped him for nothing. That was all your doing, brother. You and your tendency to gossip."

"What do you mean?" Jon bellowed loudly. "I heard him and Geoffrey arguing! They nearly popped each other's corks then and there."

"Do you mean to say you heard the argument I had with Geoffrey? And that was the reason you . . . all of you, kidnapped me? That and my propensity toward murder?" The last words were hurled at Alison's head.

For the first time since Jon's arrival silence prevailed.

Justin's angry glare went first to Morgan, who was supposed to be the older, wiser of the lot. His black eyes moved on to Jon who flushed guiltily. Thomas' jaw nearly reached to his belly button. Alison bit her lip, all anger and defiance gone from her stance. She lowered her eyes. "Father always said gossiping was the worst of all the mortal sins. I believe him."

"There seem to be many defects to your character, Alison." Geoffrey stood, multicaped and windblown in the doorway. "First, lust and now gossip." He shook his head sadly. "What would Father say if he were here?"

Alison was far too distressed to note the teasing note behind the words. She was only conscious of the hard, mocking expression which was on her husband's face.

Geoffrey entered the room and began peeling off his

322

gloves. "It seems I've joined quite a crowd." His eyes moved about the room, settling a bit longer on Thomas than the others. Jon mumbled something about the boy at an inn where he was asking unintelligible questions about Alison. It seemed safer to take the brat with him than to leave him loitering about the countryside, spreading conjecture about his sister. Geoffrey made no answer to that. His gaze moved onto Morgan. "At least you took care of her. Had I gotten my hands on you, I would have throttled you."

"Of course I took care of 'er! Ain't I always?"

"That's debatable." His gaze swept to Alison. She stood in the center of the room, confused and afraid. His anger relented. "My words were meant as a jest, Alison," he said softly. "You're only human and have as many faults as any of us."

Jon snorted unsympathetically and moved to pour himself a drink. He was sipping from the glass when he took in his first full view of his sister. He lowered the glass and his eyes grew wide. Snickering, he said, "Alison, you're getting fat!"

Jon regretted the words immediately. He hadn't been treated to his sister's tears often, but when he was, he felt far worse than she did. Moisture shimmered in her eyes and she backed to the door. Jon set the glass down and moved toward her. "I didn't mean that, Ally."

With so many eyes gawking at her she felt like a freak. Her troubled gaze wandered over each person, but whatever words she wanted to say seemed to choke her. Turning before she disgraced herself, she ran from the room.

Geoffrey made a move to follow her, but Chatham's

hand on his arm stopped him. "I'll go to her. You'd be better off teaching your little brother the facts of life."

"She needs me."

"No, she needs me. She was perfectly content until all her relatives began showing up."

"'at's right, melord," Morgan offered cheerily. "She was perfectly 'appy until Jon challenged the Marquis to a duel."

"That's right! Of all the lame brain . . ." Chatham turned an incredulous gaze on Wilton. "Do you know why these rogues kidnapped me?" he demanded of Geoffrey. "Because they wanted to stop us dueling over Eileen. They thought to disgrace me and humiliate you, but in their eyes it was better than either of us ending up dead."

"What?" Geoffrey glared at his brother and servant. "What do you think I am that I can't even fight my own battles? If I wanted to duel Justin, two dozen kidnappings would not have prevented me doing so. I can't believe my own family interfering like that . . ."

Chatham did not wait to hear the rest of the tirade. He met Mrs. Banks in the hall as he was about to slip up the stairs to his wife. "Fix something for our guests to eat, will you, Mrs. Banks? And put something extra on that tray for the child. He looks as though he hasn't eaten in months."

Alison was sitting on the edge of the bed, wiping remnants of tears from her eyes when Justin entered. Awkwardly she jumped from the bed and moved to stand beside it. She could not meet his eyes. "Once again I must apologize. I not only listened to gossip, but I spread it also."

She peeped up at him quickly, but his expression was

324

forboding. "Your . . . your reputation was such that we thought Geoffrey might be killed. We . . . I couldn't think of anything else to do but kidnap you . . . and it didn't seem so awful at the time. I just wanted to keep you out of the way."

He was steadily advancing on her and she as steadily stepped away from him. "About the other . . ."

"Of course, you couldn't have kidnapped Geoffrey. He might have recognized you."

"Please don't mock me, my lord. I am very ashamed of myself."

"You ought to be. That is the most harebrained scheme I've ever heard of. I suppose it would take you, Morgan and Jon to think of it. Do you really understand how dangerous it was?"

"Yes, I do understand now. My lord . . . about what Jon said . . ."

"Ah, yes, my murderous inclinations. Aren't you afraid I'm tempted to murder you right now?"

Her back came up against the wall and she stopped, summoning the courage to lift her eyes to him. His fingers went to her throat and stroked lightly. His touch was not that of a murderer but a lover. Incurable honesty came to the fore. "I think you are tempted to do me bodily harm and I cannot blame you. But you won't hurt me. You've been angry with me before and I was not harmed. To accuse you of murder when I knew little of the facts was a horrible thing to do."

"It was."

"Oh, please, Justin," she loped her arms around his neck and pulled him closer. Her eyes filled with tears and begged him earnestly. "If you'll forgive me this one more time, I promise to make it up to you. I know you didn't have anything to do with my parents' deaths, you couldn't have. And if I'd known you better then, I would have been sure long ago."

"You were a horrible little brat and hated me then."

"No, I was jealous. When you were around, Geoffrey forgot he had a little sister. I just wanted some attention."

"Charming way you went about getting some. Running off with my clothing, hiding my shoes, threatening to tell your parents about the sleigh . . ." Pain clouded his face at the remembrance of what was to have been a happily glorious day that ended in so much tragedy.

Her fingers stroked the side of his face and she reached on her toes to press a kiss against him. "'Twas an accident, better forgotten."

"It was no accident, Alison. Geoffrey and I built a good sleigh under Morgan's tutelage. Nothing escaped his notice, especially not a weakness in the yoke. I was accused and convicted by that damned Squire. In one fell swoop I lost the closest family and friends I ever had. I spent years learning to handle my hurt and bitterness. And now, to think you thought of me as a murderer all this time . . ."

Alison rained kisses all over his face and neck in an effort to wipe out the pain she caused. "Forgive me, forgive me. I was so wrong and I love you so much. Let me make up for the false accusation, my love." Suddenly the kisses stopped, her words ceased. Lowering herself to the soles of her feet, she stared thoughtfully at him, musing aloud, "If it wasn't an accident, then it was on purpose. Who could have done such a monstrous thing?"

"That's what I've wondered for years. But if you recall I was banished from any proximity with your family. Until a few months ago, I had only seen Geoffrey from a great distance. I thought to put the lot of you from my life. And then I was kidnapped . . ."

"And I was ravished . . ."

"I thought only of murdering you, until I saw you bare. You were too much of a temptation to let slip through my fingers. And then I did the most foolish thing, I learned to love you."

At the softly spoken words, Alison smiled enchantingly. "You love me?"

"Yes, I love you. And if you ever so much as consider anything like that doltish scheme again, I will beat you within an inch of your life."

Throwing her arms about him, she buried her face in his neck, turning to meet the sweet moistness of his lips. "No more schemes, I promise," she whispered when she reached for air. Her fingers tugged at the buttons of his shirt and where she freed his chest, she pressed moist kisses. "Geoffrey and Jon will wonder where we've got to . . ."

"You're suffering a decline," he replied swiftly, lifting her into his arms and carrying her to the bed. "And I, as a dutiful husband, am assisting you in recovering."

Alison had to giggle. "A very dutiful husband, my lord."

"I've been wondering how to get you alone since Morgan knocked on our door this afternoon." The gown fell from her shoulders and waist, his fingers following behind, cupping soft skin and teasing lightly. "It's been sheer torture watching you move. All I could think was how you looked and felt beneath that gown. How I was aching to have more of you."

Her lips parted for his tongue. He moved slowly within her, caressed by the silken sweetness of her mouth. Her thighs parted and cradled his body intimately. He moaned his pleasure, his tongue thrusting hotly into her, his fingers searching out her secret places. He was breathing heavily as his mouth lowered and closed over the taut nipple. Alison whimpered with pleasure as his mouth took the other one and tantalized.

"I'm so glad you have a lustful nature, my lord," she breathed wickedly into his ear.

"Ah, yes, a nature to match your own."

The ache within her loins spread rapidly. Her fingers went to his breeches and began to tug on them urgently. "Love me, Justin, please. Forgive me my wicked gossip."

"Forgiveness must be earned, my love," he rasped hoarsely as he kicked the breeches free.

Her hands caressed the sculptured muscles lining his back and waist, lowering to his buttocks and kneading gently. "Gladly. How?"

Never had she witnessed such a devilish smile as the one which crossed his features. With a lithe movement, he was the one lying on his back and she was astride him, her eyes wide and brilliant at the swiftness of his move. His iron-hard arousal pressed between her thighs, riding her moistness. "How's that for a hint?" His voice was rough and breathless, his eyes and hands predatory.

With the ages old assurance of a woman greatly desired, Alison smiled meaningfully as she slowly rotated her hips. "I'm not sure I understand what you mean, my lord. Do you want this . . . or this?"

His raspy voice gasped her name and his hands brought her face low, next to his, for a lengthy kiss. His hands moved to her hips, carrying her high until his arousal met her tempting places. "This is what I want, love," he groaned, his hand urging her lower. She lowered just a bit, teasing him with the heat of her and the heavy thrust of her breasts, lifting herself when he barely touched. He was panting for the inner depth of her and she was exhilarated by his primitive need. Barely touching, she teased him unmercifully, letting his mouth suckle whenever he could reach her fleeting nipples. Fiercely he muttered a groan and brought her hips over his. Her body jolted with the fiery impact of his strength and she arched, enveloping him within her fully, taking his hardness greedily and coaxing him for more.

Like a goddess, she raised over him, her form astride his hips and proud of her shape and texture. His fingers closed over her aching breasts, molding, kneading, gleaning from her a shuddering response he could feel deep within. She took a deep breath and her hips began to move in an undulating rhythm as old as mankind. Her eyes glazed over as the sweet heated pleasure ran through her veins, flooding her with naked passion.

His hands guided her rhythm, lowering from her breasts to her ribcage, to her hips. Like a master he timed her strokes, allowing her hips to raise until her moisture caressed all of him, then lowering her hips until they encompassed his iron hardness fully. Her mouth opened and a soundless gasp of pleasure escaped at each forceful thrust. She couldn't get enough of him. His finger lightly rubbed against her bud of womanhood and the cry escaped. Deep within her once more, he felt her wetness flowing and his finger played and tantalized until he captured her shudders with his hands and pulled her down, against him, so he could share in her torrent of sensation.

When she quieted, when she lay still and breathless against him, he rolled her over and took his own sweet pleasure within her taut, sweetly caressing body.

And when they were done, Alison curled against his side and slept. And Justin, like the dutiful husband he was, he soothed her declining nature and slept alongside her.

Chapter Thirteen

The chaise rolled through the cobbled streets of London, the wheels echoing rhythmically. The Earl's head relaxed against the leather seat, his eyes were closed and his long limbs stretched before him. Familiar, chanting noises of late afternoon London and its peddlars intruded and he wakened gradually. He raised himself and lifted a hand to the curtain, sliding it aside so he could see for himself the distance they had yet to travel. He was very nearly to his destination, his London townhouse.

He spent three days at Chatham's hunting lodge. He hadn't laughed so much since he was a boy. Finally he had the time to come to know his brother and sister. Jon had grown up, almost. Perhaps the time had come to consider a commission for him. He was certainly eager to do his country's bidding.

And Alison was blooming with health and happiness. She still had a good bit of the devil in her. Geoffrey could understand why Jon was so impatient where she was concerned. Sibling rivalry, now that was something he remembered from childhood. Her husband would have his hands full and the Earl chuckled to admit how Justin deserved every moment.

The first night they stayed up late talking. Jon never did get it through his thick head the reason Alison was growing fat. But when she and Justin returned to the study she was rested and glowing with confidence. Nothing Jon said worried her. She laughed him off with an "oh, pooh, Jon!" which infuriated her younger brother all the more.

Another snowstorm hit the second day and the afternoon was filled with snowball fights, sledding and cocoa. That night they played cards. At first the games were sedate and dignified. Then Thomas wormed his way in, Morgan joined them and the next thing he knew, they were on the floor playing spoons. The quicker and nastier a person was, the better his chances of winning. Thomas won, Jon came in second. He and Chatham had not stood a chance. Alison informed them they were sadly out of practice.

A bittersweet memory of his mother and stepfather was rekindled. As children, they'd had evenings like these often. Until now, he hadn't realized how much he missed them.

And the last night, Jon played the pianoforte. In most families the pianoforte would be played by the females, but not in his. Alison was all thumbs. Jon was a tolerable musician but his real advantage was his extensive repertoire of songs. All learned from fellow students at Oxford, and few of them fit for decent folk's ears. They all joined in the singing.

Morgan hovered in the background, as usual, his protective instincts sharp when it came to his Alison.

Geoffrey laughed aloud as he recalled Justin's handling of the old man. The Marquis had taken so much in good stride: unwelcome guests, snow and cold, childish games far into the night. His limit was reached when Morgan thought to interfere with his wife though. The old man was shocked to find them sharing a bedroom and lost no time informing Alison so. Milord Marquis erupted at that and Morgan knew to keep his mouth shut, forevermore.

The snow melted too quickly. Thomas and Morgan were sent back to the cottage for Alison's things and Jon returned to school. Geoffrey thought he took the hint rather well, and was gone by the next morning, too.

But gone to where? Back to Eileen and the emptiness of his life. The time to return to duty could not come quickly enough.

He'd been considering divorce. But that meant petitioning Parliament and reading sarcastic cartoons of himself and his wife in the *Times*. Why bother? After this marriage, Geoffrey could never bear to marry again.

Separate residences would have to do. At least that way he would never have to see her again.

The briskness of the late afternoon bit into his skin as he alighted from the chaise. A curricle he recognized as belonging to Dr. Pares stood in the road. One of the servants must be ill, he decided.

Even more curious was the aura of quiet about the house as he entered. No footman ran out to open the carriage door, no Willis stood in the entry in mute welcome. Geoffrey closed the door behind him and tossed his cape onto a chair. He wanted a drink. He saw the mud he tracked in and decided to remove his boots and set them beside the door. In his stocking feet he crossed to the study and poured himself a brandy, tossing it off in one swallow.

He would have to find out what was going on, after another drink. The quiet was ominous.

As Geoffrey poured the second, a muffled sob sounded from upstairs. A moment later, the air was rent by a pain filled scream, so horrible that Geoffrey dropped the glass and watched it splinter into a thousand pieces. He was motionless for only a second, then ran from the room and took the stairs two at a time, until he reached the upper floor. His head jerked at the sight which greeted him. Mistress Mobley and several of the other servants waited outside Eileen's door. Willis was the first to see him and moved apart from the others. "My lord . . ."

"What the hell is happening here?"

"Her ladyship . . ." Willis hesitated, but there was nothing which would make this easier. "It's believed she's dying, milord."

The servants moved aside to let him through. Geoffrey opened the door to Eileen's room and saw Doctor Pares standing beside the bed. Eileen's personal maid, Gale, was behind him, sobbing into her handkerchief. One of the other maids stood in the background, her hands clasped together. On the floor by the foot of the bed were bloody rags. More blood stained the sheets and blankets, spilling onto the white bedspread. Geoffrey closed the door behind him, and heard a frightened Eileen cry, "I can't see! Oh, my God! It's black in here!"

Gale clasped a trembling, white hand and pressed it

to her lips. Geoffrey crossed slowly to the bed. Eileen's beautiful features had become puffy and plain in her suffering. The bright blue eyes were red and clouded, her hair streamed about her neck in a wet mass. Her free hand clutched at her belly and her mouth was distorted as another scream of pain threatened. Doctor Pares lifted her head and poured something into her mouth from a cup. The taste must have been vile, for she weakly attempted to pull away from him, moaning her anguish in being forced to drink it.

"Take it, my lady. It's morphia. It will help the pain."

She whimpered at that, but sipped, her expression losing some of its anguish as she did so. Dr. Pares laid her head gently on the pillow and nodded to Gale to take her place beside Eileen. He saw the Earl then and motioned him from the room. Geoffrey opened his mouth as though to speak but the physician cut him off by mouthing silently, "Not here."

Geoffrey nodded abruptly and led the way from the room. With a curt order he stopped any questions they might have faced from the servants outside the door. Geoffrey led the man across the hall and into his own sitting room. The strain of the day was evident on the physician's weary features. "I need a brandy," was the first thing the man said. "You'd better pour yourself one, and sit down. What I have to tell you isn't pleasant."

For some reason Geoffrey found his hands shaking as he poured the drinks. He handed one to the physician and asked, "Is she dying?"

"I'm afraid so."

"My God! But how?"

"She had an abortion . . ."

"No!"

The physician lifted his head and met Geoffrey's anguished gaze. "She was well along with the child. Did you not know?" the doctor asked softly.

Geoffrey took a deep breath and shook his head. "She couldn't even face having a child? What kind of a woman is she?" he asked bitterly.

"She's a woman who was very afraid of you finding out about either the baby or the abortion, I would guess. Now, she's simply a dying woman and I would like to see her die in some comfort. I've drugged her heavily, but at the rate she's losing blood, she can't live much longer." The physician's features suddenly softened and he said ruefully, "Don't judge her too harshly, my lord. Whatever sins she may have committed in the past, she is paying for them now. Whoever did this to her, deliberately butchered her. She never had a chance of living from the moment he took the knife to her. The pain she is suffering should atone for a lifetime of sins."

"Oh, my God!" Geoffrey's shoulders slumped and he turned away from the physician.

"My lord, there is one other thing. She didn't want you to know about this, she begged us not to tell you. She said you have enough hate for her. Perhaps you would remain here . . ."

"No, I won't let her die alone."

"She won't be alone. Gale and I will be with her," the physician reasoned simply. "Please, do this one last thing for her. She grows very agitated at the thought of you returning while she still lives. I believe her last concern is that you not think too harshly of her, my lord."

Geoffrey placed his forehead against a cold pane of the window and remained there for some time. He heard the door close behind the physician.

Eileen did not waken again.

Hours later Geoffrey was summoned to her room. The muslin sheet covered a very still form. Beneath the bed were the rags which absorbed the blood from her body. Gale hovered in the background, crying softly. The screaming had stopped hours ago, the morphia saw to that.

Doctor Pares assured Geoffrey the cause of death would remain between themselves. News of Eileen's death must surely spread fast, but as to the cause . . . there was no reason for that to go any further than this room. The servants could only guess the truth. Both the maids who attended Eileen's death were trustworthy. There was nothing to fear.

Geoffrey listened numbly as the physician spoke, but he realized the man had spent many hours in this house today, and those, out of consideration for the Earl, not for the fee he could expect.

For a long while after Doctor Pares left, Geoffrey remained there, blunted of all feeling.

In a short time her body would be gone from here as would her belongings. This bedroom would be just another room in the house. After all these years of hating her and anything to do with her, it seemed hypocritical to feel such a sense of loss.

From the foot of the bed her body appeared still and white, so unlike Eileen that he shivered at this proof of mortality.

Anger grew on him then. This was his wife, a woman who died aborting another man's child. Geof-

337

frey had not touched her since the first night of their marriage, that was when he first began to hate her. After this, he would never have to look on her again. A divorce would have been preferable to this gnawing regret which tore him apart.

Gale stood in the shadows and he ordered, "Dress her in a fine gown and the diamonds. Let her be buried as she lived. She looks obscenely naked."

Gale answered slowly, a grave sorrow in the flat tenor of her voice. "She has no need for the diamonds, my lord. Let her set aside the vain trappings which have brought her to this state."

"God will not judge her by her appearance. Only mortals do that. He will not forgive any woman who could allow this to be done to her." Geoffrey spoke bitterly.

"She did not do this alone. Her father sent her to that physician. He insisted she not carry the child. And you know her ladyship, she always did as her father ordered. She never loved wisely, my lord. She loved where she thought she was loved in return."

Geoffrey turned and glared at the woman. "What do you mean, 'he sent her'?"

Gale's hand were shaking, her eyes were red rimmed from tears. She looked so weary, the Earl insisted she take a seat before she told him anything more. Gale would be the only one to truly grieve for Eileen.

"I went with her this morning to see her father. I waited while they argued. I could hear her crying and begging him not to insist. I did not understand what she was talking about, I didn't realize her trouble." Gale lifted her head and her eyes beseeched the Earl to understand. "What she did was none of my concern, she told me that often enough. Lord Belden came out with us and gave orders to the driver and the next I knew, Eileen was being taken in to see a physician."

The grey head fell into the servant's hands and she sobbed quietly as she spoke. "They kept me in the waiting room. Later, a man carried her out and set her inside the carriage. He told me to take her home and put her to bed. She looked so horrible I was immediately frightened. I questioned him but he refused to answer and left us. I did not see Naylor Belden again, my lord. By that time, Eileen was crying with the pain and all I could think to do was fetch Dr. Pares." The tear-filled eyes lifted. "Her own father did this, my lord."

Geoffrey stared hard at her, speechless as the chaotic thoughts milled around in his head. Could she be right? Coudl Naylor Belden have plotted his own daughter's death? Why? As punishment for what he did to them in revoking their allowances? Could any man be so horrible? Geoffrey crossed to the window and stared through it, unseeing, his mind working feverishly. If Naylor was capable of this, he was capable of so much more.

"What shall I do with her clothing and other belongings?" Gale's softly spoken words broke into his thoughts.

"I don't care. Give them all away."

"Not the jewels. You'll want them someday. I'll give her clothing and other belongings to the servants. Her jewels I'll store in the safe."

Geoffrey shook his head. "I never want to see them again."

"You'll marry again, my lord."

Geoffrey emitted a mocking guffaw. "No. This once was more than enough." A strained silence followed and Geoffrey regretted his outburst. He'd always disliked Gale, but that was because of her faithfulness to Eileen, not because of the woman herself. The servant had been with Eileen since she was a child, and it was easy to blame Gale for many of Eileen's shortcomings.

"You don't have to worry about your future. I'll see to a pension for you," Geoffrey said gruffly. "You were good to her and earned it."

"Thank you, my lord. I've always known you would deal fairly with me." She hesitated, "And if I can ever do anything for you . . ."

Geoffrey shook his head. He would need no reminder of his disastrous marriage.

Suddenly the room felt stifling. Eileen's body seemed nothing more than a caricature of a once breathing, laughing woman. He'd wasted many years of his life with her tied around his neck like a millstone, and now he was suffering the guilt of gaining his freedom in such a way. He had to get away from this paltry thing which had once been his wife.

He quit the room and descended to his den. There he locked the doors and proceeded to get roaring drunk.

Chapter Fourteen

The carriage lurched its way over a rocky patch and Alison shifted uneasily. Weary of sitting so long, she leaned forward to the window and peered outside for what must be the umpteenth time that day. A shiver escaped her, in spite of the woolen cloak, lap rug of fur spread across her lap, and the warmed brick beneath her feet. The further north they traveled, the whiter and colder it became.

Dropping the curtain, she frowned and turned in her seat. Her eyes met those of her husband who sat beside her and she could see laughter lurking there.

"It won't be long now, Alison."

"No, I suppose not," she answered with a forlorn sigh. Two days ago they left the cottage and had been traveling since. At the moment, Alison was wishing herself and Justin back at the cottage, in London, or anywhere else for that matter. She was not certain she had the courage to face whatever was ahead of her at Chatham Park. The prospect of meeting Justin's grandmother was daunting.

"Nor as difficult as you might think," he responded to her unspoken fears.

"Oh, yes, it will," she said vehemently. "Your grandmother must be expecting someone more . . . someone, well, someone . . . competent! Instead she'll be getting me!"

"Oh?"

"Will you stop laughing at me? I've just remembered how wealthy you are. We're going to one of your houses, we have just left one, and I know of the one in London. How many more do you have?" Alison demanded, her voice reaching a higher pitch.

"Four," came the calm answer.

Alison's eyes closed as though in a nightmare. "I can't do this, Justin. I won't even be able to keep track of the number of sets of sheets there, let alone wax and wicks and blankets and servants. Why, I've never given an order in my life."

"I know better." Justin laughed outright at that. "Just because you don't think of them as orders doesn't change their nature. No one would dare say you no. And I have enough servants to see that you won't have to count sheets and wax and wicks. You did no such thing in Geoffrey's homes."

Alison's chin lifted a notch. "I have been in only one of Geoffrey's homes, and there I was treated as a child. I'm no mistress, and frankly, I can't imagine me telling your housekeepers a thing!"

"Why not? You managed Mrs. Banks."

"I did not manage Mrs. Banks, she managed me, in case you did not notice. And I never order Morgan about, I always request." She ignored the strangled sound Justin made and continued, "Mrs. Banks never needed to be asked, whatever needed done was done before I even thought of it."

"You liked Mrs. Banks, so what do you think my other housekeepers are like?"

"A lot like you, toplofty and difficult to please. No, don't try to frighten me with that scowl of yours. It's all I can do, remaining calm enough to meet your servants. I swear, if you don't behave, I'll have an attack of the vapors."

Justin gave a crack of laughter. "Do that. I've a cure I've always wanted to try."

She grinned then. "I don't think I want to know what your cure is, do I? I thought not. Oh, well, I'm not exactly the vaporish type." A thoughtful gleam entered her eyes and she tilted her head to one side to study her husband. "Do you know you're the first and only man I've ever hit? I was proud of that black eye. I wish I could have had a better look at it."

"Yes, you did take off rather soon, didn't you?"

"Not as far as I was concerned. You were far too dangerous for my peace of mind."

That devilish grin surfaced and his hand slid to her belly. "Now we know how dangerous."

Alison's calm fled. "Dangerous enough that I've now seven houses and one grandmother to worry about."

His shoulders shook with laughter. "I thought you were braver. If you're worried about my housekeeper, think what she's wondering about you."

"What do you mean?"

"We are newly married, so to speak, and she's probably thinking you can wrap me around your little finger. She must wonder if you'll like her and keep her on. At this moment she's probably wondering if you have some relative who might aspire to take her place, by tomorrow she might not even have employment. Poor Mrs. Chesney, she's been with my family for years. She's as honest a woman as they come, keeps her book in the strictest order. I never even have to ask her for them. Once a month she sends them to my man and he tells me that the business of the house couldn't be better."

"Oh, dear, she sounds terribly efficient."

"Not about everything, I'm afraid. I must confess lately she's developed this terrible habit of misplacing things. Especially keys." He shook his head sadly. "That can be a nuisance."

"She doesn't wear a key ring about her waist?"

"Not lately. She forgets to put it on and the entire household is disrupted while she searches for it. When I was a lad she wore one and I could always hear her coming, it was wonderful. Small and slight she may be, but she's a martinet to a young boy."

Alison lowered her voice to a whisper. "Do you know what I think?"

"No, what?" Justin responded just as softly.

"I think Mrs. Chesney has never worried over keeping her position for so much as a second. She knows you would not trade her for a hundred of my relatives. I also think either the redoubtable Mrs. Chesney or your many governesses were very remiss with you when you were a child. They seemed to have failed to take a willow branch to the seat of your breeches and break you of the habit of telling such shocking faradiddles." She spoke firmly, her eyes flashing.

"I had many a governess who tried, but never Mrs.

344

Chesney. It would have broken her heart to have harmed me in any way," Justin grinned. "Tears in the eyes always suffice with that lady. Try it if you find you need something. Much more effective than the vapors!"

"I can imagine you as a child, spoiled, terribly dignified and . . ."

"Toplofty?"

"Yes."

"Sometimes, but I tried terribly hard to please . . ."

"Oh, so it hasn't been until recent years that you realized you had no one to please but yourself?"

"You hit hard, sweet. I have at times considered others."

Alison reached out a gloved hand and touched his arm. "I am sorry, Justin. I was teasing you, that's all. You're so good at it, I wanted to get some of my own back."

Justin looked down on her worried, flushed face and at her hand tugging on his arm so earnestly, and shook his head. His hand came to cover hers. "You take me too seriously, Alison. I have an extremely thick hide. Your little nettles cannot prick it."

The coach slowed its movements to take a narrow turn. Justin thrust the curtain aside and peered out to find the bright sun glistening over the white snow. "We've only an hour or so to go," he said, satisfied. "We've turned toward the west. Come here," he tugged her closer to his side and pointed out several items which might interest her. "There, see that mountain? That's where I fought the crusades at the side of Richard the Lionheart. And you can't see it from here, but there's a valley just beyond, that's my Camelot. I never did find a Guinevere, though I had a mare once

345

came close. And around the next bend . . . Ah, yes, the sun has agreed to exhibit it for us. There's the old abbey. It has some of the most gruesome ghosts. Headless monks, nuns without legs, all of them hurtling curses at Henry the Eighth."

"We should have brought that book on witchcraft. It tells how to get rid of ghosts."

"Get rid of them?" Justin was clearly shocked. "Why should we want to do that? They're practically family."

Alison's eyes twinkled. "Yes, you're right. We'd better save them for the children."

Moments later, she asked the question hovering in her mind all day. "What's your grandmother like, Justin?"

"She's an old lady now. My earliest remembrance is of her leaving for a ball, garbed in lace and diamonds, smelling like a garden of roses. I was enchanted. I wanted to touch her, to be held by the fairy queen. Instead, my hands were slapped soundly and I was sent to bed without supper for being so naughty as to crush a piece of her gown." He spoke bitterly, his mind on some distant thought. "She was always very busy, had many concerns, the chief one being herself. Children bore her. She wouldn't tolerate them, except they buy her a bit of posterity. Children should be locked away with nannies and governesses, kept out of the adults' way, that was her belief. Even if the child was a lonesome little boy who was still confused after the loss of his parents." His eyes were cold when they returned to her. "You have nothing to worry about. She won't bother with you. You have proper breeding to marry into the family. She might appreciate the fact that you're carrying another piece of her posterity. She

346

thought she would go to her grave without it being assured. She'll expect a great grandson . . ."

Alison could stand the bitter expression on his face no longer. Interrupting, more tartly than she realized, she spoke her mind. "Both your posterities can go to the devil, I'm having a girl."

His hands hauled her into his arms and laughter rumbled from deep within him. "I think I would like a daughter, or two, or as many as you choose to give me, but do you think it's possible to fit a son in somewhere?"

"Perhaps, one day."

He grinned, bringing her hand to his mouth and kissing her fingertips. "You are good for me, Alison. You remind me what's important."

Alison couldn't help herself. When Justin spoke to her so intimately and so caressingly, she felt her insides begin to melt. "We'll have your son, I promise."

The first sight of Chatham House had her tingling with nerves. Snowcapped evergreens and shrubbery lined the drive to the house. Justin pointed to the arches lining the road and told her by early summer they would be covered with roses. Alison was touched by the fond note in his voice. He left no doubt that he may have seven houses, but this was home.

The house was of grey stonework, three stories high and with a profusion of white, mullioned windows. Justin explained the original structure had been added onto over the years. Two chimneys marked the corners of the original house. The low rambling additions were added for comfort rather than conformity. South of one of the additions was a solarium where, Justin informed her, he took breakfast.

"Your home is beautiful," she stated, awed.

"Our home. And I think so, too. I haven't spent much time here since I was a lad, but now I think is the time to change that. This is where I would like our children raised."

"It's perfect," Alison agreed, her eyes filled with the expanse of the lawn and forest behind the house.

"There are so many nooks and crannies inside and outside. I thought I'd found a priest's hole once when I was a child, but my grandmother informed me it was no such thing. An old stove had been removed from there was all. I still call it my priest's hole."

Alison's fingers tightened on his hand. "We'll put a door on it and tell our children that's exactly what it was."

"I knew you'd understand."

Justin helped his wife alight from the carriage, tucking her arm in his to lead her into his home. Alison's grip tightened as the front door opened and revealed the most elegant creature Alison had seen since London. The butler was very tall and erect, his bearing as regal as a king's. His neatly trimmed moustache curled at the corners yet did not give the impression of a smile. Black coat, breeches and white gloves were impeccable in their neatness. His expression did not alter one bit as he said sternly, "Welcome home, my lord."

"Thank you, Wallace." The butler assisted milord in removing his coat and gloves and waited patiently to help the lady with him. "Alison, your cloak," milord prompted.

She knew what they were waiting for, and heartily she wished she possessed enough dignity to see herself through the rest of this day. However, her hopes were rapidly dwindling. She did not want to remove her cloak, not before this intimidating person.

The Marquis moved nearer his wife and his hand worked the buttons on her cloak. "Wallace, this is my wife, Lady Alison. Her brother is Earl of Wilton, do you remember him?" At the older man's nod, Justin continued, "Do you think you could arrange for my wife to meet the staff sometime this afternoon?"

"Of course, milord." The butler's demeanor remained very stiff and correct, until the cloak was removed. Almost imperceptibly, he started.

"As you can see, Wallace," the Marquis said softly, "we are expecting an increase in our small family very shortly. I imagine my wife will want to see the nursery."

After a slight pause, Wallace began to smile broadly. His beaming face turned to the Marquis and he said earnestly, "Congratulations, my lord, my lady. I hope you will be very happy."

Alison's face was pink with embarrassment, but she smiled at him in return, relieved that finally he was showing signs of being human. Her attention was captured by the paintings on the staircase and she was already beginning to wander from Justin's side and eyeing the inside of the house with curiosity. Impulsively she said, "I want to see the entire house, not just the nursery." They stood on the entrance landing and on either side of them were circular staircases leading to the opposite wings of the house. An enormous hall was before them, and from it veered the main rooms.

Justin followed her glance and said, "Our rooms are up those stairs. The nursery is beyond that. On the other side of the house are the servant's quarters. Come,

I'll show you through." He tucked her hand in his arm and led the way through the foyer.

Against the walls in the massive foyer stood bare wooden benches, all polished to a fine sheen. The brick floors must be waxed daily, Alison thought in some chagrin. Nowhere was there a smudge or a smear or a speck of dust. She thought of one or two years from now and the little fingerprints which would be everywhere. The wainscotting and all the fine carvings over the mantelpiece were safe for a while, she thought, the baby would be too short to reach them for a few years. Mrs. Chesney was appearing more and more the dragon lady in Alison's mind.

Justin led her through room after room, parlor, study, the morning parlor, dining room, the blue parlor, the billiard room, a drawing room, the conservatory, until, finally they reached the den. "Mrs. Chesney will have to show you the kitchen and its rooms. She hasn't allowed me in there since I ate both pies she cooked for dinner one night."

"Confess. The truth is your feet hurt."

He relaxed in his chair and put his feet up on a well-cushioned ottoman. He grinned. "I confess."

Alison threw him a caustic glance and seated herself. "If your feet hurt, imagine hers. I've never seen such a perfectly kept house."

"Who? Oh, Mrs. Chesney. She has help, I assure you."

"Oh, dear. Are there so many of them to face?"

"Quite a few."

"And every one of them as perfect as Wallace?"

Justin laughed. "He can be most imposing, can't he?

I used to shiver whenever he came into a room. He's always addressed me most politely, even his thrashings were polite."

"He thrashed you?"

"Yes, oh, don't look so shocked. I assure you I did my best to deserve every blow. In fact, when I think of some of the things I used to do, I'm surprised he was so polite about it all. He never once forgot my dignity. He has my utmost regard, I assure you."

"Well, I don't want him thrashing my children," Alison declared stoutly.

"Oh, he won't. He informed me once how glad he was when I reached full maturity and he was relieved of the duty. He warned me at the same time that if there were ever again any youthful figures, as he phrased it, running about Chatham, they would in all possibility be my fault, therefore only my responsibility. He may cut a branch or two and hand them to me, but he won't wield them."

"You sound very fond of him."

"I am. He was my father's batman years ago. I remember little of my father, but Wallace has always been here. Did you see his face when he noticed your condition? He's probably in the kitchen right now, spreading the news, as though it's his accomplishment instead of mine."

"Won't they all be shocked. This is rather sudden."

"My sweet, they've known me since before I grew into short pants, I've always shocked them. I don't imagine they thought I would have a conventional wooing, so, no, I don't think they'll be too surprised."

"Good. We'll say it was all your doing."

A rap sounded on the door and at Justin's words,

Wallace entered, bearing a tray of tea and cakes.

"Apricot tarts," Wallace announced. "Mrs. Chesney understood you were fond of them, milady."

"Oh? I am, but who . . ."

"Henry Mordaunt was here not so long ago, he told us about the marriage, so you weren't such a great surprise. Of course, he didn't tell us everything. Mrs. Chesney particularly asked your favorites."

"That must have taken most of the day," Justin drawled.

"How thoughtful of her."

"Shall I assemble the servants, half an hour, perhaps?" Wallace questioned.

"A bit longer than that. My wife will dawdle over tea. Her appetite, you understand?"

A ghost of a smile lit Wallace's face and he nodded.

"Just for that I'm only going to have one tart."

After two cups of tea and the tart Alison was able to relax against the cushions of the sofa and take her leisure to look about the room. Deep blue velvet drapes covered a massive set of double glass doors which led outside. A thick rug covered the floor before the massive hearth in which a fire burned brightly. The paneling and wainscotting were of a deep hued English oak. Massive bookcases of the same wood lined the room and these were filled with books and trinkets, a collection of music boxes were nestled on the highest shelf. A large Chippendale desk stood to one side of the double doors, a lamp of gleaming brass and glass sat atop it. Leather chairs and matching ottomans stretched against one wall, Justin clearly at home in one of them. Across from the chairs, separated by a low table, was the sofa on which Alison sat. The tea tray was laid out before her on the massive table. In all, but for the music boxes, this was a man's room, well kept and well used.

Justin watched her perusal of the room. "Do you like your new home?"

"It's beautiful."

"Not so frightened now?"

"Out of my wits, but for you, I'll brave anything."

"That's the way."

It was much easier than Alison could have imagined. Several of the higher ranking servants made small speeches of welcome. All Alison had to do was smile and say a few words of appreciation. Even Justin seemed to have patience with these people. He stood beside her and never once was bored or weary of all the falderal. For a usually abrupt man, his consideration of these people touched her.

Mrs. Chesney was a tiny woman with a cherubic face that beamed the moment she saw the Marquis. She not only curtsied, but was caught up in a quick hug against him.

"Alison, I'd like you to meet this very special friend of mine." Mrs. Chesney was a woman whose kindly nature matched her face. Later, Alison would wonder what had ever frightened her about coming here.

Justin led Alison down the line of servants and personally made all the introductions. He knew every one of them, though they came in all ages and he had not been to Chatham for awhile.

They were nearly at the end of the line when they heard a carriage coming up the drive. Justin muttered beneath his breath, "That didn't take long."

Alison's curiosity was satisfied moments later when Wallace returned, escorting an older woman Alison

353

realized must be Justin's grandmother. She was tall and stately, her white hair piled high in an elaborate coiffure and topped with a broad brimmed hat, trimmed of mauve ribbons and feathers. A day gown of heavy brocade, embroidered about the waist and skirt, completed her ensemble. The low neckline and quarter length gathered sleeves framed an underdress of deepest mauve. In her hands was a parasol and on every finger dangled rings. Around her neck and on her wrists were chains of gold, pearls and emeralds. Her carriage was imperious, as she swished her way into the room, her eyes only for her grandson. The eyes were wary and lined with great age. The dowager Marquesa seemed uncertain of her welcome.

Justin brought her to meet Alison. "Grandmere, this is my wife, Alison. Alison, my grandmother."

The dowager's eyes were bright as they scrutinized the young girl carefully. "Your brother is Earl of Wilton?"

Alison's chin lifted. "My half brother."

"Ah, well, at least you've an acceptable birth." The dowager turned from Alison and commented to her grandson, "I could use a sherry, it's a dry journey from the dower house."

"Oh course. Wallace," he nodded to his man, "see to it." They were seated in the morning room when Justin addressed his grandmother again. "Well?"

"She's not a bit of what I expected. You took your sweet time bringing her here to me." A lorgnette lifted to her eyes and she studied Alison through it. Her head came up swiftly on seeing Alison's slight swelling and she speculated drily, "You've been busy, I see." Justin laughed but Alison stirred uncomfortably in her seat.

354

The old lady went on relentlessly, "She's much younger than I thought."

"But Henry must have told you . . ." Justin began.

"Bah! That man! He's so besotted with her I could not believe a word of what he said. He described her in terms I was not even aware he knew. He described her pulchritude," this was said with a sneer, "her felicitous nature, her benevolence. Bah! By the time he was done I was sure you had married yourself a freak."

"I don't ask you to approve of her, Grandmere, just to welcome her," Justin said coldly.

"I didn't say I wouldn't, Justin," she said defensively. "But I can't help but wonder about . . . about this condition she's in. There's bound to be talk."

"There always is, even when there are no grounds."

"And there are grounds here, or else why have you given those strange orders?"

Justin flushed uncomfortably. "There's nothing so strange . . ."

"Nothing strange about wanting a marriage ceremony performed when the girl's already so obviously pregnant?" The dowager demanded shrilly.

Milord bit his lip. "I wish you would refrain . . ."

"Justin?" Alison turned to him. The truth was easy to read in his sheepish expression and she flung herself into his arms. "You want to marry me all over again?"

His arms tightened at the fragrance of her and his lips caressed her hair. "I want to wipe out the horrible memory of that other time. I don't want our lives together beginning in such a way."

"Oh, Justin, and I thought you thought I was just being silly."

"Sweetheart!"

"Justin!"

"My Gawd! Fetch the minister now. I can't stand anymore of this," Grandmere said tartly.

"Sorry, Grandmere, but you know how it is with newlyweds."

"Actually it's been too long for me to remember anything. Besides, you shouldn't be *that* newly married."

"Well, we were separated for quite a while . . ."

"She couldn't stand the sight of you, eh?"

"Our ideas of marriage didn't agree . . ."

"I can see there were other things on which you agreed very quickly."

Justin grinned. "Yes." Hugging Alison closer, he peered into joy filled eyes. "I thought my vicar should perform the service. We've been friends all our lives and he'll not ask too many questions of us."

"A real vicar this time?"

"As real as his claims and he has all sorts of papers proclaiming his position. He can show you those if you wish."

Grandmere's brows rose. "You mean you weren't married by a real vicar before?"

"Of course he was real, he was just a bit too inebriated for us to tell our grandchildren about." Justin bent his head to Alison and took her hands in his. "I admit the ceremony seemed a farce. You should not have been married in a backstreet shanty and I'm sorry I arranged matters as I did. My only excuse is I was very angry and I wanted to hurt you. What I didn't bargain for was the bad taste it would leave even in my mouth. So tonight, we will be married, again, in my home, with my grandmother as witness. I hope that will erase completely the memory of the other ceremony."

"Not completely, I trust," Grandmere said drily, her disdainful gaze resting on Alison.

"No, not completely. I have fond hopes for the future, in spite of it."

"Ah, yes." Finally the old lady smiled. "My great grandson!"

Justin's eyes met Alison's. "Or great granddaughter."

"Yes." Alison smiled intimately at him.

"Sweetheart . . ."

"Don't start that again," Grandmere cried. "I can't stand anymore."

"No, Grandmere, we won't." Reluctantly he released Alison. "The day has already been a long one for my wife and it promises to be a long evening. You will excuse her while she rests?"

"I am very tired," Alison agreed, moving slowly to the door. Her steps were not as sprightly as they had been that morning and some of the luster was gone from her eyes.

"Don't worry, my dear," said Grandmere. "I'll see to everything for you. It will be a beautiful ceremony, I promise you."

"Thank you," Alison murmured, meeting Mrs. Chesney just beyond the study door.

Grandmere turned to Justin when she was gone and commented, "Henry was right, she is quite acceptable." The old lady sipped at her wine. "Am I to understand all your differences have been resolved?"

Justin laughed. "The statement is too sweeping. All our differences will never be resolved, we keep finding new ones. But I have faith that someday I can make her see reason."

"You seem besotted to me." A trace of spite was in

the old lady's tone. "I would say she knew the manner by which to make you see her way."

Justin grinned ruefully. "There is that, too."

"And you don't mind being led around by a child her age?" Grandmere's brows rose haughtily.

Justin's grin swiftly faded. "Don't try to make trouble between us, Grandmother. I'm a fortunate man. I have deserved to lose her. I will do all in my power to see that nothing comes between us again."

The old lady shrugged her frail shoulders. "I do not wish to cause trouble."

"A word here, a word there. It amounts to the same. You'll not put doubts in my mind now. I know her too well."

"You are besotted," she sneered.

"I admit it. I love my wife, and I trust her. She is capable of loving unequivocally, not merely trying to possess." His voice was risen in anger and he downed his sherry quickly to drown that anger. He knew better than to be angry when he handled her. He had many bitter memories of his childhood, most of them caused by a manipulative woman who tried to own him, yet was never capable of loving him. That woman stood in the room with him now.

"We've reached an arrangement, you and I. We do not interfere with each other's lives. We tolerate each other fairly well. If you want to remain on such terms with me, get along with my wife. Do not try to come between us, I know the signs too well. If I find you are ever responsible for so much as one untoward word between Alison and myself, I will never see you again. Is that clear?"

"I have no intention of causing trouble!"

"I believe that. Just as I believe you are too foolish a woman to realize what it is you do. Whether it's because of jealousy or possessiveness, I don't know, nor do I care. But I do not want Alison to suffer for our differences. She is not accustomed to a family such as ours. Perhaps it's time we buried what has already passed between us."

"Whatever ill feeling there is, it's on your part! You've never forgiven me for not taking more of an interest in you when you were a child."

"And that should be in the past, too. Alison comes from a loving family. She has two brothers, both love her dearly. I would be embarrassed for her to see the acrimony between us. It shames me."

Grandmere rose and looked coldly at Justin. "You should know me well enough by now to know that I cannot abide children. I have never liked them. I am sorry you feel that I neglected you, but I promise to do everything by your wife that is correct."

"That's all I ask."

"Is my help needed for the arrangements?"

"No longer, you have arranged for the vicar. Mrs. Chesney and Wallace have been given their orders."

"Very well." The old woman rose and turned to quit the room. "I will return about eight this evening. Is that the time?"

"Yes, thank you, Grandmere."

She turned for one final look at him. "You may think I'm a silly, selfish old woman, and perhaps that's just what I am. But I do love you, Justin. I will do whatever I can for your wife."

Chatham bounded up the stairs two at a time, his pace not slowing until he reached the bedroom door.

He swung the door open cautiously and saw Alison sound asleep in the center of the bed, lying on one side. Her hair spread over the pillow and one leg was curled in front of her. Stirring restlessly, she lifted her hand and brought it to rest on her belly. Justin crossed the room and crawled on the bed beside her, sliding his hand over the slight swell and felt the movement of their child. Her eyelids fluttered open.

"Busy little beast, isn't he?"

Alison smiled at him, stretching and stifling a yawn. "Always," she agreed. "And he's the busiest when I'm not." Sitting up slowly, she broke into another huge yawn. Suddenly her eyes lit up and she straightened, asking, "Is it time yet?"

"Time for what?"

"The wedding. My wedding."

"Our wedding," he corrected. "And yes, it's almost time. I thought you might like your dinner first."

She grinned. "How did you ever guess?"

"Intuition," he answered drily.

Alison laughed aloud as she scrambled from the bed. "What shall I wear? What's proper for a second wedding like this?"

"I'm not exactly certain what's proper, having never done this before myself, but I had Henry see Madame Renaud in London and bring back something for you to wear tonight." From the closet he selected a gown of white satin and seed pearls. Lifting it over his arm, he displayed it for Alison.

"It's beautiful," she gasped, scooting to the edge of the bed and tucking her feet beneath her. "But white? For me? I can't even see my feet, Justin."

"You don't need to see your feet as long as your shoes

match. Here, get off the bed and take off that crumpled chemise and put on a fresh one. I had to guess on the waist size . . ."

"There is no waist on this gown."

"That's how I compromised."

"Justin, it's white. I shouldn't be in white."

"Yes, you should." His eyes softened and the lean fingers lightly stroked her cheek. "This ceremony is for us, as the first one should have been."

"I wasn't in white that day either."

"I was in too much of a hurry to wait. I wanted to make you my wife. On my mind was the memory of making love with you that first time. You were so sweet and innocent, this ceremony is my way of celebrating our lives together."

"You didn't think I was so innocent then."

"I quickly learned differently. But Alison, you must understand how dangerous kidnapping me was. I was a perfect stranger . . ."

"I know how dangerous you are." Her smile was seductively intimate. "Look at the trouble I'm in, and all because of you."

"And I wasn't so bad."

"I thought you were horrible, especially when I couldn't keep my food down. And you were so mean in London . . ."

"I know I was. But that's all behind us now and I want you to promise me you'll take care in the future and never do anything so foolish again. If you need something, if anything worries you, I want you to come to me. Do you promise, Ally?"

"I promise to never kidnap anyone unless you're with me. You would make a wonderful culprit."

"Baggage!" he retorted softly. "Turn around so I can reach your buttons."

"Somehow I don't think it's proper for the bridegroom to help the bride fasten her wedding gown." But she did as she was told, holding her hair out of the way for him.

"It's even less proper for the bride to arrive at her wedding unbuttoned."

She giggled. "That would shock your grandmother."

He finished the task and Alison stood before the large cheval mirror. "Your Madame Renaud is wonderful. I look . . . beautiful, and so slender," she breathed.

"Only from the front. From the side you still protrude. Here, sit down and I'll put on your slippers."

"I can reach my feet, I just can't see them."

"There's no need to do either with me here."

The slippers were of white leather and sheathed her slender feet like gloves. The gown rode low on her shoulders, emphasizing the creamy mounds of breasts, and the fitted sleeves added a long grace to her silhouette. Alison felt so beautiful that she twirled around before the mirror, admiring herself.

Justin left for a moment, returning with a black velvet box tucked beneath his arms. From within he extracted a single strand of pearls which he slipped over her head. The cold beads slid enticingly between her breasts, disappearing in the clevage.

Alison fingered them gently. "They're beautiful, Justin."

"They were my mother's. They haven't been worn in over thirty years."

Her eyes grew somber. "How did your mother die?"

"When I was born. My father died a few years later of a fever. I barely remember him."

"I've been lucky my entire life," Alison said simply. "I had both parents for a while, and now I have you."

"And you will soon have a child of your own."

Her smile disappeared and was replaced by a worried frown. "Will you mind if we have a girl? I really don't have any choice in the matter . . ."

"I know that, Alison. Believe me, it won't matter in the slightest. I shall be pleased whichever we have."

"Oh, good." She gave a sigh of relief. "I thought because I threatened to have a girl, you might think I did not want a boy and I really want either one, just as long as she's healthy . . ."

"Hush." His arms loped about her. "You're making a muddle of your explanation but somehow I follow your reasoning. And no, I still don't mind which we have. We can always try again."

"I was reading about Henry the Eighth, that book in the library, and he was so upset with Anne Boleyn . . ."

"Another of my favorite books. I revel in beheadings. Don't fret, Henry was an old fool, my love. I promise to neither behead nor divorce you."

Her only comment as they left the room was, "Good, because if you did, Geoffrey would probably challenge you to a duel and we'd be right back where we started."

The vicar, Thomas Neville, arrived for dinner. A man of middle years, his frame was sparse, almost gaunt. The warmth of his greeting left Alison in no doubt that he was a good friend to her husband. His good natured smile and easy grace put Alison at her ease quickly.

The dowager carried her lorgnette to her eyes as she

greeted Alison, her lips curling into a sulky pout. "Justin, not your mother's pearls!" She'd been trying to get them for years.

"My wife's pearls now." He carried Alison's fingers to his lips. "Don't they look splendid?"

"Yes, splendid," came the tart answer.

After dinner, Justin took Alison by the hand. "Shall we begin the ceremony now?"

"Yes, please," she answered simply, her eyes shining.

The small chapel was a relic from earlier days when church services had to be held in the manor house. Tonight it was festively decorated with hothouse flowers and brightly colored ribbons. Wallace, Mrs. Chesney and the other servants waited in the pews as the Marquis led his bride to the altar. Words intended for his wife only were whispered in her ear, "I've always promised them they would see me wed. We did nothing properly the first time, so this repeat performance is necessary for more reasons than one."

Justin smiled and spoke his vows without hesitation. Alison's eyes sparkled as she gave her hand into his and repeated her vows in a much softer voice, but one just as certain. She had no lingering doubts over the vows she spoke this day. This was what she wanted for the rest of her life. There was no timidity in her now, just the certain knowledge that her fate lay with this man.

The service was over and the small group of merrymakers removed to the parlor for the remainder of the celebration. Champagne was served and the Marquis and his bride were toasted several times before the rug was removed and a space cleared for dancing. For the first dance, Justin led his bride onto the floor, after that he had to relinquish her to many others. Even the dowager smiled and clapped gaily throughout the evening, her feet not as nimble as they once were, but happily dancing just the same. Justin finally intervened when Thomas requested his third dance with the bride. "She's danced enough, Thomas. We must remember her delicate condition."

The vicar pursed his lips and looked down on his partner. "I hadn't thought about that. Are you tired, my dear?"

A dreamy smile lit her eyes and her feet tapped to the gaiety of the music. "I'm not in the least tired. I could dance away the night."

Thomas' gaze roved over Alison and onto the Marquis. A sly grin crossed his face. "I think, what your husband is trying to tell you is that if you dance three times with anyone, it'd best be him."

Milord grinned, and to the delight of everyone present, whirled his wife onto the floor several more times that evening.

The festivities over, they climbed the stairs, arms entwined. Alison's head rested on his shoulder as she recalled the perfection of the evening, the celebration and the wedding. "Justin, I'm so happy. I didn't think I'd ever feel like this. I mean . . . I didn't think I'd ever want to be married, it's so permanent!"

"See what you missed by running away from me?"

She replied solemnly, but with a twinkle in her eyes, "You're right. Morgan and Thomas were nowhere near as interesting."

"I should hope not. I can do so much more that is interesting."

He sent his wife's maid to bed though she waited to help her mistress undress. "Kate looks to be falling asleep on her feet. Too much dancing for her too, I'll wager. It seems I must help you to bed, wife."

"Don't muss the gown, Justin. Isn't it the most beautiful thing you've ever seen?"

"I had no idea that Henry would prove so adept at choosing women's clothing," he answered drily, helping remove the gown from her shoulders. "Perhaps I've given him the wrong sort of tasks all these years." Alison sat on the edge of the bed and unclasped her garters and rolled the silk stockings down her legs. "Face me," he said. "I'll unbutton your chemise."

Alison stood before him and his fingers worked their way down the tiny buttons which enclosed the chemise. She smiled as the garment parted invitingly and said softly, "I love you, husband."

"How many glasses of champagne did you have?"

"Two."

He laughed softly. "No wonder. Into bed with you, now."

"I need a gown."

White teeth flashed a wicked grin. "Not tonight, you don't."

"If I don't get one, you don't either." Then she laughed because he never wore a stitch to bed.

"Fair's fair, I always say." Doffing his clothing as quickly as he could, he followed her into the bed. "And now, my lady wife . . ." His arms reached for her. "Demme, I forgot!" Abruptly he spoke and jumped hurriedly from bed. He crossed to the chiffonier, all the while shuffling his feet, and searched through the top drawer for a small packet.

"That's a clever little dance. You should have done it downstairs for all of us to enjoy."

366

"It's cold out there," he retorted, scrambling for the warmth of the bedcovers and pulling her against him. He deliberately pressed his cold feet against her thighs and she squealed in agitation.

"Just you wait, my lord," she warned.

"Stop squirming. Aren't you interested in your bridal gift?"

Her movements abruptly ceased and her eyes took in the packet in his hand. "But I have nothing for you."

"That's because I haven't given you any hints on what I want. Don't worry, you can make up for it later, I love presents. Here, take it. Surely with your imagination, you can think of something else to give me. Something warm and soft and cuddly . . ." His mouth nibbled at her nape and his hand moved suggestively to her breast.

Her head tilted and she gazed at him in awe. "You must have been a very successful rake. How could any lady resist you?"

"Ah, so you admit you cannot resist me?" Teeth nipped at the base of her neck, sending delicious sensations up her spine.

"I admit it. Even when I didn't want to, I found you irresistible."

He gave a mock growl and pressed her on her back, his thighs covering hers and leaving her in no doubt what he wanted. His lips played with hers. "I find you irresistible, too. I thought of this moment all night. I had you in my arms, but I wanted you in my arms as you are now, only for me. I wanted your body bare so I could look on you, so I could touch your breasts and feel them swell for me. I want your body as hungry for me as mine is for you. I have never felt like this about a

367

woman. If I weren't so besotted already, I swear, I'd be frightened out of my wits."

"How can you talk like that? You have nothing to fear from me. I love you."

"It's about time you admitted it. I thought you were too shy." He gave that devilish grin and laid back, his arms beneath his head. "Convince me. But first, open the gift. Then prove you love me."

Alison's thoughts were on things other than gifts, like the glint in his eyes, the firmness of his arms around her. But he was adamant. Reluctantly she sat up, brushing hair from her eyes and unwrapped the parcel. "Justin," her eyes flared up at him, wide and shocked. "Mama's jewels! I never thought I'd see them again."

"If you like them so much, why are you crying? I thought you'd be pleased."

"They do please me," she murmured, the tears shimmering in her eyes. "It's just that you're so wonderful to me and when I think that I had you locked up for a whole week," she spoke between sniffles, "and how much trouble I was for you . . . I can't tell you how sorry I am for what I did to you . . ."

"Don't be silly," he said fondly, drawing her close. "I don't regret a moment of it. You may have been a trifle harsh, admittedly, trying to starve me to death, sending Morgan around to beat me to a pulp . . ."

Her tears rapidly dissipated. "I did not . . ."

"Yes, you did. Morgan knocked me cold. That horrid little brat you adopted bit me on the shins. Your older brother wanted to take me apart piece by piece, and your little brother nearly challenged me to a duel. And all because of you." He spoke in a soft voice, his teeth nibbling on her earlobe and nape, sending spirals of pleasure through her. "Now that we're legitimately married I can tell you how impossible it has been for me to recover from your harshness. Your punishment should encompass the rest of our lives. Your worst crime was making me want you so badly I ached with it, yet you'd have nothing to do with me. You ran from me."

"You chased me away, you scoundrel! You and your temper . . ."

Her words ended on a gasp as he rolled over and parted her thighs, entering her swiftly and deeply. "The first part of your punishment is to teach you what it is to ache for the feel of my body next to yours, just as I ached for you. Did you know when you ran from me that I could make you feel like this? Or this?" The words sounded rough and raspy in her ears. From the first touch of him, she was ready for his loving. His hips thrust and drove inside her, again and again. That he restrained himself was proven by the tautly drawn cords lining his neck and arms. His face was harsh in the candlelight, the arms on either side of her offering a haven of protection and love. Her sense of pleasure was heightened at this proof of his regard. He wanted her desperately, but held himself in check to keep from hurting her. Lifting her hips, she met his thrusts and drew him closer to her heart. Her fingers learned each sculptured line of his back and buttocks, her lips tasting his mouth, neck, shoulders, and chest. The beating of her heart pounded against her brain and she panted his name, her fingers tugging on his arms demanding more of him.

His movements slowed and his mouth tasted the pearl drops of sweat on her temples as the words slowly spewed from him, "Oh, no, my love. I said you needed to ache for me and ache you will." His fingers slid between their moist bodies and found her most secret place, swollen and throbbing. Piercing pleasure swamped through her at his touch and her whole body quivered. She heard rather than saw his devilish grin. "Do you like what I do to you, my lady?" The fingers probed and teased until she whimpered with desire and need. The intimacy of his kisses deepened. "What more do you want, my lady?" His breath was hot where it wafted over her skin. "You'll have to tell me, for I swear I do not know."

How could he not know, she wondered desperately, her senses careening wildly. She wanted him. Against her thighs she felt the heat and pride of him. If she ached for his touch, what would he feel at her touch? The same fierce pleasure? Tentatively, she reached a hand and covered him. His groan seemed almost to be of pain, but instead of recoiling, he melted into her caress, the raspy noises from his throat sounding like those of a starving man.

"Stop," he moaned huskily.

"Why? Don't you like this? Or this?" Her tongue flitted over his lips, settling boldly between them, coaxing an opening to within.

"I can't stand it," he groaned. "You're driving me mad."

But Alison felt a heady sense of power at this torment she caused and was not about to stop. "Just a little more," she begged, her fingers stroking lightly over the drawn skin which pulsated with desire.

His hand covered hers and tugged it free of him as his hardness probed her thighs for her heat and depth. His

370

mouth closed hotly over her nipple as he thrust within and felt her body jolt at the explosion of their joining. He stroked deep within her. Her answering caress was more intimate than her fingers had been and more tormenting, too. His touch was poignant with tenderness and at odds with the savage expression on his face. Through hazy eyes, Alison watched him, awed by his control when she knew where he was concerned, she had none. The tremors started deep within her, spiraling wildly until she heaved in his arms, his name a cry on her lips. He held her tightly and knew when her need exploded, his would wait no longer. He moved deep within her, practicing the fine art of giving and taking. He gave and now he took. Her cry mingled with his as he thrust deeply once more and the world began its wild spiraling of the senses. Each thrust sent new tentacles of sensation through him and he rode each sensation, his arms keeping Alison in the center of his careening world.

Until exhausted, they slept in each other's arms.

Chapter Fifteen

Bounding down the porch steps and racing toward the waiting coach, the Earl cocked his head to one side to allow the gathering rain to fall from his tricorne in rivulets. His thick, black cape was plastered to his clothing by the time the coach was reached. A footman, barely visible beneath his own enveloping cape, held the door open for his master, slamming it once Wilton was inside. The coach swayed with the weight of the footman as he once again swung into position on the rear of the equipage.

The carriage lurched as the wheels began turning, soon settling into a rhythmic motion. Great puddles of water gathered in the cobbled streets, but the wheels traveled briskly through them.

Inside the coach, the Earl of Wilton drew his tricorne from his head and, shaking it free of most of the rain, tossed it on the seat across from him. He loosened the frog at his neck, but decided the early spring night was too cold and damp to remove the cape.

His spirits were high tonight. Since early fall he'd

been in London and the formalities of society were stifling him. Today he'd received word, within two weeks he would be returning to the colonies. In the Americas a man could be wild and independent, free of the conventions of his birth and responsibilities.

One day he'd have to return to England and take up his duties as Earl, but at the moment he was of more value to his country waging war against the French.

One thing he would miss though, and that was the warm comfort of Anne Ellingsworth. He'd set her up as his mistress almost immediately on his return, and in all these months had not grown weary of her. She was comforting and undemanding, rare traits in a woman.

Even tonight, when he'd told her of his impending departure, she had not sulked and hinted for more of him than he was willing to give. She offered him a very satisfactory preliminary farewell, her words and actions promising an even more pleasant farewell each night until his departure. And for being a woman of such self-possession, he would settle more on her than he ever intended. Such generosity should be rewarded.

He was pleasantly tired. The early evening had been spent over the gaming tables, fine brandy always at his fingertips, and later evening in Anne's arms. He was replete. His head lolled against the squabs and his eyes wavered closed.

The rain pounded harder now. Its steady drumming against the roof of the carriage was somehow soothing to his resting mind. He began to doze off when a harsher note sounded, jarring this pleasantness. It took a moment for him to fully rouse and realize it was a bullet he heard whining through the air. His eyes flew open.

A frantic voice he immediately identified as that of his own footman shouted, "Ben! Ben, did 'ey 'it ye?"

The dull pounding of horses' hooves against wet pavement loomed nearer.

The carriage jerked and Wilton felt a heavy weight fall from the top of the carriage. He could only guess that Ben must have been hit and fallen from his driver's seat. The horses picked up mad speed. Wilton tucked his hand in the supporting strap by his head in order to keep his balance. His eyes flew upward. Right where he placed them were the two loaded pistols he carried since the last attack on his life. He should have known David would fight one last time to try and gain the succession.

After Eileen's death, Geoffrey tightened the noose around David's and Naylor's fates. Eileen was no longer here to save them from the most desperate of their creditors with her allowance. Geoffrey had taken steps to remove them from any inheritance beyond the title, drafting a new will for the property which was not entailed. And that property was the most profitable. Naylor and David would inherit an empty title and the home in Wiltonshire, but they would not have enough funds to keep it properly. And he'd made certain their creditors were aware of that fact.

Now they were in hiding to avoid capture by their creditors. Fleet prison was not a life either man could survive, and other than himself there was no one to pay their debts. Geoffrey wanted to see them rot in prison. He would not lift one finger to help them.

The coach lurched wildly and Geoffrey heard the frantic screams of the horses as they ran on, unfettered. The wails lengthened and their tenor changed from one of fury to one of stark terror. Wilton recognized the change of pace when the horses tired, but the coach was hurtling on, at top speed.

He gripped the strap more tightly. Being cooped inside this coach was maddening. He would far rather face his adversaries and whatever that brought than be tumbled about inside here like a puppet with no string.

The animals screeched once more. The sharp rending of wood splintering and breaking pierced the air. The carriage lurched again and hit something. Wilton thought it must be one of the horses and hoped the poor animal died instantly. The other one cried out, but he was bound to his partner by the strength of the yoke. The carriage lurched to a slow swaying. Wilton made a grab for the pistols and tucked them securely inside his waistband. He held onto the strap for dear life. The carriage hovered ominously, giving one final lunge before hefting over to its side and settling there.

Pain shattered through the Earl as he was tossed on his hip and his head cracked against the door of the coach. For only a moment he lay numb, then heard John's voice just outside, "Be ye alright, milor'?"

With an effort, Wilton raised himself and pushed the door of the coach open. A great rush of water poured in. Where he had lain moments before was now a pool of icy water. Lifting his arms, he balanced his body on the side of the coach and hefted himself up and through the door. Lithely he bounded from the side of the coach, landing on his feet beside John. The Earl glanced about himself, but a curt warning issued from the footman and he ducked, barely in time to see John raise his pistol and fire wildly. Two shots answered this sally. Fired in quick succession, the first missed his ear only by a hair's breadth and the other imbeded itself in the body of the carriage.

Wilton pulled the pistols from his waist and aimed toward the direction from which the shots came, keeping his head low. His unseen enemy had not gauged the character of his opponent well. The Earl was a crack shot, years of practice against an enemy saw to that. And the enemy Wilton had faced often enough were the wild Indians of the colonies, savages who struck and ran. He well knew how to hold his fire until he was certain of his targets.

Moments later, his training stood him in good stead. Movement was barely perceptible through the thick downpour and the cover of the forest, but it was enough. Aiming the pistol, he pressed his finger gently to the trigger. That the ball found its mark was certain from the familiar cry of a man and the sound of his body falling. "Here, reload this," he ordered curtly of the footman. Through the steady droning of the rainfall, an uneasy horse snorted its protest loudly. Wilton aimed in that direction, correcting his hold at the next sound and firing. Another man fell, cursing the greed for money which brought him out on a night such as this.

"'ere be two more of 'em," John whispered. "I got a gander at 'em when 'ey be chasin' us." His breath came heavy and fast through the dark dampness of the night. Crouching low, he pulled his greatcoat over his hands to keep the powder dry as he poured it into the barrel and rammed it home. He gave the loaded flintlock to the Earl and quickly began reloading the other one.

"Keep low. There are two men coming at us, John. Keep watch on your right." Before the assailants reached within firing range, they split up, each one riding in a different direction to circle around the coach. Hooves hit the muddy earth and thudded dully, the steady droning of the rain muting the sound. Wilton kept low and strained his eyes to see through this wet blackness. A sudden glinting of metal captured his attention and Wilton spun around, firing quickly but hitting nothing. A bullet whined and John doubled over with a gasp, clutching at his belly. Only the long reach of the Earl's arm prevented him from keeling face first into the mud. From John's limp fingers he took the other pistol, firing it just as another of the attackers came into view.

Frantically he searched for John's own pistol, but was hampered in this by the weight of the man's body and the darkness. Not that it mattered any longer, by now the powder would be wet and useless. Wilton pressed his ear beneath John's nose for some sign of life but could hear or feel nothing. In the distance the last of the highwaymen came steadily toward him. Reluctantly he set the footman's body beside him, propping it against the coach. Wilton poured powder down the barrel of his pistol and rammed the wadded ball home. The gun was cocked and he was beginning to fill the priming pan when he sensed the man approaching. Shifting the pistol in the direction of the enemy, Wilton pulled the trigger. The gun jerked as a burning pain bit into his side. His eyes closed on a gasp and his hand fell to the earth beside him.

He breathed in pain-filled gasps, knowing he was as good as dead now. He had no pistol, only a wound which made it impossible to reload, if by chance he found one. With supreme effort he lifted his fingers and

377

held them up before his eyes. The red blood of his wound was barely discernible through the sluicing rain. The water hit his fingers, diluting the blood into rivulets of pink which dripped steadily onto the earth. The moments ticked by and Wilton wondered where the last of the assailants was, and what he waited for.

His body trembled with the cold. A wet cape provided little protection from the elements. In spite of the pain, he knew he must rise and move from this place. Groping to his feet, he clung to the bottom of the carriage and felt his way to the front. His feet labored through the thickness of mud and cold, dragging his heavy body with them. A blessed numbness spread through him, giving him renewed strength. The severed yoke came up against his shins and he bent over to learn the length of it. Just when he decided he must climb over it, his hand felt rough cloth. Peering through the darkness, he barely made out the shape of a man. His fingers ruffled his clothing, searching for some sign of identity, but came away with only a long bladed knife. The knife was tucked into Wilton's waistband. This must be the last of the highwaymen, the one the Earl thought would kill him. Confused, Wilton tried to make sense of this and decided his last wild ball must have found its mark. Apparently, his luck hadn't run out yet.

Relieved, he allowed his exhaustion to overtake him. Finding a dryer spot sheltered by the driver's seat, Wilton collapsed there, hoping time and rest would see him safely home. Pulling his tricorne low over his face, he relaxed, his fingers pressing against the wound to assuage the pain. His eyes closed.

A long while later, a slight sound alerted him. The

downpour seeped through his clothing relentlessly. He tried to move, but his extremities were numb from the cold and loss of blood.

The mud gave way, sluicing beneath the tread of footsteps. Someone was slowly moving toward the carriage. Wilton brought his head down to his knees and tucked his arm inside this curvature of his body. His fingers slipped to his waistband.

Black leather boots crept into his vision. A rough hand swept the tricorne from his head and grasped a thick handful of golden hair. With a harsh tug, the hair was pulled back and Wilton was brought up to face this last attacker. As his head came up, the Earl gathered the last of his strength and took a vicious swipe with his arm, finding a mark and driving deeper and deeper with the dagger. Only when his strength was completely spent did his hand fall away.

The body of David Belden collapsed at his feet, the silver blonde head lolling freely, smeared with blood. The knife was where Wilton thrust it, in David's neck.

The effort exhausted his strength. Wilton straightened his legs, pressed his head against the coach and knew nothing more.

He wakened in his own bed and was immediately conscious of the cleanliness and safety in which he lay. The pain had steadied to a dull throb, spreading through his back and belly and left arm. At first he thought he'd lost the arm, but lifting his right hand across his chest, he found bandages running the full length of the arm and knew it was still there.

His eyes closed in relief and he found the faces of Ben and John appearing in his dreams. Eileen and the horror of her death tormented him endlessly. His mother and stepfather were there, as was the sleigh and great chunks of ice and water drifting wickedly on a snow capped lake. The nightmares swamped him and more than once he wakened from this pain-induced stupor and found sweat pouring down his forehead and temples. At some point the nightmares ended, leaving behind a blissful emptiness. Geoffrey slept.

His eyes opened to find Doctor Pares at his bedside. The man smiled and glibly said, "After sleeping like a babe, you've finally decided to join the real world? High time!"

For the first time Geoffrey noticed that when the good doctor spoke, his chin and beard moved in pointed unison. He almost laughed, until pain turned the laughter into a grimace.

"How do you feel?"

"Like I've been shot, stabbed and sat on by a horse."

"Nothing quite so bad. A bullet that took a deal of probing to find and you lost a great deal of blood."

"Ah, that much I do remember."

"No, don't try to sit up yet. Give the wound some more time to knit. Perhaps tomorrow."

"How long have I been like this?"

"A few days. If you'd had a restful sleep, you'd recover more quickly. Instead you tossed and cursed like an old sea dog. Your fever did much of the talking."

Full memory returned while the doctor spoke and Geoffrey's lips thinned. "I should have killed David!"

"You did," the physician affirmed drily. "Henry Mordaunt found him lying across you. 'Twas his warmth and the weight of his coat which kept you alive."

Geoffrey closed his eyes wearily. "And John? Ben?"

Doctor Pares shook his head. "To find you alive was a miracle."

"They were good men, both of them." Geoffrey's tone was grim. "David may be dead but Naylor is every bit as responsible for the deaths of my servants. He will pay. I'm done with waiting. Where's Henry Mordaunt now?"

"Somewhere in this city, looking for your father-in-law. Oh, and he sent one of your men to Chatham Park to let the Marquis know about this."

"No!" bellowed Geoffrey, sitting up abruptly. He gasped as the pain shot through him.

"I told you to stay down."

"I can't," came the unequivocal reply. "Alison will insist on coming here and seeing for herself I'm alive. I don't want her in the middle of this. I want to find Naylor first."

"Your opinion of my abilities is not very flattering," drawled a voice from the doorway. My lord Marquis lifted a gloved hand and motioned airily. "Crawl back into your sickbed, I beg of you. I did not bring my wife." His large frame loosened from its position by the doorjamb and sauntered to the bed. "I remember the deplorable tendencies she has to try to protect you, and you are correct, it is imperative she be kept where she is, and safe."

Geoffrey looked at him in surprise. "And how did you manage to leave her behind?"

"Only by the sheerest of cunning. I did not tell her why I needed to come to London."

Geoffrey grinned, his hand tightening against his wound and the pain. Glazed eyes lifted to the

Marquis. "You didn't tell Morgan either, I hope?"

"Give me credit for a tad bit of intelligence. I left Alison very encumbered at the moment. I promise she can't move fast enough to kidnap anyone else, not for a long while." Black eyes rested on Geoffrey and the lips softened in a semblance of a smile. "And I promised Morgan I would personally tear him limb from limb if she so much as moved a hair from Chatham Park."

Geoffrey had to laugh. "And how is my sister?"

"In wonderful spirits, happy, healthy, looking forward to the birth . . ."

"Alison is with child?" Doctor Pares questioned, surprise in his voice.

"I'm sorry, I neglected to introduce you. Justin, this is Doctor Pares, a physician of undoubted skill, as you can see, and trustworthy reticence, as you must have guessed. This is Alison's husband, Marquis of Chatham. And yes, they are expecting a child. Soon."

"Congratulations, my lord." The physician spoke earnestly. "I have known Lady Alison since her parents brought her to London as a child. I wish you both the best."

When the doctor was gone, Justin pulled a chair to the bedside. His dark eyes studied Geoffrey as though to gauge his strength. "Perhaps the time has come to speak frankly."

"As we should have done years ago," Geoffrey haltingly responded. Pain settled over him in waves, causing him to breathe harshly, his voice coming in a whisper, "As we might have done anytime these last months. I allowed my concern for Alison to temper my judgement. While I was in the colonies I decided one of my first tasks when I returned to England was to find you and apologize for what I put you through when we were children. I was waylaid in that task," he added drily. "Not once, but several times." Justin's shoulders shook, but he had the grace not to laugh aloud. "You took the brunt of unspoken blame for the deaths of my parents. I knew at the time you were not responsible, but I was in too much pain to care about anyone or anything, even myself. And Naylor, what a clever devil he is! Years passed before I finally understood what happened that Christmas. And when I did, I had no proof, only conjecture."

Justin nodded, his face growing serious. "You were alive and seemingly unharmed, except for that dreadful marriage. That's the one thing I never understood, why did you marry her? You hated her, we both hated her! Why?"

Geoffrey shrugged and his eyes closed wearily. "The way to reach me was through my family pride, my family responsibilities. Naylor knew that. He was appointed a trustee of the estate because of his relationship to my father. It was he who pointed out my duty to marry Eileen, to save the impoverished branch of the family. He claimed my mother would have wanted it. I was child enough to swallow that nonsense. Mother was such a good woman, it seemed he spoke the truth. If marriage with Eileen was not in my mother's mind, why were Naylor, David and Eileen invited that Christmas? I was only seventeen when we were betrothed, nineteen when we married, barely old enough to wed without permission of the trustees.

"I believed him. He was my only living male relative other than Jon. Idealism may seem a desirable trait to teach the young, but it can have dangerous consequences. So I married Eileen. Even before that fateful day, she, David and Naylor had free access to all that I owned, my houses, my fortune. I gave freely, I was raised to be a generous creature." Geoffrey's eyes closed and his facial muscles tightened against another assault of pain. Moments passed before he was able to continue, "I saw little of them between the betrothal and the marriage.

"To this day, I swear, I do not know how I realized Eileen was not a virgin that first night. I think back on it and I don't know which came first, my accusation or her admission. All I remember was realizing I was not the first. I was so young, I expected so much of the woman I would call my wife. But life goes on and by the next morning I admitted it was too late for any choice in the matter, I had to live with the marriage. And I would.

"I could not touch her after that. I thought, given time, I would grow accustomed to her and resume that part of our marriage. Then she began laughing at me, at everything I felt, or thought, or did. More time passed and I could not rouse any desire for her, all I felt was a growing contempt.

"Naylor and David were there, too, always in the background. I felt them snickering behind my back with Eileen. I was confused, hurt. I wanted to flee from my own home.

"And then, I fell ill. It was the flu, Naylor insisted. When I worsened, Naylor casually reminded me of how my father died, and his father died. Both were healthy men, suddenly attacked by a fatal illness, an illness strangely like my own. The sickness lingered long and painfully with them. It was a relief to everyone

384

when their bodies finally expired and there would be no more suffering. What more could I expect? I inherited good from them, it seemed I was also inheriting the bad.

"And my wife," mockery entered his tone of voice, "dutifully cared for me. She hovered about, tucking blankets beneath my chin, making a grand display of her concern. Two days of that was all I could stand. My contempt for her grew the more I saw of her.

"Finally, when I had enough, I told her to leave me in peace, that Simmons would care for me. And then she had a most peculiar request, she asked if she could still carry my food, claiming that doing such a small task gave her great pleasure. I accepted the offer, but I began to wonder. What was this wifely concern and why so sudden? I felt a damned fool at what I was thinking, it couldn't be possible. I ignored my own thoughts and ate whatever she brought.

"Until I became too ill to even eat. I accepted the tray though I would not let her feed me. I insisted she leave it, that Simmons would feed me. So, she left the room and I told Simmons to go, that I would keep nothing down and I wanted no more torture. He set the tray on the floor by the bed. The cat wandered in and I let her eat of it, hoping the disappearance of even a small amount of food would convince my wife I had eaten enough. It worked. She returned, claimed immense pleasure over my attempt to eat anything, and took the tray."

Golden eyes formed black pin points in the center as they lifted to Justin. "By morning the cat was as ill as I, and by afternoon was dead."

"My God!"

"Oh, yes, all those horrible, unbelievable thoughts were true. Thank God Simmons was a man to be trusted, a man who disliked my wife and her family almost as much as I now did. After that I partook of food only from my servant and he brought it directly from the kitchen. My strength began to improve immediately. A few days later I was well.

"I sent my dear relatives and my wife as far from Wiltonshire as I could. I gave orders they were never to set foot there again, particularly, I did not want them near Jon or Alison. Naylor was relieved of any responsibility to the estate. I shared my story only with my solicitor and he clearly thought I was mad. From that moment on, I kept my thoughts to myself. I was still a prisoner of my own guilty thoughts and felt I had to keep them on allowance or else they would embarrass my family.

"I bought a commission and proceeded to forget all about my wife and her relatives, except for the gossip they stirred. It was galling to hear talk of my wife's indiscretions as far away as the colonies, but I grew accustomed to that also. It was far preferable than having to return and take her in hand. For almost twelve years I lived that way, the only way I could face my marriage and the disaster I made of my life. Eileen remained in London, with her family, my only requirement being that she make a strict accounting of monies to my solicitor. I didn't care how she behaved as long as I never had to see her again. Naylor never forgave her for losing the inheritance for him. He had long ago begun to think of it as his."

Justin rose from the chair and strode agitatedly

about the room. "You should have disowned all of them."

Geoffrey grinned. "I had thought of murdering each one. They really weren't worth the risk. I separated my life from theirs, forever. And then came the talk about a marriage between Alison and David. Naylor had grown too confident of his powers with me gone. I had to return to show him I was no longer a young boy, threatened by his words or deeds, that I was fully capable of facing them. I did not foresee Eileen's death, nor the pain it would bring me. I would regret a dog dying so painfully."

Geoffrey fell silent. When next he spoke, his voice seemed to come from a great distance. "I did a great deal of thinking over those twelve years. I have learned not to discount my instincts, they are usually right. Have I ever told you how my father died? A bleeding ulcer, the physician said. It began with the flu and grew progressively worse. No one knew exactly what it was or what caused it. Everyone thought it must be inherited because my grandfather died of the same thing. Peculiar that it only affected those two generations, never before and never after, until my bout with poisoning.

Geoffrey's voice lowered. "I did some checking, Justin. At the time of my father's and my grandfather's death, Naylor was at Wiltonshire."

"Are you saying . . ."

"Do you remember that Christmas? You once said you thought my mother was afraid of Naylor. Justin, I believe she thought exactly what I think now, but she had no proof either. She believed Naylor killed my

387

grandfather to eliminate one person standing between him and the title. Two years later he killed my father, never dreaming my mother carried me. She kept him away from me those early years. I don't know how he inveigled an invitation to the house that Christmas, but I know now it was not with the intent of marrying me to Eileen. Remember how she kept an eagle eye on me that whole time?"

Justin paused in his pacing. "Yes, she had never done that before."

"And then she died in an accident, an accident where the yoke was weakened by the blade of a saw."

Justin's lips thinned and he glared at Geoffrey. "I did not weaken that yoke . . ."

"Of course you did not. I knew that then, but I was too mired in self-pity and misery to pay any attention to your sufferings."

"Then if you know I didn't . . ." his eyes began to alight with understanding.

Geoffrey nodded. "But I believe Naylor capable of doing such a thing." Haltingly, Geoffrey told Justin of Eileen's brutal murder. "My uncle is a more wicked man than ever I knew. He was so angry for the loss of his allowance and so afraid of what I would do if she gave birth to another man's child, he had her killed. His own daughter. And he threw his son into the fray. He wants the title desperately. He will do anything to gain it. Anything."

The golden head lifted to Justin. "Are you certain Morgan understood Alison was not to leave Chatham House?"

Justin nodded. "I threatened him with hanging and quartering. Besides I'm returning in two days, I will

388

keep her safe. Henry can remain with you. I'll send another man to warn Jon."

"Was it you who had Henry following me when I was attacked?"

Justin nodded. "Yes, I guessed something was amiss. Good thing, too, or Naylor would be Earl this very moment."

Chapter Sixteen

"Morgan!" Alison called breathlessly, stumbling across the cobbled yard and toward the stables. "Morgan!" she cried again, her voice catching on a sob as her fears threatened to overtake her. The old man came out of the barn, wiped his fingers on a soiled rag and watched her progress.

Burdened as she was, her movements were cumbersome. The day dress of blue muslin fitted loosely about her, draping in folds from her bodice to her feet. The neck was high, the lace ruching tickling around her throat and wrists. The full-length sleeves puffed at her shoulders, tapering to the wrists. But for a few tucks and folds, the gown was free of adornment.

"Whoa, lassie," Morgan held a hand high to slow her. "Wot d' ye mean, runnin' like thet? Don' ye ken ye could 'urt yerself? The babe . . ."

"Morgan," Alison drew a deep, agonized breath as she slowed to a stop. Clutched tightly in her trembling hands was a letter which she thrust at him. In her eyes was a haunting fear Morgan longed to erase. "Read this, please! It's from Uncle Naylor!"

Morgan gave her a quizzical glance as he accepted the letter. "Yer Uncle Naylor?" he questioned aloud, his eyes perusing the length of the missive. Impatiently he thrust it back at her. "I canna read 'alf these words, girl. Ye'll 'ave to tell me wot it is 'e wants."

"He says that Geoffrey has been badly wounded in an attack by highwaymen."

Morgan paused for only a moment, but long enough that Alison realized he'd been keeping this from her. "You knew. You've known all along!" she accused, her voice trembling with fear and rage.

"'Twas for yer sake, lassie. The Marquis thought it best that ye'd not know. 'e's gone to make sure Lord Wilton be well."

"He said he needed to go to London on business. He said nothing about Geoffrey!" Alison bit her lip to keep from crying the words aloud. Seeking some sort of protection from the fear assailing her, she crossed her arms over her chest and tugged at her shoulders with shaking fingers. Her spine curved at the terrible ifs running through her mind.

"Course 'e said 'at. Ye'd insist on goin' to Lunnon with 'im and when 'e refused, ye'd go all sulky and mad. Ye're in no condition to travel, not now," he said flatly.

"But Geoffrey has been asking for me. In the letter Naylor says he has come on a mission of mercy, to escort me to London. I only wish my own husband was as willing! How dare he treat me like a child, even now, when my brother may be dying! How could he have done this to me? At the very least he could have confided in me!"

"Yer in no shape to travel . . ."

"Of course not! But not knowing is what's so frightening, having to guess, to imagine what must be happening with my brother! The least Justin could have done was be honest with me! I could have handled the truth!"

"Now lass, don' ye cry," Morgan consoled, taking her stiff form in his arms. "I wanted 'im to tell ye the whole of it, but 'e thought yer not knowin' was better. 'e be a good mon, yer 'usband. I didna take to 'im at first, but 'e loves ye. 'e meant it fer the best."

Alison's body yielded against the comfort of Morgan's embrace, the tears falling freely now. "Naylor says in the letter that the wound is very bad. Geoffrey is not expected to live, which is why I must go to London."

"I canna believe Lord Wilton 'ad want ye to come right now. Not when it means riskin' the babe . . ."

"If he's dying, he's not thinking normally."

"'e Marquis will remind him of the child. Yer brother will understand," Morgan spoke with certainty.

"Yes, he will." Alison lifted an earnest gaze to the old servant. "I see that I cannot travel to London, but I can go to the Coach House and speak with Naylor. He'll know more than he says in his note and I want to know everything." Morgan looked doubtful and Alison placed a hand on his arm. "I owe Uncle Naylor a debt of gratitude. He's traveled all this way to see me, to give me the message from Geoffrey. That cannot have been a comfortable journey for him. I'm sure he'd much rather be at Geoffrey's side through this. The least I can do is thank him personally for his trouble."

Morgan was filled with doubts. The Marquis had left strict instructions that they were not to leave the grounds of Chatham Park. Still, it was a relief that she did not insist on traveling all the way to London to be beside her injured brother. He could see no harm in what she asked.

"Well, as it's no more'n a short jaunt to the village, I see no reason we should not go 'ere. Now, ye go along and put somethin' warmer on ye. Go on."

A youthful friendship was rekindled during the days Justin spent with his brother-in-law. As Geoffrey recovered his strength, they stayed up late and spoke intimately of their lives, past, present and future. They reminisced, laughing at memories of mischief made during their stay at Eton. They discussed mutual friends and where each was today, argued good-naturedly over politics and religion. They even managed to disagree about Justin's handling of his courtship without exchanging blows.

This was the last night Justin would be in London. Geoffrey was well on his way to a full recovery and he had to return to Alison. Their child would come any time and he would be beside her. Justin offered Geoffrey Chatham Park in which to recuperate, but the Earl refused. He still planned on traveling with his regiment in a few days.

"Do not be gone from England for so many years, Geoff. Your sister and I would like to see more of you, and I'm certain she'll want to show off the child before you leave," the Marquis said lightly, rising. The hour was late and he needed his sleep if he wanted to ride all day tomorrow.

"Four more years, I think then I'll settle down. I enjoy what I do, Justin. I fear England will seem sadly tame when I do settle for good." Geoffrey laughed and clapped his brother-in-law on the back. "Take good care of Alison and my nephew, will you?"

"She threatens the baby will be a girl." Justin grinned.

"She would."

The Earl stiffened as wild shouts and screams for help penetrated the thick walls of the house. Both men ran swiftly toward the kitchen, for the cries seemed to come from the rear of the house. From other parts of the building, Justin could hear doors slamming and cook shouting for her robe. Several barely dressed servants hobbled to their bedroom doors and followed the commotion.

One of the stableboys met them at the rear door and frantically gestured toward the stables.

"Fire!" he panted. "'Tis spreadin' fast!"

The blaze could be seen from a great distance. Even as they raced toward it, the glow expanded and mushroomed like a great, huge breath. On reaching the stable doors, each man wrenched one open. The heat clawed at them, driving them back.

"Oh, my God, look up there!" Geoffrey's horrified gaze followed the direction of Justin's finger. In an upper window, with the eerie glow of the fire silhouetting them, were the three men who tended the stable and lived in the rooms above. The fire crept closer to them and they climbed further out on the ledge of the window. Frantically, they pleaded for someone to help.

"They're going to jump!" Geoffrey croaked, helplessness in his voice. "They'll kill themselves!"

Justin swung on his heels and faced the servants who stood about and gaped at this deadly scene. "Fetch some sheets, and be quick about it!" His eyes flew back to the window, his face as pale as his friend's. "It'll be too late. They have to make a choice now. Death by burning, or risk a crippled life by surviving the jump."

Rage swept through Geoffrey, tormenting him much like a physical blow as the first of the men jumped and landed in a broken heap beneath the window. Several men stopped their task of throwing water on the barn and watched in silence. The water did not reach far enough inside to quench the fire. The servants arrived with the sheets and were in time to only gape at the sight. They spread a sheet wide for the next man to jump onto but he hesitated at the sight of the broken body Cook covered with a blanket.

Geoffrey turned to Justin and spoke in a tight, hard voice. "If something happens to me, promise you'll kill Naylor. Promise me!"

"You think it was he who did this?" At Geoffrey's curt answer, Justin nodded his head. "I promise. No, don't go in there!" Justin frantically grabbed at Geoffrey's arm to stop him, but the Earl was enraged beyond reason. Justin had to shout to be heard over the roar of the fire. "You'll be killed!"

Geoffrey did not pause as he ran to the barn, but his voice could be heard above the roar of the inferno, "Remember your promise, Justin!" Several long leaps led him into the belly of the fire. Justin could only watch.

A great roar thundered and the creak of wood splintering hit the air. The frenzy of the horses inside increased in nightmarish volume. Parts of the roof rose as though in protest, before tumbling slowly into the barn. The bright glow of fire grew brighter, and within seconds, licking flames of soaring heat burst forth and seared the night air.

In the upper portion of the barn, where the two men once stood, was nothing. The window hung onto the side of the barn, adrift among licking flames.

Justin doffed his coat and dipped it in the trough, holding it over his head as he gave a shout and roared into the barn after Geoffrey. Black smoke filled his lungs and eyes. The distraught horses whinnied and cried, but of Geoffrey there was no sign. The smoke grew blacker and thicker in here, creeping painfully between his eyelids and into his eyes. If he didn't find Geoffrey quickly, he'd have to get out or die in this with him. The heat increased its intensity the deeper he went, but the smoke-induced blindness was more frightening. The fire popped loudly and embers flew at him from different directions. His shoulder rammed against a stall and the frightened cries of the animal inside touched him painfully. He wrapped his fingers in the ends of his coat and unlatched the gate. He could only hope the horse might find his way out of this hell.

Finally, he had to admit the task was hopeless. His throat burned from the heat and smoke as he dropped to his hands and feet and crept toward the direction he entered from. Nothing could be seen in this smoke. As he moved forward, his hands unexpectedly touched a soft mass. Justin felt frantically around and realized that by the grace of God, he'd found Geoffrey. A beam lay across his hips. They were very near the door and Justin guessed he'd been unconscious almost from the moment he entered. Precious time was wasted removing the heavy beam before he could lift Geoffrey's body over his shoulders and make his way to the door. What was left of the roof missed them by inches. Justin fell face forward onto the earth once he felt the fresh air hit his face.

Helping hands were there, pulling them further from the inferno. Justin came to his feet, struggling a few steps, only to collapse by the trough, a spasm of coughing overwhelming him. Geoffrey's body tumbled beside him, to the instant care of the many servants. A horrendous roar split the air. Winds of tremendous strength reverberated through what was left of the barn. Flames burst their bounds and leapt from all directions, feeding on barnwood and air. A moment later, what remained of the walls of the barn collapsed in one dust-laden heap.

Justin's throat and mouth were parched and burning from the acrid smoke, but he stared, mesmerized by the collapse.

" 'ere, drink this!" someone shouted and he was given a glass of liquid which burned as it trickled down his throat. As he covered the hands of the other man with his own, he saw how black his hands were. He shifted his body and could see Willis bending over Geoffrey.

"Is he alive?" Justin's voice was thick and raspy and it hurt to speak.

"He'll live," answered Willis. "He's unconscious and his hands are badly burned, but his wound has not reopened." The relief in Willis' voice echoed that which Justin felt. "He's coming round now."

Justin sighed in relief and fell backwards onto the cold ground. His head turned to see how far the fire had spread. The house was untouched, though the outbuildings behind the barn burned wildly. His eyes lifted to the rise behind the outbuildings, where the road leading to the inner city was located. A chaise and four waited patiently there and beside it stood an erect, elegant figure. The glow of the fire gave the black clad figure a laughing face.

"I'm going after him. Now." The voice was barely recognizable as the Earl's, it was fill with such pain and mucus. Geoffrey was conscious and sitting up, though his body was wracked with coughing. His eyes spied Naylor at the same moment. "Give me your kerchief, Willis, and take the cravat from my neck."

"Why?" The butler asked, doing as he was told.

"Because my hands hurt like the very devil. And because I need them to ride. And because I'm going after that bloody bastard, now." He was assailed by a coughing fit that took time and water to assuage. When it was over, he wiped his mouth with the back of one blackened hand. "Tie them around my hands, Willis."

"Let's go to the house and clean them . . ."

"No, now."

"Milord," Willis spoke urgently. "The skin will peel off them if they're not properly bandaged. They may never heal right."

"I'll go after him," Justin said, rising. "You're right,

398

he must be stopped."

"He's mine. He's standing up there watching this waste of lives and laughing at us. It will be the last time he laughs." Geoffrey's eyes met Justin's in unspoken communication. He turned to Willis. "Get two horses from Lord Ashton. And don't waste time with explanations."

The cook fetched a cream which she spread on the badly burned hands before wrapping the cloth around them. By this time, Willis had returned with the two horses, both saddled and eager to be gone. Geoffrey mounted painfully, his eyes returning to the now empty hillside. "He's gone. If he thinks he will not face me . . ." With a brisk kick to the horse's flanks, he was off. Justin followed closely behind.

It was a simple matter to follow one lone coach at this time of night. The riders remained on the high road while Naylor's coach swept to the lower roads and traveled toward the center of town. The bright moonlight captured the clouds of dust which followed in the wake of the chaise.

The coach rolled across the bridge and the two riders swept lower, drawing nearer their prey.

From beneath the bridge and up the sloping sides rode four men furiously toward them. Geoffrey laughed grimly, "The bloody bastard's still plotting!"

Justin reached into his coat pockets and took the two pistols Willis placed there. His aim was unerringly accurate.

"I could have used you a fortnight ago!" Geoffrey jeered and two men were hit and turned away. A bullet whined by his head and he turned his attention to their foes. He missed, but the two remaining highwaymen spun their steeds around and disappeared into the darkness.

Their task was almost too easy now, the way they maneuvered the coach into position and Justin climbed aboard, taking the reins from the coachman. The man would not risk his life to protect Naylor. He leapt from the coach as the Marquis reached him, and he too disappeared down murky streets. Chatham pulled tightly on the reins and the coach slowed and stopped.

"Keep your pistols loaded," Geoffrey hissed. "With Naylor Belden you never know where to look to find a murderer."

"Give me yours. I'll do the loading. How are your hands?"

"I can feel nothing."

"Let's take this bloody bastard to your house and decide what to do with him there."

"No, let's take him to the country where revenge can be swift and justice isn't so particular," Geoffrey answered, joining Justin on the driver's seat.

"Sorry, my friend, but I'm sworn to uphold that justice. We'll take him to your house and question him before turning him over to the magistrate."

"There's not enough evidence to convict him, Justin. All there is is my word against his."

"That's not quite true. Most of the servants saw him on that rise tonight. There's Eileen's maid. She can swear to the old man's involvement in her death. And we can both testify to his access to the yoke many years ago. Morgan will confirm our words."

In spite of his claim that he could feel nothing, the

Earl's face contorted with pain as he gruffly croaked, "I won't risk a trial or a judge setting him free. If that pits us against each other, Justin, so be it."

Frustrated, Justin had to shout to be heard over the horses' hooves. "Dammit! Let us question him before we argue over the matter . . ."

The coach was slowing its movements as Geoffrey's house was reached. His residence and the neighbor's, Lord Ashton's, were brightly lit in anticipation of their return. The servants milled around the front lawns.

"Geoffrey . . ."

"Oh, damn the words. Let's see the man first, and then we'll decide." Geoffrey hauled himself from the seat and approached the carriage door.

Willis moved to stand beside him now. "Your hands will be scarred forever," he declared, as the blood dripped from the open welts.

"It's a small enough price to pay for justice."

"Is he in there?"

"Yes."

"Don't open the door until I hold a pistol on him," Chatham snapped, handing Geoffrey a pistol for his own use. The touch of cold metal against his skin brought fresh torture. "And stay out of the line of fire."

"Can you keep your pistol aimed?"

"It will be a pleasure."

Justin chose an angle at which to stand which gave him a good view of the door, yet offered protection, too. Geoffrey sidled against the side of the coach, a pistol in his right hand. He reached the door and tugged the handle down. Not a sound came from within. He released the handle and the door swung

401

open. Still nothing.

The silence was eerie, almost as if the coach was empty. Around him, many eyes watched closely.

Chatham could stand no more. Placing a loaded firearm in each hand, he swung himself in the doorway in a sudden movement. His aim was dead on the man who occupied the coach.

But the man's body was crumpled like so much dirty linen, lying on the floor of the carriage. He wore a black frock coat and breeches, like always, but instinct warned Justin something was wrong. He kept the pistol aimed at Naylor's head as he climbed in. Dangling from Naylor's right hand was an empty bottle. The old man's face was turned toward the squabs. All Justin could see was stubble of a black beard . . .

But Naylor had a fetish about grooming and cleanliness. He had never been poorly shaven in all the years Justin had known him. Justin grabbed the man by the neck and pulled his face back to take a good look at him. As he did so he cursed loudly. This man had Naylor's build and general appearance, but there all similarity ended. Again Naylor avoided capture.

The old man was barely breathing when Chatham released his hold. In a language purely from the gutters of London, the scum spoke bitterly, "'at swine!" he croaked, swallowing a painful cough, "'e poisoned the rum, just so's 'e'd not 'ave to pay me!"

The empty bottle and the man's deathly pale skin verified these words.

"You should have been more particular whom you trusted. If a man hires you to murder, believe that he, too, is capable of murder."

The old man moaned grimly. "So high and mighty,

melor'? I 'as 'ired to give ye a message, I 'as. Com' 'ere, closer, so's I can see yer face when I tell ye. Let's see if yer so high then." The old man's eyes were pinpoints of sadistic humor as he waited for the Marquis to lower his long frame beside him. The evilness of the man was epitomized in the grin he wore. Geoffrey climbed in the coach and squatted beside both men. The old villain's words were slurred from pain and more difficult than usual to understand.

"'e cheated me, 'e did."

"Why were you hired to impersonate him, old man? What was the purpose of your display tonight?"

A wicked cackle that weakened swiftly answered his question. A sudden chill assailed the Marquis. The villain crooked his little finger and whispered, "Come close. 'e wanted me to tell ye aboot yer sister . . ."

"I haven't got a sister!" Justin roared.

"Ain't ye the Earl?" snarled the old man.

Justin savagely recoiled from the old man, his whole body tensing with anger. "My God, you're talking about Alison!" The Marquis grabbed the old man by the neck of the frock coat and pulled his face up to meet his. The old man gurgled and with difficulty managed to swallow. "Naylor said to tell ye 'at 'e 'as yer sister, and 'at ye won't see 'er alive again. Ye may 'ave the money and the title . . ."

Geoffrey pressed his body against the old man's, his hands moving threateningly to the wrinkled throat, and demanded, "What are you saying, you bloody old fool?"

"'e's already got 'er. 'e said by the time I saw ye, she'd be dead. 'e said to tell ye 'at 'er condition won't stop his pleasure . . ."

Horse's hooves pounding off into the distance brought Geoffrey back to reality. Justin was mounted and already on his way to find Alison. Geoffrey snarled as he dragged the old man's body to the door of the coach and dropped it onto the hard earth. "See to this damned cur!" he ordered of his stupefied servants.

He was mounted and right behind the Marquis.

Chapter Seventeen

The wrought-iron gate of Chatham Park was swung wide to allow the light curricle and pair to step high and lively through. The matched pair cantered briskly and the finely boned horses took dips and mounds in the road with the same ease they took curves.

The quirt crackled over the horses' heads and the speed of the curricle increased as it tackled a straight stretch of road. Beyond the forested area was a series of tight curves and the curricle slowed its momentum to take them with a smooth gait. The clip-clopping of the horses' hooves reverberated in the stillness of an early spring afternoon.

Seated atop the curricle, Alison pressed her bright blue cloak tightly against her belly to keep it still in the breeze. Several strands of golden hair unfurled and rapped gently against her cheek as she gazed about herself, at the waning day, and found beauty in the now familiar surroundings of her husband's birthplace. Everywhere her gaze settled brought evidence of renewed life in freshly sprouting fields and newly born lambs and calves, suckling at their mother's teats.

Impossible to even think her brother was near death on a beautiful day such as this.

They'd reached the outskirts of the village when, abruptly rending the stillness of the afternoon, came several riders approaching them. The swift hoofbeats could be heard but as yet the riders were unseen. As Morgan snapped the reins, the curricle glided around another bend and four riders were visible in the distance. Their direction seemed to be straight at the curricle. They rode with determination, their heavy black coats billowing against the wind.

Morgan cursed at himself for being such a fool. Growling angrily, "Git ye down, Ally," he hefted the quirt high, snapping it determinedly. The pair of horses lurched forward. There was no turning back, not on this narrow stretch of road. Morgan's only choice was to bravely ride through the four men and pray the curricle would stay together long enough to outrun them. The horses bolted ahead, taking a curve wildly. The curricle bounced in the air and landed heavily, the wood creaking with the force of the jolt. Alison crouched low in the curricle, beneath the seat, her fingers gripping tightly onto its ledge.

One of the approaching riders pulled a pistol from his belt and bandied it about his head in a threatening manner. Morgan's hand slid to Alison's fair head to press it down. "And stay down," he roared.

The curricle careened wildly now, seemingly out of control, but it sped through the riders, causing them to waste precious moments turning and following.

A crackling noise rent the stillness of the forest. One of the front wheels of the curricle hit a boulder and an

406

inner spoke splintered. The curricle jerked to a stop, flying up in the air and landing on its side as it hit the solid earth. Morgan was tossed from his seat, but was thrown clear of the wreckage. He shook his head from the impact of the blow and was instantly on his feet, running to the horses' heads in an attempt to calm them. The animals were frightened and snorted angrily, their hooves frantically beating against the air as Morgan grabbed for the reins and spoke softly to their heads in an effort to soothe them.

The riders came steadily on.

"Be ye 'urt?" Morgan shouted gruffly. Alison's fair head popped up from the wreckage and the sight of the small round bundle at the side of the curricle answered his question. "Run to the trees, Ally! Run, quickly!"

Instead she sped toward him. "I've got a pistol, Morgan!"

"Good Gawd! Wot . . . Git yer 'ead down!"

"But . . ."

"Git over to the trees," he ordered roughly, taking the pistol from her hands. "Git there now! They'll give you protection, girl, go!"

Alison shivered at the tone he used on her but did as she was told. Her progress was somewhat slower than Morgan would have liked but her speed was greatly encumbered.

Morgan watched until she was hidden then he climbed beneath the rear wheel of the curricle. With Alison's pistol tucked in his waistband and his own dangling from his fingers his position was such that he could keep anyone from penetrating the woods where she was hiding, and he could keep them from surrounding him, unless there were more of them than

407

he knew. They were sure to have seen her go into the forest. With any luck they would assume he joined her there.

Forcing himself to wait patiently for the riders, he realized he recognized none of the men. So what could they want? Were they merely common thieves? Instinct told Morgan that was not so. He allowed them to advance closer before shouting, "Hold!"

The man who bandied his pistol so easily moments ago seemed to hesitate on learning Morgan was near. His pistol was still primed and cocked, now wavering between the forested area where he knew Alison was and the curricle where Morgan nestled. The pistol lowered. "Save yerself, man. All we wants is the girl."

"Nay, ye beggone," Morgan rasped.

"'ere's four o' us. Ye've not even a decent 'orse to make good an escape on. Our quarrel's not with ye. We want the girl and we'll 'ave 'er. Ye could live through this, yet." As the man spoke, he urged his horse nearer Morgan a step at a time. They other three men seemed to understand his intent for they moved in much the same threatening manner, slowly circling the curricle.

"One more step and I'll shoot ye down," was Morgan's grim answer.

A bullet whined past his shoulder and embedded itself in the wood of the curricle and Morgan knew the time for words was past. Lifting his pistol, he took careful aim and dropped the man who fired the ill-chosen round. His hands were quickly filled with powderhorn and pistol but his eyes darted rapidly between them and his adversaries, gauging their next move. Ducking, he barely avoided the next ball and reached into his waistband for the loaded and primed pistol. His shot missed, but several more shots rang out, in quick succession and from different locations. Morgan gaped up in surprise to see another of the men fall.

Two more men rode into the clearing, coming from the direction of the village. Morgan fumbled with the powder, sure he did not recognize these newcomers anymore than he did the others. Of the first four men who attacked them, two were still mounted. On the arrival of the newcomers who offered succor to Morgan and Alison, they spurred their horses and fled the fight.

Morgan was confused. He had these men to thank for his life and Alison's, but he did not know them, nor was he sure he could trust them. One of Morgan's saviours, a man with a wooden leg in the stirrup where flesh and bone should be, rode nearer, his chin jutting forward as his eyes sought Morgan in the maze of broken wood and wheels.

Morgan gaped as the man lurched in the saddle. He looked . . . foxed! But no one that inebriated could have made as sure an aim as it took to drop that last fellow! What the devil was going on here, Morgan wondered. But he didn't think they'd seen Alison.

Both men approached the curricle slowly, though without grace. Morgan scrambled from beneath the curricle, keeping the pistol hidden in the full swath of his coat. The lass better remain right where she was. Nodding his head curtly, Morgan boomed, "I owe ye me thanks, sir."

The man with one leg swung hard, narrowed eyes to Morgan. Drunkenly his body teetered as he lowered to rest an arm across the saddle. "Save your thanks, Mr.

Hull. I am not overly concerned with your hide. Now, where is your mistress," he demanded abruptly. Morgan guessed he'd been drinking most of the afternoon. Drink made a man very unreasonable. His companion watched the proceedings quietly, a silly smirk on his lips and eyes brightly glistening with the effects of spirits.

By his dress, Morgan knew the companion to be a servant. Both men were young, but Morgan would not be fooled by that. They could be every bit as dangerous as older, unscupulous demons. The combination of curly red hair and youthful freckles on the servant made him seem harmless enough. But the other man, something in his eyes spoke of hatred and danger.

The servant straightened suddenly, stammering, "Milord, I ain't . . ."

"Shut up, Fletch." Stacey Fielding's gaze didn't waver from Morgan. "Now, where is the Earl's sister," he questioned softly. No answer came and his intent eyes moved to the forest, putting an end to all Morgan's hopes that she had not been seen. "You, Lady Alison, come out of there, now, unless you would see me put a bullet through his head."

"There's no one there . . . ," Morgan began, taking several swift strides toward the man. The pistol aimed on him bobbled once and Morgan stopped.

"Shut up," Stacey ordered curtly, lowering the threatening weapon. "Fletch, go in there and get her . . ." The sentence was left unfinished for Morgan growled once and brought his hand up, the pistol in it aimed directly at the servant's heart. Stacey Fielding suspected Morgan held a pistol long before it lifted, and his own came up at the same moment. A retort

410

sounded and smoke billowed around Stacey's hand. Morgan cried aloud as the impact forced the pistol to fly from his hand, shock shearing through his arm to his chest. He flexed his hand and was surprised to find that he was not hit. The searing heat of the ball as it impacted against his pistol was what he'd felt.

Fletcher blinked twice, his slurring words leaving no doubt in Morgan's mind as to the state of his total inebriation. "Blimey! An exact 'it! Ye did'na even wound 'im!"

"Get the rope and tie him up," Stacey ordered coldly. Morgan had other ideas though and quickly sped down the road. Fletcher and Stacey rode after him, trapping him between their horses. After a good deal of tussling, Morgan was returned to the curricle and bound, all the while straining and cursing to the busted wheel. Nearly breathless from Morgan's struggles, Stacey crouched beside the wheel and leveled a pistol to Morgan's head. His eyes glared into the depths of the forest as the words spewed from him. "Come out, Lady Alison, and I'll spare your man. If I must come chasing after you, he's dead."

Barely a moment passed before the rustle of leaves accompanied Alison as she left the shelter of the forest. Her cloak enveloped her from head to toe and long strands of blonde hair hung in wisps around the hood. A woebegone picture, she held her hands tightly in her lap and attempted to speak with dignity. "We have little money on us but you may have it all, if you would only leave us to go on our way."

Stacey Fielding smiled brittlely, pleased to see her so frightened. He would have her even more frightened before he was done. "So, you're sister to the

411

Earl of Wiltonshire?"

Alison flushed beneath such harsh scrutiny and lifted her chin a notch, tugging the cloak more tightly about her as if it offered protection from this man. "How do you know that?"

"I make it a point to know of the Beldens," he answered, meeting her clear gaze directly. The pistol lowered and he continued to scrutinize her. "I know much of you Beldens, more than I ever desired to know. For instance, I know how the Belden women are faithless and cruel. Shallow women with no thought of morals or right or wrong, no thought of the future and what their present actions will bring rise to." Contemptuously he spoke, his mouth twisting with hatred. "And the Belden men! They are just a notch better. Why, your uncle wanted to hire me to kill you. An amoral act, admittedly, but perhaps you'd pressed him too far. I decline to judge the man, though he, too, is a Belden. He even went so far as to tell me the details of where you were living, how he thought you could be lured out, even the gory details of how to commit the deed." The lines around Stacey's mouth deepened as he watched his captive's eyes close in fear. Alison bit her lip and he savoured the taste of having a Belden in his power.

His voice lightened. "But I refused. Much as I detest the Beldens, I will not compromise my values to rid the world of such scum, not to please another of them at any rate. Curiosity got the best of me though and I followed him here to see how far he would go. It seems he really wants you dead. He simply looked elsewhere for his murderer, and found four of them. Makes me wonder what horrible thing you've done to him. Of course I know what you Beldens are capable of, look what your brother has done to me." With his hand, he gestured to where his leg should have been.

"Geoffrey did that?" Alison's eyes were widened in horror, first by the thought of Naylor conspiring to kill her and now by this seeming proof of Geoffrey's cruelty.

Stacey nodded. "Tell me, is your soul as ugly as your brother's and his wife's?"

Morgan roared angrily against his bonds, his chest heaving with the effort to be free of them. Being pursued for vengeance was an ever more dangerous matter than being robbed.

Alison could only watch his efforts, knowing that even if he freed himself they would not be saved. Not against two armed men. She wanted to go to him and soothe his anguish, but could not drag her leaden feet from this spot. Her head came up and bravely she met Stacey's eyes. "I don't believe Geoffrey harmed you without provocation. He wouldn't."

"I don't give a damn what you believe. All I care about now is teaching one of you Beldens a lesson you'll never forget. Before I'm done with you your brother will come begging me to spare you. When he's sufficiently penitent, I might."

"But . . . ," her mouth opened and on the tip of her tongue was the news that Geoffrey was badly hurt, but perhaps that was a lie, too. So one comforting thought came of this confrontation. Somehow Naylor's treachery did not surprise her, though she did not understand why.

"Now, up on the horse with you," Stacey ordered abruptly, grasping her upper arm and pulled her with

413

him to his animal.

"Where are you taking me?"

Stacey savoured the note of pleading in her voice, but for the first time since he and Fletcher had interfered he wondered just what it was he was doing. Where was he taking her? Damned if he knew, he hadn't given it any thought. He merely acted when he followed the four men and saw their intent. Stacey had a lot to drink this afternoon, as much as Fletcher, though he handled it better. But he was sobering now and realized how little planning he'd done. But he'd think of something later. All he knew now was he had one of the Beldens at his mercy and would bring the others to heel with her as his weapon. The thought was invigorating. Ever since his involvement with Eileen, his self-confidence was sapped. This would renew it.

Alison was deceptively docile, until he released her to free his stirrups. Then she turned and gathered her skirts, running with as much speed as she could garner. Unfortunately, Fletcher was watching. With a swift kick to the flanks of his horse, he was before her, the horse dancing around to prevent her escaping into the forest. Finally, she realized she could not avoid him. She stopped and raised moist eyes to the servant, her low lip trembling.

"Yer comin' with us, milady."

"Oh, please, don't do this," she begged.

"On yer way," Fletcher grumbled low, watching as her shoulders sagged and she turned. His mouth drooped open as she moved toward the horse waiting for her.

"She's waddling," he remarked incredulously. Fletcher lifted a hand to his nape and rubbed. He was

414

beginning to wish he could think straight. "Master Stacey, I donna think we ought to take 'er with us. I think . . ."

"Don't do anymore thinking. I've been waiting for this moment for a long time. I'm going to enjoy watching Geoffrey Belden squirm."

"Mebbee we ought to go after 'im and leave 'er alone . . ."

"We aren't going to hurt her. I just want a Belden at my mercy for a change."

"Sommat tell me we'll be sorry if'n we do this."

"I didn't ask for your opinion," Stacey snapped. "Come here," he told Alison, cupping his hands so she could climb into the saddle.

Alison sank into the soft leather wearily. Her legs and back were aching. Valiantly she kept the tears at bay. The hood slipped from her face and caught at her neck, freeing loose strands of hair. For a moment she seemed unbearably young and frightened. Just for a moment. Another woman had touched him once, too, and Eileen Belden used him badly. This woman was a Belden, just like Eileen. "Don't start crying," he jeered. "Show a little backbone."

Alison bit her lip and turned her face from him. He knew the tears were falling though she was too proud to admit as much to him. In spite of his hate for her family, he was touched. Gruffly he inquired, "What are you doing out at this time of evening, anyway?"

"Naylor sent me a note that Geoffrey has been wounded and he needed me. In the letter Naylor said he would wait for me at the Coach House Inn and escort me to London."

Stacey grimaced. "Probably just a lie. That old man

is full of lies."

Her breath caught and she turned to face him, the tears staining her cheeks, but for the first time since this horrible fiasco began a ray of hope entered her eyes. "Oh, do you think so? I pray Geoffrey is not hurt. He has had so much to bear . . ." The words came tumbling out, only stopping when Stacey pulled on the horse's reins and caught her attention. Of course he would not want to hear of Geoffrey's travails, not when Geoffrey was responsible for the loss of his leg.

"Never mind. Here, take these," Stacey gave the reins into her hands. "I'll ride one of the bays." The horses were still tethered to the yoke, milling around the area, nibbling on the fresh grass. Stacey captured one and leaped onto the animal's back, his hand holding tightly on the mane for support and guidance. Whirling the bay around to Alison, Stacey commented idly, "What a fool you were to fall for your uncle's plan. You should know him better than that."

"I know him barely at all. Geoffrey did not like him to be around Jon or myself." Alison turned in her saddle once they were on their way and waved to Morgan. The old man's eyes watched her, the fear in them palpable.

Fletcher took a deep breath. "Where to, Master Stacey?"

Stacey gave the matter much consideration now. Somehow he didn't think the Fox and Hound Inn would be appropriate. "My uncle has a cottage not too far from here . . ."

"Yer uncle? The one who's the London magistrate?" Fletcher laughed grimly. "Lordy, I'd love to see 'is face when 'e learns you've turned kidnapper!"

416

"Shut up, Fletch."

"Mebbee 'e'll throw ye in Newgate, 'is own kin."

"I'll take you with me," Stacey growled.

Alison wondered grimly where she would be by then as she rode between the two men. "Who is your uncle?"

"Sir 'enry Fielding," Fletcher boasted proudly, instantly regretting opening his mouth, for Stacey glared hotly at him.

"Shut up, Fletch. You don't have to announce our identities to the whole world."

"Sir Henry Fielding is your uncle? But he's such a stickler! How can *he* be related to *you?*"

Stacey's eyes grew cold. "And it's said your brother is a stickler for the proprieties where his sister is concerned. How can *he* be related to *you?*"

"If you think he's a stickler, wait until you meet my husband," Alison added sadly. "He's worse. And he'll be livid when he hears of this. Oh, please, won't you allow me to go home? He has such a terrible temper . . ."

"Will he beat you?"

Alison considered a moment. "No, but he'll be chillingly polite and very distant. I've been such a lot of trouble to him . . . I couldn't stand it if he stopped loving me." Tears filled her eyes.

"Please, canna we take 'er back," Fletcher howled. "I don't want no part . . ."

"Shut up, Fletcher."

"Wall, 'ow do ye plan to intr'duce our guest 'ere to Sir 'enry's 'ouse'old?"

This whole plan was seeming more and more like lunacy to Stacey as the evening lengthened and he sobered, but he was too stubborn to give it up. "We're not going to the house. Lord, they'd find it strange if I arrived with the two of you in tow! No, there's an empty cottage on the estate. We'll stay there."

"I don't think I can go much further. I'm very tired." Alison was slumping in the saddle.

"It's not too far now."

"My back hurts."

"Are you going to cry again?" Stacey demanded in exasperation.

"She donna look too well, Master Stace." Fletcher uttered the words just as Alison swayed and his arms flew up to catch her. "'ere, lass, 'ere, ye must sit up." Anxiety filled his voice.

"Please, let me go home."

"Leave her to me," Stacey ordered briskly, dismounting. Hauling himself up to sit behind her, he spoke in her ear, "Put your legs over and you can rest against my chest. Don't fret so much. I'm not going to touch you anymore than I can help."

"I'm so tired."

"We're almost there. If it's any comfort you'd have further to go if we took you home now."

"But I want to go home," she wailed again, "especially before Justin gets there."

The effects of the ale dissipated swiftly, replaced by a hazy cloud of doubt. What was he going to do with her now? His inclination was to turn about and immediately return her to her home, but now he had his pride to consider. The morning would do just as well, he thought. And she would learn a much needed lesson. All the Beldens would. Stacey Fielding was not always such a fool as he had been the morning of the duel.

They drew up before the cottage. Stacey dismounted

418

first and reached up his arms for Alison. Wearily, she tumbled into them. It was at that precise moment that he first realized exactly how misshapen she was beneath that voluminous cloak of hers. Many little things seemed to come together in his mind. His eyes slowly widened in terror.

His head bent and he looked down on the curling tresses which separated in wisps on his jacket. He cursed loudly. His uncle wouldn't just imprison him in Newgate for this, he'd hang him from the rafters! Alison gave an exhausted shudder and his arms tightened. "Why didn't you tell me?" he croaked.

"What?" she questioned, sleep uppermost in her mind.

He turned to Fletcher, his face a vision of someone expecting the wrath of God to descend any moment. "She's increasing," he whispered in a terse voice.

"I thought she walked kinda funny," Fletcher said without thought. His eyes lit with accusation and he turned to Stacey, snarling, "I tol' ye we'd just be gettin' into more trubble, but no, ye 'ad to take 'er. Bah! Ye and the Beldens! Who cares now? If ye think I'm 'arming a woman carrying a baby . . ."

"Shut up, Fletcher. We'll take her home, right now." He lifted her and would have placed her right back in the saddle, but a muffled protest sounded.

"I can't. I'm too tired. Besides, my back hurts."

"I thought you wanted to go home?"

"I do, more than anything. But if I don't get some rest, I'm going to be sick. I can't ride any further."

Fletcher listened to this and a nagging worry gnawed at him. "Milady," he queried, doffing his hat. "When's the baby due?"

"Anytime."

"Damn!" The men cursed simultaneously. Stacey turned to Fletcher. "I'll get a carriage and some food. You see she rests until I get back. We're getting her home, fast."

"I've 'eard tell as 'ow Chatham's a fair man with the pistol," Fletcher commented idly.

Alison opened one eye and glared at him. "If you're thinking what I think you're thinking, don't. Do you hear me? You will not harm one hair on his head . . ."

"I was thinking more about mine."

"None of this is his fault and I don't want him hurt because of it."

"Just don't you go having that baby on us."

"I certainly won't. My child will be born at Chatham House."

"I hope so," Stacey roared. "But for now, you can get yourself inside that cottage and sleep while you can. Fletcher, watch her for awhile. I won't be long." He mounted his horse and disappeared into the night.

"Cum on in, milady. We can make ye comfy for a time," Fletcher invited.

"I don't suppose there's any tea? I'm so hungry . . ."

Later, Alison was replete and sleeping soundly in a freshly made bed. The feather stuffing tickled her nose but she was warm and full and knew she'd be home in hours. Her fear of Stacey and Fletcher had fled. Whatever bothered Stacey needed sorting out but he was not an evil person. He wouldn't harm her, he never had any intention of harming her. And now, her initial fear of him seemed slightly ridiculous.

Patting the pillow so the feathers would spread more comfortably beneath her head, Alison thought how

420

much more comfortable her bed at Chatham House was. That reminded her of Justin and how she had to be home soon, before he knew of this latest trouble. Closing her eyes for the last time, she thought how, if he were here, in this bed with her, his arms would hold her and his shoulder would make her head comfortable . . . how he had such a warm body and was so nice to cuddle with. He'd smell of lemony soap and leather . . .

A strident chaos seemed bent on interrupting this pleasant dream. Alison rolled onto her side and pulled the pillow over her head to shut out the noise. And suddenly, the quiet was more ominous than all the shouting and scuffling. Fully waking, Alison sat upright in bed and listened. Nothing. Then a muffled noise and a thud. Next thing she knew Stacey and Fletcher were scrambling into her room and shutting the door tightly behind them.

"Get the chair, Fletch."

"What's happening?" Alison questioned breathlessly.

Stacey turned to her, his face grim. "Your uncle and his hired thugs followed us here. They want you pretty badly, I'd say." The color drained from her face but his attention was diverted as he became busy placing the heavy chair beneath the door knob. The light lock on the door would keep no one out for any length of time.

"How much powder d'ye have, Fletch?"

In answer, Fletcher shook his head sadly. "Not 'nuff. But 'ere's some in the kitchen."

"I didn't think or I could have refilled at my uncle's house," Stacey blurted in angry frustration. "I vow to swear off juice in the future, makes a man too careless." He glanced toward the bed and saw Alison wide eyed with fear. More softly he spoke, "You'd better put on your stockings and shoes, my lady. We may have to run for our lives."

"Where is my uncle?"

"He and his men are outside the cottage. The first I knew of them, they blew off the front door with gunpowder. I'm afraid this is where we face them."

"Come out, gentlemen." Their adversaries were no longer outside the cottage. The voice from the other side of the door was low pitched and refined, the words so softly spoken that Stacey had to strain to hear. "I want the girl and I will have her. You may as well save yourselves. If you set me to too much trouble, I will not hesitate to put an end to your lives as well. Just give me the girl and you can go free."

Stacey and Fletcher glanced at Alison at that very moment. She sat very still on the bed, only her lips and fingers showing any sign of life. They trembled with fear.

Stacey crossed to her and knelt on the floor beside the bed. His fingers tugged her stockings over her feet. "Don't be so frightened. We will not give you over to him."

"But . . ." she was shaking so badly her lips could barely form the words. "'Tis me he wants. I don't want you and Fletcher harmed over something not even your affair."

Shoes slid smoothly over the stockings. "'Twas my carelessness brought you here. You'd be safe at home by now if I hadn't been so foolish. Nay, my lady, we'll see to your protection. Trust us."

Tears welled in her eyes. "You're a good man, Stacey Fielding. I would like to thank you . . ."

"Thank me by saving my life with your brother and husband. Later. Were I in their shoes, I'd want to slit my throat, too."

"Milord," Fletcher spoke in an undertone. His ear was pressed against the wooden door. "'ey've gone around the cottage. At most 'ere's only one man in 'ere now. This may be our best chance for escapin'."

Stacey glanced at Alison and smiled briefly. "He's right. Are you ready to run?"

Nodding, she rose from the bed and followed Stacey's motions, tucking herself behind him and Fletcher. Both men readied their pistols and Stacey removed the chair. The lock was quietly released and the door gently pressed open. Forming a line of people, they stealthily crept out of the room and into the parlour.

Glancing around himself, Stacey was satisfied they were not yet in danger. He did not believe Naylor and his men were gone, they simply waited outside. The sun barely peeped over the horizon but gave them enough light to find their way. And gave Naylor the light to find his prey.

With a motion for silence, Stacey moved left, toward the kitchen and the others followed him. Inside, he reached into the pantry, to the shelf where they kept powder and balls. His searching fingers found nothing.

"Is this what you seek, Master Fielding?"

At the eerily spoken words, Stacey spun around and took the lead, thrusting Alison into a position behind himself and his servant. A grim smile was settled on Naylor's face and in his hands were the bags of powder and balls.

"As soon as I found these," Naylor carelessly tossed them onto the table, "I knew patience would bring you to me." In opposite corners of the room stood the two hired men, each with a pistol in his hand leveled at the captives. Naylor motioned to them. "I suggest you drop your own pistols. A few careless shots and anyone could be hurt. Of course, my niece would be the first to die. She is the reason we are here, after all."

Stacey nodded to Fletcher and both men set their pistols on the table.

Alison had time now to study Naylor, until her protectors returned and she was forced to stand on tiptoe to see over Stacey's shoulder. Naylor was garbed in lengths of black superfine, the only relief a touch of white lace at his collar and cuffs. He was as she always remembered him, cold and menacing, a distant figure which seemed to mock everything and everyone. A chill crept down her spine as she realized he could easily kill her and feel nothing. She doubted him capable of feeling anything. "Why are you doing this, Uncle? What have I ever done to you?"

Naylor's lips thinned. His smile was bone chilling. "You? Why, you've done nothing."

"Then why this?"

His expression grew uglier. "Because of Geoffrey, of course." He rasped the words fiercely. "Because he was born, and from that moment on he's been a thorn in my side! I went to the trouble of ridding myself of my own brother and his son and then what happens? Your mother announces she's increasing. His birth took everything that was mine, the title, the money, the power. I wasn't able to get near him when he was

424

growing up, not until the accident." His rare smile was sudden and deep. "Fortuitous, heh, that accident? Though it was meant to cause Geoffrey's death, not your mother's, richly though she deserved it. And then Geoffrey took himself out of my reach, left the country even. That was fine, Eileen had access to the money and I could wait as long as necessary to be rid of him permanently. And then he returned from the colonies." Nostrils flared with anger. "He'd grown up and done too much thinking with it. He cut off my access to the money, *my* money, and I swore then to be even with him. Damn him! And damn you for your brother. I vowed to hurt him so badly he'd prefer being cut to ribbons to what I would do." The black eyes deepened. "What could possibly hurt him more than killing his beloved little sister, the sister he went to such ends to try and protect? And to make my revenge sweeter, I would kill her while she carried a child. What a heinous crime! And so perfect!"

Alison gasped and stepped back, her hand going to her belly.

"Stay behind us, Alison. I won't let you take her," Stacey rasped angrily.

"You'll have no choice," Naylor answered, a self-satisfied smirk on his face. "You see, you and your friend here will hang momentarily. Then, I've promised these two men a bit of time alone with my niece. Seems they're enamoured of her, in spite of her condition. And when she's beyond caring, I'll hang her. Just imagine her brother's face when he finds the body. He'll hate me even more then, much more."

"Leave 'er be!"

425

"Move outside, Master Fielding . . . and take your servant with you." Naylor sounded almost bored now as he motioned the way out the back door. "My man can shoot you as you stand just as easily as he can hang you."

Stacey glanced from Naylor to the first of the thugs, then onto the second man. In the man's hands was a length of rope and in his eyes was a nasty gleam. The time it took to walk through the door might give him the precious time he needed to think of an escape.

Morgan tugged on the binds with all his strength, but after hours of this, all he managed to do was tire himself. He kept seeing Alison's frightened face as she rode off with those two men. Never in his life had he regretted anything so much as agreeing to take her to the inn this evening. By the bright light of the summer moon he could see the last of the curricle horses grazing not but a few feet from him, little good that did. His mind wandered, vainly trying to reason where the men might have taken his Alison.

The man missing the leg mentioned both Naylor and Geoffrey. Perhaps Geoffrey would recognize a description of the man. A faint hope and one which might prove too late for Alison anyway. What did that man mean, Geoffrey was responsible for the loss of his leg? Was he one of Geoffrey's men in the colonies? No, that couldn't be it, not if Naylor played some part in this. Nothing made sense. All Morgan knew for certain was that none of them would have traveled too far. They were too drunk and Alison too slow.

426

The more he considered, the more he realized there was only one thing he could do when he finally did gain his freedom. Return to Chatham Park and get help. Many men could scour the countryside much more quickly than one. With help, she'd be found. Any other thought was intolerable.

The morning sun began its ascent over the horizon and beat down on Morgan's head. Jerking to attention at the sound of riders approaching, he recognized Lords Chatham and Wilton. In spite of what was to follow, he'd never been so glad to see anyone in his life.

The men reined in and explanations and questions flew among the three as Morgan was released. "The man who 'as 'er 'as a wooden leg. 'e mentioned as 'ow 'e knew ye, me lord . . ."

"Stacey Fielding," Geoffrey rasped.

The Marquis stared hard at Morgan. "Was she harmed?"

"More frightened than 'armed when I saw 'er last. But that was 'ours ago! I thought to git 'elp . . ."

"Stacey's uncle has an estate not too far from here," Justin informed Geoffrey.

"Which direction?" In moments all was agreed. Morgan would return to Chatham House and rouse more men for a search. Justin and Geoffrey would seek Sir Henry.

They'd ridden through the night, nonstop from London. Both men were near exhaustion, but their grim thoughts kept them going.

The sun rose higher.

Ahead was a small village. Slowing their pace, they rode through the main thoroughfare, mindful of other

427

wheeled traffic and pedestrians. Once on the other side, they again increased their speed.

From the main road, they turned onto a narrow, winding lane. Nestled among the hills in the distance was a large, Tudor style home. The sight of their destination had them spurring their horses and racing toward the house. Suddenly, a woman's cry rent the stillness of the early morning and the anguish in the dearly familiar voice sent fear spiraling through Chatham.

Pulling on his reins with all his strength, he turned his steed in the direction of the cry, heedlessly breaking through branches and thick undergrowth to reach his destination.

In a clearing rested a small cottage. Voices of several men came at him from the rear of the house. More cautiously he approached now, bringing his horse to a stop at the sight which greeted him. Stacey Fielding and another man, their hands bound, were being led to stand on kitchen chairs beneath a large maple tree. Justin recognized the purpose behind the ropes hanging from the thickest branch. Alison watched this sight, tears streaming down her cheeks. Naylor stood beside her, a pistol pressed against her belly and his arm resting casually on her shoulders.

The sight enraged Justin. He had no doubt, if confronted, Naylor would happily pull the trigger and watch Alison and his child die.

A movement behind Alison captured his attention. Geoffrey stood there, taking in the full scene. Lifting a white face, he gave a brief nod to Justin. The Marquis swallowed heavily, knowing full well he had to go into this with bravado if he were to have a chance of success at all. In the pit of his belly was a cold, chilling fear for his wife.

Alighting from his horse, he stepped from the cover of the forest into the clearing. He did not bother to silence his movements and the others all turned to watch his approach. "Give me my wife, Naylor, and I'll see you have anything you want."

"Justin . . ." The word quivered from Alison. On her face was etched such hopeless despair that Chatham wanted to simply hold her and soothe her fears. He couldn't, not as long as the pistol was pressed against her side.

"And what have you that I might want," snickered Naylor. Now he had both of them in his clasp. His revenge couldn't be more perfect.

"How about the news that Geoffrey is dead? Don't look so surprised. That was what you and David planned, was it not? He barely survived the attack. He did not live through the recovery. You're a titled man, Naylor Belden. Of course Geoffrey willed most of the wealth to Jonathan and away from you. But if you let Alison live, I'll give you whatever else you need. I have enough money to go around . . . to all of you." His hand motioned to include the two thugs and piqued their interest also. Alison's head dropped and, even from this distance, he could hear her sobs.

Naylor's black brows lifted and he smiled speculatively. "So, finally, my nephew received his just desserts! What a pity he couldn't have gone sooner. 'Twould have saved you and Alison much pain."

"You need my money to live, Naylor."

"Do you really think I'm fool enough to believe you

429

would reward me for this day?" Naylor shook his head sadly. "No, I'll simply have to go after Jonathan. He should be simple enough to eliminate. He has not a great deal of understanding, you realize."

"And, of course, these men will be willing to wait until Jon's estate is settled for their earnings. You live very close to the vest, Uncle."

"Wot d'ye mean, " rasped one of Naylor's co-horts. "We're to be paid tonight. 'at's the deal!"

Alison gasped as the pistol dug forcefully into her side. "Remember who has the game in hand, my lord Marquis. You may live and I may die, but I take Alison with me. Do not incite my men any further."

Chatham spread his arms wide and smiled enticingly. "I mean no harm, Naylor. I simply offer you a trade. Money in return for our lives."

The temptation of Chatham spread wide as a target was too much to resist. Angling the pistol to where Chatham stood, Naylor tightened his hold on Alison and pulled the trigger. A simultaneous shot rang out and Alison was dragged to the earth with Naylor as he fell. Tangled within the grasp of his hands, Alison's frame trembled with tears and fear. Blood flowed and stained the fabric of Naylor's coat.

Naylor's ball was wide of his mark. Justin hurried to her, crouched low and swept her free of Naylor, into his comforting arms and allowed her to weep wearily against his broad frame. "You're safe now, Alison. I have you. I promise I won't allow any harm to come to you." His words soothed her fears, but the flow of tears was not stemmed. Chaos reigned for a time as the men with Naylor realized others were watching from the cover of the forest. They ran to their mounts and rode fast and furiously to escape capture. Stacey cursed loudly at the bonds which prevented him giving chase. At that moment Geoffrey emerged from the forest, battered and bruised, certainly, but not dead. Glaring angrily at Stacey and the man with him, his eyes promised explanations and penance if they so much as moved a finger. Stacey's flow of words subsided abruptly.

"Alison, don't cry so," Geoffrey soothed, crouching beside her and Justin. "You'll make yourself ill. As you can see, if you'd care to look, I'm fine."

Alison turned her face to him. She could see nothing through the rain of tears and wiped her eyes with the backs of her hands. Her shoulders shook and trembled as she attempted desperately to control herself. When, finally, she could see him, though he was a blur, she threw herself into his arms and wept again, this time in relief. "Justin said you were dead," she accused mournfully.

"He had to say something to gain Naylor's attention. I thought it very clever of him. I couldn't shoot until the pistol was taken off you."

Alison lifted her eyes and gazed at him. "He . . . Naylor was going to kill me. He said . . . some horrible things . . . about you and Mother . . . and the accident . . ."

"I know," Geoffrey's grasp tightened. "I should have warned you long ago and this might never have happened. They were a murderous bunch, that family. I'm ashamed to own a relationship to any of them."

"Geoffrey, did he kill Mother and Father? He said

431

you were the one meant to die . . ."

"He did, Alison. He was an evil man."

"And I blamed Justin for years," she wailed, turning and clasping her husband tightly. Pressing kisses across his forehead and face, she pleaded earnestly, "Can you ever forgive me for my wicked, wicked thoughts? I was so vain I set myself up as your judge and I have never regretted anything so much in my life!"

"Hush, Alison. We've been over this before. Believe me when I say you are my life and my love. I forgive you anything."

"Even my disobeying you last night? It seemed harmless enough to ride to the Coach House Inn and meet Naylor . . ."

"Yes, I forgive you that, too. I should have told you about Geoffrey's injury and my suspicions. I will share everything with you in the future. But if you ever dare to disobey me again, I promise you'll regret it! I never want to spend another night as I did this last one! Never!"

Rising, he gave Alison over to her brother. His black eyes on Stacey sent chills down the younger man's spine. Chatham spoke angrily. "And you, sir, you have me to answer to for your conduct last night. My wife might have died because of you!"

Stacey swallowed. "I know. I regret my actions. I regretted them almost instantly, but was too foxed to admit it. We were on our way back to Chatham House with her when Naylor and the men arrived . . ."

"We were," Fletcher agreed eagerly. "We saved her, too. Naylor would'a gotten to 'er earlier if it 'adna been fer us! Don' ferget 'at in yer anger, melord."

"They speak true, Justin," Alison confirmed, standing beside him. "They protected me as best they could, and nearly lost their lives in defense of me. I don't think you should be so angry with them."

"I think I need a stiff drink, breakfast and my bed," Geoffrey announced, "in that order. We'll sort this out later. Personally, I'm thankful they came along, drunk or not, and gave her some sort of succor. Morgan certainly fouled up!"

Justin buried his face in his wife's hair. Relief flowed through him and he felt an unfamiliar weakening of his strength now that the danger was past. This day might be forgotten sometime in the future, but at the moment all he could do was touch her and hold her and thank God she was still alive. A wan smile lit his face. "Yes, let's go home."

Alison hugged him once more and he groaned, hauling her to him and kissing her soundly on the lips. "If you ever put me through this again, I'll beat you soundly!" Relieved to hear him sounding much more normal, she grinned broadly.

"I swear I will always obey you implicitly . . ."

"Done go blamin' 'e lassie," Fletcher implored earnestly.

A glint entered Chatham's eyes. "Another champion?" he chuckled softly.

"They're really very nice people, Justin. But Stacey seems to think Geoffrey is responsible for the loss of his leg . . ."

"Chatham House, a drink, breakfast and bed," Geoffrey repeated stoutly. "Explanations will wait."

"I have a carriage around front, but I can't very well drive with my hands like this," Stacey pulled his hands to his side and motioned to the fact that he was still bound. "If you'd release me, we'll get you home fast. Truly, my lord, we did not plan to harm her," Stacey spoke earnestly.

"Oh, give me your hands," Chatham snapped, "I'll untie them."

Chapter Eighteen

Naylor's body was left with Henry Fielding. The magistrate accepted a statement from each of the men and Alison before allowing them to go on their way. Stacey took the reins and Fletcher rode on the driver's seat of one of Sir Henry's most comfortable equipages. Geoffrey was stretched out on one seat of the coach and was soon sleeping. He was barely recovered from his bullet wound when the fire was discovered. Now he suffered from exhaustion. The horses were tied behind and following the coach.

Every time they hit a bump, Geoffrey slid further down in the seat and, across from him, Alison shifted around, trying to get comfortable. "You're a much better driver than he is, Justin. Perhaps you should give Stacey a few tips."

Justin could envision that. He closed his eyes momentarily and his lips twitched. He did say, "Don't you think that might be a bit dangerous, presuming to offer someone with Stacey's temper criticism of his driving?"

"Probably," Alison said with resignation. "I don't understand his propensity toward dueling at all."

"I'll make you a bargain, Alison. If I promise, no, if I *vow* not to get into anymore duels, do you promise to behave with more discretion? No more late night excursions, no more kidnappings, no more riding across the countryside to save some unfortunate soul?"

Alison nodded her head eagerly. "I agree. I can't tell you how weary I am of being in trouble, but when I think of you or Geoffrey in danger . . ."

"I can understand that. I can even understand what made you want to see Naylor. I accept being partly at fault. I promise to tell you everything from now on, or at least everything with few exceptions. I cannot prevent your worrying or caring, but please prevent some of mine. I love you. The thought of being without you frightens me near to death. I could not bear it."

Snuggling in his arms, she sighed and said, "That's how I feel. I love you so much it hurts. And when you're not around, it's as though some vital part of me is missing. I exist, barely, but I don't live. And I don't laugh."

Chatham shuddered, "If you knew the thoughts I've had . . ."

"Shhh," Alison placed her fingertips over his mouth. "If they were like mine when I received Naylor's letter, you would have been scared clear through your toenails. I promise this will never happen again. I have learned my lesson." He brought her fingertips to his lips. "Justin, there's something else I should tell you . . ."

"Yes, my love?"

"Well, I think we need to hurry home. The . . . the

436

baby is coming."

"Of course he is, sweet. Anytime now."

"Not just anytime. Pretty soon, I would say."

"Today," he croaked.

"Not right this minute, of course, but I would be very grateful if we could be home soon."

"How soon?"

"Well, I feel a bit peculiar."

"Very lucid as always," my lord snapped impatiently. So much for vows of patience, Alison thought. "How peculiar?"

"My back hurts. It's been bothering me all night. And ever since early this morning I've had the queerest sensations, here." Her hand slid over her lower abdomen.

"Oh, my God! That must mean something."

"I think so, too." Cuddling nearer, she confided in him, "My back is the worst. Could you rub it, just a little?" His palm was warm and soothing. "I confess I would like to have the baby today, I'm so tired of being fat."

"As long as you wait until we reach Chatham House, you can have the baby whenever you want."

The rhythm of the coach made both drowsy enough to fall asleep. When Alison woke, it was because of a more intense drawing in her belly. She glanced at her husband who still slept soundly and thought that if they had a son she would want him to look just like his father. The carriage swayed deeply and Alison caught her breath. The drawing was no longer mere sensation. Carefully, she removed Justin's arm from her waist and scooted to the window. Chatham House was just coming into view, and not a moment too soon.

"Justin," she whispered in his ear. "We're home."

Opening his eyes, he sat up and rubbed lines of fatigue from his forehead before turning to her and inquiring abruptly, "How do you feel?" Silly question, he thought. He could see how anxious she was. Her face was tightly drawn, beads of perspiration dotted it.

"Like I'm going to have a baby."

The coach stopped in front of the house and the door was immediately opened by a footman. Justin jumped out and snapped at the man to go fetch the physician, immediately. He took his wife into his arms and strode toward the portico. "What about Geoffrey?" she asked.

"Someone will waken him. You're going to bed." Mrs. Chesney met them in the hall just as my lord was beginning to lose his calm reserve. "She's having the baby!"

Mrs. Chesney took one look at the two of them and in her most bland tone responded, "Then, we'd better get her cleaned up and in bed, milord. If you would care to take her upstairs . . ." She waved him ahead of her with a brisk movement of her hand and milord, taking the hint, hurried up the stairs. Mrs. Chesney followed and in her crisp, efficient manner set about preparing the bed and linens.

Justin helped Alison strip herself of the cloak and the blue muslin dress. He wanted her to crawl beneath the sheets immediately, but she threw him a speaking glance and crossed to the washstand. "I refuse to have this baby as dirty as I feel."

Markedly impatient, he waited while she washed her face, neck and arms. When she would have done her feet, he growled and lifted her to the bed.

"Justin, I never to go bed with dirty feet."

438

"There's nothing dirty about them."

"There is. I haven't washed them since yesterday."

"You are the most obstinate female," he rasped, setting her carefully on the edge of the bed and proceeding to wash them himself. When he was done he rose and tossed the cloth into the basin. His eyes were bright with anger. "Is there anything else you need washed? Your belly, perhaps? Though that might take the better part of the day!"

Alison flushed at this angry remark and reached for a sheet with which to cover herself. Justin could have bitten off his tongue at the embarrassment which flamed her face. He reached for her hand, "Alison, I . . ."

Mrs. Chesney had no use for men in a birthing, especially men careless with their tongues. Irritation laced her voice and she snapped, "You'd best see to yourself, milord. I'll see to milady."

"But I want to help!"

"Help all of us by leaving the room, please. I think you should imbibe in a brandy, or several. I've delivered a fair number of babies in my time, yours won't be the first," the housekeeper responded briskly. She tucked the sheets around Alison and turned, expecting the Marquis to be gone. "Now, go away with you. You'll just be in the way."

"But I want to help," he repeated.

"With your tongue running away with you? No, milord!" She practically chased him from the room. "Your lady will be much more comfortable without you to worry about. Come back later, after you've washed and changed your clothes. You look like you slept in them all night." With her hands she pushed him

439

into the adjoining room. Her head was shaking as she returned to Alison. "Don't worry about what he said. He didn't mean it. He's frightened and worried, and men are impossible when they are that way. They think they should be in charge all the time, even when they don't know what they're doing. Men are all the same, my dear. I should know, I've had four husbands. Buried every one of them, and I tell you now, I will never marry again!

"But you and I have better things to do, my dear, than talk about our common affliction. We have a baby to birth. I hope the Earl of Wilton joins your husband. Maybe they'll both get foxed and stay out of our hair."

"Mrs. Chesney, I'm having another pain . . ."

"Yes, dear." The housekeeper laid a comforting arm on Alison's shoulder. "It won't be long now."

In the adjoining room, Justin hurriedly washed and was changing his clothing when the first cry came. He froze momentarily and his mouth went dry. It suddenly seemed to dawn on him that he was not ready to be a father. Another muffled cry sounded and he tucked his shirt in his breeches and hurried to the other room.

His face was contorted with the fear he felt. His first thought was that the doctor was not here yet. Mrs. Chesney glanced up at him and snapped impatiently, "Everything's happening very fast, so if you must be here, go to your wife and hold her hand!

He did as he was told, sitting beside Alison, his long fingers brushing the damp strands of hair from her face. She grabbed for his hand and gripped tightly as pain enveloped her. His free hand instinctively went to her back and rubbed firmly. Mrs. Chesney instructed

440

Alison to take short, deep breaths, to pant with the pain.

My lord Marquis received scant attention, only once and then was instructed curtly, "My hands are full, if you can't stand the sight of blood, leave now, or I'll leave you where you fall."

"Then leave me," he responded gruffly as Alison's grip tightened.

Their child would enter the world any moment and he had every intention of remaining. His mouth went to her ear and whispered comforting words of love for her and pride at her courage.

"Justin . . . Mrs. Chesney . . ." Alison gasped once more. "I . . . oooh . . ."

"That's it, my lady. Push now and you'll soon have a fine baby. "That's a good girl . . . yes. Again . . . It won't be long now . . ."

Their daughter came into the world squalling healthily. She was a red, wet bundle of fury at being so rudely cast out of her comfortable home. Alison was weary, her features moist with sweat from her labors as Mrs. Chesney cleaned the child. Justin lovingly wiped her face with a damp cloth. The child was wrapped in a light blanket and set in her mother's arms. "Isn't she beautiful?" Alison asked in a tone of awe, her gaze taking in the light blond fluff which would be hair one day. Gently she unfurled the blanket and counted fingers and toes and found her daughter to be perfect.

Justin wasn't so sure. The tiny bundle emitted the most gruesome sounds. She surely had a temper. And that face, that red, squalling face. Was that beautiful? He hardly thought so, but recalling his last ill-chosen comment, and the banishment which followed, he

441

wisely kept his tongue. As the blanket was peeled away and Alison studied the child, he bent nearer and did so also. The fingers were perfectly formed and long, they moved with a grace reminiscent of her mother. And the skin was a bright pink, not red, wrinkled, yes. Beautiful? "Yes," he said without a qualm, kissing his wife's forehead. "She is beautiful. Almost as beautiful as her mother. Thank you."

Alison sighed and closed her eyes. "I'm so glad you like her."

"What a silly statement," Justin said as he picked the baby up and held her in his arms. She fit perfectly. The squalling stopped and a fist waved mightily in the air, her whole body squirming. He had to laugh with pleasure. "I think she has your eyes, look at those long lashes! And that temper."

Alison smiled sleepily. "Yes, your temper. Can't you hear it?"

Mrs. Chesney chuckled at this. Her work was almost done. She gathered spoiled linens and prepared to take them downstairs with her. "I'll be back with clothing for the baby. Nurse will want to see her. They'll all want to see her." The door closed softly behind her.

"We're a real family now," Alison said contentedly.

Justin grinned. "I felt like a real family the first time I felt her move. What shall we name her? Your father's name won't fit. She's too tiny."

"I've been so convinced we were having a Bradwell, I never gave any thought to a girl's name."

"I did. How about Mary Kathleen, after my mother?"

"Oh, I like that!"

Justin smiled at his wife. "Will you always give me

442

my way so easily?"

"When I can."

He laid the baby beside her and lifted her fingers to his lips. "I love you very much, Alison." Laughing to himself, he thought that she'd have to be awake the next time he told her. He didn't want her forgetting that important fact.

Mrs. Chesney bustled into the room. "They're begging for a glimpse of the babe downstairs! Can't we show off the newest member of the family?"

"Of course we can," Justin answered swiftly, lifting his little daughter to his arms.

"At least let me dress her first," Mrs. Chesney chided.

"I almost forgot about that," he laughed, giving the baby to the housekeeper's care. She was returned to him in a white, voluminous dress of muslin and lace. "I can barely see her for all this material."

"A lady must look her best at all times."

"Mary Kathleen does that," he replied proudly. "Suits her, doesn't it? Her name, I mean."

"Ah, yes."

A very proud man left the room, his daughter in his arms. Mrs. Chesney glanced about, to see if there was anything she might have forgotten. She found nothing.

"Mrs. Chesney?"

"Oh, my dear, I thought you were asleep." The housekeeper moved swiftly to the bed. "Are you in pain?"

"No, but would you do something for me?"

"Of course. What is it?"

Alison hesitated for a moment. "I'm afraid Morgan's about to be fired again and all because of me.

443

Would you please tell him to go to his sister's and stay there until I send for him?"

"But my lord gave orders that he wants to see him immediately when he returns."

"I'm sure he did, but don't you think this once he might forget about orders? If we can keep Justin and Morgan separated for just a while, just until he calms down . . ."

"My lord was very emphatic about it."

"I'm sure he was, Mrs. Chesney. But Morgan meant no harm. He has a very important job ahead of him, taking care of Mary Kathleen."

Mrs. Chesney clucked her tongue. "I don't think the Marquis will let him near her."

Alison's eyes were mischievous, but weary. Slowly they drifted closed. "We'll have to see about that, Mrs. Chesney. We'll have to see."

SEARING ROMANCE

REBEL PLEASURE (1672, $3.95)
Mary Martin
Union agent Jason Woods knew Christina was a brazen flirt. But
his dangerous mission had no room for clinging vixen. Christina
knew Jason for a womanizer and a cad, but that didn't stop the
burning desire to share her sweet *Rebel Pleasure*.

CAPTIVE BRIDE (1984, $3.95)
by Carol Finch
Feisty Rozalyn DuBois had to pretend affection for roguish
Dominic Baudelair; her only wish was to trick him into falling in
love and then drop him cold. But Dominic has his own plans: To
become the richest trapper in the territory by making Rozalyn his
Captive Bride.

GOLDEN ECSTASY (1688, $3.95)
Wanda Owen
Andrea was furious when Gil had seen her tumble from her
horse. But nothing could match her rage when he thoroughly
kissed her full trembling lips, urging her into his arms and filling
her with a passion that could be satisfied only one way!

LAWLESS LOVE (1690, $3.95)
F. Rosanne Bittner
Amanda's eyes kept straying to the buckskin-clad stranger opposite her on the train. She vowed that he would be the one to tame
her savage desire with his wild *Lawless Love*.

(1716, $3.95)

Now you can get more of HEARTFIRE right at home and $ave.

Preview Four Brand New ZEBRA *Heartfire* Romance Novels...

FREE for 10 days.

No Obligation and No Strings Attached!

♥

Enjoy all of the passion and fiery romance as you soar back through history, right in the comfort of your own home.

Now that you have read a Zebra HEARTFIRE Romance novel, we're sure you'll agree that HEARTFIRE sets new standards of excellence for historical romantic fiction. Each Zebra HEARTFIRE novel is the ultimate blend of intimate romance and grand adventure and each takes place in the kinds of historical settings you want most...the American Revolution, the Old West, Civil War and more.